I0788447

The Assassin

Denver

Jim West

Copyright by Aurora Publications

The mounted cowboy over the state of Texas is the trademark of Aurora Publications.

This is a work of fiction. Names, characters, places, and incidents either are product of the author's imagination or are used fictitiously, and any resemblance to any actual persons, living or dead, events, or locales is entirely coincidental.

My special thanks go to my longer than time itself friend, John Fleenor, whose satirical wit keeps me straight. Thank you, John.

ISBN
Hardcover: 978-1-964289-96-0
Paperback: 978-1-964289-95-3

Other books by Jim West

DNAlien
DNAlien II
DNAlien III
Living Within a Strange Mind Vol. I
Living Within a Strange Mind Vol II
Genocide by GMO
The Making of an Assassin Atlanta
The Assassin Baltimore
The Assassin Chicago

Prologue

"American 2344 contact Fort Worth Center 126.7," the FAA departure controller at Dallas Fort Worth (DFW) Airport directed.

"126.7, good day," Captain Mike Knox answered as he entered the frequency into the secondary head of his radio.

"Fort Worth, American 2344, with you passing 7 for 10," Mike said, taking a glance at the altimeter.

"American 2344, radar contact. Climb and maintain Flight Level 230. Turn left, heading 355," the controller directed.

"Up to 230 and left 355," he responded as he watched First Officer Jim Lashley enter the altitude and heading into the control display that provided direction to the autopilot.

Moments later, they were passing 10 thousand feet, and Mike reached up to press the button on the overhead panel that caused a chime to be heard in the cabin of the McDonald Super 80.

"You got the radio," Mike told Jim as he removed the handset from the rear of the center pedestal.

"I've got the radio," Jim said as he took a quick look at the control panel and made sure the autopilot was performing as directed.

Listening to Mike tell the passengers how much he appreciated their flying American Airlines and that he would do everything possible to make it a smooth ride and anticipated an early arrival, Jim smiled as he watched Mike make rude gestures during his rehearsed announcement before turning the seatbelt sign off.

As soon as Mike replaced the handset, Jim looked at him and said, "Lovely speech."

"I've been practicing. I've got the radio," Mike acknowledged as he turned his overhead speaker up and tested the volume. Satisfied that he could hear the radios, he pulled his headset off and hung it on the lever that opened the sliding side window.

Jim quickly followed suit, pulled the handset microphone from its holder, and hung it where he could reach it easily. Almost simultaneously, the overhead speaker came to life as the controller directed, "American 2344, contact Fort Worth 122.7. Good day."

Taking the aircraft microphone from the holder on his left, Mike responded, "122.7. Good day."

Entering the frequency into his radio, he continued, "Fort Worth, American 2344 with you out of 180 for 230 heading 355."

"Roger American 2344, continue up to Flight Level 330 and proceed direct Amarillo," the controller directed.

"330 and Amarillo," Mike replied as he watched Jim change the control panel to match the altitude assignment and change the navigation from the previous heading of 355 to the course in the GPS that would take them across the VOR at Amarillo.

Jim rechecked the control panel, and once satisfied that the airplane was performing as he wanted, he slid his seat back and reclined it slightly as he took his almost empty drink glass from the cup holder beside his seat. "Any big plans for tonight in Denver?" he asked, glancing at Mike.

"Nope," Mike answered as he slid his seat back slightly and reclined it one notch. "You?"

"Meeting a Marine buddy for dinner," Jim answered. "Same guy from last night."

"I'll probably see if the girls want to go out for a drink again," Mike said, nodding. "If not, I'll just grab something to eat at the hotel and catch a movie in my room."

"They're a good crew," Jim told him. "Merna is one of the best number ones I've ever flown with.

Mike smiled and said, "That she is. If I wasn't married, very married, I might be a little tempted. But too many of our pilots have found out the hard way that everything they do with the ladies on the road gets back to the home front."

"I noticed that you only mentioned the ladies," Jim told him, shaking his head. "What about the sweet boys back there?"

"I think I'll leave them for you, Marines," Mike answered, smiling at Jim. "You guys spend months on end at some lonely airfield in the middle of nowhere. Thousands of miles from the nearest woman. I've heard it's an acquired taste."

"Navy. Marine. You're at sea with them. We're on land with them," Jim said, laughing. "But I'll stick with the feminine side. I never could understand what a guy would see in another guy. Now, the lady-lady thing I find interesting."

"Now that might be interesting," Mike responded, nodding in agreement as the radio came to life and the controller directed, "American 2344, Oklahoma Center now on 118.6. Good day."

"118.6 for OK Center," he acknowledged as he dialed in the frequency. "Good day."

"OK, Center, American 2344 with you at 330," Mike said after switching frequency.

"Good afternoon, American 2344. Proceed direct Lamar for the Quail 4 arrival. Maintain 330," the controller directed.

"Lamar for the Quail 4," he acknowledged, watching Jim make the change to the GPS that would take them to the Lamar VOR. "Any ride reports?"

"Some light chop on the arrival below 230," the controller answered.

"Thanks," Mike said as he replaced his microphone.

Jim looked out the side window at the flat terrain that was passing beneath the airplane and started thinking about what was going to happen that night in Denver. Contrary to what he had told Mike, he hoped that this afternoon would finish the assignment that he'd been working on for over a month.

Tonight, his team would hopefully remove a threat to one of the assets that Black Water had been tasked with providing security. The assassin that had been sent to eliminate the person Black Water was guarding had to be eliminated himself.

Page Left Blank Intentionally

Chapter One

American Airlines flight 248 landed just a few minutes early at the LaGuardia Airport (LGA) in Queens, New York, having left the Dallas Fort Worth International Airport (DFW) 3 hours and 10 minutes earlier.

After taxiing to the terminal, Captain Paul Kachmar set the parking brakes and shut down both engines once the ground power was connected to the airplane. After completing all the checklist items, he turned to Jim Lashley, the First Officer (FO), and asked, "Do you want to say goodbye to the passengers? It was your leg, and the landing was pretty good. For a Marine."

"I'll let you have the honors, sir," Jim answered, smiling. "I know how you Air Force types need your egos stroked continuously. Besides, I know that you'd stand at the door if I had screwed it up. So, please. I'll just sit here quietly until it's time to go find the hotel van."

"Not a problem," Paul said, smiling as he got out of his seat and opened the cockpit door. "Just remember that I offered you the chance to smile and act like you really care. Maybe you'd even meet some cute little lady that would make your night here in the city memorable."

Jim turned in his seat and watched the passengers as they filed past the cockpit, nodding as they left the airplane. Paul stood there smiling and saying thanks to most of them or "You're welcome," depending on the passengers' response to seeing him standing there.

When the last passenger had left, Paul returned to his seat and began picking up all of his items that had been used during the flight. After putting everything in his kit bag, he stood up and asked, "Ready for an exciting evening in another hotel?"

Jim stood, picked up his kit bag, and followed Paul out onto the jet bridge, answering, "Always ready for an exciting hotel stay. Maybe this one won't smell like cheap aftershave or mildew."

After winding their way through the terminal, they met the Flight Attendants standing on the curb waiting for the van that would take them to the Holiday Inn.

"How'd it go, ladies?" Paul asked as he set his kit bag and suitcase down.

"Just peachy," Gay Lynn answered. "Over three hours of smiling and listening to bitching and complaining. I can't imagine any other job that would compare to the joy I get from never being home and living out of a suitcase."

"I understand," Paul told her. "But you could be in a cubicle in some office somewhere staring at a computer screen and shuffling papers 8 hours a day and fighting traffic getting to and from work. I don't know about you, but I'll take this over any other job I can think of."

"Oh, don't get me wrong. I love my job," Gay Lynn replied. "It's just after 3 legs in 1 day and full airplanes, I get a little frazzled. I'm with you on the 9 to 5 office thing. At least here, if you're dealing with an asshole, you know he'll be gone on the next leg. Not so if he's in the cubicle next to yours."

"What are you doing tonight, Captain?" Terry, the Flight Attendant who took care of the cockpit and first-class passengers, asked.

"Not much," he answered. "Jim and I are meeting for dinner at the hotel. Then hit the sack. You guys are welcome to join us, of course."

"Thanks," Terry told him. "But we've sort of planned to meet in my room for an informal debrief of the day. But we appreciate your offer."

"The offer still stands," Paul told them as the van pulled up to the curb in front of them. "If you change your mind, just come down to the restaurant and join us if we're still there."

As the van driver came around to the back and opened the door to the luggage area, Amanda, one of the flight attendants who worked in coach, looked at Jim and smiled as she left her bags for the driver to put in the van.

"What was that?" Paul whispered as he handed the driver his kit bag and suitcase.

"What?" Jim asked, waiting for the driver to turn and get his bags.

"That sly little smile," Paul asked quietly. "I know a flirt when I see one. And that was a flirty smile."

"I don't think so," Jim said as they headed for the door to the van. "She's probably just a friendly sort of lady."

"Either you're blind or full of shit," Paul said, smiling as they took the seats at the rear. "If she had smiled at me like that, I'd be sitting beside her on the way to the hotel instead of being back here wondering."

"I'm not wondering," Jim said, shaking his head. "I try to look at all the flight attendants as if they were either my sister, my daughter, or my mother. And it seems that lately, most of them remind me of my mother. Or an ugly sister."

"You're probably missing out on several adventures," Paul told him. "That's one of the advantages of this job. There's nearly always the opportunity for an adventure."

"And it's those *adventures* that usually cost pilots half of their retirement, their house, and child support," Jim replied, smiling. "No thanks. I'll wait until I get home to star in any *adventure*."

"I know," Paul said, nodding in agreement. "But it's soooo very good for a man's ego. Sort of like going to the Lamborghini dealership and getting a test drive. I know I can't ever justify buying it, but the memory of driving it will last forever."

"And you know very well that any little *adventure* could cost you a new Lamborghini every year for the rest of your life," Jim said, laughing.

"Yeah, I know," Paul said, shaking his head. "Maybe I should have been a car salesman instead of a pilot. I'd get to test drive any of the cars that I wanted to."

"With my luck, I'd probably wind up as a Volkswagen salesman," Jim said, laughing. "On a used car lot!"

"Could be worse," Paul told him as they were pulling up to the Holiday Inn. "Could be a used Yugo car lot."

Chapter Two

Jim and Paul were standing behind the Flight Attendants as they were signing in for their rooms when Jim heard a voice behind him say, "It's about time you got here, Mr. Lashley."

Turning at the familiar voice, Jim responded, "Didn't know I was late, General."

"Not late," General Gene Barker told him, extending his hand. "I just said it's about time. Didn't say late. Didn't say early. Just about time."

Shaking his hand, Jim turned to Paul and said, "Paul, this is General Gene Barker. He was the Commander of the Marines in Vietnam when I was there."

As Paul shook his hand, Jim continued, "General, this is Captain Paul Kachmar. He's the unfortunate gentleman that has to put up with me for the month."

"Good to meet you, Captain," Gene said as he shook his head. "I know full well the trials that you must endure with Jim. I've known him for too many years to admit. You have my condolences."

"Nice to meet you, General," Paul said, smiling and nodding. "I'm sure you have some interesting tales about Jim if you've known him for that long. I've only known him for a couple of weeks now, and I'll have to say that he's a different breed than the standard co-pilot I've flown with."

"I'm sure he is," Gene told him as they stepped up to the desk to register for their rooms and get the keys. "I admire your restraint in just saying that he's a *different breed*. I've heard him described in some not-so-flattering terms over the years. Most of them I wouldn't repeat in front of mixed company."

"Listening to you two, I'm feeling sort of unappreciated," Jim said, smiling. "Not to drift off the subject of demeaning me, but what brings you to New York, General?"

"Actually, I'm here to discuss some issues with one of my company's clients," Gene said as they stepped back from the desk. "I talked to your lovely wife Jennifer this morning to see how things were back in Mesquite, and she told me that you were on a trip. When she said that you were laying over in New York tonight, I decided that I'd try to get a room here since I knew that American had a contract with the Holiday Inn."

"Well, it's certainly good to see you," Jim told him, knowing that there was more to the story and that Gene had come here specifically to talk to him. "Paul and I had planned to have dinner here tonight, and you're more than welcome to join us."

"I would enjoy that," Gene told them as they walked to the elevators. "But I'll only join you if I can pay for our meals. Will any of the Flight Attendants be joining us as well?"

"Probably not," Paul answered as the elevator doors opened. "They say they've got other plans. I did give them the option to come down and join us if they changed their minds, but I doubt that we'll see them until tomorrow morning."

"That's fine," Gene told them as Paul stepped into the elevator. "Why don't you guys go change clothes, and I'll go get us a table at the restaurant? Is 15 minutes enough?"

"That's plenty of time," Paul answered as Jim got on the elevator. "We'll be there."

"Good," Gene said, nodding at Jim as the elevator doors began to close. "I'll be waiting."

Chapter Three

Gene was sitting at a table near the rear of the restaurant when Paul walked in, looking around. Spotting Gene, he waved the Maitre d' away and headed for the table.

Gene stood as he approached and motioned for him to take the chair opposite his saying, "Please have a seat, Paul. I was going to order a bottle of wine for us but remembered that you guys aren't supposed to drink while on a trip."

"That's the general rule," Paul answered as he sat down. "But it's more or less an unspoken agreement between members of the crew that some relaxing of the *rule* is tolerated as long as you've got at least 8 hours from when you had a drink until you come down for pick up the next day."

"That's sort of like it was flying in the Marines," Gene replied, taking his seat again. "What's your background?"

"Air Force," Paul answered. "I was a T-38 instructor and then flew 0-2's before I got out and came to American."

"So, you were a Forward Air Controller (FAC)," Gene said, nodding. "Where were you stationed?"

"Tucson," Paul replied. "Three years in the Arizona desert."

"There are worse places," Gene told him as the waiter approached their table. "The Marines have FACs as well. But we use the OV-10."

"That's a much better plane," Paul said before looking at the waiter. "Could I get a Heineken, please, sir?"

"Of course," the waiter said, nodding. Looking at Gene, he asked, "And for you, sir?"

"I'd like a bottle of Chardonnay and three glasses, please," Gene told him. "And an order of baked clams and the bacon-wrapped shrimp."

"Excellent, sir," the waiter said. "I'll have the wine right out with the gentleman's Heineken. The appetizers will be out shortly."

"That's fine," Gene said, laying the menu on the table.

"So, you and Jim go back years," Paul said, leaning forward and putting his elbows on the table, cupping his hands. "Did you fly together?"

"No," Gene answered. "Jim was a mud grunt when I first met him."

"Oh," Paul said, surprised. "All he told me was that he flew F-4s in Vietnam before coming to American. I think he also said that he was in the Reserves."

"That's true," Gene said, leaning back in his chair. "But he was part of a Marine Recon Team when I first met him in Vietnam."

"That's a far cry from being a pilot," Paul said, shaking his head. "I'm assuming that he was enlisted at the time."

"That's correct," Gene said. "His team was sent to the wrong place and was virtually wiped out. Matter of fact, Jim was the only man to make it back alive."

Paul sat back and said, "That's quite some story. Jim never mentioned anything about that. What happened to the other men?"

"Jim carried them down the hill and put them on the helicopter that was sent to rescue them," Gene told him. "Matter of fact, one of the men who died on that hill was my nephew. If not for Jim, all of those Marines would probably be still listed as Missing in Action."

"I guess Jim was lucky to get out alive," Paul said as the image of Jim carrying the Marines down a hill under fire entered his head. "How did you come to know about Jim?"

"I was flying lead of a flight of F4s that was sent in to provide air support while the chopper tried to pick up Jim's team," Gene explained. "I didn't know exactly who made it out until the chopper got back to base. That's when I found out that Jim had made ten trips up and down that hill trying to bring everybody home."

"I guess you never know some things about the people you fly with," Paul said, amazed at the story. "I never knew he was an enlisted man or what he did. I just assumed that he was like most of us who finished college and joined the military to fly. You just never know."

"No," Gene said as he saw Jim approaching. "Most of us don't want to talk about some of the things that happened over there. Even though he was awarded the Silver Star and his second Purple Heart for that little incident, he doesn't want to discuss it. And I'd appreciate it if you wouldn't mention that I talked to you about it."

"I understand," Paul said. "I had some of my pilot training classmates go there, and they feel the same."

"Been waiting long?" Jim asked as he arrived at the table.

"About time," Gene said, winking at Paul as Jim sat down. "We were about to give up on you and eat the appetizers I had ordered."

Jim looked around the table and said, "I see. Probably about to drink the wine that hasn't arrived yet also."

"You always were a smart ass," Gene said, laughing as the waiter arrived with the wine and beer. "It's good to see that you haven't changed with your cushy job flying airplanes with toilets."

Chapter Four

As the waiter sat the wine and beer on the table, he asked Jim, "Would you care for anything, sir?"

"Have you guys ordered?" Jim asked Gene.

"No," he answered. "We were waiting for you. I just ordered the wine and some appetizers, and Paul ordered the Heineken."

"The wine will be fine for me," Jim told the waiter as he picked up the menu. "Any recommendations for the meal?"

"The baked rigatoni bianco is one of our specialties," the waiter told him. "It's sauteed in garlic and oil with broccoli and chicken."

"That sounds good to me," Jim said, handing the menu to the waiter. "And I'd like the Caesar salad also, please."

"Excellent," the waiter replied. "And for you gentlemen?"

"That sounds good to me," Gene told him, handing him his menu.

"Same for me," Paul said, returning his menu also.

"Very well," the waiter told them as he turned to leave. "Your appetizers will be here momentarily."

As Gene poured a glass of wine for Jim, Paul took a sip of his beer and asked, "You said you were here to meet with some of your company's clients. What does your company do?"

As he poured his glass, Gene answered, "I work for an international security consultation firm, and my specialty is physical security."

"What does that entail?" Paul asked as Jim glanced at Gene.

"Pretty much everything from the design, implementation, monitoring, staffing, whatever the company that's hired us needs," Gene answered, smiling.

"Do they just work with private companies?" Paul asked as the waiter brought the baked clams and shrimp dishes.

"Oh no," Gene explained as he took a couple of clams and two bacon-wrapped shrimp from the dish. "We also work with governments or occasionally an individual."

"Interesting," Paul said, taking some of the appetizers. "What's the name of the company?"

"Black Water," Gene answered.

"That name's familiar," Paul told him as he took a bite of the shrimp. "Weren't they involved with something in Iraq a few years back?"

"Yes, we were," Gene answered. "We were contracted by the US government to provide certain services as military contractors. But our security business is available to almost any government agency or country. Depends on their relationship with our government. Most of our employees are former military, and their expertise covers everything from physical patrol to computer security."

"That does sound interesting," Paul said as their salads arrived. "Are most of the people there Army or Marines?"

"Actually, no," Gene told him. "We hire people from all the services and civilians as well. Depends on your background and what we need. Some of our people start out as part-time when we're contracted to provide some unique services. For example, we may be contracted to set up a computer program and ensure its security.

We may need several experts for that contract for a short period because of the time constraints imposed by the client," Gene added. "But once the program is up and functioning as the company requested, we don't need all those employees. They're released and may or may not be used on another contract."

"I don't guess you need any pilots," Paul remarked as their meals arrived.

"Actually, we have several pilots on our staff," Gene told him as the salad was set on the table. "Some of our operations require moving security personnel between locations. Since there may not be either commercial service or pilots with the security clearances available, we're forced to have both fixed-wing and helicopter pilots."

"I wish I'd known about companies like yours when I got out of the Air Force," Paul remarked as he took a bite of his pasta. "That sounds like more fun than being a high-speed bus driver."

"Not me," Jim said, glancing at Gene. "I had enough of the 'fun' while I was in the Marines. Being an airline pilot isn't very exciting, but as you mentioned, there's a toilet and Flight Attendants to bring you coffee. Try to find that in the middle of some godforsaken desert or a mosquito-infested swamp where there are more varieties of snakes than channels on your TV. If you even have a TV."

"No, I'll take the boring flying where I'm sleeping in a nice clean bed when I land," Jim continued. "And there's always a bar with cold beer and usually a restaurant with good food. Not to mention, some of the Flight Attendants are cuter than a whisker-faced nomad, and I'm not trying to sleep in a rat-infested hut eating fish heads and rice. And then there's the pay."

"Jim's right," Gene said as they enjoyed their meals. "Most of our pilots would gladly swap places with you guys. I'd be willing to bet that any of them would rather be here with us right now than what Jim just described. Not to mention the risks associated with their jobs."

"And then there's the pay," Jim said again, raising his wine glass. "Here's to no risk and high reward."

"We all took the risk in our former lives," Gene said as he raised his glass. "Now's the time to enjoy life and let the kids have all the 'fun.'"

"To the good life," Paul said, raising his beer. "I guess the grass is always greener...."

"That green may be pond scum," Jim said as he smiled and took a sip of wine. "And there may be an alligator hiding beneath the surface just waiting."

Chapter Five

After 30 minutes of enjoying dinner and the conversation, Paul announced that he needed to get back to his room and call home. Thanking Gene, he told Jim he'd see him in the morning and excused himself.

As soon as he had left the table, Jim asked, "So, what's happening that brings you to my layover hotel instead of waiting to come to Texas to see me?"

"You don't think I came here to work with some company clients?" Gene asked, finishing his glass of wine.

Jim leaned back in his chair, holding his wine glass, and answered, "Not a chance. And I know that you guys can locate me at any point in time that you want. All the little *coincidences* over the years have made me somewhat skeptical."

Gene motioned for the waiter and told Jim, "Well, for your information, you are correct. But I didn't want to wait three days to talk to you. Even though I do enjoy coming to Mesquite to visit you and Jennifer, we have an issue that I want you to start thinking about."

"What's that?" Jim asked as the waiter arrived with their bill in a folder, asking if they wanted anything else.

Gene handed the waiter his credit card and told him, "No, thank you. Everything was perfect."

As he left, Gene continued, "Let's wait until we get outside. A short walk would do me good and give us a chance to discuss a rather delicate matter. I've brought a folder with most of the information for you to read when you get time."

After signing the receipt and leaving a cash tip, Gene pushed his chair back and asked, "Shall we?"

Jim slid his chair back and followed Gene out of the restaurant and onto the sidewalk. Once outside, Gene crossed the road in front of the hotel into the parking lot and stopped beside a black Suburban with dark-tinted windows.

"I'm surprised that you'd drive this thing," Jim said as Gene unlocked the rear passenger door. "You normally prefer something a little less conspicuous."

"I didn't drive it," Gene replied as he took a large manila envelope from the back seat. "I had one of our local agents pick me up at the airport. And you're right, I'd prefer a nice town car if I've got to drive it myself."

"Where's the driver?" Jim asked as Gene locked the car and leaned against the side.

"In his room, I presume," Gene told him as he handed him the envelope. "Don't bother opening this until later. We'll just talk in generalities for now."

"Okay," Jim said, leaning back against the car parked next to Gene's Suburban. "What sort of time frame are we looking at?"

"That's one of the problems," Gene said, looking toward the north and watching the constant flow of airplanes arriving and departing LaGuardia. "We got the tasking two days ago but don't have all of the details."

"I guess I don't understand," Jim responded with a quizzical look. "How can the company contract to perform without knowing what they're required to do?"

"That's not as strange as you'd think," Gene told him. "At least half of our contracts are somewhat open-ended. Meaning that the client gives us a concept and simply says to develop the plan and be prepared to implement it when notified."

"But don't they tell you something about what they expect?" Jim asked.

"Of course," Gene answered, nodding. "Sort of like this one. Basically, it's a babysitting job. We're to accept the *package* and keep it safe until further notice."

"Don't tell me that you want me to actually sit in some safe house taking care of a guest of the client," Jim told him incredulously.

"Of course not," Gene answered. "You're much too valuable to have you sitting around watching *Gunsmoke* or *Little House on the Prairie* on TV and bringing coffee to somebody. We've got plenty of people for that."

"Good," Jim said. "So, what do you need me for? You guys know where all the safe houses are and have plenty of ways to transport the *package*, as you call it. I just don't see why we're having this discussion. Especially since this seems to be a routine personal protection operation."

"This is everything except routine," Gene told him as he looked around the parking lot. "The *package* is one of the most sensitive operations that Black Water has been assigned in years."

"What's so sensitive about this one?" Jim asked, getting anxious to read the material in the envelope.

"She, the package, was extracted from North Korea last week," Gene explained. "The company sent a team from

Dark Water in to bring her to the US. She arrived this morning."

"What's so important about her?" Jim asked as his curiosity mounted. "And who's tasking us?"

"She has certain knowledge about a program inside China that could have a major impact on international relations," Gene told him. "You'll get some idea about what happened when you read the material I've given you. And, as far as who we're working for, I guess that'd be the Secretary of State."

"Why not the CIA?" Jim asked. "They normally contract with Black Water for overseas operations. I understand about Dark Water's involvement, and I can see why Muddy Water is picking up the tasking now that it's become a domestic issue."

"I'll just say that this is way above the CIA," Gene told him. "I'd guess that there're only two people within the government that even know what we're doing. And I've told you that one of them is the Secretary of State."

"And I can guess who the other one is," Jim said, nodding. "And if this goes south, he'll disavow any knowledge, and the Secretary of State will take the fall."

"I certainly can't confirm that," Gene said, pushing himself off the Suburban. "But that's generally the way things work at that level."

"Okay," Jim said, following Gene toward the hotel. "But why do you guys need me?"

Gene stopped just short of the entrance and answered, "You don't think that our friends in China are just going to sit at home twiddling their chopsticks, do you? I'd guess that within the week, if not already, they'll know that she's missing, and the trail back here could be discovered. You're going to plan for the probability that they'll send a team here and develop plans to remove them before they can eliminate our guest.”

“Do you want the answer now or tomorrow morning?” Jim asked sarcastically.

“Good night, Jim,” Gene said, opening the door and heading for the elevator. “I’ll contact you when you get home.”

Chapter Six

Three days later, Jim was sitting at home rereading the file that Gene had given him in New York. Jennifer had gone to work almost two hours ago, and he was finishing his fourth cup of coffee when the phone rang.

"Hello," Jim said as he turned down the volume on the television.

"Good morning, Jim," came the all too familiar voice of General Barker. "Enjoying the fruits of your labor?"

"As much as possible, sir," Jim answered, smiling to himself. "But it seems that the few days I get off to enjoy anything seem to evaporate as fast as a drop of water on the sidewalks of Yuma in the summertime."

"Hell, a drop of water will never hit the sidewalk there," Gene said, laughing. "I swear that I watched a man try to water his yard, and the water coming out of the hose evaporated before it hit the grass."

"That may be stretching it a bit," Jim remarked as he remembered his time at the Marine Corps base there. "But it damn sure was hot on the flight line. Something about standing on a concrete pad when it hasn't been less than 100 degrees for three months. I don't miss it a bit."

"But it was a dry heat," Gene said, laughing. "Not like the sweltering jungle where the humidity and heat fought to see which one could get to be the highest. Ninety-five degrees and 98 percent humidity were a recipe for misery."

"Toss in the insects, the rice paddies, and those gentlemen that seemed to resent our presence in their country, I guess Yuma was a little slice of heaven," Jim told him.

"I don't think I'd go that far," Gene countered. "But there certainly were worse places. I seem to remember your disparaging description of a little trip to Syria a few years back."

"Yeah, you and your folks at Black Water seemed to go to extraordinary lengths to find the most God-forsaken hell holes for me back then," Jim said, remembering all of the missions he had taken working with Dark Water, the covert enforcement arm of Black Water.

"And now, look at you," Gene countered. "Plush lavish lifestyle. The only time you break a sweat is when you're washing and polishing your little Corvette. I should have it so good."

"You've got to be shitting me," Jim retorted. "Flying around the country in a private jet. A limo driver to take you wherever you want. An expense account that rivals several small nations' annual budgets. I'm not sure you even know how to spell sweat."

"Maybe we both should admit that life has turned out pretty good," Gene admitted. "Better than a giraffe with a sore throat."

"Or a frog with hemorrhoids," Jim replied. "Having to hop everywhere he goes and land on his ass."

"Maybe an elephant with a stomachache," Gene countered.

"That's true," Jim told him as he walked back into the kitchen to refill his coffee cup. "However, I don't think you're calling today to discuss animal husbandry. Or reminisce about our mutual histories regarding the past."

"You are correct, sir," Gene answered. "How about I take you to lunch today? I can be there in about an hour if you're not too busy."

"I believe I can squeeze you in this morning," Jim told him, smiling. "I'll have to cancel some very important conferences dealing with a multitude of international issues involving the life and livelihood of millions of people, but I'll be ready in an hour."

"How's your grasp of the issue we discussed in New York a couple of days ago?" Gene asked, shaking his head.

"I have some thoughts," Jim answered. "But I probably have more questions than answers."

"That's to be expected," Gene told him. "I'm hoping that our lunch will be a good chance for me to hear your thoughts and possibly answer the questions that may have arisen since you've had time to read all of the material."

"It could be a very long lunch if you're going to answer every question," Jim said. "Have you made reservations for the rest of the day?"

"No," Gene answered. "I've got to be in San Francisco this evening, so we've only got a couple of hours. I'll be there shortly to pick you up."

"I'll be ready," Jim replied. "Do I need to bring the material?"

"Only if you need it," Gene answered. "I'm very familiar with it, and this is just going to be a look at some possibilities to resolve the problem."

"I'll bring it anyway," Jim said. "Just to make sure we're on the same page about what I think you're asking me to do."

"Good enough," Gene told him as he hung up. "See you in an hour."

Chapter Seven

Jim slipped on a clean pair of starched Wranglers, a long-sleeved button-down starched shirt, and a well-worn but polished pair of Tony Lama boots. Just as he was making sure the coffee maker was off, the doorbell rang. Knowing it was Gene, he switched the TV off, grabbed the file from the coffee table, and headed to the front door.

"Venice Pizza good with you?" Gene asked as Jim made sure the door was locked behind him.

"Sounds good," Jim said following Gene to the Suburban waiting at the curb. "As long as you're buying, you can pick the restaurant."

"I like their food," Gene said as they got in the car. "And there's usually a little privacy in the back room. And I also know it's one of your favorite restaurants."

Jim smiled, shaking his head, and asked, "Is there anything in my life that you, or the company, don't know?"

Gene appeared thoughtful for a second as he drove and finally answered, "We're not sure if you wear your tightie whities to bed or go commando."

"Depends," Jim answered.

"You wear Depends when you go to bed?" Gene asked incredulously, turning to look quickly at Jim.

"No," Jim replied, laughing. "Depends on what Jennifer's wearing."

"I should have known you'd have a wiseass answer," Gene said, laughing along with him. "After all these years, occasionally, you're still a pain in the butt."

"Ah, there's the secret," Jim said as they pulled into the parking lot. "As long as it's only occasionally, you'll never really quite know when I'm pulling your chain."

"It's good to see that you've retained your sense of humor," Gene told him as he opened the door. "Sometimes that's a luxury I can't afford."

"Gentlemen, welcome back," the waitress said as they walked in. "It's been a while since you've been here. Still want a table in the back?"

"Yes, please," Gene answered as they followed her. "And I believe we're ready to order. Right, Jim?"

"I'd like the lasagna and unsweet tea with lemon," Jim told her as he took a seat.

"Same," Gene repeated, taking the chair opposite Jim. "And a basket of your rolls, please."

"I'll have the tea and bread right out," the waitress told them as she turned to go.

Waiting a moment, Gene asked, "So, what's your theory on how the Chinese are going to resolve their little problem?"

"The first question should be, what's the real problem? Is it what she knows or if she's either told someone or she's left information somewhere for someone else?" Jim answered as he opened the file.

"Let's assume they believe removing her will solve their problem," Gene said. "What would you do if you were them?"

"If it's purely a removal problem, I'd either hire a local or send someone in to take care of her," Jim answered. "I'm sure they have their own people or have access to companies like Black Water."

"They do," Gene agreed as the waitress returned with their tea and a basket of bread.

"Right out of the oven," she told them as she put plates and silverware in front of them.

"Smells great," Jim told her, selecting a roll and a pat of butter.

"As always," Gene concurred, taking a roll. "I look forward to every trip down here just so I can come here."

"Thank you," the waitress said, turning to leave. "Your lasagna will be out in about ten minutes."

"The company thinks they'll send someone over that's part of one of the government teams," Gene said, buttering his role. "We continue to believe they want to control every aspect of their operations without any information leaking into the private arena."

"Okay," Jim said, nodding. "I can understand that, given their propensity for absolute control. And I'd be willing to bet that the company already knows who's either on their way or is already here."

Gene paused a second and admitted, "Yes, we think we know who he is, and we're watching him very closely."

"Well then, you may already have a problem," Jim told him.

"And what would that be?" Gene asked, taking a bite of the roll.

"You just told me that you know who 'he' is," Jim answered. "By that, I'm assuming you're referring to a single person."

"Yes," Gene replied, looking directly at Jim. "Why would they send more than one person? There's only one target as far as we know. If it was our contract, I don't see the need for additional resources."

"That's one of the problems with our organization," Jim told him. "You naturally assume that every other organization, whether it's private or governmental, conducts business as we do."

"And, since you guys have had some very elite people to pick from and have access to some of the best intelligence in the world, you can get by with only one operative for something like this," Jim continued. "And, if your operative determined that additional resources were required, you'd have a communications system that would ensure that his or her requirements were met."

"Okay, let's say I agree with you," Gene said, nodding his understanding. "How would you arrange the solution?"

"If my tasking was to merely eliminate a single woman, I'd send a single man," Jim answered.

"I thought you just said that a single person wouldn't be able to do the job," Gene objected. "Or am I missing the point?"

"A single person can do the job," Jim told him. "But I think you're forgetting about their need for absolute control. And that includes control of information. To do that, you need another person to remove the shooter you sent to remove the lady. Otherwise, there's someone out there who knows you arranged the hit."

"So, you're saying that you think there's another player," Gene said as the waitress approached their table.

Waiting for her to leave, Jim answered, "No, I don't think there's another player. I think there are at least two more. One is to eliminate the lady. Another, who has no clue about the lady who's there to remove him. And a final operative to remove the man who killed the man who killed the lady."

"Is there anything else?" Gene asked, taking a forkful of lasagna.

"Of course," Jim answered, smiling. "You asked me to look at some sketchy data and develop a plan. I wasn't sure if you wanted to know how I'd approach eliminating the *package* or if you wanted to know what I'd do to protect the *package*. Which I personally think is what you really want. If, as I'm assuming, due to the level of interest, it is the most important part of the operation."

Chapter Eight

"All right. Let's say I agree with your three-shooter theory," Gene said as they continued eating. "Who are the second and third?"

"You've admitted that you know the first shooter," Jim answered. "Now, I'd use someone like Black Water to remove him. Probably one of the Albanian groups that operate over here. I'm sure you guys have the names and contact information of every foreign or domestic contract security group operating not just in the US but elsewhere in the world."

"That's possible," Gene admitted, wondering if Jim was just guessing or had somehow obtained some very classified company information. "Let's say that I can probably do some investigating and see if an operative from one of these yet-to-be-determined groups is snooping around the US."

"You might want to contact the NSA and see what kind of communication traffic is bouncing around between China and any of these *yet-to-be-determined* groups," Jim proposed. "That might be somewhat more productive than looking for direct links from those *yet-to-be-determined* groups to someone here in the US."

"The NSA doesn't have the authority to monitor or capture any communications between sovereign nations or between them and private US citizens or corporations," Gene explained.

Jim looked amused as he replied, "And a frog's ass isn't watertight. I'm not about to get into a discussion of legal or ethical issues regarding some of our intelligence agencies. And I'm sure that over your 30 years in the Marines, especially when you were privy to numerous intelligence briefings, both on the record and off, you've been given information that could only come from an…. expansion of the agency's original charter."

"Okay," Gene told him as he sat back in his chair. "You think they'll bring in a contract operative to remove the original shooter. I can agree with your premise. What about your third man? A different contractor? Or, back to their internal assets?"

"How much do you know about the drug operations controlled by the Chinese Mafia?" Jim asked, scraping the last of the melted cheese from his dish of lasagna with a piece of bread.

"Some," Gene admitted, sipping his tea. "How do they figure in?"

"Right now, they probably don't," Jim admitted. "But those fine Chinese citizens holding temporary green cards or student visas are most likely the same ones that are bringing in truckloads of underage girls from Thailand, Korea, the Philippines, and countless other southeast Asia countries."

"Agreed," Gene concurred. "And you plan to get them involved by threatening their supply chain?"

"Seems logical to me," Jim agreed, nodding. "Or maybe better to just let them know that shooter number two is over here looking to establish another avenue to bring the girls and drugs to America. Just the threat of competition could be the catalyst to get the reaction we want."

"And what is the reaction we want?" Gene asked.

"To make the Chinese believe that their first shooter completed his assignment, the second one also did, and the drug gang finished the job so that no one can tie anything back to China, or more importantly, the information that our lady brought with her won't be made public," Jim answered.

After pausing for a few seconds to let Gene mull over his thoughts on what the operation might entail, Jim continued, "Still, that doesn't do what you're really after. And by you, I mean someone way up there above the Secretary of State and, therefore, the company."

"And that would be?" Gene asked, smiling at Jim's grasp of the situation.

"Preservation of the asset," Jim answered, knowing that Gene and the people at Black Water had probably figured out everything before Jim received the file in New York.

"Yes," Gene agreed, nodding. "If we lose the asset, we lose everything. Protecting her is the job. Everything we've discussed up to this point is how we think they will come after her. And I agree with everything you've mentioned. Some of it is either under investigation or the investigation has been concluded with the data on file back at Quantico."

"I figured as much," Jim told him. "I've always been amazed at how you seem to use me as a sounding board for your plans. One of these days, I wonder if you'll just give me the completed plan and ask for my opinion."

"Doesn't work that way," Gene told him. "If I gave you a plan, you'd start out looking to see how it would work. And maybe not seeing the missing pieces. This way, you work through the problem with no preconceived conceptions and arrive at the conclusion. For example, we developed a plan to eliminate the first shooter before he could get to the asset. We also planned on looking for a second shooter with the same reasoning as you used. But we never factored in using one of the gangs here to eliminate the second shooter."

"I just figured that the Chinese wouldn't want anybody with ties to them to ever be in a position to reveal what had happened," Jim explained. "Shooter one had to go, and he probably knows it. That complicates his problem because he has to have an escape plan that gets him away from our forces once he accomplishes his mission, but more importantly, to evade who he knows the Chinese are sending. And he hasn't a clue whether it's one of his country's people or an organization like Black Water."

"He's got a problem," Gene agreed. "What do you think he'll do?"

"If it was me, I'd take a month or so to watch her. See where she's being kept. Give her guardians a little time to relax their guard. Then find a long-distance method of elimination," Jim answered. "And I'm guessing that you've already figured that out since you told me you know who they've sent."

"Yes," Gene told him. "If he's who we think he is, and we're pretty damn sure unless it's just a coincidence that a Major in the People's Liberation Army Special Operations Forces would be in San Francisco for a vacation just mere hours after our asset arrives."

"That would be a coincidence," Jim agreed. "Sort of like all of the coincidences that put you at the same hotel where I'm spending the night while on a trip."

"Sort of," Gene said, smiling.

"What else can you tell me about our Major?" Jim asked. "I'm betting that he's not some shoe clerk from the personnel division of Hang Chang Dang province."

Laughing at Jim's obvious attempt at humor regarding the Major's background, Gene explained, "No. Major Sun Bin is a very accomplished soldier. One I wish we had working with us. He was a member of the Guangzhou Military Region Special Forces Unit, known as *South Blade* or *South China Sword*. They're much like our Navy Seals. Currently, he's one of the 3,000 members of the Beijing Military Region, known as the Oriental Sword, which is probably their most elite unit."

"Pretty impressive," Jim admitted, listening to the man's accomplishments. "South Blade, that unit had a lot of sniper training if I'm not thinking of another unit."

"That's them," Gene confirmed. "That's why I think your long-range elimination theory has merit. But we've pretty much got a handle on everything within a two-mile radius of where we're keeping our lady. I really doubt that they, or we, have anyone that can take a shot from that far out."

"I agree with the two-mile shot being almost impossible," Jim said as their waitress came back to check on them.

"Anything else, gentlemen?" she asked as she approached the table.

"No, thanks," Gene said as he put two 20-dollar bills on the table. "Once again, you've exceeded our expectations. And I look forward to my next visit."

Gene smiled at her as she turned away and told Jim, "I've got some additional information for you in the car. I'll give you a couple of days to go over it and see if you have any further ideas. Ready to go?"

"Yes, and thanks for the lunch," Jim said as he slid his chair back. "I'm looking forward to seeing what else your brain trust back in Quantico has come up with and seeing how it matches what we've discussed."

Chapter Nine

Friday morning, Jim was back from another three-day trip and was using his first day off to take care of the various little items on Jennifer's 'to-do' list that she inevitably compiled every time he left.

This time, one of the items was that the garbage disposal had quit working. After turning on the water in the sink, he flipped the switch for the disposal. Hearing the obvious strain of an electric motor that was trying to turn but couldn't, he turned the water off and got a flashlight from beneath the sink.

Pushing the rubber flaps aside, he looked into the opening to see if maybe a spoon or fork had gotten wedged in the blades. Not seeing anything obvious, he went to the small closet down the hall from the kitchen.

Taking a broom from the closet, he was headed back to the kitchen when the doorbell rang. Carrying the broom with him, he changed course and went through the living room to the front door. As soon as he opened it, Gene remarked, "Glad to see that you're keeping up with your domestic chores."

"Please, come in," Jim told him, holding the door open. "I'm a little surprised to see you this early in the morning and especially so soon after our last visit."

Shutting the door behind them, Jim headed for the kitchen and said, "Now, if you just follow me, I've got a small problem to fix before I solve all of your problems. Care for a cup of coffee?"

"Coffee sounds great," Gene answered. "Since I can see how busy you are, I'll get it myself. I'm somewhat knowledgeable regarding where the cups and coffee maker are in your kitchen."

"Help yourself," Jim said as he looked in the sink where the malfunctioning disposal was installed. Putting the end of the wooden handle into the opening, he tried to rotate it around the small opening in a clockwise direction.

"What the hell are you doing?" Gene asked as he walked over to watch.

"Garbage disposal is stuck," Jim explained as he put additional force on the broom handle. "Not sure if Jennifer dropped something in there or if something else is binding the motor."

"And you believe you can twist the blades with the broom handle?"

Gene asked, watching him struggle to clear the disposal.

"I've done it before," Jim answered. "Sometimes it's something somebody dropped in the sink accidentally. Sometimes, it's a piece of bone. Once, I found about three feet of nylon string that had gotten wrapped around the shaft just below the blades."

"How'd you see the string?" Gene asked, leaning over to get a better view.

"Once I got the blades to turning, I changed directions and saw a bright orange piece sticking up beside the blades," Jim explained as the blades gave slightly. "Then I got a pair of needle nose pliers and pulled it out a little at a time."

"Looks like you're getting it to turn," Gene said as he watched the broom handle slowly slide around the outside of the opening.

"I think I've about got it," Jim agreed, reversing the turning to counterclockwise. "Just a little more, and I'll try it again.

Reversing the turn again, the blades suddenly moved freely as Jim stirred the broom handle. "That should do it," Jim said, removing the handle from the opening.

Turning the water back on, he flipped the switch and was satisfied to hear the disposal spinning freely. Turning it off but leaving the water running, he looked at Gene and asked, "So, what brings you to town today?"

Shaking his head at Jim's unconventional method of home repairs, he answered, "I wanted to talk some more about our problem. As you know, I was in San Francisco the last couple of days, and we've verified our number one shooter as Sun Bin. He's a descendant of another Sun Bin, who was a descendant of Sun Tzu."

"I'm familiar with Sun Tzu," Jim said, nodding. "He wrote *The Art of War*."

"Yes, he did," Gene confirmed. "General Sun Tzu then had a descendant named Sun Bin, who also wrote a military treatise known as *Sun Bin's Art of War*. Anyway, the current Sun Bin is most likely the guy who is here to eliminate our asset."

"So, our target is Sun Bin," Jim replied. "And he's been confirmed to be in San Francisco. Is our *package* there, and what's her name?"

"Hua Mulan," Gene answered. "Ironically, she's named after a legendary Chinese female warrior. We're in the process of relocating her, but for now, she's still in San Francisco."

"Pretty risky if Sun and Hua are both there," Jim noted. "Where are you going to move her?"

"Not sure of the final location. We're still working on that," Gene answered. "But given there's almost 35,000 Chinese or Asians in the Chinatown area where she's being held, we don't think she'll be noticed for a little while."

"Let me bring up another issue," Jim said, ready to discuss an area that had been bothering him. "You know that she's going to have to disappear again."

"By again, I'm guessing that you were counting when she disappeared in China as the first one," Gene replied.

"Yes," Jim confirmed, nodding. "Now, since they obviously know she's here, they won't rest until she's eliminated. Therefore, if you're to protect her, she's got to disappear again. But this time, she has to be confirmed dead, or they'll just keep coming. And it has to be Sun Bin who notifies his boss that the job is done. Otherwise, you just postpone the problem."

"And then we'll have another Sun Bin coming over," Gene said, agreeing. "What's your idea?"

"There are two scenarios that I can imagine that would give us the result we desire," Jim answered. "The first one is that we use a doppelganger and let Sunshine kill her. Then he can report back that she's gone, and we let whoever is after him take care of that problem. Then that shooter is eliminated, and the Chinese think things went according to their plans."

"And the second?" Gene asked.

"We convince Sunshine that it's in his best interest to leave Hua alone, help us identify his executioner, and we let the third man take care of him," Jim explained. "Then we can take care of that man, and you may get your wish regarding Mr. Sunshine."

"And what wish would that be?" Gene asked, refilling his coffee cup.

"You told me that you wish you had him working for you," Jim said, grinning. "Surely you remember what you told me when we were having lunch at Venice Pizza right before you went to San Francisco."

"I remember," Gene answered. "I'd certainly like having a man of his caliber on our staff. Especially since the company is getting quite a bit of contract work in the Asian nations."

"If it was up to me, I'd try to intercept Sunny before *his* executioner gets here and see if you can't make him an offer he can't refuse," Jim said, pouring his cold coffee into the sink. "At least let him know that we're aware of his choice of vacation spots and explain what'll happen if things play out the way we've hypothesized."

"You don't think that we can hide Hua until we get what we need and then let her go?" Gene asked hypothetically.

"You can," Jim admitted, getting another cup of coffee. "But you're taking a chance on not getting the maximum value out of her, whatever that may end up being. And it sets a pretty poor example of how the US takes care of asylum seekers who risk everything to provide information that's critical to us. It's an option, but I'd at least approach Sunny Boy and see if we can't get a better resolution."

"You're probably right," Gene told him. "That idea was kicked around a little bit when we learned that Sun Bin was here. But the Chinese culture is quite different than ours, and their loyalty to their Commanders is difficult to overcome."

"I understand," Jim replied. "But, as you mentioned, he knows that his *Commanders* will probably be sending someone after him. If there's an avenue to exploit, it's that if he continues with his mission, either they will get him, or we will. Maybe you should do a little research on Pang Juan."

"Who?" Gene asked.

"Pang Juan, a Chinese General and supposedly friend of Sun's namesake, the original Sun Bin," Jim explained. "Pang was jealous of Sun and ultimately had his face tattooed, branding him as a criminal, and also had his kneecaps removed. I'm sure today's Sun knows the story. Just reminding him of how unquestioned loyalty can be detrimental to one's health may provide enough incentive to abandon his current course of action."

"There are times that you surprise me," Gene said, putting his empty cup in the sink. "How much research did you do on Sun Bin after I gave you his name last week?"

"I was bored," Jim answered, smiling at Gene. "It was either that or housework. I chose to spend an hour or two at the library."

"You must really hate housework," Gene said, turning to leave. "What other sage advice can you provide?"

Walking with Gene to the front door, Jim said, "I also recommend a review of Sun Tzu's *Art of War*. Pay particular attention to chapter 7 on maneuvering. Especially his point of leaving an outlet free when you've surrounded your enemy and not pressing a desperate foe too hard. Give Sun Bin a way out. Especially since it benefits us."

Shaking his head as he walked to his car, Gene said, "I'll contact you as soon as I discuss your ideas with the folks back at Quantico. We may want you to come for a visit if you've got the time."

"You know my time is always available for you, General," Jim said, standing on the porch. "And spending time with you sure beats the hell out of housework."

"Comparing time with me to housework isn't much of a compliment," Gene said, getting into his car. "Especially since I know how much you hate housework. I'll give you a call this evening."

Chapter Ten

The phone rang later that evening when Jim and Jennifer were clearing the dinner table. "I'll get it," Jennifer said as she set the dirty dishes she was carrying into the sink.

Jim finished taking everything else from the table into the kitchen when Jennifer walked in smiling a few minutes later and held the phone out, saying, "General Barker would like to talk to the housemaid."

"General," Jim said, shaking his head as he took the phone. "To what do I owe the pleasure?"

"We're going to Virginia," Jennifer whispered, kissing him on the cheek.

"I just asked Jennifer if she could take a day or two off and come out to visit," Gene answered. "And I mentioned that she could bring her maid if he was available."

"How good of you, sir," Jim said, smiling at Jennifer's happiness. "I'm so happy to be included in the plans that you and my wife have made. I don't suppose you've made travel arrangements?"

"Private jet," Jennifer whispered again. "I'm going to pack."

"You need to be at Love Field tomorrow morning at 8 o'clock," Gene answered. "The plane will get there sometime tonight, and the crew will be staying somewhere around the airport. I've also reserved a room for you and Jennifer at the Inn at Evergreen about 30 miles from Quantico. You should get here about noon. I'll meet the plane, and then we'll head to the Inn for lunch before you and I come back to the base."

"I suppose this is just a two-day visit since I've got to fly Monday," Jim told him as he looked at his schedule that was posted on the refrigerator.

"Of course," Gene told him. "Something has come up, and we need to make a quick decision. We'll talk more about it on the drive back from the Inn after we have lunch and let Jennifer have the afternoon off to relax."

"Anything special I should know?" Jim asked. "Do I need to bring a coat and tie, or is jeans the appropriate attire?"

"Jeans and a sports coat will suffice," Gene answered. "The Inn is part of a country club, and the dining room is reasonably relaxed. Although maybe not quite as relaxed as some of the restaurants you take me to when I come down there."

"I can handle that," Jim replied. "Since you know that I've got a trip scheduled for Monday, do you think there's any chance I may need to make other arrangements?"

"No," Gene answered. "This shouldn't take more than a few hours Saturday afternoon before we take Jennifer to dinner. If necessary, we can come back Sunday morning and wrap it up. I've planned for the plane to take you back home Sunday after lunch."

"Good," Jim told him. "I'll go see if I can convince Jennifer that she doesn't need to pack for a week, and we won't be going anywhere that requires formal attire."

"Good luck with that," Gene said, laughing. "I'll see you about noon tomorrow."

After hanging up, Jim walked into the bedroom and watched Jennifer laying several dresses on the bed along with numerous blouses and pants. "It's only going to be one night," Jim said as she put different pairs of shoes on the floor in front of the dresses.

"I know," she answered as she shifted the shoes around. "I just want something nice to wear to dinner tomorrow night. It's not often that I get to dress up for an evening."

Jim shook his head and took his well-used suitcase out of the closet. Selecting a pair of freshly starched Wranglers and a white button-down collar shirt, he tossed them in the suitcase along with two pairs of socks and underwear. "I'm done," he exclaimed, snapping the suitcase shut.

Jennifer looked at him with disapproval written on her face as she asked, "You need something nice to wear tomorrow night. I'm pretty sure you need to bring a jacket and maybe a tie."

"I'll wear the jacket on the airplane," Jim explained. "Gene said jeans and a sports coat are all I'll need at the restaurant."

"If you plan on eating with Gene, that's fine," Jennifer said as she selected a silk blouse and matching skirt. "But, if you plan on dining with me, you'll wear some slacks and a nice shirt. And a sports coat. And a nice tie. And make sure you polish your boots before we leave."

"Anything else?" Jim asked, reopening his suitcase.

"Nope," Jennifer answered as she put her selection of clothes in her suitcase. "I just don't want to be embarrassed when we're sitting in a nice restaurant. And I'm sure the General will be properly dressed, so you need to look like you didn't just walked in from the pasture."

Taking a pair of gray slacks and a light pink silk shirt from his closet, Jim folded them and put them where the jeans and white shirt had been. Then he held out a dark blue corduroy sports coat with a striped, grey tie, asking, "Is this all right with you?"

"Those are fine," she told him. "But I think you need to bring a pair of your black boots instead of those old brown ones you like."

"Not a problem," Jim said as he put the jacket and tie in the suitcase. "I'll just wear the ones I fly in. They need to be polished anyway."

With a slight shake of her head, Jennifer remarked, "You may need to get a new pair of black boots anyway. Those are getting a little old."

"They're fine," Jim said, closing the suitcase once again. "Nobody notices what kind of boots I wear, and American only requires that footwear be black. And I like brown boots."

"I know you do," Jennifer said, smiling and kissing him on the cheek. "That's one of the few things I like about you. You're a simple man with simple tastes."

Jim put his arms around her and said, "I may be a simple man with simple tastes in most things. But I obviously like exotic beauty in my women."

Jennifer looked up into his eyes and replied, "You're extremely lucky that you found one of the very few exotically beautiful women that find you somewhat attractive."

Kissing him firmly and then pushing him away, she continued, "Now, you go do whatever you need to do while I finish packing."

Jim shook his head as he picked up his suitcase and headed for the living room, saying, "And don't think that I missed that little remark about the *few* things you like about me. You may need to do some '*splaining* about that. And the *somewhat attractive* thing as well."

"How about you meet me in the shower in about 30 minutes so I can '*splain* everything I like about you?" Jennifer said as she put another set of clothes in her suitcase.

"That'll be just fine," Jim said, smiling at her. "I just hope you're ready for a lot of explaining. Being a simple man, I may not understand right away. You may have to '*splain* it to me four or five times."

"Now you're dreaming," she said, laughing. "The way I'll explain things, you'll know all you need to know the first time."

Chapter Eleven

Jim and Jennifer arrived at Love Field in Dallas just a little after 7 o'clock the next morning. After parking by the General Aviation section of the terminal, Jim carried their bags into the lobby area to wait for the crew that was going to fly them to Quantico. Just after setting their bags down, he walked over to the door that opened to the ramp and looked out.

Seeing the familiar Gulfstream 3, he turned and looked around the lobby. Just as he started toward two men standing by the complementary coffee maker, one of them glanced at him and said something to the other man.

Jim approached them and asked, "Going to Quantico this morning?"

"Yes, we are," the older of the men said. "I'm Kerry. And I assume you're Jim Lashley, and that's your wife, Jennifer."

"That's right," Jim said, shaking his hand. "If it's all right with you, I'll take our bags out to the airplane, and we'll be ready anytime you want to leave."

"That's not necessary," the other man told him. "I'm Samuel, the copilot. My job description is to carry bags and keep Kerry out of trouble."

"Nice to meet you, Samuel," Jim said, shaking hands. "But it's no problem for me to take them out."

"No deal," he said, smiling and shaking his head. "I've got to go check out the airplane, and I'll take your bags with me. Come out with Kerry, and I'll have everything ready to go."

As he took their bags and headed out to the airplane, Kerry said, "He's a good guy. Very thorough. He hasn't been with the company very long and is sometimes a little over-aggressive.

"That's not a bad trait to have," Jim said. "Is there anything I can do to help?"

"Not really," Kerry answered. "I've checked the weather, filed the flight plan, and the only thing left is to make a quick call to my boss and advise him that we're going to be an hour or so early. If you guys are ready to go, that is."

"I'd rather be in the air than sitting here for the next 45 minutes," Jim told him as Jennifer walked over. "Jennifer, this is Kerry. He'll be our pilot to Quantico this morning."

"Nice to meet you, Kerry," she said, shaking his hand. "Good weather?"

"Should be as smooth as a baby's butt," Kerry said, tossing his coffee cup in the trash. "If you guys want to go on out, Samuel will get you settled while I make a quick phone call, and we can get out of here."

No sooner had Jim and Jennifer gotten settled in their seats when Kerry stepped in and told them that they would be airborne in 15 minutes. Five minutes later, the engines were running, and they were headed for the runway.

Once in the air, Kerry came on the speaker and told them that they were free to move about the cabin, and there were snacks and drinks in the rear of the airplane.

"Want me to go get you anything?" Jennifer asked as she unbuckled her seatbelt.

"Not yet," Jim said, reclining his seat. "And, I know he said you could get up, but I'd feel better if you waited another 10 or 15 minutes. There's a shitload of little airplanes flying around here, and if Kerry had to dodge one, it could be pretty drastic. So, please, stay in your seat and put your seatbelt back on."

"Okay," she replied as she refastened her seatbelt. "I'm sure you know what's safest with all of your time doing this."

"Rarely happens," Jim said, smiling. "But I'd hate to lose that exotic lady that likes a *few* things about me. Not sure if I'd ever find another one."

"Not like me," Jennifer told him, sitting back in her seat. "Certainly none of those *Flight Attendants* you fly with all of the time."

"Trust me," Jim agreed. "I can't think of any that would come close. Except maybe one or four."

Jennifer stuck her tongue out and said, "Well, there goes your chance for another membership in the mile-high club."

"I'll take another shower with explanations instead," Jim said as Kerry announced that they were passing 10 thousand feet.

"And now," Jim said as he unbuckled his belt, "I'll be glad to get you something from the back if you so desire."

"Dr Pepper and a kiss," Jennifer answered. "And let me know what kind of snacks they have."

A few minutes later, Kerry stepped from the cockpit and told them that there were sandwiches in the small refrigerator behind the curtain as well as a microwave. As he returned from the lavatory, he told them they would probably be landing about 11 o'clock East Coast time, about an hour earlier than expected.

For the rest of the trip, Jim and Jennifer spent the time reading the magazines and talking about how much time she would have for sightseeing.

As Kerry announced that they would be descending into Quantico, he told them that it would be a quick approach and that they needed to put everything away and buckle up.

Thirty minutes later, they were clearing the runway and headed for the ramp, where Jim noticed a familiar black Suburban. As they taxied to a stop, Jim saw General Barker step from the Suburban and head toward the left side of the airplane.

As the engines were winding down, the stairs lowered, and Kerry stepped from the cockpit to shake Jim's hand, saying he hoped they'd have a chance to see each other again.

"We're going back tomorrow night," Jim said as he nodded at Samuel. "Maybe we'll see you then."

"We've got to go to San Francisco tomorrow morning and won't be back until Monday or Tuesday," Kerry informed him. "Maybe some other trip."

"I'll take your bags down," Samuel said as he shook Jim's hand. "Thanks for flying Unknown Air."

As Jim followed Jennifer down the stairs, he watched Gene come to give her a hand as she stepped down, asking, "How was your flight, Jennifer?"

"Great, General," she answered, giving him a slight hug. "I still don't know why you don't just give Jim his own airplane, and we can come anytime you need him."

"I'll give that considerable thought," Gene told her as he shook Jim's hand. "What do you think, Jim?"

"That would mean that I have to fly the damned thing," Jim answered, smiling. "No, thank you. I'll just sit in back with the lady, eating Milton's crackers and drinking Dr Pepper."

"Sorry, Jennifer," Gene said as they headed to the car where Samuel had left their bags. "The boss says no."

"Do either of you really think he's the boss?" she asked them as she climbed into the rear seat.

"Of course not," Gene replied as he shut her door. "Men give up the right to be the boss when they get married. And they say that women are the weaker sex. What fool ever thought that was true?"

Forty-five minutes later, as they pulled into the Inn at Evergreen, Jennifer looked around and said, "Now, this is nice. Sort of different from the last hotels we stayed in when we visited."

"I thought you'd like it," Gene said as he led her up to the entrance. "Makes it nice since it's close and the food's excellent."

He turned to Jim and handed him a key, saying, "Your room is ready. If you guys will please hurry, we can grab a quick lunch here before we head over to Quantico."

"Why don't you take Jennifer to the dining room, and I'll toss the bags in the room and be right back," Jim said, looking at the room number on the key.

"Good idea," Gene answered. "We'll see you in a couple of minutes."

The waiter was standing by the table where Gene and Jennifer were looking at the menus when Jim sat down, saying, "Nice rooms. Pity we're only going to be here for one night."

"Maybe next time you can stay longer," Gene said, handing the menu back to the waiter. "I'd like the Chop House salad and iced tea, please."

"Certainly, sir," he said, nodding. "And for the lady?"

"I'd like the House salad with grilled shrimp," Jennifer answered, handing him her menu. "And tea as well."

"Yes, ma'am," he told her and looked at Jim. "And you, sir?"

"I'd like the Caesar salad with grilled sirloin, please. And tea," Jim answered, closing his menu and handing it to him.

"Excellent," the waiter told them. "I'll be right back with your drinks."

"This is pretty nice," Jennifer told them as she looked around. "I'm glad I brought some nice clothes for dinner tonight. I wish I'd had time to change into something nicer for now, though."

"You're the only woman here," Jim said as the waiter returned with their drinks. "That makes you the best-dressed lady in the place."

"I don't think you're scoring any points with that argument," Gene said, raising his glass. "But here's to a nice visit and hopefully a productive meeting."

"To a good visit," Jennifer parroted, raising her glass. "I'm still not sure what you Marines do when you have your little 'meetings,' but I'm sure it's always productive."

"Always," Jim said, raising his glass. "But you should remember that it's these little 'meetings' that give you a chance to get away for a few days every now and then."

"Well, then," Jennifer said, laughing. "Why don't you boys have more meetings? Maybe you need to meet in Paris. Maybe Tokyo. I could enjoy that."

"We were thinking of Fort Worth," Gene said, joking as their salads arrived. "I'd enjoy a few days hanging out with you guys in the evenings. What do you think, Jim?"

"Now that's a good idea," he answered, looking at Jennifer. "We wouldn't even have to go out. I've got a great grill, and Jennifer just loves to cook."

Chapter Twelve

"I hate to eat and run," Gene said as he signaled for their check. "But Jim and I need to get back to Quantico if there's any hope of finishing what you guys came here for."

"That's all right," Jennifer told him. "I'll take this afternoon to relax by the pool and maybe just walk around the grounds. What time do you plan on being here for dinner?"

"I'm hoping that we'll be back by about 7," Gene said as he signed their check. "I'll call and let you know if that changes."

Jim smiled as he handed her the key to their room, saying, "I'll make sure we get back by then. All I need to do is remind him that you're the boss and you'll never let me come back up here to play if you don't get to dress up for dinner tonight."

"We'll be here," Gene assured her as he rose. "I've already made dinner reservations and I can't disappoint both you and the Maitre d'. Ready to go, Jim?"

"Ready," Jim answered as he and Jennifer rose. Kissing her on the cheek, he continued, "I'll even try to get back early enough to clean up since you've made me bring a jacket."

"I'm sure the General will be dressed appropriately," she said, turning to Gene. "And I know he'd be embarrassed if you weren't as well."

"Of course," Gene said with a slight bow. "We Marines are always the epitome of fashion. Now, again, we've got to go, but you enjoy your afternoon."

Jennifer gave him a hug and kissed Jim before heading to the elevators and waving.

Once on the road toward Quantico, Gene said, "Reach under your seat and take out the envelope there."

Jim did as directed and extracted a 9 X 11 thick envelope stuffed with typewritten pages and a couple of photographs.

"Take your time looking at all of that," Gene said as Jim pulled sheet after sheet from the envelope. "We've got almost 30 minutes before we get there, and I want you up to speed on everything we now know."

Jim read each page and carefully laid each one on the seat when he finished. Looking at each photograph, he put them in a separate stack. It took almost 20 minutes before he finally finished reading each page. Picking up one of the photographs, he turned it slightly so Gene could see it and asked, "Is this Sun Bin?"

Gene took a quick glance at it and confirmed, "Yes. Our number one suspect to be the shooter."

"What has he done since he's been here in the States?" Jim asked as he studied the picture.

"Pretty much blended into the population in Chinatown," Gene answered. "If we weren't paying attention, he'd appear as any other Chinese citizen here for a visit."

"Has he located Hua?" Jim asked.

"Not that we know of," Gene told him. "But he's only been here a couple of days. We've managed to get a tap on the phone he's using, and there's been nothing that leads us to think he knows where she is."

Sorting through the stack of papers, Jim pulled one out and said, "It looks like he's already picked a couple of favorite restaurants. What do we know about the staff in them?"

"We're running checks," Gene answered. "The owners are third and fourth-generation descendants of Chinese immigrants who've been here for decades. There's nothing in their background or current activities that would make us suspect that they're anything except loyal American citizens.

Now, the staff is a little harder to get concrete information about," Gene continued. "Most of them are young, some here on student visas, other members of the owner's family, and occasionally a Caucasian working part-time."

Jim gave Gene a quizzical look and asked, "Why would a Caucasian be working in Chinatown? Especially part-time? That seems a little out of place."

"We're not sure," Gene admitted. "There simply hasn't been enough time to do a thorough background check on all of the people working in the restaurants."

"It might be nothing," Jim concluded, rereading the page. "I just look at it as I do the restaurants I'm familiar with. Most of the Mexican food restaurants I know of are predominately staffed with Mexican people. And Venice Pizza? The owner is Albanian, and just about everyone working there is Albanian. Mostly family members."

"I agree," Gene replied. "That's why we're putting more emphasis on the Caucasian, but it's just going to take a little more time. What else do you have questions about?"

"Let's start with Sun," Jim answered. "Since you've got a tap on his phone, I'm assuming that you have a record of all of the calls and a transcription of the conversations."

"You are correct," Gene agreed. "We even have tapes of every call going out or coming in. You can listen to them if you want to."

"A transcription will suffice," Jim said, changing the pages he was holding. "Listening to the taped conversation would be akin to trying to determine what a dog meant when it howled. My Mandarin is just a little rusty."

"I suppose you haven't mastered Cantonese either," Gene joked. "You're disappointing me, Jim. I was hoping to use you as the translator if we decide to bring him in."

"Good to see you still have a sense of humor," Jim said, smiling. "I'll bet the man speaks as good English as I do."

"Better," Gene said, laughing. "He doesn't have that damned Texas drawl that you can't seem to get rid of. What else do you want to know?"

"Getting back to the transcripts or the tapes, do you have your geeky spooks going over them?" Jim asked.

"Of course," Gene answered. "They're feeding each conversation, each word, and even the pauses between words or sentences into their magic machine. That damned thing is more advanced than the enigma machine was during World War 2. It compares the cadence of the conversation with similar words or phrases to see if there's a variation that could be a code."

"How would that be a code?" Jim asked.

"Like morse code," Gene answered. "For example, if you pause one amount of time between two words and a different amount between others, it could represent dots and dashes, like morse code."

"Wow," Jim exclaimed. "I would never have thought of that. Guess I need to spend a day or two with one of those mushroom people down in the cellar where they work. Maybe I'd learn something."

"That's not even half of it," Gene continued. "If you do get a pattern, then you have to determine which is the dot and which is the dash. Then, you have to figure out what language they are using before you can start seeing if that is a code. Trust me. You don't want to even start trying to understand what those folks enjoy doing."

"No shit," Jim said, shaking his head. "I can't even do a crossword puzzle in English unless it's words with four letters or less. So, I guess there's nothing you've learned from the phone calls."

"Very perceptive," Gene confirmed. "But, again, it's only been a couple of days."

"Okay," Jim said laying the picture of Sun down. "What about the second shooter? Any information or clues as to who he or she is?"

"No," Gene answered. "And frankly, that worries me more than Sun. Him, we know and can handle. It's the unknown player that is always the biggest problem."

"I certainly agree," Jim said, nodding. "What have you done to help solve the problem?"

"Nothing yet," Gene admitted. "Remember, it's only a couple of days, and he could already be here. Or he could have been here for years. We just don't have a handle on it yet."

"Understand," Jim replied. "Now, here's what I think we need to do to smoke him out. And, it has the benefit of reassuring us about Sun."

"What's that?" Gene asked as they approached the gate into the Marine Corps Base Quantico.

"We need to move Hua," Jim answered. "And we need to ensure that Sun sees her and knows that we have her. Then, when we move her, he has to follow."

"That sounds like it has possibilities," Gene told him as he presented his ID to the gate guard. Returning the salute before proceeding onto the base, he continued, "I'm guessing you think that it will force shooter two to follow Sun."

"Exactly," Jim answered. "It may take three or four moves before we can really isolate any particular individual. But I can't think of any other way unless we get lucky and intercept a conversation that mentions killing Sun."

"We'll present that to the other members when we meet," Gene said as they came to a small, fenced area where another guard stopped them. Presenting his ID again, they drove through the first fence and waited for the gate to close behind them. When the next gate opened, they continued to a nondescript building and parked.

"Here's another twist," Jim said as he followed Gene to the building. "What if Sun is actually shooter two, and shooter one is already here?"

Gene stopped beside the steel door and started entering the code before turning and asking, "Why is it that you always present more questions than answers?"

"I'm blessed," Jim answered, smiling as they entered the small enclosure where they again had to present identification to a man behind a glass in the wall beside the locked door.

Chapter Thirteen

Once cleared in, Gene led the way to one of the many conference rooms that were scattered throughout the building. As they entered, a man wearing a black short-sleeved knit shirt with the logo of Black Water stitched above the left breast pocket approached them.

"General Barker," the man said, extending his hand. "I'm glad to see you again, and I'm assuming this is Jim Lashley."

"Good to see you too, Don," Gene said, shaking his hand. "And this is indeed Jim Lashley."

Don turned to Jim and said, "Good to meet you, Jim. We heard you were coming to give us a hand with our little problem."

"Nice to meet you," Jim said, shaking his hand. "And from what I've read, it seems that you guys have things pretty well in hand."

"We're trying," Don told him as he guided them to a table at the front of the room. "There are drinks and snacks on the table by the wall if you're hungry. We'll start the presentation as soon as you're ready, General."

"I'll just grab a quick glass of tea, and we'll be ready," Gene told him as he headed for the snack table. "Anything for you, Jim?"

"Tea will be fine," Jim answered, looking at the stacks of paper on the table where Don had escorted them.

As Gene returned with two glasses of tea, they both sat down and waited for the presentation to start. Don motioned to a man wearing a white knit shirt with the same logo and said, "Tim will start the brief, sir. All the current material is on the table, and it's arranged chronically to follow the speaker's presentation."

"Good afternoon, General," Tim said, taking the podium at the front of the room. "Mr. Lashley, welcome also."

"This is Hua Mulan," he began as a picture of her came onto the screen to his right and behind him. "As you may know, she was a very high-level scientist at a microbiology lab located in the Hubei Province of China. Her position was regarded as very unusual for a female at the Wuhan Institute of Virology. Even more so since she has no political connections and her family isn't of any particular importance. She's there because she possesses one amazing trait."

Tim paused as he looked from Gene to Jim before continuing, "She has an eidetic memory, what some call a photographic memory. She has near total recall, at least of the biological processes she manages. Her ability to retain virtually everything she sees or reads is amazing. Combine that with an intellect on a par with Stephen Hawking, and you've got an amazing lady."

The screen changed to pictures of six Asian males as Tim explained, "These men are Hua's handlers. They are employees of Black Water, and there's no reason to mention their names. The pictures are only so that if you are involved with Hua, you will be able to recognize them. Their job is more like a security force, but they are kept informed as to our plans. There are individual copies of their photos for you to keep if you need."

"How are they handling the security?" Gene asked.

"There are always two men with her," Tim explained. "If she needs to go out, one will be by her side, and the other will be a few feet ahead of them to look for anything suspicious. If they're at a restaurant, one sits with her and the other takes a table with a view of any entrance and their table. That allows them to have three teams working eight hours per day. Or, all six of them can respond if necessary."

After a couple of minutes of letting Gene and Jim look at the men, Tim had the screen change to a photo of Sun Bin, saying, "And, as you know, this is our primary suspect as to who is actively searching for Hua. And I'm sure you've seen all the data that we've managed to obtain. The only new information since yesterday is we've determined he has an additional phone that we didn't know about."

"So far, he's used it to make a single call," Tim continued. "And all we heard was that we assumed was a synthesized voice. Whoever responded to the call used a single word, also synthesized."

"Excuse me," Jim said, holding up his hand. "Are you maintaining visual contact with Sun?"

"Yes," Tim answered. "As much as possible. The only time we don't have him under observation is when he's in his hotel room. And we've got it bugged. What are you thinking?"

"If you've got him under surveillance, and you haven't seen him purchase another phone, that would suggest he brought it with him from China," Jim told him. "I'd venture that he's using it to communicate with someone in China. And since he's using it, it would appear that he knows he's under surveillance. Which would give me reason to doubt any information you get if he is indeed using a code, as the material I read on the way here suggests."

"Are you suggesting that he may be attempting to provide misleading information because he knows his phone is tapped?" Tim asked, looking from Jim to Gene.

"That's what I'd do," Jim answered. "And I'd be changing my phone every day. As far as the one he's currently using, I would even suggest that tomorrow he's given it to someone else to give you another false trail to follow."

"That's possible," Tim agreed, nodding. "But, if someone else uses that phone, our voice recognition program will alert us to the change. I don't think we'd be wasting much time with it."

"Understand," Jim responded. "But, if he does give it away instead of destroying it, it would make me even surer that he knows the original phone is tapped. Which brings me back to the probability that he's feeding you false information during those conversations that you're trying to decipher in some coded message."

"Do you have a tap or trace on the number he called using the new phone?" Gene asked.

"Not yet," Tim admitted. "Like I said, we just found out about it. Our research into the called phone is ongoing, but it may take another day or two. We've programmed our computers to record any calls to or from that phone whether or not it's Sun. But for now, there's only been one call from him."

"Do you know where that phone is located?" Jim asked.

"We think it's in San Francisco," Tim answered. "We know which towers it's using, and they are all within the Chinatown area. But it could just be a relay connecting to another phone anywhere."

"Okay," Gene interrupted. "I'm sure your guys will figure it out. But, in the meantime, is there anything else you need to show us?"

"Not really," Tim answered. "I was planning on talking about our progress on the possibility of determining if there is a code hidden in Sun's calls, but that seems to be of questionable value if Jim's theory is correct."

"I wouldn't discount any information you get if you do crack the code," Jim told him. "It's possible that I'm full of crap, and he's using the new phone to mislead us. I'm not sure if you're old enough to remember *Mad* magazine, but there was a cartoon in every issue about spy versus spy. One was dressed in white, and the other one was dressed in black. You never knew which one was going to be the good guy when you initially looked at it. Even if we think there's a possibility Sun is gaming us, there's always value in any information. Even if it's false. If it's determined to actually be false, it may eliminate a course of action.

I'd suggest proceeding as you've been doing," Jim continued. "Then comparing his actual activities or other conversations to the ones we find suspicious will sooner or later let us know if he's using either phone to mislead us."

"I think that's a good approach," Don said, stepping up to the podium beside Tim.

"I agree," Tim said. "Anything else?"

"Tell them about your thoughts regarding the shooters and moving Hua," Gene told Jim.

"You think we need to move her?" Don asked, looking from Gene to Jim.

"Yes," Jim said, nodding. "Even more so now that we need to figure out if Sun is trying to misdirect us. The other reason for the move is to flush out the second shooter, if there is one. Which I fully believe is the case. As well as a probable third shooter sooner or later."

"How is moving her going to do that?" Tim asked.

"It's going to take several moves," Jim acknowledged. "We move her to some out-of-the-way location, such as Omaha. We get a chance to see who follows within the next day or two. Then we move to some other Podunk place where we weed out any false positives just in case of a coincidence. I might even change modes of transport. Fly to Omaha, then drive to Nowhere USA."

"Sounds good," Don agreed. "How do we make sure Sun follows?"

"We've got to expose her," Jim answered. "He's got to see her going to the airport or somehow find out that she's moving. I'd probably make sure he sees her today or tomorrow at the latest. Since you know which restaurants he frequents, have Hua ready to move when your people advise you that he's going to one of them. Then, have her walk by the window or something so that he sees her."

"Don't you think that's an unnecessary risk?" Tim asked. "If he's here to eliminate her, that's playing into his hands."

"He's going to find her sooner or later if he doesn't already know," Jim explained. "This way, we know where he is and can whisk her away immediately if he makes any move. Or we can eliminate him on the spot if there's truly a threat. But it's imperative that he knows where she is so that we can lead him, and the probable second shooter, to where we move her. Then we control the game. Right now, we don't know if he's located her, if the second shooter is here, or anything other than he's here and now using a second phone. We need to start controlling things. If we're not the lead dog, all we see is another dog's butt. The time for just sitting back and analyzing is over. It's time for us to take some action. If this lady is this important, and you tell me she is, the clock is ticking, and we're already late."

"One more thing," Gene said, standing up. "Jim has an additional wrinkle to toss at you."

"Go ahead," Don said, shaking his head. "It looks like we need to get a new game plan started, and I'd hate to be going down a road that leads nowhere."

"Just a thought," Jim said, standing. "Is it possible that Sun is the second shooter here to eliminate the actual guy that's going to kill Hua? I think that exposing Hua and then moving her will give us some insight."

"How's that?" Tim asked.

"If Sun shows little interest in following Hua, he may be watching someone else to see what they do," Jim explained. "If we figure out who's actually following her, then we might know what role Sun is really playing. I bring this up because he seems to be too valuable an asset to the Chinese to be sent here to just to be eliminated. The more I think about it, the more I'm leaning toward him being the second shooter. Or the third. Or maybe just as an insurance policy in case the first ones don't do their jobs."

"The good thing is that monitoring the phones, exposing Hua, and all of the moves should give us that answer," Gene said. "Now, Jim and I need to get back to Haymarket, and you guys need to start coordinating flights, rooms, and everything necessary to put Jim's plan with Hua into motion within the next three days. Two, if possible. We'll be back tomorrow morning to review those plans to see if we can help implement them. Have a good evening, gentlemen."

66

Chapter Fourteen

As Gene and Jim were driving back to the Inn, Jim spoke up, saying, "I feel as if I need to apologize to Don and Tim."

"Why?" Gene asked.

"I just feel like I took over their presentation and ordered them to look at something that may not be the way to go," Jim explained. "It looked like they had spent a lot of time planning a different approach, and they probably think I'm trying to take over the entire operation."

"Don't worry about it," Gene said with a quick glance at Jim. "First off, Tim is part of the research department. He has no operational experience. Did you hear him say anything except quoting information they had gathered? I didn't. He gets his orders from the operations people. They develop the plan and request information. Tim is a downstream researcher. All he did today was present the information that others gathered. Don't worry."

"What about Don?" Jim asked. "Isn't he Black Water? I thought this was a domestic operation. Normally, Muddy Water handles that."

"Don is Black Water staff," Gene explained. "So is Tim. The operation began overseas and was carried out by Dark Water. Once it came ashore, it fell into the purview of Muddy Water. That's why you're involved. But Black Water is overseeing the operation. However, Don isn't in the operations area either. He is more like logistics. He's there to make sure we, Muddy Water, have everything we need from an operational standpoint. He serves the same function for Dark Water. You just keep looking at it from an operational point of view. You did exactly what I brought you up here for."

"You brought me up here to destroy their work?" Jim asked. "That's what I think I did."

"Absolutely not," Gene emphasized. "You even kept them on the path regarding the phones and how to use the information they were gathering. The information they have will still be used. No waste of time. The waste would have been if they hadn't been pointed in the direction of moving Hua. Refocusing their perception of Sun could be beneficial as well."

Glancing at Jim to see if he was getting through to him, Gene continued, "If they don't look at the possibility that he isn't who they believe he is, it could skew the entire operation if he's not the primary shooter. That's why you're here. To see what isn't obvious even though it appears to be. From the time I found out what you did in Vietnam on that hill, I knew that you didn't just see the obvious."

"You have an uncanny ability to see things that most people don't see," Gene told him. "That's why I recruited you to Black Water. That's why I bring you in more and more at the planning stage. You've developed well beyond a simple field operator. If I didn't trust you to point out the potential flaws or see what others have overlooked, I wouldn't have brought you here."

"If I'm more than a simple field operator," Jim said with a serious face, "does that mean I'm getting a pay raise?"

Gene glanced at Jim and laughed, saying, "Of course. How about if I buy you dinner every time you and Jennifer are here? Or when I come down to Mesquite to visit? How's that for a pay raise?"

"Toss in the private jet, and it's a deal," Jim said as he watched the countryside slide by. "That'll keep Jennifer happy. That and nice hotels. And a chance to dress up. I'll consider that a pay raise."

"I don't think the company will go along with that private jet deal," Gene replied. "But you've got to know that I've sent it more times than not. And usually, Jennifer can come along if she's not working. That's the best I can do."

"Not to change the subject," Jim said, "But how's Jewell? I haven't heard much since she was injured in that car wreck during our assignment in Chicago. I hope Black Water is taking care of her because she's too valuable as an agent not to try to bring her back."

"She's out of the hospital," Gene answered. "She's still going to have months of rehab. I'm keeping an eye on her, and the company will take care of everything she needs."

"That's good," Jim responded. "She was, or still is, a good field operator. She had a keen sense of timing that helped immensely on the assignments where we worked together."

"I know," Gene told him. "And I know that she was more than just another agent to you. I'll tell her that you asked about her next time I talk to her."

"Thanks," Jim replied. "She's been a good friend for a lot of years."

"I understand," Gene said. "Now, what's your idea on the movement of Hua?"

"I'm still in favor of someplace like Omaha," Jim answered. "Toss in a couple of smaller and smaller towns. Maybe two or three days in each location. Then, once we see who's following her, we can set up a trap to take out whoever's identified."

Gene asked. "Even if we take them out, don't we still have the problem of China not resting until she's eliminated?"

"I certainly think so," Jim agreed. "I still think we need to convince shooter one that she's dead and give him time to report it to his boss. Or there's still the possibility of turning Sun if we determine he's shooter one. The only problem is that shooter two is still a threat. And number three. It's sort of like a line of dominos. If one of them is removed, the rest of them may not fall."

"Agreed," Gene said. "It appears that learning who the shooters are is probably the smallest of the problems. Hua herself is going to be a problem if she stays alive. And keeping her alive *is* the most important thing. That is the contract."

"Why?" Jim asked. "If we, or the government, get the information she possesses, isn't that the goal? The information?"

"Partially," Gene admitted. "But the impact of her live testimony broadcast around the world would be hard for the Chinese to dismiss. Showing a sheet of their activities is too easy to deny. No, we need her to be seen testifying."

"Yeah, I can see that," Jim agreed. "Then, we'll still have the problem of her safety. You know they won't stop until she's dead. Even if we pull off convincing them now that she's been eliminated by one of the shooters, they'll return with a vengeance later after she's gone public."

"I'm sure they will," Gene agreed. "But, for right now, the operation is only concerned with getting her to the point of testifying. That's all the company was contracted to do."

"Don't you think we have some responsibility once the contract is fulfilled?" Jim asked. "As you know, once the administration that hired us gets what they want, they'll soon forget the residual problems caused by their actions."

"In some ways, yes," Gene answered. "I've been working with my boss to have some sort of follow-on program when we're involved in one of these types of operations. Not only will it be the right thing to do when we're finished with a person like this, but it will also be a way to safeguard people that need to disappear due to other operations."

"Are you talking about some sort of witness protection program?" Jim asked.

"More than that," Gene told him. "What we're discussing is more like what the Nazis did after World War two. Thousands of high-ranking officers escaped via what were known as rat lines to South America. I'm looking at something like that."

"What would the people you are assisting do then?" Jim asked. "They still need to live. How do they get jobs to support themselves? How long will they be expected to go without ever seeing their families again?"

"Those are some of the issues we're working through," Gene answered as they pulled into the parking lot at the Inn. "But the company will include the cost of what we think is necessary in the initial contract. So, Hua, for instance, would be given a new identity and relocated to someplace like Sao

Paulo, Brazil, which has a large Asian community. As far as expenses go, it would be something like our Social Security program. They would get a monthly amount that allows them to maintain the same lifestyle they had before we interrupted their lives."

"Do you think that will happen?" Jim asked as they walked toward the building.

"I think so," Gene told him, holding the door open. "It even has possibilities of becoming another branch of Black Water."

"What would you call it?" Jim asked, getting into the elevator. "Bottled Water?"

"I was thinking Clear Water," Gene replied, laughing. "But Bottled Water may be more appropriate since we're basically holding them captive. Bottled Water. I like it. Now, I'll see you guys in the restaurant in about an hour."

Chapter Fifteen

When Jim and Jennifer arrived at the restaurant, Gene had already gotten a table for them and was talking to the waiter. As they approached, he stood and said, "Jennifer, you look great. Please, have a seat. I'm just about to order a bottle of Merlot unless you prefer something different."

"Do you have a Malbec?" Jennifer asked the waiter as she took her seat.

"Yes, ma'am," he told her. "We have an excellent Malbec from Argentina."

"Is that all right?" she asked, looking at Gene as Jim sat down across from him.

"Of course," Gene answered. "Could we get two bottles, please?"

"I'll be right back, sir," the waiter said with a slight bow.

Picking up the menu, Jennifer asked, "What do you recommend, General?"

"The grilled filet mignon is excellent," Gene told her. "But I know how you and Jim like yours mesquite grilled. The chicken is also very good, but Jim doesn't like chicken.

That sort of leaves the crab cakes, which are delicious, or the Ponzu seared salmon."

"What's Ponzu seared?" Jim asked, looking at the menu.

"Ponzu is a soy-based sauce with citric juice," Gene explained. "Toss in a little crushed red pepper, and you can use it for a salad dressing like vinaigrette, a dipping sauce for various seafood, or when you sear the salmon. It's one of my favorites here."

"Sounds good to me," Jim said, nodding. "I'm guessing that it's an Asian dish."

"Japanese," Gene told him as the waiter arrived with their wine.

"I think I'll have the crab cakes," Jennifer announced, laying her menu on the table.

"Shall I pour?" the waiter asked as he opened the first bottle of wine.

"Please," Gene said, watching him holding the open bottle.

"Of course, sir," the waiter answered, handing Jennifer a glass with a small amount of wine. "Madam, let me know if you approve."

Sipping the wine, she nodded and answered, "Excellent, thank you."

As he filled her glass, he asked, "Are you folks ready to order?"

"Yes," Gene answered. "The lady would like the crab cakes. Jim and I both want the Ponzu seared salmon."

"Excellent," the waiter said as he set the wine down. "And what vegetable would the lady like?"

"Could I get the Julienne vegetables?" she asked.

"Of course," he answered with a slight bow. "I'll turn in your orders and be right back to check on you."

"Thank you," Gene told him as he raised his glass. "To my friends and another chance to enjoy your company."

Jennifer raised hers and said, "To you, General. For your hospitality. It's always a joy to spend time with you."

"Well put, Jennifer," Jim agreed, raising his glass and looking at Gene. "And to many more evenings with my beautiful wife and you."

"Thank you," Gene said, tipping his glass toward both of them. "But it's easy to be hospitable with you guys. Let's just say to a long-lasting friendship and many more times together."

"Indeed," Jim said, tipping his glass. "Friendship."

"And to two of my favorite gentlemen," Jennifer said, tipping her glass.

As they took a drink, Jim set his glass down and looked at Gene, asking, "Did you hear her refer to us as gentlemen? I think we may need to see if there's a house doctor. She normally refers to us as knuckle-dragging heathens."

"That you are," Jennifer said, laughing and patting Jim's hand. "But occasionally, you dress up sort of acceptable. But that's to be expected of a Marine. And I've come to love both of you."

"I'll take the compliment at face value," Gene said, setting his glass down. "Did you enjoy your day?"

"It was great," Jennifer answered excitedly. "The room is amazing! And when I went out for a walk, I decided that I needed to take up golf so I'd have a reason to walk around outside. It's just beautiful. And I've decided that we'll stay here every time we come."

Gene smiled at Jim and announced, "We've created a monster. I knew I should have never put you guys anywhere except Motel 6 by the airport. And no more private jets. And only coach. No first class. No more pampering."

"You started it," Jim said, shaking his head. "Now you have to pay the piper."

"I guess I'll have to go back to the board of directors and get an increase in my budget," Gene said, laughing as the waiter arrived with their meals. "I may have to fudge my numbers a little to make it appear as if I'm using a company of Marines instead of just Jim."

Jennifer put her hand on Gene's arm and told him, "I'll be glad to stay at Motel 6, General. As long as Jim and I get to spend time with you."

"You better take care of this lady," Gene said, patting Jennifer's hand. "This is one rare lady. I'm not sure even you deserve her."

"That I know," Jim told him as he took a bite of his salmon. "Just look at the transformation she's done to me. What was a mud-crawling, knuckle-dragging, beer-swilling heathen is now a polished gentleman sipping fine wine at an ornate club with white cloth tablecloths. It's a long way from the jungles where you and I met."

"That it is," Gene concurred. "It's a long way from our former lives. And a welcome improvement. From leaky tents in a jungle to an Antebellum home with nobody shooting at us. A welcome improvement."

"What are you guys doing tomorrow?" Jennifer asked, taking a piece of Jim's salmon.

"I thought we'd have a quick breakfast and then Jim and I will head to Quantico," Gene answered. "We'll come back for lunch and get you so you guys can get back to Mesquite."

"I think I can find something interesting to do for a few hours," Jennifer said, smiling. "Just walking around the Inn is amazing. This is something I never thought I'd really get to see. It's sort of like that house in Gone With the Wind."

"That's a pretty good analogy," Gene told her. "This place was a plantation with about a thousand acres and was built back in the 1820s. But I don't think Jim comes anywhere close when compared to Rhett Butler."

"At least I'm not Ashley Wilkes," Jim countered. "That guy was a little too refined for me."

"I can think of a more appropriate word instead of refined," Gene said, smiling. "But there's always a place in this world for people like that."

"Aren't they all in the Coast Guard?" Jim asked, laughing. "Or the Air Force?"

"You two quit it," Jennifer told them, laughing along. "I thought he was sweet."

"That's what we're saying," Jim said, looking at Gene. "He was sweet."

Chapter Sixteen

After breakfast the following morning, as they were driving back to Quantico, Gene said, "I bet the team was up half of the night trying to set up a schedule to move Hua."

"That's fine with me," Jim said as they drove along. "I hope that when they're flying, they pass through at least one airport requiring a change of planes. That will give us a good look at any passenger that changes to the same plane."

"Do you think that's important?" Gene asked, glancing at him. "We'll have the passenger manifest of each flight well in advance and can check any names that appear on each one."

"I understand," Jim answered. "But matching a face to the names is important. Being able to watch them while they're waiting for the connecting flight could help. Getting a picture that we can use to do a facial recognition check may show that they're flying under an assumed name. Lots of benefits to having an hour or so to study the adversary."

"Sounds like you remember your training as a Long Range Reconnaissance Patrol," Gene told him. "I guess we taught you something that stuck with you."

"Partly that," Jim admitted. "But there was something else I remember from reading Sun Tzu's *Art of War*."

"Pray tell," Gene said smiling at him.

"It's first to measure. Second, to estimate quantity. Third, to calculate. And the final thing is victory." Jim told him. "If we can watch the people getting off the plane, we might figure out if there's more than one following her and what we'll need to do to protect Hua and make sure whoever's in China thinks she's dead."

"Do you think that's possible?" Gene asked as he thought about what Jim had just said.

"It's what I'd do," Jim said, nodding his head for emphasis. "What if you're the one following her, and you need to use the restroom while you're waiting for the connecting flight? You come back out, and she's gone. What do you do?"

"Wait for her to show back up to board the next plane," Gene replied.

"What if she took off?" Jim posed. "What if the scheduled flight was a diversion, and she was actually going on a different flight to another city? Would you take a chance on losing her just because you didn't want to send a team instead of just a single person? I wouldn't. Hell, I'd probably send three or four."

"I see your point," Gene agreed. "I'm guessing that you've changed your mind about how many people we're going to have to deal with."

"Yes," Jim answered. "I still think there are probably three shooters. One for Hua. One for that shooter. And a final shooter to sever the possibility of anyone linking all of them together."

"Does that mean you think there are three teams?" Gene asked.

"Not necessarily," Jim answered. "But I'd be damn sure I had enough force to eliminate the primary target, Hua. After that, sure, I'd like more options. Eliminating shooter one is only a precaution against discovery. As is eliminating that guy. Neither are the prime objective."

"Good point," Gene admitted as they approached Quantico. "Let's see how much we upset the apple cart with this."

"Boy, those guys are going to just love me," Jim said as they cleared the security at the gate and parked. "I can't wait to see the looks on their faces when you break the news."

"I break the news?" Gene asked with a laugh as they were cleared into the building. "No deal. It's your idea. You'll break the news."

Entering the same conference room as they used the day before, Don greeted them and said, "Good morning, General ... Jim. There's a table with coffee, juice, and some pastries available."

"Thanks, Don," Gene said. "I'll go grab a cup of coffee while Jim gives you an update on moving Hua."

Shaking his head as Gene walked away, Jim said, "There's a possibility that there may be more than one initial shooter. By that, I'm suggesting that there may be more than just the shooter following Hua. I'm suggesting that there could be as many as four people who will follow when we move her."

"Okay," Don said thoughtfully. "How does that change things?"

"Not a lot," Jim answered as Don followed him to the table where Gene was pouring coffee. "But I think we need to make sure that on the initial move for Hua, we pass through at least one airport with a connecting flight so we can see who and how many are following. I'd prefer two connecting flights to get her to the destination, but one will work if there's sufficient time between flights."

"I think that can be worked into our plan," Don told him. "Matter of fact, it might be better than our original idea."

"What do you mean?" Gene asked as Jim was getting a cup of coffee.

"Well, what if we left San Francisco heading for Atlanta, for example," Don explained. "Then, when we get to Dallas for the connection, we use a different ticket to Chicago."

"That's a great idea," Jim told him enthusiastically. "I have been wondering how our shooter, Sun, was going to get a ticket to follow her anyway unless he knows where she's going. That seems to me like it would be impossible unless we have a leak.

But there is a way," he continued as he visualized the possible plan. "And it fits with my concept of a team following Hua. I don't see any other way. Unless, as I said, we do have a leak, which I doubt."

"How do you think they'll do it?" Don asked, getting some coffee.

"I'd send three or four people to follow her as we start the move," Jim explained. "Then, when she arrives at the airport, they can determine which terminal she heads for. That limits her possible destinations. One of the team goes to the ticket counter and buys a ticket to any destination leaving that terminal.

He then gives the ticket to another team member who'll enter the terminal and locates the gate, therefore the destination," Jim continued. "Then the guy at the ticket counter buys tickets for all of the members to that location."

"And I guess you can repeat the process at each stop," Don said, nodding. "That makes sense."

"I don't see any other way they can follow," Jim agreed. "But we need to make sure there's at least an hour between flights until the final flight. That one should be with as little wait time as possible so they don't have time to get tickets."

"What do you think, Don?" Gene asked as they headed for the table at the head of the room. "Is this going to cause a major revision of your plan?"

"Not really," Don answered as Tim joined them. "It just means that we may need to add a few people to our team as well so we can keep an eye on each of their teams. I'll get more tickets and make reservations for more rooms at the hotels. Oh, and add a couple of cars at each location they may need. Shouldn't be a problem."

"Good morning, General ... Jim," Tim said. "Have we made some changes to the plan?"

"Nothing that will change anything for you guys," Don advised him. "Mostly a logistical issue. For now, we'll go ahead with the briefing as if everything is the same."

"Sounds good," Tim said as Gene and Jim took their seats. "I'll give you a quick update on everything and see if you have any questions, and then I'll get with Don to go over anything he may need from me and my team."

Chapter Seventeen

"Okay," Tim began, "The folders in front of you have been updated with what we learned last night. I'll give you a moment to take a look at what's new. And, as before, I'll present the material in the same order as in your folders to make it easier for you to follow on the screens. But please don't hesitate to interrupt if you have any questions." Tim waited until both Gene and Jim were looking at him and then told them, "The biggest thing that's happened is regarding the second phone. As you can see, it's actively being used with an increased frequency."

Jim raised his hand to interrupt and asked, "What about the original phone? Have you found any code or anything that would be considered suspicious?"

"If you wait just a minute, I'll answer those questions, sir," Tim said. "I'd like to finish with this phone before we move to the first phone."

"Not a problem," Jim apologized. "I just had a question, but it can certainly wait."

"The phones are all shown here on the screen," Tim told them. "But, to try to keep it as simple as possible, I'll try to summarize what seems to be how they are being used."

Tim paused as they looked at the four phone numbers on the screen with listings of calls to or from each one and then said, "Sun has two phones. The first one is using a code. The second is using a synthesized voice, as I told you earlier. And the response is synthesized."

"Does that mean you can't even determine if it's Sun talking on it?" Jim asked.

"Yes and no," Tim answered. "We're still working on it using some of the same techniques we are using about the codes you were asking about earlier. We're developing an algorithm that looks at cadence, pitch range, and other characteristics that we can measure. We overlay those with recordings from Sun on the other phone and try to get enough matches to give us assurance that it's him."

"Anything so far?" Gene asked.

"A little," Tim answered. "We've seen an almost imperceptible delay between words that almost perfectly matches his speech pattern. It's still a little early to say for sure, but if we get another ten or so recordings, I'm positive we'll be able to guarantee if Sun's the speaker."

"What about who's on the other end?" Jim asked. "Is there anything you can use to try to identify him?"

"No," Tim answered. "But whoever Sun is calling always answers with a single word."

"What do your guys think about that?" Gene asked.

"Sun speaks two or three sentences," Tim explained. "And then there's a short pause, and we hear a word. Nothing more until Sun talks again. We think Sun is giving orders to whoever he's calling."

"Or he could be providing information," Jim offered. "We used to use a technique we called zipper. It was used in conjunction with our Have Quick radios, and whoever was being given coordinates or something would just key the microphone."

"I'm familiar with Have Quick," Tim said, smiling. "Frequency hopping radios going to random frequencies that are prearranged and coordinated between them using a word of the day and a Mickey, or time sync. But there isn't any hopping here. No frequency changes."

"I was referring more to the single-word response," Jim explained. "The actual word may not have any significance. It may possibly even be binary. One syllable word response may mean yes and a two or more syllable word could mean no. Or vice versa."

"That would make it difficult to talk about anything," Tim said. "But I can see where it might fit what we're looking at. I'll make sure we do a little more research on the recordings regarding the number of syllables in the words being used by each phone."

"It's not that difficult," Jim explained. "For example, I tell you to go to location A. You give me a one-syllable word answer, meaning yes. Later, I may ask if you're there, and you give me a two-syllable word answer meaning no. I'll ask again until I get a one-syllable word answer."

"I understand," Tim said. "We'll add that to the algorithm when we run all of the recordings again tonight."

The screen changed again, and Tim said, "Now, in regard to your earlier question about if there's a code being used by Sun. We think there is."

"Have you broken it?" Gene asked.

"We think so," Tim answered. "It appears to be in Mandarin, which isn't surprising since Sun is Chinese, and we're assuming he's talking to another Chinese person. However, some of the 'words' appear to be numbers, and we haven't been able to decode them."

"What sort of numbers are you talking about?" Jim asked. "Do you have an example?"

"Yes," Tim said, taking a page from the folder he had on the podium. "I didn't include it in your folders because we don't know what it means yet."

Stepping down, he walked to where Gene and Jim sat and laid the page on the table in front of Jim. "We think we're looking at a simple alphabet number code. Maybe Z is 23, and G is a 7. Possibly, it's tied to the phone keyboard where A, B, or C is 2, and T, U, or V is 8."

Jim looked at the numbers for a couple of minutes and then asked, "Do you have a Latitude Longitude (Lat-Long) map of San Francisco?"

"I don't know," Tim answered as he turned to Don.

"We do," Don said as he turned to leave. "I'll be right back."

"What are you thinking, Jim?" Gene asked.

"I think these numbers are coordinates," Jim answered. "I'm pretty sure San Francisco is about 37 or 38 degrees north and 122 or so west. These numbers may represent a location. These numbers, if I'm correct, could give you an exact location."

"Like a GPS," Gene added.

"Exactly," Jim agreed as Don came in with a map of San Francisco.

Spreading the map on the table, Jim pointed to the San Francisco airport and announced, "See, the airport is 37.62 north by 122.36 west. That could help you determine what the code for the numbers is by using the 3, 7, 6, and 2 for the first four numbers."

"And the same method for the five numbers representing the longitude," Gene told them. "If you have two 3's, three 2's, and two 6's in the order as the lat-long for

San Francisco, you've got a third of the numbers identified in the code."

"But our numbers have several more digits," Tim said.

"GPS," Gene told him as Jim tried to pinpoint the location described by the numbers Tim had provided. "It has three sets of numbers for each direction. For example, it could be 37 degrees, 46 minutes, 26 seconds north and 122 degrees, 25 minutes, 52 seconds west."

"That's right," Jim agreed as he pointed to the map. "And the more numbers, especially the third set, make it more accurate. If you had 37, 46, 26.4322, you'd probably be at the front door of a building."

"Or a restaurant," Gene added. "You guys need to get on this. Sun could be giving information on Hua's location to somebody."

"But that would mean that he's not the shooter," Tim argued.

"Exactly," Gene said, standing and turning to Jim. "That's exactly what you were talking about yesterday. Sun may be shooter two."

"Yes, sir. Or number three," Jim acknowledged as Gene turned to Don.

"Don, you need to get some more resources involved," Gene told him. "We need to go to every one of the locations identified by these coordinates. And I mean immediately. If any of them are Hua's location, get her handlers to get her out of there ASAP. Find another place to hide her until we start moving her around."

"Yes, sir," Don responded. "Anything else?"

"Yes," Gene said. "Get the tickets, hotels, cars, and anything else we need for the movement. We may be moving her tonight if those coordinates match her location."

"You have anything else, Jim?" Gene asked, turning away from Don.

"Not right now, sir," Jim answered.

"Then we'll get back to the Inn," Gene announced as he headed for the door. "I'll follow up after I get you on the plane back to Texas."

Chapter Eighteen

"If any of those coordinates prove to be Hua's location or places she's been, we've got major problems," Gene said as they were driving back to get Jennifer.

"That's for sure," Jim agreed. "But the thing that bothers me the most is who Sun is calling. Because if Sun is shooter one, and if he's sending locations to someone else, that doesn't change our plan for Hua."

"What do you mean?" Gene asked.

"If Sun is shooter one and he knows Hua's location, it's irrelevant whether he shoots her or another shooter does it," Jim explained. "Which leads me back to the probability that he isn't shooter one."

"I'm not following you," Gene replied with a glance at Jim.

"If he's shooter one," Jim told him, "Why would he be talking to anyone about her location? But if he's shooter two, he could be sort of like the spotter on a sniper team. The real shooter wouldn't suspect that his spotter is going to eliminate him after he takes out the target, Hua."

"I got it," Gene said, nodding. "If Sun is number two, he furnishes locations knowing where shooter one will be.

Then, he can ambush him after Hua is eliminated. That would be smart of the Chinese to make the shooter believe that he has a partner. Then that partner, Sun, doesn't have to guess at when the hit will be, where it will take place, and where the actual shooter will go after it's over."

"Yes," Jim said, nodding. "Otherwise, Sun would have to be following both the shooter and Hua. The only thing we know for sure is that Sun is using another phone to communicate with someone. And that could mean two different people, which is what I suspect."

"Let's assume that Sun is talking to the real shooter in code. That would explain the coordinates being encrypted," Jim continued. "Then, he's giving updates to whoever sent him here on the phone using a synthesized voice."

"Let me see if I've got this right," Gene said, shaking his head. "You think Sun is talking to the real shooter in code."

"Yes," Jim answered. "That's because he needs to use a code to give instructions and the coordinates. As I said, that only makes sense if there is another shooter who is here to take out Hua. I can't think of any other reason for Sun to be providing both coded information and locations."

"What if Sun isn't the guy using the synthesized voice?" Gene asked. "What if there's another player that we don't know about?"

"Tim said that they've overlaid his voice on both recordings, and there's enough of a match to believe it is Sun," Jim said. "He sort of hedged his bet by saying they want a few more recordings to match, but I'm willing to believe it's Sun. If we start adding more people to the mix, it means that there are unnecessary people who would know what's going on. I don't think whoever sent Sun here wants that. I'll go with my assumption that there are at least two people involved. Shooter one and shooter two. Possibly, there's a shooter three, but only if they don't trust Sun as shooter two."

"Say you're right," Gene replied, nodding. "Sun is directing the real shooter in code. Then he's relaying information back to his bosses via synthesized voice. But why not just code?"

"Voice recognition," Jim explained. "Maybe whoever Sun's briefing doesn't want his voice heard. Or just another precaution."

"That's logical," Gene said. "Now, I think it's even more imperative that we move Hua as soon as possible so that we can identify the real shooter."

"I agree," Jim replied. "Now, here's how I think things will go. We move Hua. Sun follows, and we know because we're watching him. When we get to location A, we get a chance to see if anyone else follows us to location B."

"Or on the next move," Gene added.

"Yes," Jim agreed. "Now, there's always a possibility that the real shooter is waiting for Sun to send him Hua's location once she's settled. That makes it easier for him to show up there instead of traipsing from airport to airport."

"How will we know that?" Gene asked.

"If there are coded communications every time there's a movement, we'll know because the geeks at Quantico will pass us the decoded message," Jim answered. "If it includes coordinates of where we are, it's proof that someone is waiting for the final destination."

"Sounds good," Gene said, nodding in agreement. "Then we just wait for the trace on Sun's phone to show that he's close to us."

"That's the plan," Jim told him. "However, we still have a major problem."

"What's that?" Gene asked, shaking his head.

"Confirmation of Hua's death still has to be given to Sun's boss," Jim answered. "Like I said earlier, until they receive word that she's no longer a threat, they'll just keep sending shooters."

"Then we're back to square one," Gene said, exasperated.

"More or less," Jim agreed. "But we'll have made some progress."

"What do you mean?" Gene asked.

"We've gained time," Jim answered. "Let's look at the problem from the end back to the start. The end is when Hua has provided the information in front of the world, and we have her at your supersecret hideout down in Argentina."

"Hopefully," Gene told him.

"So, our current goal is to keep her safe until she testifies," Jim said. "Since we don't know when that is, we can't keep her safe indefinitely unless the people that want her dead think she is. That leads us back to she has to die as soon as possible, as far as anyone knows."

"What are your thoughts on that?" Gene asked.

"Number one, no matter how we do it, it has to be convincing to Sun," Jim answered. "He'll eliminate the shooter since the job's done. Then, he'll probably head home. Unless there's a shooter three who takes care of him."

"Okay," Gene said. "Where and when do you want to plan her *demise*?"

"Let's initially plan for her to be moved for at least three days," Jim answered. "That will give us time to determine for sure there is another shooter, and Sun is controlling him. The where should be someplace that allows us the opportunity to force Sun into chasing us into a position where we'll stage the *accident*. Then we'll know he's fallen for it when he uses the coded phone to relay the information to the real shooter."

"I guess further proof will also be when Sun uses the other phone to notify his boss," Gene replied. "Then, we can put Hua somewhere safe until she exposes what the Chinese are up to regarding their biological programs."

"That's my thought," Jim agreed as they pulled into the Inn. "I just hope you and the company have your *Bottled Water* program up and running by then. Otherwise, another team from China will be here to exact their revenge on Hua for divulging their little secrets."

Chapter Nineteen

"I'll get us a table," Gene said as they entered the Inn. "If you'll grab Jennifer and meet me, we'll try to get back to Quantico in the next couple of hours."

"I'll go get her," Jim said as he headed for the elevators. "Hopefully, she's got her bags packed. But it won't take long after lunch if she hasn't."

As they walked into the restaurant a few minutes later, Gene spotted them and stood. "Jennifer, did you enjoy the morning while Jim and I were working?" he asked, pulling out a chair for her.

"Yes, I did, thank you," she answered, taking her seat. "I think I could become a lady of leisure if given the opportunity."

"You'd be bored by the week's end," Jim told her as he sat down. "You keep working when you certainly don't need to. You'd go crazy sitting around the house. Nope, you'll never be a lady of leisure. You don't have the temperament."

"I agree with Jim," Gene said as the waiter approached. "I've known you for several years, almost as many as Jim, and you're not happy with nothing to do."

"Maybe I could learn," she countered, looking at the menu. "Especially if I had an unlimited budget, a private jet, and a husband who wanted to follow me around the world."

"Now you're asking for Ashley Wilkes," Jim said, smiling. "I don't think Rhett Butler would be happy traipsing around the world carrying your luggage and waiting on you hand and foot. Even if his name was Butler, he would never ever be one. Never."

"Besides," Gene told them, "Jim doesn't have an unlimited budget and never will with the airlines. They pay a good salary, but not near enough for your world travel dream."

"Are you folks ready to order?" the waiter asked, standing by the table.

"I need a moment," Jennifer answered, picking up her menu.

"I'd like a glass of tea, the Bull Run burger, medium rare, American cheese, mushrooms, and French fries, please," Jim answered, handing the waiter his menu.

"Iced tea and the Evergreen Club," Gene told him. "And sweet potato fries."

"The Crab Cake sandwich, please," Jennifer said. "And ice tea."

"Will there be anything else?" the waiter asked, gathering the menus.

Gene looked at Jim and Jennifer before he answered, "Not right now, thank you."

As the waiter walked away, Jennifer looked at Gene and said, "Well, you know you could hire Jim as a permanent advisor. Then he'd be available any time you needed him. We could move up here, or you could keep a jet in Dallas so we could be here just mere hours after you call."

Gene looked at Jim and smiled as he answered, "You think Jim would be happy sitting around the house waiting for me to call? If it wasn't for the three or four days a week he has to go fly, I'd give him a month before you'd find him in the garage sucking on a hose connected to the exhaust pipe of his Corvette. And you know he'd never leave Texas."

"Oh, I know," she said, putting her hand on Jim's arm. "And Jim's right about me never being a lady of leisure. But it sure would be nice to have a few days like this every couple of months. Just to spend time with no dishes to wash, laundry to do, toilets to clean, you know, everyday life stuff."

"But everyday life stuff is what makes these days special," Jim countered. "I enjoy flying for American Airlines, sometimes. I enjoy mowing the yard, sometimes. And I don't really mind those other little chores, sometimes. But, not having to do them for a few days is something to look forward to."

"Jim's right," Gene agreed as the waiter came back with their teas. "If you spent every day with nothing to do, you'd probably want to mow the yard or do the laundry sooner or later."

"Do you really think I'd ever wish for a toilet to clean?" Jennifer asked him, laughing. "You may be right about looking for something to do, but laundry and toilets? Not a chance."

"Okay, I didn't mention cleaning toilets," Gene said, laughing. "And laundry may have been a poor choice also. But you're just like Jim. You need a purpose in life. I think that's why you two fit together so well. You both have a drive to accomplish something. It may just be to contribute to your financial well-being or just to do something for other people. But both of you look for ways to make life better for yourselves or for others. That'll never change."

"What about if I have the leisure life I'm talking about, but I also have a mission to make life better for others? Maybe I could start a charity to help dogs without collars?" Jennifer countered as the waiter came back with their sandwiches.

"Dogs without collars?" Gene replied, laughing. "I suppose you'd travel the world meeting the animal control people of every city and make sure every stray dog would have a collar. Now, that sounds like a worthy ambition."

"Oh, you know what I mean," Jennifer answered, shaking her head. "Any purpose. Orphans. Cancer. Abused people. The elderly. I could find something worthy of my time."

"How about husbands without wives?" Jim asked as he picked up a French fry. "Because that's what I'd be if you were out running around the world. Because, again, I'm not cut out to be a manservant."

"I think you're both perfectly suited to the lives you've got," Gene told them. "The only thing you guys really care about is each other, and neither of you would change anything because you've seen how the other half lives. It's always the little things that make life special. The touch of your husband's hand, the look you give him, the little smile when you remember something special.

Some of the unhappiest people in the world are people who don't have someone who will give them those small things. Money, fancy vacations, yachts, nothing can compare to the feeling you get when you have the moments you guys have," Gene concluded. "Now, let's try to finish lunch so I can get you back to Mesquite in your *private* jet. At least it's your private jet for this trip.

By the way," Gene asked, looking at Jennifer, "have you already packed your bags?"

"Yes, thank you," Jennifer said with a slight hint of sarcasm. "And I packed Jim's also. So we'll be ready for *our* jet when you take care of *our* bill."

Jim shook his head and looked at Gene saying, "I'm starting to agree with your thought about staying at the Motel 6. She never would have wished for a life of cheap motels and rental cars."

"Probably not," Gene acknowledged. "Now, if you're finished eating, I'll go bring the car around while you're bringing your bags down."

"They are already here," Jim said, standing. "I left them with the desk clerk. So, unless Jennifer needs to wash her hands or something, I'll meet you out front."

"I'll walk with you, sir, if you don't mind," Jennifer said to Gene as she got up. "My *butler* will bring the bags."

Chapter Twenty

The following Thursday, Jim was putting his empty coffee cup in the dishwasher when the phone rang. "Hello," he said as he shut the dishwasher door.

"Good morning, Jim," Gene said. "What do you have planned today?"

"Good morning, General," Jim answered. "Just hanging out until Jennifer gets home. Do you have something in mind?"

"I have some updates on things," Gene answered. "How about if I swing by and we talk about it? Then, if you'd like, we can get Jennifer and go to lunch."

"Sounds fine with me," Jim replied. "When do you plan on being here?"

"Probably 30 minutes or so," Gene told him.

"That'll work," Jim said. "I'll call Jennifer and make sure she can get away for lunch."

"Great," Gene replied. "I'll see you then."

After hanging up, Jim called Jennifer and told her of the plan. "Not a problem," she said. "What's the General doing here? We were just with him four days ago."

"Not sure," Jim answered. "He just said he was in town and had some time before he had to go back to Quantico. I think he enjoys your company."

"More likely, he enjoys sitting around with you and talking about the old days when you were both Marines and making the world safe for us poor civilians," she said, laughing. "But I'll be happy to have lunch with you guys. Any idea of where?"

"Why don't you choose," Jim answered. "Gene and I normally have lunch at Venice Pizza, but we'll go anywhere you want."

"How about Sushi?" she asked.

"If that's what you want," Jim answered.

"Good," she said. "There's a place close to the office that's supposed to be good. Kaze Shushi and Hibachi."

"What time?" Jim asked.

"I can get off any time after 11," she answered. "Just give me a call before you leave the house, and I'll clear it with my boss."

"Great," Jim said before hanging up. "Love you, baby."

"Love you too," Jennifer replied.

A few minutes later, the doorbell rang, and Jim opened the door, saying, "That was a rather short 30 minutes. Come on in."

"I was closer than I thought," Gene said, walking to the couch. "I didn't want to call before I left Virginia because I figured you'd still be asleep."

"I probably was," Jim said as Gene opened his briefcase. "By the way, Jennifer wants sushi for lunch. I hope that's all right with you."

"That's fine," Gene said, handing Jim a folder. "Here're the transcripts from the phones that the spooks have compiled since you left Quantico."

Opening the folder, Jim took out several sheets and read through them. "How certain are they that they've broken the code?" he asked as he finished the last page.

"Probably 90 percent," Gene answered. "What do you think they're planning?"

"Not sure," Jim answered. "The coordinates Sun keeps sending still lead me to believe that he's not the shooter. But sometimes the rest of the conversation doesn't seem relevant to what I'd send if I were the spotter."

"What do you mean?" Gene asked. "It seems like just a normal conversation about what he's doing or where he's going."

"Yes, it seems perfectly normal," Jim agreed. "But there's something about the way Sun asks those questions.

Here, for instance," Jim said, pointing to a conversation on the page. "Sun appears to be asking if the shooter needs anything."

"Okay," Gene said, looking at the page. "What's so strange about that?"

"What would the shooter need if he's just waiting for the location to be provided?" Jim asked. "If I was the shooter, I'd have everything as soon as I got here."

"Okay," Gene said. "What do you think it means?"

"I don't have a clue," Jim answered. "But it's just odd for Sun to be asking the shooter that. The shooter should have been ready days ago."

"Anything else?" Gene asked as Jim put the page back into the folder.

"I don't see anything here about the second phones," Jim answered. "Have they been used lately?"

"A couple of times," Gene told him. "Still no clue as to who is on the other end, but they are sure it's Sun on the one making the calls."

"That's fine," Jim agreed. "But it doesn't help unless we know who he's talking to. What about the real location of that phone? Do they still think it's in San Francisco, or possibly it's just a relay to somewhere else?"

"They say, San Francisco," Gene answered. "They used some cosmic timing computer stuff to rule out the distance between the phones due to the length of time between transmissions."

"How the hell do they do that?" Jim asked. "The time between transmissions could be just how long the callers wait before saying anything."

"It's not just that," Gene explained. "There's something about wavelengths, bandwidths, and unique characteristics of each tower. I don't understand it, but they're sure it's in San Francisco. Maybe not in Chinatown, but very close."

"Then we can rule out Sun communicating with someone back in China," Jim said. "Who the hell else would he need to talk to here?"

"Is it possible that he's communicating with someone from their embassy?" Gene asked. "Then that person uses one of their secure phones to talk to China?"

"I suppose," Jim said, nodding. "That might explain some of the delay in the responses. Sun has to wait for the embassy to send the message and for them to give him the response. That's entirely possible."

"Does that make any difference in what you think about Sun and the actual shooter?" Gene asked.

"Not really," Jim answered as he thought about the embassy being involved. "I'm more worried about those coded conversations. I'm starting to get an uneasy feeling about them. It almost seems too personal for Sun to be giving instructions to whoever we think is the actual shooter."

"What do you think we need to look for?" Gene asked, seeing the concern on Jim's face.

"That's the problem," Jim answered. "I don't know. But something is off about it. Maybe we'll learn more from additional calls."

"Anything about the other phone?" Gene asked. "The one we now think may be going through the embassy."

"Not really," Jim answered. "I don't think it matters whether it's direct to Sun's boss or relayed to him. Unless there's some conversation that we can use to figure out who he or she is, it's irrelevant. And I would bet it's coded, also.

Having another person knowing what's going on with Hua isn't in anyone's best interest."

"What do you want from the spooks back at Quantico?" Gene asked as he put everything back into his briefcase.

"Hell, I don't know," Jim admitted. "More precise locations on the phones would be beneficial. A tap on the embassy phone would tell us if they are relaying information back to China. Try to determine if it's also coded. Maybe that's the phone Sun is using to pass information to the shooter. The only thing I can think of to do without more information is to move Hua. At least that would give us a chance to see if other people are involved."

"She's going to be moved tonight," Gene told him. "They have her booked on a flight from San Francisco to Dallas and then to Omaha."

"What about her six handlers?" Jim asked. "Are they going also?"

"No," Gene answered. "Omaha isn't well known for its Asian population. Too many of them showing up together might raise some unwanted interest."

"Agreed," Jim said, standing. "I'll tell Jennifer we're on our way."

Chapter Twenty-one

As they were headed to get Jennifer, Jim asked, "Have you made sure that Sun knows where she is right now?"

"Yes," Gene answered. "Yesterday, he went to lunch at one of his normal restaurants, and we had one of Hua's guards follow him in. He called the others, and they brought her down there."

"Pretty damn bold," Jim remarked. "What happened?"

"That's what's interesting," Gene answered. "Nothing."

"What do you mean nothing?" Jim asked incredulously. "Did Sun seem surprised? What did he do?"

"Nothing," Gene repeated. "Absolutely nothing. He barely noticed her when they walked in. After he finished his meal, he paid his bill and walked out."

"What about Hua?" Jim asked. "Did she notice him? Or recognize him?"

"Same," Gene answered. "She followed her team in and sat there eating. I'm not even sure she saw him."

"But surely she's been shown a picture of Sun," Jim argued. "I can't imagine you'd not let her know who we think is trying to kill her."

"Of course, she knows who he is," Gene explained. "Now, there's one other thing that happened yesterday that isn't exactly in line with the way things have been up to this point."

"What's that?" Jim asked.

"The phone that Sun normally uses to send synthesized messages got a call," Gene answered. "It was from the phone he usually calls."

"So, it sounds like his boss is calling him," Jim mused nodding. "Did it go through the Embassy?"

"We're still not sure," Gene admitted. "But the spooks said it seemed to originate from the same location, and the delays we've been discussing have remained constant. So, they surmise it's still being relayed."

"And Sun didn't follow her from the restaurant when she went back to her apartment?" Jim asked.

"No," Gene answered. "What do you think?"

Pausing for a moment, Jim answered, "I think it confirms my thinking that Sun isn't the shooter. He's here to remove the shooter after he eliminates Hua. Or he's here in case the shooter fails."

"I can see how that explains what we saw," Gene agreed. "Sun didn't need to follow her because either he knew where she was going or the shooter already knew."

"That would be my guess," Jim said. "Which makes it imperative we get her out of there before the shooter makes his move."

"We agree on that," Gene said, nodding. "Tomorrow, she will be in Omaha. If nothing else, we may have forced the shooter to change his plans."

"What are your security measures from the time Hua gets to the airport and when she arrives in Omaha?" Jim asked.

"Her team will take her to the airport in San Francisco," Gene explained. "We have a couple of people who'll be on the plane with her to Dallas. Then, our people will be waiting for her arrival and watch to see if anyone is following her. Our people on the airplane with her will be debriefed as soon as they land to see if they noticed any unusual attention being paid to her during the flight.

Two more people will be watching her as she changes gates," Gene continued. "One of them is a Flight Attendant who'll be on the flight to Omaha and will be spending the night there with the rest of the crew."

"You have another American Airlines Flight Attendant working for the company?" Jim asked.

"Of course," Gene answered. "Did you think you were the only one at American that worked for us? We have pilots, Flight Attendants, mechanics, ramp workers, and some in management positions."

"Hell, why don't you just buy the airline and use all of us?" Jim asked, realizing the enormity of Black Water's operations.

"Too expensive," Gene answered. "Plus, we'd be picking up too many people we don't want or need. We also thought about starting our own airline, like Air America was in Vietnam."

Jim laughed and said, "That wouldn't work. Everybody knew they were a CIA operation. Your secret would be out before the first takeoff."

"Yeah, that's what we concluded," Gene replied, smiling. "Not to mention we would need gates at every airport, publish schedules, and way too much other crap that we avoid by using the established airlines."

"So, you have agents with the other airlines," Jim said, nodding.

"Of course," Gene said, looking at him. "We can't depend on just American to go where we may need. You should have known that."

"I guess I suspected it," Jim said. "I remember all the times someone on the ground or at the gate at an airport would hand me something. And Jewell was a Flight Attendant as well as an agent. So yeah, I guess I knew."

"As a matter of fact, you know the Flight Attendant that's going with Hua," Gene announced, smiling.

"Really?" Jim asked as he saw Jennifer's office ahead. "Who?"

"A lady named Millicent," Gene answered. "You've flown with her before. And I'm guessing you remember her."

Jim nodded and said, "Tall, good-looking lady with dark hair. Sort of exotic looking. Yes, I definitely remember her. But why would you guess that I remember her?"

"Because she's tall, good-looking, and exotic," Gene answered, laughing. "Don't forget that I've known you for almost 20 years. I know you better in some ways than Jennifer."

"Oh, I'll bet she knows the type of lady that gets my attention," Jim said as they pulled in to park. "I've caught her watching me if there's a lady like you're describing around. She may not know I see her watching, but I do. But she also knows that I'd never do anything except look." "If she knew about all of the ladies you've worked with on the assignments you've been on since you were transferred to Muddy Water," Gene said as they got out of the car, "she might not be so trusting."

"If you're referring to Jewell," Jim responded, walking toward the office building. "You know I look at her as just a friend."

"That wasn't always true," Gene countered. "There was a time I had some doubts about putting you two together. But I was also referring to an agent that worked with you in Chicago."

"Who was that?" Jim asked, opening the door.

"Marie Laveau," Gene told him as they walked in.

"Oh yeah," Jim said, smiling. "Another good-looking exotic lady. But you have to admit that I've demonstrated enormous restraint. And there were certainly never any females that tempted me when I was with Dark Water."

"That's not surprising," Gene told him as they approached Jennifer's office. "You were always in Turkey or Syria or some other middle eastern country and generally in some shit hole location where goats were more populous than women."

"And better looking," Jim replied, laughing.

"Who's better looking?" Jennifer asked as she walked out of her office.

"Gene was just talking about some of the assignments we were on in the Marines," Jim told her. "And I told him that you were better looking than any of the women we ran into overseas."

"You're such a liar, Jim Lashley," Jennifer said, smiling. "You men. You Marines. You think we don't know that you talk about all the women you've met all around the world. We know. Trust me. Any woman involved with guys like you two knows what you're like when you get together. Now you better take your *better-looking wife to lunch,* or you'll wish you were back where goats are better looking than the women."

Chapter Twenty-two

Just as they were walking into the restaurant, Gene reached into his pocket and pulled out his phone. Looking at the number, he told Jim and Jennifer to go ahead and get a table, and he would be there as soon as he returned the call.

After being escorted to a table as far from the door as possible, Jim pulled Jennifer's chair out for her and told the waiter, "Could we get three iced teas, please? We'll order as soon as our other party comes in."

"Certainly, sir," he said, placing the menus on the table. "Please take your time."

"What would you like?" Jim asked, looking at the menu. "I think I'd like the smoked salmon, crab roll, and shrimp tempura roll."

"I think I'll have the spicy Alaskan roll and the calamari tempura roll," Jennifer answered, setting her menu aside as Gene took the seat across from her.

"Everybody decided?" he asked, picking up his menu.

"Except you," Jim answered as the waiter arrived with their teas.

Gene glanced at the tea and asked, "No Sake?"

"I have to go back to work," Jennifer answered. "But you guys can get some."

"Too early for me," Jim said, sipping his tea.

"And I've got some work to do also," Gene told them, setting his menu down. "So, thanks for ordering the tea."

"Are you folks ready?" the waiter asked as soon as Gene put his menu down.

Gene motioned for Jim to start, and he said, "Spicy Alaskan roll and calamari tempura roll for the lady. Smoked salmon, crab roll, and shrimp tempura roll for me, please."

"And you, sir?" he asked, looking at Gene.

"The snow crab and sweet shrimp," Gene answered. "And could we start with the seaweed and squid salad and three plates, please?"

"Definitely, sir," the waiter said with a slight bow. "I'll have that right out. Will there be anything else?"

"Not now," Gene answered, handing the waiter all three menus. "Thank you."

"You've got a couple of days off, don't you?" Gene asked Jim as the waiter left.

"Yeah, I'm pretty sure I've got three more days before my next trip," Jim answered. "Why? Do you need something?"

"No," Gene told him. "I'm just going to be staying in Dallas for a couple of days and thought I'd take you guys out to dinner tonight and maybe tomorrow if you can put up with me."

"I have a better idea," Jim said, looking at Jennifer for her approval. "What if we have dinner tonight at our place? I'll cook some steaks, maybe baked potatoes and asparagus."

"That sounds nice," Jennifer agreed. "And please don't tell me you're planning on staying in some hotel. You'll stay with us."

"I'll agree under certain conditions," Gene said, smiling at Jennifer. "First, Jim and I will go to the Crowd Cow, and I'll pick up some Wagu Striploin. Also, if you don't mind, I'll also get some corn on the cob. And I'll grab a couple of bottles of wine. Would you like the Malbec again or something else?"

"How about a Pinot Noir?" she asked.

"That's fine with me," Gene told her. "There's a Total Wine in Plano that I'm sure will have Goldeneye Pinot Noir. I'll grab a couple of bottles. And finally, If I'm still here tomorrow night, I get to take you to dinner."

"I think I can go along with that," Jennifer said, nodding as the waiter arrived with the salad. "Jim didn't tell me why you're here today. I'm just sort of surprised to see you again so soon."

"I may have to meet some people at the Dallas Fort Worth (DFW) Airport this evening," he answered. "And it's possible that they'll need to spend the night. Their schedule is still rather uncertain, so I'm here to make sure things go smoothly."

"Well, it doesn't matter," Jennifer told him. "We're always glad to have you here. Regardless of why, you'll always be welcome."

"Thank you, Jennifer," Gene told her as he took some of the salad. "Jim and I will have everything ready for dinner when you get back home."

After dropping Jennifer back at work, Gene headed back to Jim's house, saying, "The call I got was from Don. It seems as if one of Hua's handlers suddenly disappeared."

"What do the folks at Quantico think?" Jim asked.

"They don't have a clue," Gene answered. "None of the team had any knowledge as to why Hua was here. All they knew was that they were to escort her and keep her safe until we relieved them. So, as of right now, I don't see any connection between the man disappearing and Hua being moved."

"How sure are you about the man?" Jim asked. "How long has he been with the company? And, most importantly, are you absolutely sure he has no knowledge about Hua?"

"I'm not sure how long he's been with us," Gene admitted. "We have several teams like his around the country that are more or less part-time. We only use them when we have a situation like this."

"Not to tell you how to run your business," Jim replied, "but don't you think she's a pretty high-value target to risk using part-time help?"

"I understand your point," Gene explained. "Maybe part-time is a misnomer. They are more or less like you, called when needed. You're technically a part-time agent. They may or may not have other jobs, but they are always on call if we need them. We have teams like them scattered across the country. All around the world as well."

"Okay," Jim said, nodding in agreement. "Now, remember when I mentioned having a leak?"

"Yes, I remember," Gene answered. "But you were talking about how the shooter might know where Hua is being moved."

"Yes, I was," Jim acknowledged. "But it just seems suspicious for one of her handlers to just disappear. I'm not saying that he's the shooter, but is it possible that he's been watching her and providing information to someone else? Not necessarily to the shooter because we now think that's what Sun is doing."

"Who else could be involved?" Gene asked. "We've agreed that China is probably trying to limit who knows what's going on regarding Hua. Nobody else knows she's here or why she's being protected. It could be just a coincidence."

"I don't really believe in coincidences," Jim said as they pulled into his driveway. "This needs to be figured out before tonight. I know you said he didn't know anything about the operation, but what if he did? We've had some sleepers in the organization before. I think you need to get someone out there in San Francisco to find the man. And I just hope that he was involved in a car wreck or something. There are too many loose ends. This move tonight was designed to try to figure out what's going on regarding the shooter and who else may be looking for her. Now we have a missing man who knows we're moving her. That's making me as nervous as a long-tailed cat in a room full of rocking chairs."

Chapter Twenty-three

After dinner that evening, everyone was relaxing in the living room talking about General Manuel Noriega, Operation Nifty Package, where he was captured, and his trial for drug trafficking when Gene excused himself again to answer his phone.

Minutes later, when he returned, he said, "Sorry, but I've got to go to DFW and check on some people. I hate to leave you with the mess to clean up, but these folks are sort of why I'm here."

"That's certainly okay," Jennifer said, getting out of her chair. "Would you like Jim to go with you? Since you guys cooked everything, I'd planned on letting you sit around while I cleaned anyway."

"That would be nice," Gene said, looking at Jim. "Would you mind?"

"Not at all," Jim answered, standing. "How long do you think you'll need to be gone?"

"Probably an hour or so," Gene answered. "How long does it take to get there?"

"This late, maybe 30 minutes," Jim replied. "Maybe another 10 minutes or so, depending on which terminal we go to."

"Couple of hours," Jennifer said as she walked them to the door. "That should give me plenty of time to get everything done. I picked up some Blue Bell Pistachio Almond ice cream on the way home, and we can have a bowl when you boys get back."

"Sounds good," Jim said, kissing her cheek. "We'll see you then."

"Okay, what's happening?" Jim asked as Gene drove west toward the 635 Loop around the north of Dallas.

"Nothing new," Gene answered. "With the uncertainties we're dealing with, I want to be there when Hua arrives and then talk to her escorts. If there's any new information, I want to be there to hear it."

"And I'm glad Jennifer suggested you come with me," he continued. "I was going to suggest it, but it's better when it's her idea."

"I'm glad to be coming along," Jim told him. "I'd like to meet this lady anyway. How's her English?"

"I understand that she speaks perfect English but with a slight accent," Gene answered as he maneuvered around an eighteen-wheeler. "I just hope that someone from the flight is going to be going to Omaha so we can get a good look at him."

"Did the folks at Quantico give you a passenger list?" Jim asked.

"Yes, for the inbound flight," Gene answered. "But it didn't seem necessary for the Omaha leg because our targets wouldn't know where Hua's going until they get here."

"How long is the wait for the Omaha flight?" Jim asked.

"Almost two hours," Gene told him. "Isn't that what you recommended? To give them enough time to go out and get new tickets?"

"Yes," Jim assured him. "And, since we're meeting the flight, we can see who leaves the boarding area and goes out to ticketing. How many people do we have at the airport that can help?”

“Not many,” Gene admitted. “The two that came with her from San Francisco, Millicent, the Flight Attendant who you know, a photographer, and us. I wish we had more, but this was a rather quick setup.”

“I guess we’ll just have to pay attention as they get off and be there for the boarding when they get to the gate for Omaha,” Jim said, nodding. “And I’m sure Millicent can get an updated passenger list before they start boarding. That will give us a little advantage on spotting them.”

“It’ll help if they’re Asian,” Gene added. “That should substantially reduce the people we need to watch.”

“If we’re looking for an Asian,” Jim offered. “I wouldn’t if I could avoid it. It would have been an asset in San Francisco, but here, it makes them stand out in Omaha.”

“I’m betting they never considered that we’d move her to somewhere like Dallas or Omaha,” Gene countered. “They probably planned on everything taking place in San Francisco, if not actually in Chinatown.”

“Maybe,” Jim told him. “But they really didn’t know where we’d put her when she got here. It could have been any city in the United States.”

“I see your point,” Gene agreed. “Even the passenger list may be misleading if whoever’s following her doesn’t have an Asian name. Could be Smith by marriage or a false name.”

“That’s true,” Jim said. “It’s good to have the photographer, but we’ll have to wait for the facial recognition folks to do their magic. Maybe it’ll help the people in Omaha. Or when we move her again.”

“Any little piece of information will be welcomed at this stage,” Gene replied as they approached Highway 121 leading into the airport. “I’ve had to run operations with less, but I had a little more time to do the intelligence work.”

"Me too," Jim agreed. "And the outcome wasn't always to my liking."

"I know what you mean," Gene said as they took a parking ticket at the entrance. "It's never a guarantee for success, but knowing your enemy is a major factor in any battle."

"I hope you're not going to quote Sun Tzu," Jim said, laughing as he looked at the signs showing the terminals for the various airlines.

"Looks like Terminal A," Jim told him. "That's good. It's the closest and will give us time to see where the Omaha flight is departing. How much time until it arrives?"

"Maybe thirty minutes if it's on time," Gene answered as he looked for a parking spot at the terminal. "Tell you what, you jump out and go find the gate. I'll park and meet you there."

"Okay," Jim said as the car stopped. "I'm guessing Millicent is going to meet Hua at the arrival gate."

"Yes," Gene confirmed. "And if she's as smart as I know she is, she'll have a passenger list for both flights. That gives us a starting place."

"Not only that," Jim added, "but when we get the final list, we can compare it to the one she'll have now. Then we can see which names have been added."

"That's a good idea," Gene said. "Now, I'll see you inside as soon as I can get there."

Jim watched him pull away and headed for the closest door, entering the terminal. After seeing the arrival at gate 19, he cleared security and headed down the wide aisle, dodging the mass of passengers hurrying from gate to gate.

Approaching gate 19, he saw Millicent talking to the gate agent. Walking up quietly, he cleared his throat and asked, "Is this where the folks from San Francisco are going to be?"

Millicent turned and, before the gate agent could answer his question, said smiling, "Excuse me, sir. I think you're at the wrong airport. All San Francisco flights are scheduled for Love Field."

"Millicent," Jim said, grinning at her. "It's been a while. How are you doing?"

"Just fine," she answered as she turned to the gate agent. "He's a friend of mine. Another one of our pilots. Probably lost. We do our best, but you know."

"Hi, ma'am," Jim said to the agent. "I'm Jim, and Miss Millicent here has a somewhat warped sense of humor. I haven't been lost in over 40 flights now and I'm getting better every trip."

"Hi, Jim," the agent said, shaking his hand. "Is there anything I can do for you?"

"No," Jim answered. "I'm just here to meet an old friend that's passing through. Thought we'd have time for a beer before his connecting flight."

"Where's he going?" the agent asked, loading the departing flights on her computer.

"Omaha," Jim said. "Leaves in about two hours, I believe."

"That's the flight I'm working," Millicent told him. "It's just five gates down. Gate 24. Even you can't get lost in just five gates."

"I'll take care of him," she said, turning to the agent. "Is the copy of the Omaha passenger list on the printer yet?"

"Just now finished printing," she said as she ripped the sheet from the printer and handed it to her.

"Thanks," she told the agent as she led Jim away from the desk. "I'll see you next time I'm here."

Once away from the agent, Millicent asked, "What are you doing here? I got word that General Barker was going to meet me, but he didn't say you would be here."

"I'm here to help look for the people that are following the lady you are escorting to Omaha," Jim answered. "Now, we need to get the passenger list from San Francisco and compare it to the one you just got."

"I already have the San Fran list, and that's why I asked the agent for Omaha," Millicent told him. "Let's take a seat over here, and I'll read the inbound list, and you see if they're on the Omaha list."

They had just finished comparing the lists when Gene walked up, saying, "Good evening, Millicent. So nice to see you again."

Millicent stood and shook Gene's hand, saying, "Good evening, General. I thought I was meeting you and was rather surprised when Jim walked up a few minutes ago."

"Sort of an additional precaution," Gene told her as he looked at the lists they were holding. "What's the consensus?"

"Three names," Jim answered, taking the list Millicent had. "But the real list won't be available until at least an hour after the flight arrives."

"What do you mean real list?" Millicent asked. "Do you think there will be some changes?"

"We suspect that one or more of the San Francisco passengers will be purchasing tickets here for Omaha," Gene answered. "We just need for you to get us that list when we tell you."

"That's not a problem," she assured him. "What else do you need me to do?"

"Just pretend you don't know us when she gets off the plane," Gene answered. "I'm hoping that the new passenger list will be available before you board and we can identify any passengers you may need to be aware of on your flight. When Hua gets off the airplane, just meet her as she enters the terminal and let her know you'll take her to the next gate. She's expecting you but doesn't know what you look like.

Jim and I will be sitting just outside the door to the jet bridge, watching people as they exit," he continued. "I'd like for you to stand beside the agent when Hua gets off and then watch the deplaning passengers until everyone is off. You may need to identify the three people connecting with you when you get to your gate."

"Not a problem," she said, turning to look at the gate. "Looks like they're a few minutes early."

Chapter Twenty-four

Jim and Gene took seats as far back from the gate as possible as Millicent stood by the open jet bridge door beside the agent. Looking at the list again, Jim told Gene, "I think we need to have Quantico run the three people that are continuing on to Omaha."

"Why?" Gene asked, looking at the names Jim was pointing to. "I thought we had agreed that anyone following Hua couldn't know where she was going after getting here."

"That's probably the case," Jim explained. "But just humor me on this. Although slight, there is a chance we have a leak. It could have something to do with the missing handler. I'm trying to cover every possibility. Just have them do a quick check to see if they live in Omaha when they went to San Francisco, basic information to rule them out as suspects."

"Probably a wise move," Gene agreed, taking the list and dialing Black Water headquarters. "It shouldn't take more than 30 minutes or so to get the information."

"Good," Jim said, watching for the first passengers to come off the jet bridge. "Where is the photographer?"

"He's sitting on the other side of the waiting area," Gene answered, hanging up after telling Quantico what he wanted. "He's using a body camera that records everything that passes in front of him. It's also got a feed to Quantico, so they're seeing it almost instantaneously."

"And recording it, I assume," Jim said as the first-class passengers began to enter the terminal. "Who are the two people you had on the flight to watch her?"

"A man and a woman traveling as a couple," Gene answered. "They should be right behind Hua since their seats were in the same row. I'll meet them as they exit and get them to stick around to help us look for anyone on the flight that exits to get a ticket."

"Millicent will watch the three people connecting until they board the Omaha flight," Gene continued. "You and I will be looking at everyone else, and then we'll go to the Omaha gate to see if we recognize anyone from this flight."

"You're not asking for much," Jim said, joking as he looked at every face as the passengers passed his seat. "I hope Quantico is running a facial recognition on the pictures your photographer is steaming to them."

"They are," Gene told him. "But that's a lengthy process. Maybe someone will pop up before the flight leaves for Omaha. But our best hope is to recognize someone that purchases a ticket here."

A few minutes later, seeing Millicent greeting Hua, Gene stood and said, "There's our people. I'll go get a quick debrief and explain what we need for them to do. Maybe they'll remember some of the other passengers if they see them again at the other gate."

"I hope so," Jim replied. "I'm not holding out much hope until we get the revised passenger list."

As Gene took the couple aside and was explaining what they needed to do, Millicent appeared to be talking to Hua, but it was evident that she was watching every passenger.

When the final passenger exited the jet bridge, Millicent headed for gate 24 with Hua and Gene, followed by the other couple that had been watching her on the flight. With almost everyone coming off the flight and heading for the exit, Jim watched for anyone who remained in the terminal. Several single people were heading in both directions from the gate, but he spotted a group of three that were going in the direction of gate 24.

Nodding at the photographer, he followed the three until they waited in line for the agent at the gate. Continuing past, he went down a couple of gates and reversed his direction. When he came back to gate 24, he noticed Gene talking to the photographer and Millicent talking to the gate agent with Hua by her side.

Standing by the windows overlooking the ramp, Jim casually looked around at the waiting passengers. He spotted the three from the previous flight sitting together and talking, but no one else looked familiar. The two who were following Hua were also close to the windows and were looking around at the passengers. The photographer finally made it to the gate agent, acting like he was checking on a seat, and then slowly turned to capture everyone in the waiting area.

Still, about 45 minutes before the flight was scheduled to leave, Jim walked over to Gene and said, "I haven't seen anyone from the other flight that I recognize. And I think it's time to get a look at the current passenger list to see if there are any additions."

"I think you're right," Gene said, catching Millicent's attention and holding up the passenger list they had been using. "I'll check with everyone else to see if they noticed anybody. I'm not expecting much yet on the facial recognition, but we should be hearing on the three passengers any moment now."

A couple of minutes later, Millicent looked at Jim and nodded. He started walking toward the agent's position when she stopped by an empty seat. Seeing the empty seat beside her, Jim walked around the rows of waiting passengers and sat down. Without looking at him, Millicent slid the new passenger list across the armrest and rose. As she walked back toward the agent's podium, Jim compared the two lists.

The first thing he noticed was that there were fewer names on the new list. It was not uncommon for passengers to not make the flight or have a problem with connections, so he walked back to Gene and motioned for him to follow so they could quickly go through the lists.

Quietly reading the names from the original passenger list, Jim waited for Gene to mark each one off on the new list. When he finally finished, he looked at Gene and asked, "Is anybody new?"

"No," Gene answered. "Everyone on this list was on yours."

"Well, shit," Jim exclaimed. "This isn't close to what I thought would happen. How the hell could they have found out about where she's going? This just doesn't make sense."

"I know," Gene said as he pulled out his phone and looked at the number of the caller. "This is Quantico. Let me see if they have any information that may help."

Gene walked a few feet away, talking on the phone as Jim tried to figure out what had gone wrong. It was possible that they had missed anyone following Hua, but it seemed impossible for them to have known about her final destination before arriving in Dallas. The only logical thing he could think of was there was a leak. Maybe tied to the missing handler. But a leak seemed to be the only explanation.

"Nothing on the three people yet," Gene told him as he returned. "But there was a call on the synthesized phone."

"What did it say?" Jim asked.

"First, it was from what we assumed was the phone passing through the Embassy," Gene explained. "Not from Sun. Second, it was two words. *Spot one*."

"Spot one?" Jim asked. "What was the reply?"

"Just a tone," Gene answered. "But here's the kicker. The phone is here."

"Here? How can that be?" Jim asked. "Are they sure?"

"Positive," Gene answered. "And it's still being relayed."

"That doesn't make sense," Jim replied. "That would mean that someone else traveled from San Francisco."

"I think you're correct about that," Gene said, looking around the waiting area. "And the only explanation for the 'spot one' would be that someone followed her here and is relaying the information."

"That would probably mean that whoever made the call came from San Francisco but isn't going to follow her to Omaha," Jim said, nodding. "But there wasn't any information about where she was going. Try contacting Quantico and see if there are any coded calls. Probably with coordinates for either here or Omaha."

"Why would they be sending coordinates for Omaha?" Gene asked as he dialed.

"They followed Hua to this gate and know where she's going," Jim explained.

"Not yet," Gene said a moment later, hanging up. "What do you think is going on?"

"I'm not sure," Jim answered. "I can see someone coming here following her. I can see them calling Sun to confirm arrival here or spot one. I just don't see how that helps Sun know where she's going. There has to be something we're missing."

"What's your suggestion?" Gene asked.

"Wait until the flight leaves and try to get another passenger list," Jim answered. "It's possible that we were a little early, and there's still someone on the plane to Omaha. If nothing has changed, then we wait for Quantico to give us the information from the facial recognition or background check of the three passengers. And I'd like to see a history of credit card use or anything else they can dig up of them."

"Anything else?" Gene asked, dialing his phone.

"For Quantico, get more people to watch her in Omaha. And have them check if there are other airlines going to Omaha tonight. If so, get the passenger lists. Our guy may have come in on American and be going out on Delta," Jim answered. "And start planning another move. For us, we just go back home and wait. And eat some Blue Bell Pistachio Almond."

Chapter Twenty-five

Thirty minutes later, when the jet bridge door had shut, Gene called Quantico and asked for a close-out passenger list. Moments later, it was on his phone, and he compared it to the last list they had gotten earlier.

"Nothing new," he said, showing Jim the list. "There's no one on the flight that wasn't on the revised list or the original one. That means that whoever's following her, if anyone, either had prior information on her itinerary or they got here and sent her destination. There's no other explanation."

"I agree," Jim said as they headed for the exit to the parking area. "Now, since they know she's headed to Omaha, they may try to get someone on the ground there before she arrives. That could be a weak spot we can exploit."

"What are you thinking?" Gene asked, leading the way to where he had parked.

"Get a ticket for her out of Omaha back here," he answered. "They followed her here and told someone where she was going. I find it impossible to believe that they could get there ahead of us."

"Why back here?" Gene asked as they headed out of the airport.

"No one would expect her to come back so soon," Jim explained. "Get tickets for her and whoever was going to watch her in Omaha, book some rooms here, maybe a car, and we'll wait for Quantico to get back to us regarding the facial recognition and more details on the three that were on her flight to Omaha."

"That sounds like the safest thing to do," Gene agreed as he pulled out his phone. "Do you think the guy who was at the airport with the synthesized phone would stick around?"

"I don't see any reason for that," Jim answered. "You might have Quantico look at the next flight to Omaha and see if there were any late purchases for a single man. I'd bet that's where he'd go."

Jim listened as Gene relayed their requests to the Black Water people back at Quantico and waited for him to hang up and let him know what was happening.

Finally, Gene put the phone on the seat and said, "There isn't another flight to Omaha or out of Omaha back here until tomorrow. The company said they would make sure the team there was aware of the increased threat and change any reservations they had made just in case we do have a leak."

"That's good," Jim agreed as they headed north on Highway 121. "Anything on the three people or the facial recognition?"

"No," Gene said as he maneuvered to take the exit for the 635 loop back to Mesquite. "They need another hour or so for the people and probably four or five for the recognition program.

There was also a call on the coded phone," Gene announced. "It was to Sun. And they think it has moved, but they couldn't pinpoint it because the conversation was too short."

"Has it been decoded?" Jim asked.

"Yes and no," Gene answered. "They used the same algorithm, but the message was undecipherable."

"Looks like they know we broke their code," Jim said, shaking his head. "How long until the spooks can crack this one?"

"Hopefully later tonight," Gene answered. "Don said Tim thinks it's just a simple one-off or a variation of one of the Chinese languages."

"Okay, let's review what happened," Jim said as they headed east on 635. "Sun is still in San Francisco because we're tracking his phones. Quantico would have noticed any movement. Whoever has the other phones is moving, and at least one of them is here in Dallas."

"Agreed," Gene said. "If Sun is just the spotter, he's sitting at his base and waiting to see where Hua ends up. The call about Spot One was just to tell him she was here. The coded call was probably a follow up to give her destination. And that we won't know until the boys at Quantico can break this code."

"You know we need to start working on Hua's *accident*," Jim said. "All of this movement and listening to phone calls is necessary to move the action to the playground of our choice. But as I always do when planning, I want to start with the accident and work backward to today."

"What do you have in mind?" Gene asked.

"Remember the accident we used in Chicago to get rid of all of the gang members' bodies?" Jim asked.

"Sure," Gene answered. "Their bodies were in the van that we used to stage the wreck and then burned."

"I don't see why we can't do the same thing here," Jim said. "The only thing we need to do is make sure Sun, or the shooter, sees her get in a car and then follows it. Somewhere, we'll stage an accident, and we'll make sure he sees it."

"How can you wreck a car with her, or a double, in it and make sure nobody gets hurt?" Gene asked.

"That'll take a little staging," Jim admitted. "I'd start with the wrecked car. It should be easy to buy one sufficiently damaged. We take it to a fairly remote location and put it in a place that would seem likely for a wreck, like a sharp curve.

We'll need an identical car to use for them to be seen driving," Jim continued. "Once they start driving, we need for them to take a preplanned route and stick to a fairly rigid time frame. They'll be heading for where we've left the other car, and all we need to do is get some separation between our car and whoever's following them.

There needs to be an exit off the road just short of where the wreck will take place," Jim explained. "We'll have to do something to make sure there's enough distance between the shooter and our car so they can take the exit unobserved. Maybe have another car get between them. Maybe rig a traffic light.

Just before our car gets to the wreck, we torch it," Jim finished. "Then, when the shooter comes to the curve, all he'll see is what looks like the car he was following wrecked beside the road and on fire."

"That's going to take some split-second timing," Gene observed.

"I know," Jim admitted. "We'll need some professional drivers in both the target car and the car that gets between it and the shooter. We need an explosive guy to rig and blow the wrecked car exactly on time. And we'll probably need a couple of corpses to be in the car when it burns."

"Why would we need corpses?" Gene asked as they approached Jim's house.

"Just in case the shooter stops and runs to look at the wreck," Jim answered. "Also, even if he doesn't, there needs to be people in the car when the fire and police arrive. The car didn't get there by itself, and I'm sure it'll be on the news later. How would it sound if the news reporter said that a car crashed and burned, but there was no driver? We need the number of bodies in the wreck to match what the shooter saw drive away at the start."

"Isn't there a simpler way?" Gene asked as he pulled into the driveway.

"We get a doppelganger and shoot her," Jim said before getting out. "But getting a good enough match to fool the real shooter could be a problem. So would the inevitable news about the shooting and the identity of the victim. Simple, but it has some holes that we can't afford.

No, I think the wreck has the best chance of working," Jim said as they walked to the door. "At least until she goes public. Now, another option is to move her testimony up and keep moving her from airport to airport until it's time. I'm not sure what your budget is for this operation, but flying all day every day for a month could get to be pretty expensive."

Chapter Twenty-six

The next morning, Gene was sitting in the living room drinking coffee when Jim walked in. "I made coffee," he explained. "Hope I made it right."

"I'm sure it will be fine," Jim replied. "Did you make the eggs and bacon?"

"I wasn't sure where they were," Gene said, standing.

"I'm guessing you never looked in the refrigerator," Jim told him, heading for the kitchen.

"I thought about it," Gene answered with a smile. "But I try not to pry when I'm in other people's houses."

"Pry into what?" Jennifer asked, walking in. "Is that coffee I smell?"

"Gene was just explaining why he could make the coffee but not bacon and eggs," Jim told her as he poured her a cup.

"Well, that was very nice of him, I think," Jennifer said, winking at Gene. "Besides, I thought you said something about taking us to breakfast just before we went to bed last night."

"I did," Jim agreed, getting another cup. "But Gene didn't know that."

"I assumed it," Gene said, walking over to stand by Jennifer. "We knew that you didn't want Jennifer to have to make breakfast, clean the dishes, and then try to make it to work. Naturally, I assumed you didn't want to do all that work. Therefore, I deduced that going out to breakfast was the only solution to such a weighty problem."

"And I'm guessing that you already had a place in mind," Jim told him, taking a seat at the table.

"Yes," Gene answered, waiting for Jennifer to sit. "There's a little hole in the wall restaurant called the Texan Diner that I really like. Only open until about three or four in the afternoon, but they serve breakfast all day."

"That sounds perfect," Jennifer told him, sitting beside him. "I think Jim needs to go get his boots on and take us there. What's your favorite meal there?"

"I like the Terlingua Special," Gene said. "It's a three-egg omelet with homemade chili, fresh jalapenos, onions, and cheddar jack cheese. Top it with some of their salsa and some sour cream, unbeatable."

"That sounds like a lot of food for me," Jennifer said. "But I could go for some waffles."

"Well then, you'll love their Belgian waffles with blueberries," Gene told her. "And their Huevos Rancheros will probably rival any Jim has ever tried."

"That'll take some doing," Jim said, sipping his coffee. "The H3 restaurant in Fort Worth is one of the best. As is Mi Tierra in San Antonio."

"You can always try theirs," Gene said. "But, first, you two may need to finish getting dressed. They're pretty casual but not housecoat casual."

"You finish your coffee, Jim," Jennifer said, dumping hers in the sink. "I'll be ready in 10 minutes."

When she was gone, Jim asked, "Is she on her way back to DFW, or has there been a change of plans?"

"No, she'll get here about ten this morning," Gene answered. "I'll pick her up and take her to a hotel, and I won't get a room until she's here. I got to thinking last night about what you said regarding a leak."

"You and I are going to be the only ones that communicate with or about her until we can relocate her," he continued. "I'm not taking any more chances that someone is following her and relaying where she is."

"That'll mean you have to stay here for at least another day," Jim replied.

"I had already planned on that when I came yesterday if you'll remember," Gene told him. "The only thing different is that I'll stay with her at the hotel until we make other arrangements."

"I can relieve you when you need," Jim volunteered. "Matter of fact, I'll go with you to pick her up. We can discuss what to do next while we sit around."

"That would be nice," Gene said. "But I don't want to take up all of your days off."

"Not a problem," Jim told him. "You'd just call me or stop by anyway. The only thing we need to worry about is what Jennifer will say if you don't spend tonight here."

"I'll think of something," Gene said as Jennifer walked in.

"You'll think of something about what?" she asked.

"Nothing, really," Gene answered. "It's just that I may need to entertain a client this evening."

"Why don't you ask him to come to dinner with us?" she asked. "I seem to remember something about you taking us out since we cooked steaks here last night."

"You know, that's not a bad idea," Jim said. "A chance to relax and enjoy the evening. Maybe she'd like it."

"Oh, a she is it?" Jennifer joked. "And a client? General, what have you been hiding from us?"

"Nothing," Gene answered. "The lady is here on business and contracted us for her security. That's all."

"Well, I can't think of any better security than having her join us for dinner," Jennifer responded. "Two fierce Marines escorting her to secret dining facilities where even the waiters are required to have top secret clearances? If you're to provide top-notch service, I think you need to bring her with you. After all, your company's reputation is at stake."

Gene looked at Jim and said, "I guess it's settled. We'll all go to dinner together if my client doesn't object."

"It *is* settled," Jennifer said decisively. "Now, get your boots on. We've barely got time for breakfast, and that's if I drive my car so I can leave and go straight to work. I'll follow you guys."

When Jennifer left the restaurant for work, Gene excused himself to take a phone call. When he returned a couple of minutes later, he said, "You won't believe this. There was a call on the synthesized phone late last night."

"From Sun?" Jim asked.

"To him," Gene answered. "More important is that it looks like it came from Omaha."

"Is Hua already on the plane coming here?" Jim asked.

"Yes," Gene confirmed. "Looks like we made a good decision to bring her back as soon as possible. Now we need to figure out who is using that damn phone."

"I agree," Jim said, looking at the clock on the wall. "Maybe we better get to the airport. Who's with her?"

"Millicent," Gene answered, leaving a tip on the table and taking the ticket to the cashier. "She was scheduled to work that flight back here this morning anyway. And I don't want to get any more people involved until we determine if we have a leak. The unexpected seems to be the norm right now, and removing everybody but you and I seems to be the best course of action."

"I agree," Jim said as they headed for the car. "Maybe having her disappear for a day or so will generate some useful conversations between Sun and whoever is on the other phones."

Chapter Twenty-seven

Standing beside the gate, waiting for the flight to arrive, Gene called Quantico to check on the progress regarding the three people who had continued to Omaha the day before.

After disconnecting, he told Jim, "The people that went to Omaha yesterday are not involved. They flew to San Francisco almost a week ago to visit family. They've lived in Nebraska for two generations and have no record of anything more serious than a traffic ticket."

"The facial recognition also failed to turn up anyone that may be involved," Gene added as they watched the people around the gate. "And finally, there's still no word on the missing handler."

"Any other happy news?" Jim asked sarcastically.

"There was another coded message this morning," Gene answered. "It's similar to the others and contains coordinates."

"Please don't tell me that they are the same as here or Omaha," Jim replied.

"No," Gene answered. "They are still showing locations in San Francisco."

"I guess that's good," Jim said. "But if Sun is still there, as we know he is, and Hua is here, who is he talking to, and to whom is he providing locations? If he's the spotter, what information is he giving? This just doesn't make sense."

"All we can hope for right now is to break the chain," Gene responded. "As long as all the locations are in San Francisco, we know he's not directing anyone to Hua. But if he's communicating with the shooter, that doesn't make sense either."

"No, it doesn't," Jim agreed. "Maybe we should pick him up and see what he has to say."

"What would be our objective?" Gene asked. "Find out who the shooter is? Then what? If we get rid of him or Sun, they'll just send someone else. Then we're back to square one and we won't know what sort of communications they have and new codes to break. I don't see any benefit right now."

"You're right," Jim agreed. "I'm getting tired of chasing ghosts. Everything I thought would reveal who we're dealing with has proven to be wrong. And that phone call to Sun from Omaha. What the hell was that? We've ruled out the three people who were on the flight with her. And the odds that someone got there after Hua arrived is unlikely."

"What about private flights?" Gene asked. "We checked on scheduled flights but not charter or private. What if the shooter found out that she was going there and booked some flight with a charter company out of San Francisco?"

"No," Jim said, shaking his head. "The phone was used here first, remember? The *Spot one* call? If someone was here yesterday and in Omaha last night, they had to fly out of here. And if the coded phones are still in San Francisco, who the hell has the other phone?"

"I'll have Quantico check to see if there were any flights from the Dallas area to Omaha," Gene said, dialing. "Then maybe we can figure out who rented the plane or chartered the flight."

"I don't see any other way," Jim told him. "Unless we're completely wrong about everything regarding the phone calls and who the players are. And I don't see how that's possible."

Minutes later, Gene disconnected the call and said, "No flights. At least none out of DFW or Love Field. Or into Omaha. It could have been from some small uncontrolled airport, but there were no flight plans with the FAA."

"That's unlikely," Jim replied. "It's over 500 miles from here to Omaha. If it's a jet, it would need to file a flight plan because it cruises above 18 thousand feet. That pretty much limits it to a small plane. That means maybe three hours or more. I don't think that's the answer."

"Who else then?" Gene asked. "We've eliminated everyone else. And we know the shooter is still in San Francisco. Unless there's a completely unknown player out there. And there's still the problem of them knowing we were moving Hua. I'm starting to think that we do have a leak."

"I don't see any other possibility at this point," Jim agreed. "So, getting her here and keeping it a secret, even from Quantico, seems the only option we have."

"Where do you think we need to put her?" Gene asked as they watched the plane pulling up to the gate.

"I'm going to say the TownePlace Suites in Mesquite," Jim answered. "It gets us away from the airport area, and it's suitable for an extended stay if necessary."

"That sounds good," Gene said as the agent opened the door to the jet bridge. "We'll grab Hua and leave as quick as we can."

"What about luggage?" Jim asked as the first passengers got off the plane.

"All she has is the small carry-on she brought from San Francisco," Gene answered. "It was a quick decision, and we told her we'd get whatever she needed when we moved her. I guess we'll need to take her shopping after we get her settled at the motel."

"What's your guess at how long we need to keep her here?" Jim asked, watching the passengers.

"Let's wait and see what happens tomorrow," Gene answered as they spotted Millicent walking with Hua toward them. "I'm hoping that something will break today or tonight that will give us a clue as to what's going on."

"That would be nice," Jim agreed. "I thought I had a handle on what to do with this operation. So far, I'm 100 percent wrong."

"Hello, Millicent," Gene said as she stopped beside him. "Ms. Mulan. I hope this little change hasn't caused you too much inconvenience."

"No problem for me," Millicent answered. "I was going to be on this flight anyway. However, now I've got to get to my next flight."

Turning to Hua, she said, "I'm so sorry that this has interrupted your plans, Ms. Mulan. But General Barker and Mr. Lashley will take good care of you here in Texas. Enjoy your stay. And hopefully, it will be a little longer than the trip to Omaha."

"Thanks, Millicent," Gene said as she started to walk away.

Looking at Hua, he said, "This is Jim Lashley. He's part of our organization. We're going to take you somewhere safe until we figure out what's going on. We'll stop on the way and get you some new clothes and anything else you'll need for a couple of days."

"Nice to meet you, Mr. Lashley," Hua said with a slight bow.

"You as well," Jim told her, bowing also. "I hope we can get things resolved quickly, but your safety is the most important thing."

"I appreciate your assistance," she replied. "It's been a rather difficult journey up to this point. But I was assured that your organization is the best there is in providing personal security."

"It is," Gene told her as he led the way out of the terminal. "I'm parked just across the street, not too far away, and I'd rather have you walk with us instead of out here in the open if you don't mind."

"Not a problem, General," she replied, following them into the parking area. "This is probably the easiest part of my journey. I can't express how thankful I am for what you've done for me."

"Well, I hope we can get you back to a normal life as soon as possible," Gene said as they got into the car. "I know we can never replace the friends and family you left behind. But I hope we can give you a chance to make new friends. And, maybe someday, your family can come here to see you."

Chapter Twenty-eight

"Where should we go?" Gene asked as they left DFW North on 121.

"I'd say the Town East Mall in Mesquite," Jim answered. "They've got a little bit of everything."

Turning to Hua, Jim asked, "Is there anything in particular that you need?"

"Not really," she answered. "But clothes and some personal items would be nice."

"They'll probably have a store there that has it," Jim told her, turning back to Gene. "Just take 635 East, and it will be on the east side after you cross I-30."

"How far is it from the Towneplace Suites?" Gene asked.

"Couple of miles, maybe," Jim answered. "It'll be on the west side of 635 further south."

"Good," Gene said. "I want to get Ms. Mulan stashed away as soon as we can."

Looking at her in the rearview mirror, he asked, "Do you know why we had to get you out of Omaha so soon?"

"No," she answered with a shake of her head. "I was surprised when we had to leave San Francisco. But I'm not questioning that. I figured that moving me to Omaha was because it was a small town where nobody would think to look for me."

"That's part of the reason," Gene explained. "But we learned that someone had followed you to Omaha yesterday. We wanted to get you out of there last night, but there weren't any flights."

"Someone followed me?" she asked incredulously. "How did they know where I was going?"

"That's what we're trying to find out," Gene told her. "We think we know who's over here trying to find you, but we also think that there is more than just one man."

"I was afraid of this," she admitted. "I knew that when I decided to leave home and come here, they would never let me rest until they could get me back. Or worse."

"We won't let that happen," Jim said, trying to reassure her. "We thought we had a plan to find the men who were after you. But I was wrong. That doesn't mean we'll quit looking for them. And it certainly doesn't mean that we'll let anything happen to you."

A few minutes later, Gene took the exit that would take them to the mall. Once parked, he said, "We'll all go together, but when we get in, I'll stand by the door, and Jim will be by your side as you shop. Please get everything you think you'll need, but I prefer not to have you out in public any longer than necessary."

After going into several stores, Hua told Jim that she had everything and was ready to go. As they came to Gene, Jim said, "She's ready. Now, we'll head south and get off 635 at the exit for the Military Parkway. The hotel will be on your right just after crossing Military Parkway."

"Should be easy to find," Gene said as he maneuvered back onto 635 from the access road. "If you'll stay in the car with Hua, I'll get us rooms."

"Are both of you staying with me?" she asked him.

"No," Gene answered. "Just me. Jim lives just a few miles away, and as long as nobody knows you're here, it shouldn't be a problem. If I need him, he can be there in minutes."

After pulling into the parking lot, Gene nodded at Jim and headed for the lobby to register and get their keys. Minutes later, he returned and drove to where their rooms were located.

Opening the door to Hua's room, he handed her the key and said, "I'll be right next door in room 132. I'm sure you're getting hungry, so if you'll do whatever you need, we'll go somewhere and get something to eat."

"Yes," she answered. "I'll just take a quick shower and put on some fresh clothes. Shouldn't take more than 15 minutes."

"Take your time," Gene said. "Just call my room when you're ready. Jim will be with me, too."

They hadn't been in the room for more than ten minutes when Gene's cell phone rang. As he listened, he looked at Jim and shook his head. Disconnecting, he said, "You aren't going to believe this. Sun just got another call from the synthesized phone."

"What did they say?" Jim asked.

"Back to Spot one," Gene told him. "But the important thing is where the call originated."

"Don't tell me," Jim said. "Dallas."

"Close," Gene replied. "As near as they can tell, it's here in Mesquite."

"You've got to be shitting me," Jim exclaimed. "How the hell? Call Quantico. Have them send a team and get Sun. Immediately. Fly his ass here as soon as they can. Send a plane and get his ass on it. Don't take commercial."

Turning to the door, he continued, "And arrange for a debriefing team to get here, too. We're about to get some answers from that son of a bitch. I want the best people you have at extracting information here when they land. You might want to make arrangements to use one of the secure facilities down at Naval Air Station (NAS) Dallas also. I don't know why, but I think I know who's making those calls."

"Who?" Gene asked, following Jim out of the room.

"Who has been at every location when those calls have been made?" Jim asked, knocking on Hua's door. "There's only been one, and I was too stupid to see it."

"Who is it?" came the response from behind the closed door.

"It's Gene and I," Jim answered. "You need to open the door right now."

"What's wrong?" Hua asked as they came rushing into her room. "Is there someone here?"

"Yes, there is," Jim answered. "And it's you. Where's the phone, Hua?"

"What do you mean?" she asked, backing up.

"I mean the phone you've been using to talk to Sun," Jim answered. "You can either give it to me, or I'll tear this room apart until I find it."

"Please," she begged as she held her hands out. "I need that phone."

"You need to give it to me now," Jim said as the anger changed the tone of his voice. "You're the reason we've been running all over the country. And I demand to know why."

Hua turned and started to reach under a pillow on the bed. Grabbing her hand before she could, Jim said, "No, you don't. Gene, take her. I'll see what she was going for."

Gene took her arm and pulled her away from the bed, saying, "Ms. Mulan, please don't do anything stupid. You know we're here to help you. But you need to cooperate and answer our questions."

Jim held the cell phone up and asked, "Who are you using this phone to call?"

She lowered her head and answered, "A friend. Just a friend."

"You mean Sun Bin," Jim told her.

"Yes," she said, looking up. "How do you know about him?"

"He's the guy we think was sent here to kill you," Gene explained. "Why are you calling him?"

"You think he's here to kill me?" she asked, shaking her head. "He's the man who got me out of China and to North Korea. Why would he come here when he could have done it before we left China?"

Gene looked at Jim in disbelief and then asked, "Why would he be helping you?"

"Because he's like a brother to me," she answered. "His mother was my mother's best friend. They grew up together. They shared the same house. Sun and I grew up together. He's the only family I have left since my mother died. He's here to protect me."

Jim sat on the bed and asked, "Is that why you've been sending him a message every time we move you? So that he'll know where you are?"

"Yes," she admitted.

"Have you ever considered that we might need to know that?" Gene asked, holding up the phone and looking at her. "Do you have any idea of how much trouble we've been through trying to figure out who was using this phone?"

"I didn't think you'd know about it," she admitted. "It was just to be a precaution in case I needed help."

"What do you think?" Gene asked, turning to Jim. "Do we still need Sun here?"

"Yes," Jim answered. "I still want answers about some other issues that I don't want to discuss right now."

Turning to Hua, Jim continued, "For now, I'll keep this phone. If you need to use it, let me know. If Sun calls, I'll be with you when you talk to him. But for now, we still have the responsibility to keep you safe. And you have to start trusting us."

"I need to talk to Jim about some things," Gene told her as he opened the door. "You may not have considered it, but other people may have been tracking this phone just as we did."

Chapter Twenty-nine

"Is there anything else we need to do?" Gene asked as he shut the door to Hua's room.

"Yes," Jim answered. "We need to move again. Just because of what you told her. If we can track her by her phone, so can they."

"Where do you suggest?" Gene asked as they entered his room.

"First, we need to get out of Mesquite," Jim told him. "It's too easy to cover the motels in this area. Since we are going to take Sun to the NAS Dallas, we should head that way. There are several motels along I-30."

"Why don't you call a couple to get us five or six rooms while I go check out," Gene said, heading out. "I'd prefer if they are all adjoining, but at least get them on the same floor."

When he came back, Jim was just hanging up the phone. "What did you find?" Gene asked.

"I booked six rooms at the Marriot Residence Inn in Arlington," Jim answered. "They had six rooms on the second floor and said we could have four more if we needed them."

"Good," Gene said as his phone rang. After answering it, he turned to Jim and told him, "They are heading to Sun's place to get him. The team that's been following him said they should be there in the next 3 minutes."

"I hope you told them to grab him before he can make any more phone calls," Jim suggested. "And search every nook and cranny for other phones besides the ones we know about."

"I did," Gene assured him. "And we have a plane headed there from San Diego to pick him up. It should land in a little over an hour, which fits the time it should take the team to get him to the airport."

"Then they should land at NAS Dallas in about four and a half or five hours from now," Jim said. "That should give us plenty of time to get to the rooms and then pay a visit to the Commander at the base."

"Black Water has already contacted his office and requested a secure facility to question Sun if we think it's necessary," Gene informed him. "I'm hoping that he'll cooperate once he's confronted with what we know about his involvement."

"Have you directed the team that's getting him to let him know what we've discovered?" Jim asked as they knocked on Hua's door.

"No," Gene answered. "I don't want him to know anything. Just capturing him will be unexpected, and having his ability to contact Hua, or whoever he's communicating with on the other phone, will surely demonstrate that he has lost control."

"When will the interrogation team from Quantico get here?" Jim asked as Hua opened the door.

"Their plane should be leaving about the same time as the flight from San Francisco," Gene answered.

"We're moving you again," Gene told Hua as they stepped into her room. "You need to get everything so we can leave right now."

"Where are we going?" she asked, putting the few items she had back into the bag from shopping.

"Another motel," Gene informed her. "And this time, I hope you'll let us handle things."

"What's going to happen to Sun?" she asked as they escorted her to Gene's car.

"We're picking him up," Jim answered as Gene opened the rear door for her. "He'll be brought here to answer a few questions for us."

"Can I see him?" she asked as Gene started the car.

"No," Gene answered as he headed out of the parking lot. "Not for now. We'll see about it after we talk to Sun."

"Do you want to stop for something to eat before we get to the motel?" Jim asked as Gene headed north on 635.

"No," he answered. "I want to get away from Mesquite and put her out of sight as quickly as I can. The fewer eyes that see her, the better I'll feel. What's the fastest way to the motel?"

"Take 80 west to join I-30 west," he answered. "It's on the north side of I-30 and just past NAS Dallas. Shouldn't take more than 30 minutes."

"Okay," Gene said as the exit for Highway 80 came into view. "Once we get there, you stay with Hua while I go take care of the rooms. Then, we'll put her in the room between ours, and I'll go get something to eat."

"Not to change the subject," Jim said as they joined I-30, "but I'm going to need to talk to Jennifer. She's not going to be happy about you not staying with us as we planned. And she's going to want to know why I'm staying with you at a motel."

"I know," Gene told him. "I'll take care of that after we get Sun here and everybody settled. I'm getting you into this, so I'll try to get you out of it.

"That's not going to be easy," Jim said. "I think it may be better if I don't stay at the motel with you. You can explain why you have to babysit the customer, but she'll never buy why I need to be there."

"You're right," Gene agreed. "As soon as everybody is here, you take a cab and go home. I'll contact you when there's anything new. Then, you can come back tomorrow after she goes to work."

"That sounds like a good plan," Jim said. "I should be able to make it home before she gets there. Just call me if there's anything new."

Chapter Thirty

Jim was watching the news when Jennifer came in from work, asking, "What time does Gene want to pick us up for dinner? And shouldn't you be getting ready?"

"There's been a slight change in plans," Jim told her as he turned the TV off and followed her into the kitchen.

"What's changed?" she asked, setting her purse on the countertop. "Didn't his client, what's her name, come in?"

"Yes," Jim told her as he put his arms around her. "That's the reason our plans got changed. She was supposed to be coming to Mesquite, but something happened, and she's not going to be here."

"Oh?" Jennifer said. "What about Gene? Can't he come if she's not going to be here?"

"He's going to be meeting with some other people that are flying in later this afternoon," Jim explained. "Anyway, he said to give you his apologies and that he'd make it up to you next time."

"Well, I guess it's just going to be you and I," she said, smiling.

"You mean you still want to go out?" Jim asked.

"Of course," she answered. "First, I didn't take anything out for dinner because we were not supposed to be here. Second, I was really looking forward to dinner out. The real question is, don't you want to take me out? Even without Gene?"

"Of course, I'd love to take you out," Jim told her. "I was looking forward to it too. Where would you like to go?"

"There's a place over in Forney I heard about," she answered. "It's called Thai Pho. It's a little bit of a drive, but one of the guys said it's excellent."

"That's not that far," Jim told her. "If that's what you want, that's where we'll go."

"Good," she said, walking to the bedroom. "I'll just change clothes, and I'll be ready to go. Are you going to wear that wrinkled shirt?"

"Just going to change it," he answered. "Is this place coat and tie, or is a nice starched white shirt good enough?"

"You can wear anything you want," she said, slipping her blouse off. "You know I'd never try to tell you how to dress."

"I'll take that to mean that my Wranglers and a clean shirt are acceptable," Jim told her, smiling as he took off his shirt.

"By the way, do you need help with your skirt?" he asked, walking over to where she was undressing.

"Are you talking about helping take this one off or putting one on?" she replied, smiling as Jim stood behind her with his arms around her.

"More likely taking that one off," he said, kissing the side of her neck. "I've never developed an interest in what you're putting on."

"I know full well what you've developed an interest in," she said, turning in his arms. "It's not so much developed because I seem to remember what you've been interested in since we met in Florida."

"Well, I'm still interested," he told her as she put her arms around his neck.

"I can tell," she said, rubbing against him. "Do you think you can hold your interest until we get home tonight?"

"If I have to," Jim answered. "But I could get interested again, also."

Jennifer kissed him quickly and then told him, "I'm sure you could. But I know you, and if we don't go now, we'll be eating peanut butter and jelly sandwiches for dinner tonight."

"Okay," Jim reluctantly agreed. "But I expect something hot and spicy when we get home."

"Isn't that why we're going for Thai food?" Jennifer asked as she took a pair of slacks out of the closet. "For something hot and spicy?"

"That's not what I meant," Jim said, laughing as he put on his shirt.

"I know what you meant," she replied, pulling on her slacks as the phone rang. "Why don't you go get that while I finish dressing?"

"Got it," Jim told her, snapping his shirt closed.

"Hello," he said, answering the phone.

"Hello, Jim," Gene said. "How disappointed is Jennifer about tonight?"

"Not a lot," Jim answered. "She just insisted that I take her out. How are things over there?"

"Not much happening," Gene told him. "I've been getting a little more information out of Hua, mainly personal stuff. Sun should be landing at NAS Dallas in the next hour or so, and I've made arrangements to have him held there until we finish questioning him."

"Are the people there that will be conducting the interview?" Jim asked, not knowing if Jennifer could hear his side of the conversation.

"They just arrived," Gene answered. "Here's what I wanted to talk to you about. Did you know that the World Health Organization (WHO) is meeting in Denver next Month?"

"No, I didn't know that," Jim answered. "Why would I know anything about the WHO?"

"I guess you wouldn't," Gene admitted. "It just came up during our conversation about her work with viruses. She was originally scheduled to attend the upcoming meeting as an observer, and I was just thinking that maybe we could use that when we get serious about planning her accident."

"I can see the possibilities," Jim agreed. "Maybe if they haven't located her by then, they may think she plans to be there."

"That's what I'm thinking," Gene said. "It's something to keep in mind. If Sun is here to help her as she's saying, which I'm starting to believe, he may be able to provide some information on what we should expect from the Chinese."

"I hope you're right," Jim replied. "It sort of makes sense about the phone she was using. But I'm still wondering about who's using the other phone. What if he's playing both sides of the coin? He could still be feeding information to the shooter."

"That's just one of the many questions I'll have for him tomorrow," Gene told him.

"You're not going to interview him this evening?" Jim asked.

"No," Gene answered. "My folks back at Quantico recommend letting him sit for a few hours. The team will go in and wake him several times during the night. But the main work will begin early in the morning when he's tired and wondering what's happening."

"Jennifer will be leaving for work about 7:30," Jim said. "I can be at the motel around 8:30 or 9."

"That'll work," Gene said. "That'll give the guys four or five hours to soften him up. In the meantime, take Jennifer to dinner and tell her I'm sorry that I couldn't make it."

"Yes, sir," Jim answered as Jennifer walked in. "I'll tell her. You have a good evening."

"Let me guess," she said as she went into the kitchen to get her purse. "That was Gene apologizing for not taking us to dinner."

"You are correct," Jim said, opening the door. "As always."

"You boys are so easy to read," she said as they walked to the car. "I don't know how the government ever trusted you with secrets when you were in the Marines. I'd know everything within an hour. Maybe I should have been a spy."

"Yeah, I can see you as Mata Hari," Jim told her as he backed out of the driveway. "An exotic dancer and courtesan during World War 1."

"Why thank you, sir," she said coyly, blinking her eyes at him.

"You do know that she was discovered and shot by a firing squad," Jim told her as he headed for the restaurant.

"Yes," Jennifer answered. "But she went down in history. She's still remembered today for her beauty and refusing the blindfold."

"And I'll always remember you for your beauty," Jim told her, smiling. "That is if you'll let me blindfold you tonight."

She slapped his arm laughing and said, "You're such a pig, Jim Lashley. All of you men. Absolutely just swine."

"Now, don't go saying that all men are pigs," Jim told her as he headed east on Highway 80. "You're insulting 50 percent of the men and 90 percent of the pigs."

Chapter Thirty-one

The next morning, after Jennifer left for work, Jim waited a few minutes to make sure she didn't come back for something she had forgotten. The drive to the Marriot in Arlington was uneventful and he was soon knocking on Gene's door.

Talking on the phone as he opened the door, Gene motioned for him to come in. Taking a seat on the couch, he waited for Gene to finish.

"Well," Gene said, disconnecting the call, "how's your day going?"

"It's going well so far," Jim said, standing. "The question is, how's yours?"

"Interesting," Gene answered. "And it's just really getting started. Have you had breakfast?"

"No," Jim answered. "Where would you like to go?"

"I thought we'd eat here," Gene said, heading for the door. "They have a breakfast buffet set up, and it's quick."

"Sounds good to me," Jim said, following him out of the room. "What about the interrogation team?"

"I'm not sure," Gene answered. "I'm guessing that they've eaten and are busy at the base."

"How's that going?" Jim asked as they took the elevator down.

"Not much yet," Gene told him as they entered the dining area. "They've taken him out of his cell repeatedly just to deny him any sleep. His cell is dark, and the only light he sees is in the room where they take him for an hour or so of questions. Then it's back to his cell."

"What's he saying?" Jim asked as they selected from the buffet items.

"Not much," Gene answered, taking a bowl of cereal and milk. "They aren't pushing it. By now, he probably doesn't know if it's day or night. I figured we'd go over after we eat and talk to the leader of the team."

"Will we get a chance to ask any questions?" Jim asked, setting his plate of scrambled eggs, bacon, and English muffins on the table.

"We'll take that up with the team," Gene told him. "These guys know when a man is broken and when he's just pretending. We want him ready to sell his mother for relief."

"What if he's really here to help Hua?" Jim asked. "Shouldn't we allow for that?"

"Of course," Gene answered. "I've given that information to the team, and they'll decide when to offer him the carrot. I know you're anxious to find out why he's here, but we've got to trust these guys to soften him up if he's not here to help her."

Thirty minutes later, Gene's phone rang, and he slid his chair back as he answered, "Barker."

Listening for a couple of minutes, he said, "We'll be there in half an hour or so. Is there anything you need?"

Hearing the answer, he disconnected and told Jim, "Whenever you're finished, we'll head to the base and talk to the team. They want to know how far we should go to get information."

"I'm ready right now," Jim said, putting the last piece of bacon in his mouth.

"Then we'll go," Gene said, standing. "I'm anxious myself to have a look at Sun."

"I am, too," Jim said as they headed for Gene's car. "But I'm even more anxious to hear about that other phone."

"What about finding out if he's here to help?" Gene asked as they pulled out of the parking lot. "Isn't that just as important?"

"Of course," Jim admitted. "But until we know why he's using the phone and codes, there's still an unknown out there.

After clearing the base security and being escorted to the small building where Sun was being held, Gene and Jim were put in a room that looked into the interrogation room. Knowing that they were looking through a one-way glass, they watched as Sun appeared to be patiently waiting as two members of the team peppered him with questions.

After a few more minutes of him sitting stoically looking from man to man as they asked him various questions, he finally asked, "Who's really in charge here?"

"I'm not going to answer any of your questions until someone tells me why I'm here and what I'm supposed to have done," Sun said and then sat back and folded his arms.

One of the men glanced toward where Gene and Jim were watching and shook his head. Gene stepped to the glass and tapped on it.

The man whispered something to the other man and walked to the door. Seconds later, he opened the door to the room where Gene and Jim were and said, "He's refused to talk. He wants nothing to drink. He hasn't slept in probably over 24 hours. What would you like for us to do?"

Gene thought for a minute and asked, "Have you mentioned Ms. Mulan? Or said anything about us knowing why he's here?"

"No," the man answered. "Jeff, the guy in charge of the interrogation, just told us to keep asking random questions about what he's doing here, where he's from, nothing specific."

Gene turned to Jim and asked, "What do you think?"

"I'm not sure," Jim answered. "If he hasn't said anything up until now, I don't think he's going to say anything without pressure, and I sometimes have my doubts about forced confessions or information. Given that Hua says he's her friend, I say we give him the benefit of the doubt and give him a little information about her. Then we'll see his reaction."

"I agree," Gene said, turning to the interrogator. "What do you think?"

"That's up to you, sir," he answered. "We've been questioning him for hours, and he hasn't budged."

Gene looked at Jim and asked, "Do you want to do it, or should we let these guys have a little more time with him?"

"I think we need to go in," Jim told him. "He wants to know who's in charge, and you are the best person to give him the answer."

Gene turned to the guy who had come out of the room and asked, "Has he offered any resistance?"

"No," he answered. "We were debriefed by the crew that brought him here, and they said once he was in custody, he's been as calm as a kitten."

"Okay," Gene decided. "We'll go in. You and your partner stay in here and make sure we're filmed. If anything happens, get in there as fast as possible and subdue him by any means necessary."

"Not a problem, sir," he said as they left the room and entered the adjoining hall. Knocking on the door to the room where Sun was being held, he opened it and motioned for the other man to come out.

As soon as he exited, Gene walked in with Jim steps behind him, saying, "Mr. Bin, I understand that you want to talk to whoever's in charge. Well, now's your chance. I'm the man in charge, so say whatever you want to say."

Sun sat back and looked at Gene for a few seconds and then glanced at Jim. "I know who you are," he finally said. "You're General Barker. You used to be a Marine General, and now you work for Black Water."

Gene glanced at Jim and then asked, "Why would you think that?"

"Because I've studied you and your organization," Sun said with a slight smile. "We've known about Black Water for years. Just as we keep dossiers on your military leaders, we keep them on your intelligence operations and your pseudo contractors who are nothing more than an extension of the Central Intelligence Agency, the infamous CIA."

Gene returned his smile and said, "Just as we know about your association with the South Blade and the Oriental Sword. Now, would you like to tell me why you were in San Francisco?"

Sun sat quietly for a moment and answered, "Certainly. As soon as you tell me what you did with Hua Mulan."

Chapter Thirty-two

Gene looked at Jim, waiting for his nod of agreement, and said, "She's safe in a hotel. We took her phone to prevent her from contacting you and allowing you to tell anyone where she is."

Taking her phone from his pocket, Gene continued, "Your contact with her has caused us considerable trouble. Now, would you explain why she's been notifying you every time we move her?"

"I'll answer that," Sun said, looking from Jim to Gene. "The answer is the same as the answer to your first question: why I'm here. I'm here to ensure her safety."

"Ensuring her safety is our job," Gene told him. "Who thought she needed your help? Who sent you?"

"If your job was to ensure her safety, you've been failing," Sun responded. "She's been in more danger since you took her to San Francisco than during the entire time I was getting her out of Wuhan."

"What do you mean you got her out of Wuhan?" Jim asked.

Sun turned to look at him and asked, "And who are you?"

"Jim is one of my agents," Gene answered. "He's the one that figured out who was telling you where we were moving Hua."

"Superior intelligence," Sun said, smiling. "You figured out a phone she had was calling a phone I had. And just how long did that take you? As I said, she's been in greater danger in the hands of Black Water than if I'd hidden her in some remote village in North Korea."

"Regardless of what you think about how we've been protecting her, I asked you a question," Jim repeated. "Are you saying that you're the one who got her out of China?"

"Yes," Sun answered. "Your people, Black Water, approached her after she let your embassy know that she wanted to defect. I was the one that planned the route from Beijing to Linjiang and then into North Korea for you to pick her up at Hungnam."

Jim looked at Gene and saw him verify that was the route they had used. "How did you know she was defecting?"

Sun looked at him for a second and said, "Because she told me."

"Why would she do that?" Jim asked, shaking his head. "You're part of the reason she was trying to come here. You're a member of the Chinese Army. Would you care to explain that?"

"Why don't you ask her?" Sun replied. "You obviously trust her and not me."

"We did," Gene told him. "Now, we're asking you."

"It goes back a long way," Sun finally said. "Our families were together back during the Korean War. Her father and mine were both Mig 15 pilots. They were stationed together, and our mothers were like sisters. I'm sure you understand how it is in the military."

"Okay," Jim said. "How does that make you want to become a traitor to your country? Your family and hers were close 40 years ago."

"It's deeper than that," Sun explained. "Our fathers were both lost on a mission in what you refer to as Mig Alley, the area along the Yalu River between Korea and China."

"I'm familiar with Mig Alley," Jim said, nodding.

"Our fathers left that morning and never returned," Sun continued. "The most obvious reason was one of your F-86 Sabre jets shot them down. That left our mothers, and Hua and I, to fend for ourselves. Our mothers shared a house and worked to take care of us since the government didn't care what happened.

Hua and I became like brother and sister," he added. "I joined the military, but I always remembered how the Chinese government treated our families after our fathers died. Hua was different. She was brilliant. Where most girls are considered worthless by our society, she stood out."

"Why did she decide to defect?" Jim asked. "And why did you go along with it?"

"Once she found out that the People's Republic of China (PRC) was using her research on viruses to make biological weapons, she was determined to let somebody know that they were violating the ban on chemical and biological weapons," he answered. "She knew firsthand how deadly some of the viruses she was working with would be if they were ever to escape the lab.

She had been telling me for months," Sun continued. "I did some looking into some of our more secret internal policies and saw where we had plans for limited biological use in certain theatres. What she was telling me was the truth. My government would rather see millions of our own people die than let another country defeat us. This doomsday weapon was unacceptable to me. I agreed that something had to be done."

"And you knew that your career would be finished," Jim said.

"My career?" Sun asked, laughing. "My *life* would be finished. Do you think that Hua is the only one they're coming for? I knew that even if I managed to survive, my life would never be the same. Neither will hers.

I gave my mother a promise before she died that I'd take care of Hua and her mother," Sun told them. "And I made the same promise to her mother before she died. They were my family. Now, she's the only family I have left. If I fail now, I have no life. I'd have failed in my promise to our mothers, and now I can't go back to whatever short life I'd have there."

Gene looked from Sun to Jim and finally turned to the door. "I'll be right back," he said, motioning to the men on the other side of the one-way glass.

A couple of minutes later, he came back in and said, "We'll be taking you out of here shortly. But I have one further question before we finish. Who are you talking to on the other phone? The one where you're using a code in Mandarin."

Sun smiled and answered, "I'm not surprised that you broke the code. It wasn't that complex. The answer to your question is that I have a partner here."

"What were the coordinates for?" Jim asked.

"They were at the location of someone who was trying to eliminate Hua," Sun answered. "Tell me, have you found the body of one of her security team? The one that's been missing for a couple of days?"

"Are you saying that you, or your partner, killed one of my team members who were assigned to protect Hua?" Gene asked.

"Protect her?" Sun said. "He was providing someone else with her location. He was making sure that someone knew where she would be at any time or any day. If I hadn't had him killed, Hua would probably be dead today. That's why I said that she's in greater danger since you brought her here than when I was getting her out of China."

"Son of a bitch," Gene muttered. "You were right about the leak, Jim. Maybe I was wrong about Sun, but I was right about there being someone else out there. I need to call Quantico."

Chapter Thirty-three

"What now?" Sun asked as Gene stepped out of the room to make a report to Quantico.

"I guess we'll take you to see Hua," Jim answered. "It's Gene's call, but I'm sure that's what he'll do."

"What's your role in this?" Sun asked as he watched Jim pace the room.

"I'm the dumb ass that sort off kept us pointing in the wrong direction," Jim admitted. "I was so sure that you were here to eliminate Hua that I didn't consider any other possibilities. Maybe you were here to provide directions and to take care of things later. But never did I consider that you were here to help her."

Sun smiled and then said, "That's the problem with having to make decisions. Sometimes you screw it up. But, admitting it is the true test of a wise man."

"What's that?" Jim asked. "Some ancient wisdom from Confucius?"

"Just the teachings of experience," Sun replied. "Not to mention, all you knew about me was what you read. Sometimes, the truth about a man is what isn't written, but what is learned by association."

"Well, I'm still to blame for what you've had to go through," Jim told him. "For that, I apologize. Now, you mentioned there was someone here who was receiving directions to Hua. Do you know where he is?"

"No," Sun admitted. "But, if you will kindly get me my phone back, I can try to find out."

"That won't be a problem," Jim assured him. "We'll have to ask Gene, but I think the team that brought you here from San Francisco has them. I have another question for you if you don't mind."

"I'm at your service, so to speak," Sun said with a smile.

"I figured that the Chinese would send at least two, if not three, here," Jim said. "What do you know about how many there are?"

"Only one," Sun answered. "Why would you think there would be more?"

"One to eliminate Hua and another one to eliminate him," Jim told him. "I assumed that the first one would know who she was and why it was important to terminate her. The second would know nothing about either the shooter or Hua and just eliminate the shooter to sever the tie back to whoever ordered the hit."

"You overthink," Sun told him. "Maybe here you have people that need to know why things are ordered. In my country, an order does not require an explanation. The man who's here to kill Hua only knows that if he fails, he dies."

"So, he has no knowledge of who she really is," Jim replied.

"None," Sun emphasized. "Do you always know why Black Water sends you out?"

"Mostly," Jim answered. "Maybe earlier in my time with them, I was just given directions. Now, I generally know why an operation is necessary and given a certain amount of latitude in how to perform the tasking.”

“That is not the case with the people that run my country,” Sun told him. “Undying loyalty and absolute obedience are required, with few exceptions.”

“So, what can you tell me about the shooter?” Jim asked. “Do you know his name? Is he military?”

“His name is Li Wei,” Sun answered. “He’s former military. I knew him when we were both South Blade.”

“So, he knows you, too,” Jim said.

“Yes,” Sun answered. “He doesn’t know that I am here yet. However, I’m sure that he’ll be sent to take care of me when the party figures out that I am.”

“They don’t know you’ve left China?” Jim asked.

“Probably by now,” Sun answered. “I had requested some time off to visit the site of my father’s death. I’ve made the trip almost every year on the date he died. So, it was nothing new, and it gave me a chance to get Hua out of the country.

But I should have returned two days ago, and they aren’t stupid,” Sun said, shaking his head. “By now, yeah, I think they know something has happened. Maybe they’ll be like you, not knowing my ties to Hua, and they’ll chase the wrong rabbit down the wrong hole. But, sooner or later, they’ll figure it out.”

“Okay,” Jim said, nodding. “What about Li Wei? How will he communicate with whoever sent him?”

“He has a phone,” Sun said. “And I’m sure he has informed them that his contact, your agent, has disappeared. That, by itself, will let them know that something has happened.”

“What will they do?” Jim asked.

"They'll find another source," Sun answered. "I'm sure there are many of them here. Your universities, the embassy, and exchange programs, many of them with political ties that mean they'll do anything the party demands, including spying. Rewards will be promised. They'll have an army of eyes looking for her."

"What had you planned?" Jim asked.

"My partner was going to eliminate Li Wei, as I said," Sun answered.

"And when he didn't report terminating Hua? What then?" Jim asked.

"We would have disappeared," Sun answered. "I know that they'll never give up trying to find her, and now me. But we can go where we won't be noticed. It's not that difficult."

"What if we can convince Li Wei that you are dead?" Jim asked as Gene came back into the room. "Then he could report that she is dead, and if we do it right, he'll recognize you and tell them that also."

"How do you propose to do that?" Sun asked. "And what can you do to ensure that he calls?"

"I don't know yet," Jim admitted. "But with your help, I think we can develop a plan to let the Chinese think that both of you are dead. Maybe that'll make your disappearance easier."

"We'll do whatever is necessary to protect both of you," Gene told him. "With your knowledge of how they'll try to remove Hua, and now you, and with our assets, I think we can make it work."

"I'll cooperate as much as I can," Sun told them. "As I said, I have no life back there. Neither does she. I'm sure your government will have a lot of use for her with all her knowledge and expertise in virology. Me, I'm just a soldier. And a traitor at that."

"I think we can find a use for you," Gene told him. "But for now, I think Hua would be grateful to see you. We'll work on the rest of it later. I've gotten everything that was taken from you, and you'll be staying where she is. I'm sure you could use a few hours of rest right now."

"Just knowing she's safe is what I need," Sun told Gene as they left the room. "At least I haven't broken my promise to my mother or hers. Yet."

"And we'll help you keep those promises," Jim said, following them out into the hall.

Chapter Thirty-four

When they got back to the motel, Gene led Sun to Hua's room and quietly said, "Why don't you let her know you're here? I think that would be a very pleasant surprise."

"I'd like that," Sun said, stepping up to the door.

Seconds after knocking, he heard her ask, "Who's there?"

Saying that he was there in Mandarin, the door flew open, and Hua threw her arms around Sun's neck. As he held her, he kept talking in Mandarin as Jim and Gene walked next door to Gene's room.

Leaving the door open, Gene asked, "What's your plan now that we're back to square one?"

"I don't think we're completely starting over," Jim answered. "We've lost a couple of days, but Sun knows the real shooter. That's worth at least the days we've lost since we didn't have a clue who he was."

"You're right," Gene agreed. "And he knows where he is; that's a big jump on things."

"He knew where he *was*," Jim corrected him. "The communication link between Sun and his partner needs to be reestablished as soon as possible. I'm hoping that the partner had enough initiative to start looking for or following Li Wei so he could let Sun know what happened when they talked again."

"I hope you're right," Gene said as Sun stepped to the open door.

"Thank you," he said with a slight bow to Gene. "I promised her we'd have much more time to talk, but right now, we need to start planning on how to get rid of Li Wei."

"Come in and have a seat," Gene told him as he rose and walked to the door.

After checking to make sure Hua's door was shut, he shut his door and said, "Jim and I think you need to call your partner and let him know where you are and that the plans have changed."

Giving both phones to Sun, he continued, "I hope disrupting your operation hasn't caused your partner any real problems."

Selecting the phone he needed, he answered, "I doubt it. Wang Jong, my partner, is very resourceful. We had a contingency plan in the event either one of us disappeared. He would have revisited all the places where I had seen Li and kept trying to find him."

"May I?" he asked, sitting at the desk and taking the pen and notepad with the motel logo.

"Certainly," Gene answered. "Is there anything else you need?"

"No," Sun said as he wrote a series of Chinese symbols on the pad. "It's a fairly simple code; I just need to have it written so I can space the words as I talk. This won't take long."

A few minutes later, Sun dialed the number he needed and held the notepad as he spoke in a very deliberate and methodical tone. Finishing his transcript, he disconnected and placed the phone on the desk.

"And?" Jim asked, looking at Sun.

"He found Li Wei and has been keeping an eye on him," Sun confirmed. "He thinks that he's meeting with someone to replace your man."

"Do you have a tap on Li Wei's phone?" Gene asked.

"No," Sun answered, shaking his head. "I didn't bring any equipment of that sort and hadn't planned on needing it."

"We need that," Jim said as Gene dialed Quantico. "If for no other reason than to know when he notifies China when we convince him that Hua's dead."

"I agree," Gene said, waiting for an answer. "And having a trace would be a big benefit."

"Tell me something," Jim said, looking at Sun as Gene talked on the phone. "Why didn't you just have her disappear during the WHO meeting in Denver next month?"

"We discussed that," Sun answered. "But she would have been surrounded by so many of our people that it would have been impossible for her to get away. She was only to be there as a token of how advanced the Chinese government has become regarding females in positions of authority. And I think the government is so scared of what she would say; they wouldn't take a chance on her talking to one of the reporters that will be covering the event for your American news programs."

"They can have a tap on his phone by tomorrow evening," Gene told them as he took a seat on the couch and looked at Sun. "But you need to have Wang meet with our people at the SF Plaza Hotel at noon tomorrow. There will be a message at the desk that will tell him which room."

Sun reached for the notepad again and scribbled the information before dialing. Seconds later, he laid the phone on the desk and said, "I told him to check with the desk clerk at 12:30 and every hour after that until he gets the message."

"What else?" Sun asked.

"There's not much more we can do right now," Gene answered. "Jim has to fly tomorrow and will be gone for three days. Once we get Wang with our team, they'll start shadowing Li Wei and sooner or later get his phone's signal."

"Would it help to have your team using Wang's phone?" Sun asked.

"Maybe," Gene answered, looking at Jim. "What do you think?"

Jim sat back for a couple of minutes before answering, "It might, but I don't want to make any changes to the normal communications flow right now. Li Wei or the Chinese embassy may also have taps on his and your phones. I don't want any communications in the clear. But we could definitely provide him with a burner phone to talk to our team."

"That's a good idea," Gene said, picking up his phone. "I'll make sure our people have several with preset numbers to give him tomorrow."

"Now, if you don't have anything further for me," Jim said, standing. "I need to get home before Jennifer gets there."

"I have an idea," Gene said as he rose. "Why don't we take Sun, Hua, and Jennifer out to dinner tonight? She thinks I'm here to meet with clients, so this will make up for the dinner I promised last night."

"What do you think, Sun?" Jim asked. "Would you rather spend some time with Hua or go out to dinner with us?"

"I think your offer is wonderful," Sun answered. "It would do her good to have a chance to see how normal Americans live. We'll have plenty of opportunities to talk tomorrow and the next few days. I think that's a great idea."

"Good," Gene said. "It's settled. But you need to talk to her and make sure she understands that there's to be no mention of why she's here, her work in Wuhan, or what has happened these last few days."

"That's not a problem," Sun told him. "She and I have both had to use a fictitious story about our lives since we left Wuhan. We've posed as brother and sister traveling to visit relatives. She works in a garment factory, and I work in a factory that makes knockoff Louis Vuitton purses."

"I wouldn't tell anyone about it being a knockoff," Jim told him, smiling. "You'll have my wife and half of the wives of other pilots looking at the purses their husbands brought back from Hong Kong. Just stay with the factory job part. Now, I'll head home and wait for you guys. What time do you think, Gene?"

"How about 7 o'clock?" Gene answered. "That will give you guys plenty of time to clean up and be ready."

"Good enough," Jim replied. "Where are you taking us?"

"How about the Szechuan Chinese Restaurant?" he answered with a grin.

"How about Tucker's Grill and Taqueria?" Jim suggested. "Let them have a sample of American and Mexican dishes."

"That sounds better to me," Sun said, looking at Gene. "And I can see that you Americans have a rather devious sense of humor."

"Wait until you get to know Jim better," Gene said, laughing and turning to Jim. "We'll see you at 7."

Chapter Thirty-five

Two days later, Jim was in his layover hotel room in Miami when the phone rang. "Hello," he answered, wondering if it was the Captain of his flight or Jennifer calling.

"How are you doing this afternoon?" Gene asked. "It must be nice to just fly around the United States with pretty ladies waiting on you while guys like me work 24 hours a day to try to solve mysteries that you create."

"Good afternoon, General," Jim said, smiling. "To what do I owe the honor of your call?"

"Just to update you on a few of the things that have happened since you left," Gene answered. "If you'll come down to the lobby, I thought I'd take you out to dinner. Unless you have other plans this evening."

"No other plans," Jim told him. "The Captain was meeting his brother; the Flight Attendants were having a nail polish party or something in one of their rooms. I was just going to have dinner here in the hotel and finish reading a book."

"Sounds so exciting," Gene said, laughing. "Why don't you meet me in the restaurant and tell me all about this book you're reading?"

"I'll be there in 10 minutes," Jim said, pulling a short-sleeved knit shirt from his suitcase.

When he walked into the restaurant, he spotted Gene talking to a waiter and went to the table to join him. "Hello, Jim," Gene said, motioning for the waiter to stay. "Would you like something to drink?"

"Just ice tea," Jim said, taking a seat across the table from Gene.

"Yes, sir," the waiter said before leaving.

"I'm sure you didn't fly here just to update me on a few things," Jim said, glancing around the room.

"Yes and no," Gene replied, setting his menu on the table. "I had to meet a team that's doing some work down in Cuba, so I figured I'd spend the night and talk to you."

"Anything major going on in Cuba?" Jim asked, looking at the menu.

"Just trying to get someone out," Gene answered. "But I think you'll be more interested in what's going on in San Francisco."

"No doubt," Jim replied as the waiter came to the table with their drinks.

"Are you gentlemen ready to order?" he asked.

"I'd like the pulled pork sandwich with sweet potato fries," Gene told him. "And a small Caesar salad on the side."

"That sounds good to me," Jim said, handing him his menu.

"I'll be right back with your salads," the waiter told them, taking their menus.

"So, what's new in San Fran?" Jim asked.

"We found Li Wei's phone pretty quickly," Gene answered. "Wang had been following him since Sun asked him to. The boys at Quantico have tapped it and have some very interesting information."

"How interesting?" Jim asked, taking a sip of tea.

"Li hasn't a clue where Hua is," Gene answered. "He's been getting calls every day from someone in their embassy, and they are very upset."

"What about replacing his informant?" Jim asked. "Does the company know if Li has found someone else to work with him?"

"It appears that was a flaw in their plan," Gene answered. "They only had one man on the inside. When Sun eliminated him, they were left blind. There's been a flurry of activity at the embassy. Apparently, they're trying to find someone who knows anything about her."

"And no luck so far?" Jim said hopefully.

"None," Gene confirmed. "But the surprising thing is how many people they have been questioning. I never thought there'd be so many Chinese here the embassy thinks will help them. I'm guessing thousands in San Francisco alone."

"Any clue as to what they're thinking?" Jim asked.

"They appear to be planning on moving their operation to Denver," Gene answered. "They think she's here to blow the whistle at the WHO meeting. So, they're trying to get people at the airport, hotels, car rentals, or any other tourist activity to be watching for her."

"What about Li?" Jim asked. "Has he made plans to go to Denver?"

"As we speak," Gene answered. "He booked a flight this morning. He'll be there by noon tomorrow."

"Do we have people there to *greet* him?" Jim asked.

"They'll get there this afternoon," Gene confirmed. "And Wang will be with them."

"Have you told Sun and Hua what's going on?" Jim asked as the waiter headed toward their table.

"Yes," Gene said as their salads were delivered.

As the waiter left, he continued, "I've been using Sun as a sounding board for our ideas. The man is pretty sharp. He understands how they operate, and his insight into Li may prove to be extremely valuable."

"What has he told you about Li?" Jim asked as he tried the salad.

"He said Li is a sadist," Gene answered as he ate. "That's apparently one of the things that their government exploited."

"Really?" Jim asked, astonished. "Their military didn't condemn someone like that?"

"I guess not," Gene answered. "Don't forget, history is full of masochists and sadists. Look at Nazi Germany during World War 2. There was Franz Stangl, who referred to the prisoners as cargo and their corpses as garbage to be disposed of. And it's not limited to the men. There was Ilse Koch, known as the Bitch of Buchenwald because of her cruelty."

"I know," Jim said, sitting back. "I was just thinking of some of the things that happened in Vietnam. Guys were cutting the ears off Vietnamese and making necklaces. Having their pictures taken holding up the severed heads."

"War does strange things to people," Gene admitted. "But it appears that in China, it extends even to their own citizens. That's the frightening thing. To think that your own government will commit such atrocities on you."

"Yeah, I know," Jim said, shaking his head. "It just seems so out of place in today's society. Anything else about Li?"

"Yes," Gene said as their sandwiches arrived. "And we think it's his Achilles heel."

As soon as the waiter was gone, Jim asked, "What did Sun tell you?"

"It seems as if Li refuses to accept responsibility for any wrongdoing," Gene answered. "It doesn't matter what happens. If something goes wrong, it's always someone else's fault. He's quick to place the blame on the weatherman for a poor forecast. Or the motor pool for unserviceable equipment. Doesn't matter. It's never his fault."

"And how does Sun think that'll help us?" Jim asked as he picked up a sweet potato fry.

"Li is also prone to jump to quick conclusions," Gene explained. "If he sees the accident that you proposed, he'll call his boss and report her death. It's not a big thing, but it may give us a little advantage in hiding Hua if he thinks he's done and doesn't investigate to confirm it. Especially since he would have to admit to his boss that he was wrong."

"I see," Jim replied. "That might help us. Has there been any mention of Sun being here?"

"Not so far," Gene answered. "At least not to Li. There may be other players that we aren't aware of. But he's sure they'll figure it out sooner rather than later."

Chapter Thirty-six

The next morning, after Jim had landed at DFW, he stopped by the motel where Gene was staying. When he got to the open door, he called out to see if anyone was in the room.

Just then, the door next door opened, and Gene said, "Jim, glad you're here. I was just starting to tell Sun and Hua about our plan in Denver. Why don't you come in and explain it to them."

"Sure," Jim said, stepping into the room. "But I'd like to change out of my uniform if I can use your room, Gene."

"Go ahead," he said. "I'll just try to give a broad-brush view of what you've been working on."

A couple of minutes later, Jim came back into the room and asked, "What have you told them so far?" "Not much," Gene answered. "Just that we were planning on an accident in Denver to allow them to disappear."

"That's pretty simplistic, but it is the goal," Jim said, nodding at Sun and Hua. "It's my opinion that we need to stop any further effort to Li's finding and to kill Hua. And, if Li sees Sun in the same car, it will prevent anyone from looking for him also."

"We'll still keep you somewhere safe," Gene assured them. "But what Jim's trying to do is give us some extra time between now and when Hua is asked to give her testimony without having to keep looking over our shoulders wondering if someone has discovered her."

"When do you plan on doing this?" Sun asked.

"Next month when the WHO is meeting," Jim answered. "Gene told me that Li has already gone there, and everyone thinks Hua is trying to get there and blow the lid off their bioweapons program."

"That's stupid," Sun said, shaking his head. "Why would she walk into a place where she knows they'll be? Why would they think that?"

"Maybe they realize that we, the United States, have her," Gene told him. "And they probably believe that she's here for only one reason. To bring the question up when every nation will be watching."

"Not to mention," Jim added, "they have no clue of where she is now. That's the only logical place for her to be."

"Now, I'd like to get back to the accident," Jim said after letting them think about what he had just told them.

"I took some time looking at maps of the Denver area trying to find a location that would provide a place to stage it," Jim said. "I'd like for a team from Muddy Water to go to Denver as soon as possible to physically look at the area I've identified and see what they think.

And they need to scout the local wrecking yards to find a car that will fit the accident we're planning," he continued. "Once they find it, they need to find a matching car and buy it. I'd also like matching plates, just in case."

"That shouldn't be too hard to doctor some plates," Gene added. "And the only problem I see with the cars is finding the duplicate."

"That's why we need the team there now," Jim argued. "And don't forget that there are several small towns around Denver where a salvage yard may have just what we need."

"We'll take care of it," Gene said. "What do you think about taking Hua to Denver?"

"That's part of the plan we discussed, isn't it?" Jim asked. "So that Li could see her get in the car. It won't work without that."

"I mean this week or next," Gene told him. "Maybe two or three times."

Jim thought for a minute and said, "I'm guessing you want her to be seen at a hotel or restaurant. Something like that."

"Yes," Gene told him. "I'm suggesting that we get a room under some random Chinese name, have her seen going in and out of the hotel a few times over a day or so, and then have her check out."

"That's a good idea," Jim agreed. "If the PRC has a thousand eyes, as you suggest, someone will notice her. Then Li will be convinced that he's in the right place."

"Exactly," Gene said. "Then, we bring her back here and let Li and the PRC waste time looking in the wrong place. And it'll give us a place for her to start the accident chase sequence."

"What about Sun?" Jim asked. "Do you want him to be seen there also?"

"I don't think so," Gene answered. "I'd like to pull him out of the hat when we start the chase. When Li recognizes him with Hua as they get in the car, he'll be more eager than ever to report the accident to his people."

"I'd like to go with Hua anyway," Sun said, standing. "I still don't trust your organization with her life. If you want my cooperation, I insist on going wherever you take her."

Gene looked at Jim and asked, "What do you think?"

Jim turned to Sun and asked, "Will you be satisfied if you're there but have no contact with her? By that I mean you'll be in the hotel, but nobody can see you with her. She'll come and go with some of our people. You'll be with her on the plane, but once she's in the hotel, you can't be seen with her."

"Why not?" Sun asked. "You want Li to know it was me with her when you stage your accident. Why not let someone see me there and hope that Li finds out? Then he'll probably report my sighting and be told that I'm to be eliminated with her. Just the thought of executing the two of us will make him more eager than ever. And his overly zealous ambition may cause him to make a mistake."

"May I say something?" Hua asked.

"Of course," Gene told her. "What would you like to say?"

"I would like for Sun to be with me," she answered. "It seems to me that when the PRC starts looking into both of our disappearances, they'll discover that we traveled together at least as far as North Korea. I think that it would be strange for me to show up there without him."

Jim looked at her for a second and then said, "The lady has a point. By then, everyone will know that Sun is missing. And, as she so eloquently said, he's been seen with her leaving China. I'm starting to wish he had been seen with her in San Francisco. I think he needs to go with her."

"All right," Gene finally said after looking at the determination on everyone's face. "We'll do it your way. I can't seem to think of a single logical reason not to have both of you there."

"Thank you," Sun said with a slight bow. "I know you may still harbor some doubt about me. But this small amount of trust is welcomed. Thank you."

Hua walked over to Gene and gave him a short hug, saying, "And I thank you, too. My life has become a living hell with no family or friends. Having Sun with me is more important to me than you'll ever know."

"I understand," Gene said, nodding. "And I know both of you took a monumental risk just coming here. We'll always try to see things your way if at all possible. But, sometimes, it may be impossible."

"I know," Sun replied. "And Hua and I appreciate what you're doing for us. If I ever seem to be overstepping my bounds, please let me know. I'm certainly capable of seeing the wisdom or faults in my desires. And I'll never put her life in jeopardy just to make a point."

"Thank you," Gene told him. "We are both trying to accomplish the same thing. A common goal. Working together is always preferable. Especially when we both have unique assets and abilities. Now, if you'll pardon us, I need to talk to Jim before he goes home."

Chapter Thirty–seven

As soon as they were in his room, Gene said, "We've got another contract that I want you on."

"When?" Jim asked.

"At the first of next month," Gene answered. "Coincidentally, it's also in Denver. I was going to make sure you could bid Denver layovers for the month anyway, just in case we needed you there."

"I'll take a look," Jim told him. "Our bids for next month just came out. As of right now, I'm scheduled to fly Los Angeles and Albuquerque layovers."

"Let me know if you can arrange it," Gene said. "We can pull some strings if necessary, but I prefer not to get involved if we don't have to."

"Understand," Jim said, smiling. "I've had some experience with your *un-involvement*. Now, what's the contract?"

"Have you ever heard of a gentleman named Jay William Pride?" Gene asked, taking a seat on the couch.

"Not that I recall," Jim answered, leaning back against the desk. "Should I have?"

"Not necessarily," Gene told him. "He's a somewhat controversial city councilman in Denver."

"And we're getting involved with city issues now?" Jim asked.

"Not city issues," Gene corrected him. "Well, I guess you could call it that. Basically, the city has a problem."

"And I'm guessing it involves this gentleman," Jim said. "Just what does the contract call for?"

"His removal," Gene answered.

"Are we talking about helping to rig some upcoming election?" Jim asked. "Or some more dramatic removal?"

"We aren't in the business of rigging elections," Gene told him.

"I didn't think we were in the business of *removing* elected officials either," Jim countered.

"Really?" Gene asked. "You seem to have a rather short memory if you don't remember that our company got its start in the removal business."

"In that case, refresh my memory," Jim said.

"How many village Chieftains were suddenly missing or found no longer living when you were in Vietnam?" Gene asked. "You knew we had teams that would sneak into certain villages where the enemy was storing weapons, or the village people were harassing our troops. Then, lo and behold, there was a new Chieftain who seemed to see things our way."

"That was war," Jim argued. "If the village was siding with the North Vietnamese or the Viet Cong, they were, in effect, combatants."

"That's pretty good rationalization," Gene said. "Using that same argument, the North Vietnamese could assassinate the Chieftain of any village that supported us."

"They did," Jim replied.

"So they did," Gene agreed. "What about your first mission for Dark Water? Do you remember leaving a package beside an adobe hut? Did you ever think what was in that package?"

"I remember," Jim answered. "I was told it could be a payoff for someone in that village."

"But it was an explosive, wasn't it?" Gene asked him. "You saw the picture of the destroyed hut when you got back to New York. Who do you think was in that hut?"

"I'm getting your point," Jim said, nodding. "But that was overseas. This is different."

"Why?" Gene asked. "Black Water was founded on doing things that our government couldn't do. We, the United States of America, don't go into foreign nations and assassinate their leaders. Bullshit. We, the US of A, don't. But we, the US of A, will pay for someone else to do it. The only requirement is for there to be no ties between the government and the actions.

Remember Leonard? The pervert?" Gene then asked. "Was he at war with us? You didn't have too much of an issue with his removal. What's the problem now?"

"Removing an elected official," Jim argued. "Why are we involved?"

"Okay, I understand your hesitation," Gene said, leaning back. "Here's what's happening. First, the man is a crook. And before you say anything, I know they're all crooks to some extent. But this guy has become flagrant about his dealings.

For example," Gene continued, "if there's a city contract for anything, even if it's not in his district, he has his fingers in it. He likes to be known as 'Dollar Bill.' He's fond of saying that nothing gets done in Denver unless you've got the Dollar Bill.

Any business that tries to bid on a contract knows that there'll be cost overruns due to supply issues, labor issues, and some people even say weather issues unless you've paid the Dollar Bill," Gene said. "Then all of the bids come in at an extravagant amount in order to cover the well-known issues, and good ole' Jay William, Dollar Bill, Pride steps in with a contract slightly under the others and gives it to one of his *supporters*.

Now, in the event that someone else does get the contract, his son is all of a sudden, an employee of the company," Gene continued. "He was once a supervising engineer for a company that won the contract to repair the sewer system on the east side of Denver. Pretty good for a kid who got kicked out of junior college for allegedly dealing drugs on campus. I say allegedly because the college security guard that caught him suddenly quit and couldn't be found to testify against him.

And it just so happens that once the son was acquitted, that same guard became part of the security detail for…….wait for it……wait for it……good ole' Dollar Bill," Gene added. "Since leaving college, his son has been a systems manager, a logistical planner, a plant foreman, chief supply officer, and countless other positions where his salary would be extravagant for the CEO of a small company.

When Jay William Pride was elected about ten years ago, he was an average citizen with a small house and mortgage, meager bank account, and little to no savings," Gene told him. "Now, ten years later, he is estimated to be worth close to 20 million dollars. The city has tried everything to get rid of him. The man is coated with Teflon. Nothing ever sticks. Every time they charge him with something, the witnesses disappear or don't recall or misidentify who did what. And the people in his district keep reelecting him because he keeps them happy with trinkets. A party for one of the neighborhood children. A bank decides to make a loan they had been reluctant to do. As he says, *Shit don't get done without the Dollar Bill.*

It's been said that he once went to a custom tailor in Denver to have a bear skin coat made," Gene said. "The tailor quoted him a price of $1,500. When he asked why it was so expensive, the tailor said it would take three hides to make a man of his stature a coat.

He was in Colorado Springs a few days later and asked a tailor there about making the coat," Gene continued. "The tailor told him it would only take one hide and cost $500. When he told the tailor that the man in Denver was charging $1,500 for the three hides needed, the tailor politely told him that he may be a big man in Denver, but not in the Springs."

"Okay, I'm getting the picture," Jim said. "But, why now? Why can't this wait until we finish with Sun and Hua?"

"Because Jay William is trying to get control of the WHO event," Gene answered. "If he keeps true to form, he could disrupt everything from the janitorial services to the maid service at the hotels that'll be hosting the guests. This event is a major thing for the city. Besides the revenue that'll be coming in, there's the image. Can you imagine the black eye they'd get if the top scientists from around the world couldn't get their rooms cleaned? Or WHO officials can't get to meetings because their taxi just happened to take the wrong route and get stuck in traffic? The city has had enough. They tried to do it by the book. Dollar Bill bought the book. Now, we'll step in and see if we can't set things right."

"Okay," Jim agreed. "How much planning has been done and who'll I be working with?"

"Planning? Not a lot," Gene answered. "We just got the tasking. I'm depending on you for a lot of the planning. But, for now. Go home. I'll call you tomorrow."

Chapter Thirty-eight

Jim was repacking his suitcase for his next trip when he heard Jennifer calling his name. "Back here, honey," he said. "What are you doing home so early?"

Jennifer walked in and put her arms around Jim, saying, "Some sort of computer thing. We all got the afternoon off while the Geek Squad tries to fix it."

"What the hell is the Geek Squad?" Jim asked, turning in her arms. "Is it anything like Ghostbusters?"

"No, it's just some folks that know stuff about computers and go from place-to-place fixing things," she answered. "But what's important is that I have the afternoon off. What would you like to do?"

"I'm at your disposal," Jim told her. "It's your day off. You choose."

"Let's go to Six Flags," she suggested. "It's a nice day, and we've never been there. Come on, let's go!"

"If that's what you want, we'll go," Jim said as she grinned at him. "But I think you should change out of your office clothes."

"That won't take but a couple of minutes," she said excitedly.

"What if I help?" Jim asked, grinning at her. "Maybe it wouldn't take very long."

"God, you men," she said as she shooed him out of the bedroom. "You go find something to do for 10 minutes."

Jim headed to one of the spare bedrooms, where he had a desk and computer. Opening the link to American Airlines, he searched for the open time list of flying that was available for the pilots to pick up extra trips or trade their trip for one listed there.

Seeing an entire sequence with Denver (DEN) layovers open due to the First Officer who had been awarded the trip being on vacation, he quickly traded his Los Angeles and Albuquerque trips. The new sequence was a few hours less flying, therefore worth less to the pilot flying it, but it fit what Gene had asked for. Even if the days flying didn't match what he may be required to do, he could probably trade days with the other First Officers flying the same trip.

Just as he was getting ready to call Gene, the phone rang. "Hello," he answered as Jennifer walked into the room.

"Good afternoon, sir," he said. "How are you?"

Listening for a moment, he said, "Jennifer and I are getting ready to go to Six Flags for the afternoon."

'Gene,' he mouthed to Jennifer as he listened.

"Hang on for a second," Jim said and held his hand over the mouthpiece. "Gene is entertaining Sun and Hua. I hate to ask, but I told him I would."

"Ask what?" Jennifer said.

"If he could meet us there with them," he answered. "If you want to be alone, I'll tell him no."

"Don't you dare," Jennifer said. "Give me the phone."

Grabbing the phone from him, she said, "Gene, of course you're welcome. And we'd love to help you entertain Sun and Hua."

"It's not an imposition," she said after listening for a second. "It's only about 30 or 45 minutes from here. Where are you?"

"You're closer than we are," she said. "How long until you're ready to meet us?"

"Good," she said, smiling. "We'll meet you at the entrance in 45 minutes or so. How many people are coming with you?

This'll be fun," she finally said. "We'll see you there."

"You didn't have to do that," Jim told her as she hung up the phone. "I would have been glad to be alone."

"I know," she said as she headed for the door. "Just knowing that is enough for me. And now, we better get moving if we're going to have time for every ride."

"We couldn't ride every ride if we spent two days there," Jim told her following her to the front door. "You don't realize how big Six Flags is. It's a couple of hundred acres and probably 50 or 60 rides."

"Then we'll just have to pick the very best ones," she said as Jim locked the door.

"That's tough to do," Jim informed her. "Want to take the 'Vette?"

"My car," she said, shaking her head. "You drive."

After parking and catching the trolley to the entrance, they were just going to get their tickets when Gene called to them, waving. "I already have your tickets," he said as he greeted them.

"Thank you so much," Jennifer said, kissing his cheek. "Where are your guests?"

"They're inside looking around," Gene answered, nodding at Jim. "I told them to stay close, and we'll find them."

Spotting Sun and Hua, Gene said, "Sun, Hua, you remember Jim Lashley and his wife Jennifer."

Turning to Jennifer, he said, "And of course you remember Sun and his sister Hua."

"Of course I do," Jennifer said as she extended her hand to Hua. "So nice to see both of you again.

Both of them bowed slightly, and Hua said, "And we remember both of you. It was so kind of you to invite us to join you."

"Yes," Sun parroted as he turned to Jim, saying, "Thank you for inviting us."

"Our pleasure," Jim said, shaking his hand. "I hope Gene is being his normal cordial self."

"Gene is a splendid host," Hua said, turning to Jim. "Everybody we've met here in Texas is so very nice."

"Texans like to think they're the most hospitable people in the world," Gene remarked. "But, if we don't quit all the pleasantries, we'll never get to the rides. Jennifer, why don't you pick the first one."

"I want to ride the Texas Giant," Jennifer told them as she headed for the rollercoaster. "And then the Batman."

"Why don't we let our guests pick the next one?" Jim asked as they headed toward the ride.

"We don't know which ones to pick," Hua said. "Why don't you guys pick all of them? I'm sure whatever you pick will be fun."

"Tell you what," Gene told them. "We'll pick the first couple, and if you see something that you want to try, just speak up."

Four hours later, as they were getting off the Superman Tower of Power, Gene said, "I'm about done. I haven't been slung around, hung upside down, and felt like I was being tossed to the ground like that since I quit flying F-4s."

"I know what you mean," Jim said as they headed for the exit. "Flying the planes we do with American is more like sitting in a recliner watching TV."

"What about dinner?" Gene asked while they waited for the trolley to take them to their cars.

"How about Pappadeaux?" Jim suggested. "It's only a mile or so from here and some excellent Cajun food."

"That sounds great," Gene agreed. "I've taken them to steak houses, Mexican food restaurants, and some pure American places. They've had a sample of just about every type of food we have here. Now, they'll get to taste another unique food type."

"At least he's not trying to take us to the China Wok," Sun said, smiling.

"I can't believe you'd do that," Jennifer told Gene.

"He didn't," Hua told her. "My brother has a terrible sense of humor."

"So does my husband," Jennifer agreed as she put her hand on Hua's arm. "You wouldn't believe some of the things he says. It's embarrassing sometimes."

"Men," Hua said as they got out of the trolley. "I guess it's the same all over the world."

Chapter Thirty-nine

The next morning, after Jennifer left for work, Jim called Gene's hotel room as he was finishing his coffee. "Good morning," he said as Gene answered. "Thanks again for the afternoon. Jennifer had fun."

"So did we," Gene told him. "I think that's the first time either of them had been to something like that. Anyway, what's on your plate for the day?"

"Not much," Jim admitted. "I was basically just calling to let you know that I've got Denver layovers next month. I'll fly out around 7 o'clock on the first day to Tucson, come back to DFW, and then to Denver. The second day is about 8 o'clock to DFW, sit for two hours, and back to Denver. The third day is 10 o'clock back to DFW."

"That'll work," Gene told him. "If you're up to it, why don't you come by the motel in an hour or so? Sun and I have been looking at what to do about Li after the *accident*. Sun is in favor of eliminating him, of course. I think we need to let him go once he tells the PRC that Hua and Sun are dead."

"Sounds good," Jim said. "I'll just clean up a little, and I'll be right there."

An hour later, as Jim approached Gene's room, he saw Sun coming out, shaking his head. "Good morning, Sun," Jim said with a slight bow.

Bowing slightly also, Sun repeated, "Good morning, Jim. Again, thank you and your wife for letting Hua and I join you yesterday."

"Our pleasure," Jim said. "Is there anything wrong? You look upset."

"No," Sun answered. "Just a little disagreement with Gene about how to handle Li."

"Why don't you come back in, and let's see if we can come up with a solution both of you can live with," Jim said as he looked into the room.

"Come on in," Gene said, motioning to him as he put his cell phone on the desk. "I was just getting an update on Li."

"Have a seat, please," Gene told both of them as he shut the door. "Our friend Li has been pretty busy since he got to Denver. We've been monitoring his calls and following him since he left San Francisco. He's been getting names and locations from someone, we don't know who yet, and then he pays them a visit."

"Of course, we don't know what they talk about," he continued, "but we are pretty certain it has to do with setting up a network to watch for Hua. Most of the people he's contacted are employed at the hotels and restaurants throughout the city."

"That's logical since he lost his only source of information," Jim concluded. "But we already knew that's what he'd do. Have you picked a hotel where Hua and Sun will be seen later this week?"

"Yes," Gene answered. "We've booked two rooms at the Embassy Suites across the street from the Colorado

Convention Center, where the WHO will be meeting. We think it's the most logical place for her to be. Especially if she had intended to attend the meetings or just to get some reporter's attention."

"I agree," Jim said. "Has Li made contact with anyone who works there?"

"Yes," Gene answered as he spread a map of Denver on his bed. "Several. He's probably thinking the same as we are about where she'd want to be."

"That makes the rest of it pretty easy to work," Jim said, looking at the map. "I was looking at possible locations for our accident, and there's this little area west of Denver, just south of Golden, that's sparsely populated and has some curvy roads. I'd like the team to take a look at it. It appears to have a couple of *escape* roads for the car with Sun and Hua to exit just prior to where the accident will be staged.

It's far enough away that we'll have several opportunities to get enough distance between Li and them to allow them to get off the road without being seen," he continued. "Once he passes the accident scene, it's a couple of miles before he'll have an opportunity to turn around if he wants to get a better look at it."

"What if he just stops beside it?" Sun asked.

"It's a fairly narrow two-lane road," Jim explained. "And the wreck will be on the opposite side of the road. I'm betting that he'll go past it, think it looks like their car, and come back to verify the car or tags."

"I'll have them look at it this afternoon," Gene said. "We've also got the issue of the corpses you want in the car. It may be difficult to get two unclaimed bodies between now and when the accident occurs. Especially in that area."

"Understand," Jim told him. "But, somewhere in the country, there's a couple of them that would roughly match their size. We can move the bodies to Denver or somewhere close and keep them refrigerated until we need them."

"Quantico is looking," Gene assured him, "but we may want a backup plan if we can't make the arrangements."

"All you want is for Li to think it's us, isn't it?" Sun asked.

"Yes," Gene answered. "And for him to call in that you're dead."

"He'll make that call as soon as he's seen the wreck," Sun told them. "I don't think you need to worry about him looking too deep into it. It's just not his nature. Like I told you, he's quick to jump to conclusions, and I bet he takes one look and then makes his call."

Jim looked at Gene and finally said, "I disagree. If it's important enough, which I think it is to Li, I don't want to bet on him not coming back by and looking again. Especially if he didn't see any bodies when he first drove by."

"Okay," Gene finally said. "We'll get the bodies. We'll store them until the day of the accident. We'll worry about what to do with them after we're sure Li has called and reported both of them dead."

"If that's your decision, I still have one request. Since you're monitoring his calls, you'll know when he's reported back to his boss," Sun said, looking at both Jim and Gene. "Once that happens, he's of no further use to you."

"Yes, that's true," Gene said. "What's your point?"

"I still want to kill him," Sun answered. "You don't need him. He's here to kill Hua and me, and I don't see any reason not to once he's made his call."

"I have several reasons," Jim said, looking at Sun. "What do we do with his body? What if his boss tries to contact him to give him some other instructions? There are too many things that can go wrong if we don't let him return to China. His death or disappearance could lead to questions we don't want to be raised. Sorry, Sun. I'm with Gene on this one. I understand your desire for some sort of revenge. But the mission is to keep Hua safe. And you. Anything that would raise suspicions with the folks back in China will jeopardize that."

Sun finally said, "Okay. But if this doesn't work out as you're planning, I want to be included in any plans to eliminate him."

"And the next man they send? And the one after that?" Gene asked. "Li is just a weapon. I realize you harbor resentment about him because of your past associations and why he's here today, but just like you don't try to destroy the rifle that shot a friend, direct your attention to the ones that sent him. They're your real enemies."

"Why don't we go to lunch?" Gene asked after pausing for a couple of seconds. "Grab Hua, and we'll go to Ellen's for some chicken fried steak."

"That sounds great," Jim said. "I haven't had a good chicken fried steak since Jennifer and I were out west of here in a little town named Roanoke. There's a restaurant there called Babe's that serves either chicken fried steak or fried chicken. I've never tried the fried chicken, but the chicken fried steak is excellent."

Chapter Forty

After returning from lunch, Gene and Jim went to his room to discuss what they would need to do regarding Jay William Pride. "We've sent some people to research Mr. Pride," Gene said as they sat in the small living room area. "They're following him to see who he's working with, and we've got a tap on his phones. Right now, we're just building a profile to see if we can spot any weak points or things we can use against him."

"Do you think we can blackmail him into giving up his enterprises? Especially regarding the WHO meeting?" Jim asked.

"Probably not," Gene answered. "But it wouldn't hurt to have a brief summary of his life dropped on his doorstep. I think it's too late for anything other than an 'I know what you did' type thing."

"I'd not recommend that," Jim told him. "If it doesn't stand a chance of altering his behavior, all that would do is make him aware that he's under surveillance. If we're going to try to get close to him, that won't help."

"You're right," Gene agreed. "But we still need to develop a profile. I wish we had more time, but we don't. There have been a few interesting nuggets already, though."

"Such as?" Jim asked.

"He has a sort of Caligula complex," Gene answered. "For a man who was happily married until he started gaining power and influence, he's certainly trying to make up for lost time."

"Even in the short time we've been watching him, we've found four different ladies he's been romancing," Gene continued. "There's a rumor that he was accused of inappropriate behavior with a 13-year-old boy, but we can't verify it.

You may not like to hear this," Gene said smiling, "but his taste in women is very similar to yours."

"Why would you say that?" Jim asked.

"He prefers the more exotic looking," Gene answered. "Tall, slender, that certain look that's hard to describe. Sort of like the ones you've been attracted to. You remember that little talk we had a week or so ago about Jewell, Millicent, and Marie."

"I remember," Jim said. "I'm guessing you're thinking of using one of them. And I know it can't be Jewell. So, which one?"

"Both," Gene answered. "The man's sexual appetite is probably his weakest point. The thing that I believe will be rather unique will be having the two of them as potential conquests."

"How do you propose to do that?" Jim asked, envisioning the two ladies.

"We'll have them posing as working girls who came to Denver for the WHO meeting," Gene explained. "Since Jay is involved with the cleaning staff at the Embassy Suites, we'll have the ladies show up in the evenings and take a table in the lounge area. Sooner or later, ole' Dollar Bill will take notice."

"Will they have a room there?" Jim asked.

"No," Gene answered. "They'll arrive by limo and get a couple of chairs together in the lounge. We'll have a couple of our guys show up after 30 minutes or so and take seats with them. After a couple of glasses of wine, they'll leave together. Sometimes, we'll have one guy come in a few minutes earlier and leave with one of them while the other one waits until our other guy gets there.

We'll have different guys each night until Jay gets interested," he continued. "I'm sure he'll ask around and learn about them once he gets a look. When he's told that they leave every night with different men, he'll know why they are there."

"If he's got all of the ladies he wants without paying, why would he go for them?" Jim asked.

"You know the answer to that, Jim. Why even ask?" Gene answered. "Now, there's one other thing we're looking into, but nothing definite so far."

"What's that?" Jim asked.

"Coke," Gene said. "We're pretty sure he has a nose candy problem. There have been a couple of times we saw what we thought were transactions, but we weren't close enough to verify it. Give us another couple of days."

"That could come in handy," Jim said, nodding. "Alcohol, ladies, and drugs. What more could a man like him ask for? How soon do you want to set something up?"

"I'd like to do it on your first trip to Denver," Gene answered. "The longer he meddles in the WHO thing, the harder it'll be to get back on track. And the city is getting nervous that they won't have time to organize a first-class event."

"Okay," Jim said thinking about how little time he had to come up with a plan. "We have a couple of problems. First, we don't want it to be obvious. Second, it can't be a protracted thing because he'll still exert influence even if he's ill or it takes too long for him to succumb to whatever we use."

"What about using the coke?" Gene asked. "We could get the lab to come up with something quick acting that could be mixed in with it."

"Too risky," Jim answered. "Remember that amoeba we used on the police Captain in Chicago? And we had several practice sessions to make sure none of us got it. This must be fast acting and impossible to cause injury to our people."

"I'll have the lab do a little research," Gene said. "I'll have them look into something that needs to be injected or ingested. Something that won't harm you if you just touch it."

"What about restaurants?" Jim asked. "What type of food does he favor? Maybe we can get something that wouldn't be out of line with what he's eating."

"Nothing in particular. He's been to bar-b-q, fried chicken, Mexican, and even sushi restaurants," Gene answered. "I guess you're thinking about Baltimore or Chicago. What about cyanide?"

"Possible," Jim agreed. "But there may be some problems with administering it. What about having them look at tetrodotoxin?"

"What's that?" Gene asked, making notes.

"It's a neurotoxin that's found in certain sea animals, such as the puffer fish," Jim explained. "One of the guys I flew with a few months ago was the First Officer on the DC 10, flying mostly trips to Tokyo. There was a restaurant there that specialized in Fugu, a delicacy over there. Anyway, the puffer fish and a few others have this toxin in parts of their bodies. Only licensed chefs are allowed to prepare it."

"That may be workable," Gene told him. "Jay has been to a couple of sushi houses since we've been watching him. At least he probably wouldn't object if the ladies ask him to take them there."

"I think that has merit," Jim said. "The ladies could have him take them to dinner and somehow put it on his sushi. I think it's rather fast acting, and if it's discovered in the autopsy, it would probably be blamed on either the restaurant or their fish supplier."

"Okay," Gene told him. "I'll have the lab look into it."

"Now, if there's nothing else," Jim said, standing. "I need to get home and do a few 'honey-dos' before Jennifer gets there. Give me a call when you find out about the toxin stuff."

"I'll call when I hear something," Gene said, walking him to the door. "And I'll stay on top of the accident thing. That's going to take some split-second timing."

"I agree," Jim said, turning to shake hands. "This issue with Jay is more of a distraction than anything. I understand it's important, but we can shoot the bastard in the face and blame it on some business rival if we run into problems with being subtle."

"And to think you were questioning the wisdom of the contract just a day ago," Gene remarked, smiling. "Now you're discussing wet work."

"I've got a thing against guys who think it's all right to have inappropriate behavior with kids," Jim told him as he walked away. "Boys or girls."

Chapter Forty-one

The next morning, Gene called Jim and asked him to come over when he got a chance. An hour later, he arrived and knocked on his door.

"Good morning, Jim," Gene said, opening the door. "Please, come in."

As he stepped inside, Gene said, "You remember Marie Laveau, don't you?"

"Of course," Jim answered as she stood. Taking her hand, he said, "Marie, very nice to see you again."

"You too, Jim," she replied. "It's been a while."

"Yes, it has," Jim said as Gene shut the door and motioned for them to take a seat.

"The reason I asked you to stop by this morning is to discuss our operation regarding Jay," Gene told him as he picked up a folder from his desk.

Handing it to Jim, he continued, "The lab says it's not a problem to get the tetrodotoxin. It's commonly available through several manufacturers and can be in crystalline form or as a liquid.

If this is the route we want to pursue, the lab recommends the liquid," Gene said as Jim looked through the folder. "Easier to apply and not be noticed either on food or in a drink.

One other option we discussed was to get it in a powder form and mix it with his cocaine," Gene told them. "That is if we verify his use."

"I still object to that," Jim said, laying the folder aside. "Getting our hands on his coke could be problematic, and so would bringing our own. And we'd still have a problem if he wanted to share it. I don't think we need to put Marie and Millicent in that position."

"Speaking of the ladies," Gene said, looking from Marie to Jim, "I think you need to be with them."

"What, like one of the Johns we were discussing?" Jim asked.

"Sort of," Gene answered. "But, to make sure Jay's interested in you, we're proposing you pose as a sales representative for a service company that is bidding on the increased wait staff required at the Convention Center during the WHO meeting.

We want you to be with Millicent on one of the nights during your first Denver layovers," he explained. "We'll use the other guys at first just to get his attention. The ladies will use the excuse of a previous arrangement if he tries to arrange an evening before you're there."

"Why not use one of those other guys since they'll be there every night until we take care of our other issue?" Jim asked, not knowing if Marie knew about Sun and Hua.

Gene looked at Marie, and she answered, "I talked to Millicent, and we trust you. You've done this sort of thing many times before, and both of us agreed that we want somebody we know and trust.

Plus, I want somebody there I know will put the safety of our agents ahead of anything else," Gene added. "And you've proven that."

"And you want this all arranged in the next ten days," Jim stated, looking at Gene. "What about Millicent? Does she have a schedule that will match mine?"

"She has vacation for the first two weeks of next month," Gene answered. "That allows her to be in the lounge every evening."

"What about where we go for the sushi?" Jim asked. "Will we have any of our people there?"

"No," Gene answered. "That's one of the reasons we've selected you for this operation. We don't have time to put someone in place to make sure nothing happens or to take control if it does."

"Does the place serve sashimi?" Jim asked.

"Yes, a place called Sushi Sasa," Gene answered. "They are one of the few restaurants in the US that can order from Wako International in New York, which is the only importer of prepared puffer fish from Japan. I never realized how regulated that particular fish was until the lab sent me the report about tetrodotoxin."

"How do we make sure he'll take us, meaning Marie, Millicent, and I, to the restaurant?" Jim asked. "He may not want company."

"That's why you're representing a vendor," Gene answered. "He'll probably be more interested in getting some time with you to explain how things work in Denver than he is the ladies. How ole' Dollar Bill can make sure you get the contract. Of course, it's going to cost you a little, and you may have to hire his son as your on-site personnel manager."

"Okay, and will I be staying at the Embassy Suites?" Jim asked as he started thinking about how this would work.

"Of course," Gene answered as he took another folder from his desk. "You're going to be Raymond Fleenor, owner, and manager of Texas Professional Services. We've already booked a room for you and have prepared fill-in-the-blank contracts if he wants to see them along with a brochure about your company."

Handing Jim the folder, he continued, "Here's the information about your company, the services you can supply, and reviews from various cities and companies that have used your services. All the listed phone numbers are routed to Quantico in the unlikely event he calls them to verify your company."

"Have any contracts related to my type of services been presented to the Convention Center?" Jim asked, looking at the documents.

"Yes," Gene confirmed. "But we know they haven't made any firm commitments yet. However, they need to get it settled within the next two weeks. We selected the wait staff personnel provider as your company because Jay has been controlling most of the hotel cleaning staff and other nonunion workers in the service industry in Denver, and it fits what he knows."

"So, Marie and Millicent will be taken to the hotel every evening and sit around the lounge waiting to be noticed," Jim said, reviewing the basic plan. "We'll have a couple of guys join them later each day and escort them out. Then, I show up and engage them in conversation while waiting for Jay to make his approach.

Then he learns about my business in Denver and tries to get me to enter into a plan that ensures I'm awarded the contract for the people who clean and serve during the WHO thing," Jim continued. "We, the ladies and I, convince Jay to go with us to the sushi restaurant, where we give him a little extra with his fugu."

"That's about it," Gene said. "Pretty simple."

"Let's not worry about the body," Jim said sarcastically. "We can just call for a cab and leave him with his face in a bowl of wasabi."

"Of course not," Gene said, looking from Jim to Marie and back before asking, "What do you propose?"

"Off the top of my head, how about a 'doctor' we provide being in the restaurant," Jim offered. "When Jay starts displaying any symptoms, I'll ask if there's a doctor in the house.

I know, it's a rather tired old line from too many movies, but I'm going to need help explaining why a member of my dinner party is gasping for air with soy sauce running down his chin," Jim concluded.

"What if our *doctor* just happens to notice his difficulty and comes to the table?" Marie asked. "He could say he's a doctor and noticed the problem."

"That's a better idea," Gene told her. "That would draw the attention away from you guys. In the ensuing confusion, you guys could slip away while our doctor is administering first aid and the restaurant is calling 911."

"That's probably workable," Jim said, nodding. "Especially since the ladies could be discovered to be ladies of the evening and didn't want to be involved. And Raymond didn't want to be caught in a sordid affair. We still need to look at the transportation to the restaurant, somehow removing the evidence of the toxin, getting out unnoticed, what the doctor will do after the ambulance arrives, just a few little details."

"We'll work on it," Gene told him. "Why don't you come back late tomorrow morning after Jennifer goes to work? Millicent will be here, and you guys can discuss how you want to coordinate your roles. We can even go to a restaurant for lunch and let you simulate what we think will happen."

"I guess that's about as good as we'll get given the short time to plan this," Jim said, standing. "I'm starting to reconsider just having him shot. Simple and quick. I'll bet there are close to 100 homicides a year in Denver. What's one more? And I'll bet that's a lot more than the number of puffer fish deaths in the entire state."

"Probably so, but this one would draw too much attention," Gene answered as he walked to the door with Jim. "We'll just put that idea in the plan B file."

"Okay, but I want a weapon. Something small. Probably a .38, and I want hollow points and a light load,"

Jim told him. "I want the bullet to stay in the body if we have to do it."

"Is that all?" Gene asked.

"Not quite," Jim answered. "I want a gun that has a history in Denver, or at least in Colorado. A gun where the police have bullets that will match the ones in Jay.

"It would probably be too much to ask for," Jim continued, "but having the same gun be tied to multiple shootings would be ideal."

"Where do you suggest we find such a weapon?" Gene asked, shaking his head.

"Have some folks look into the East Side Crips," Jim answered. "I'm sure there is a shit load of pistols floating around with those folks. Any pistol you take from one of them has a high probability of having been used."

"We'll look into it," Gene told him. "If nothing else, we can get a throwdown that's untraceable."

"That, as you say, should be plan B," Jim replied. "If we have to shoot the bastard, I'd like to see some nasty ass take the fall.

Anyway, it was nice to see you again, Marie," Jim said. "I wish we could meet under different circumstances, but I guess we're destined to only meet when someone has an unfortunate event in their future."

"You too, Jim," she replied as he turned to go. "I'll see you tomorrow."

Chapter Forty-two

The following morning, when Jim arrived, Gene's door was open, and he could hear laughter as he approached. "Good morning, everybody," he announced, stepping into the room. "Am I too late for the joke?"

"Hi, Jim," Millicent said, coming to meet him and giving him a quick hug. "Not a joke, a true story about one of our Captains."

"And what did American Airline's finest do?" Jim asked, shaking Gene's hand.

"It seems as if he was seeing one of our Flight Attendants," Millicent answered. "And, of course, he's also married."

"That's not so rare," Jim said, nodding at Marie. "It's probably more rare to find a married Captain that *isn't* seeing a Flight Attendant."

"That's not the funny part," Millicent told him. "Not only was he seeing one Flight Attendant, but he was also seeing a different one at the same time."

"Again, not so unusual," Jim replied. "Probably more so with the male Flight Attendants, but it still happens."

"I understand," Millicent said as she started to grin. "But his main squeeze, Bimbo number one, is DFW based, and the other one, Bimbo two, is out of Chicago. It just so happened that Captain Sleaze flew a Chicago turn with Bimbo number one, and Bimbo number two was an extra working the leg from DFW to Chicago."

"Not good," Jim said, starting to smile. "I can guess the end of this story."

"Probably not," Millicent told him. "Bimbo two overheard Bimbo one telling one of the other Flight Attendants about her evening with Captain Sleaze the night before the trip. When the Captain called back for a Bloody Mary mix, she told the Flight Attendant that takes care of the cockpit she'd take care of it.

Anyway, the Captain was wearing a very unusually stained shirt and pants when they landed in Chicago," she finished laughing. "When the gate agent asked what happened, he just shook his head and mumbled something about turbulence."

"Turbulence," Jim replied, laughing. "I'd say more like a hurricane. Or a tornado. What did the ladies do when they landed?"

"Bimbo two stormed off the plane," Millicent answered. "Bimbo one had to fly back with Captain Sleaze, and she sort of flipped him off as she got off the plane here at DFW. And not only did the First Officer see it, but several of the passengers also noticed."

"Wonder what story he'll give his soon-to-be ex-wife?" Marie asked. "I guess I'm glad that I'm not a Flight Attendant. Too much drama."

"It can get to be that way," Jim said, smiling. "It's hard to say who's to blame, except it does take two to tango. Like my great, great grandfather always said, put little boys with little girls, and sooner or later, somebody's clothes will come off."

"If your great, great grandfather said all of the things you attribute to him, he must have lived to be 105 years old," Gene said, shaking his head. "I swear, that man had more sayings than Yogi Berra. Now, if you guys don't mind, let's get down to business."

"I think Yogi Berra stole some of my great, great, granddad's sayings," Jim whispered to Marie and Millicent. "I'm pretty sure he stole the one about being very careful if you don't know where you're going because you may not get there."

"And I guess he came up with 'Just because a man doesn't know where he is doesn't mean he's lost," Gene said, handing Jim a folder.

"No, that one's mine," Jim answered, looking in the folder. "Unless I inherited it from my great, great, grandfather."

Gene shook his head again and told him, "Not sure where you come up with this stuff, but back to business. You'll get your gun. We have one that was used in a shooting a year or so ago. A friend in the department managed to get it out of the evidence room. It was never logged in but was with the casings and slugs found where a member of the Bloods was shot."

"That's good," Jim replied. "What about the tetrodotoxin?"

"You'll have the liquid," Gene answered. "I figured you'd use it like you and Amber did in Baltimore. I think that having the ladies on either side of him during dinner would be the most natural way. I'd prefer for you to put the toxin on his food, but having you sit beside him would seem odd."

"I agree," Jim said. "And since we can somewhat control which one is his *date*, and I recommend Marie, Millicent can administer it."

"What do you think, Millicent?" Gene asked.

"Not a problem," she answered, smiling. "I'm used to doctoring men's drinks. Just a couple of drops of Visine in a cup of coffee for a Romeo pilot isn't lethal unless diarrhea is deadly."

"That does it," Jim said, laughing. "I'll make sure I never have a cup of coffee if I ever fly with you again."

"Oh, it works with a coke, tea, glass of ice, just about anything," she told him. "But you know I'd never do that to you. It's reserved for those people, including passengers, who think we're there purely for their amusement."

"All right," Gene interrupted. "Millicent is going to be the one pouring it on his food. Marie, you're his date, and it's up to you to distract him. That should be relatively easy, and you've played that role numerous times."

"But there's always a chance that Jay will want to make his play for Millicent," Jim added. "Even if he believes that I'm her John, he may want her just to prove that he can get anything he wants."

"That's true," Gene agreed. "So, we'll go to lunch and work on it. Why don't you ladies go on down to the lobby? Jim and I will join you shortly."

As Gene shut the door behind them, he said, "There's not a lot going on with Li, but we've located a white 1990 Chevrolet Corsica that was involved in a rollover accident. The top is pretty crushed, but it's otherwise in pretty good shape.

And we've got an identical Corsica for Sun and Hua to use," he continued, laying out a map. "The area you recommended looks good. Now, the biggest problem will be how we keep Li far enough behind during the chase for Sun to get off the road unobserved.”

“That and the timing of the explosion of the wreck,” Jim added, looking at the map. “We’re probably going to need two or three cars and maybe an 18-wheeler. Possibly a logging truck. I think the best way will be for Sun to take I-70 until he gets to the exit for 45, then take 40 west.”

Pointing at the map, he continued, “If Sun takes the exit and we have a car and the truck behind him, Li could see him head west on 40. Have the other car make a right turn on 40. That would put Li right behind the truck and give Sun a little time to get to his exit. As the truck swings out to make a left turn on 45, it’ll cause Li to lose sight of Sun. Sun can then make a right on Paradise Road, unseen from where Li will be sitting. If we have the explosion of the wrecked car occur just as Li turns on 40 to follow where he thinks Sun went, it will distract him from looking to his right as he passes Paradise Road.”

“I’ll send that to our Denver team,” Gene said, nodding. “We’ll let them do a few practice runs to get the timing down and make sure there’s sufficient cover for Sun’s car. Anything else for now?”

“No,” Jim answered as Gene opened the door. “I’m assuming that the girls don’t know about this part of the operation.”

“No, they don’t,” Gene said as he locked his door. “All they need to know is what we’re doing in regard to Jay. Ole’ Dollar Bill.”

Chapter Forty-three

Once they'd finished eating, Gene handed Millicent a small vial filled with a colorless fluid. "Since you're right-handed, it's more natural to reach across your body to pour the toxin on Jay's plate."

"Now, of course, this is just water," he told her when she opened the lid and smelled it. "The toxin will be harmless even if you get it on your hands but try to be careful with it anyway. And make sure to wash your hands after you use it. At least before you handle anything you put in your mouth."

Turning to Marie, he said, "You'll have to get Jay's attention for a couple of seconds so Millicent can do her job."

"The natural inclination of a person who's sitting while someone is whispering in their ear is to look slightly down, so probably touch his arm and lean in," Gene told her.

"Jim, you'll have the best view of Jay's eyes," Gene said, looking at him. "So, you'll need to be the sort of conductor. If Jay doesn't look down, let Millicent know to wait."

Turning to Millicent, he continued, "As you noticed, all you need to do to open it is to push up on the tab with your thumb. Since it's made of plastic, it won't make any sound if you happen to let it hit the plate.

And, once you're done, just use your thumb again to close and lock it," he continued. "At this point, the biggest thing is to get it out of sight before Jay looks up. You can hold it in your lap or cover it with a napkin. Just make sure it isn't visible.

Okay, I'm guessing that you'll have a small handbag and that's where you'll have the vial," Gene said, sitting back. "For now, just hold it in your lap and bring it up when Marie puts her hand on my arm. As you're moving it, pop the top, but keep your hand and arm as low as possible without hitting the plates or table."

As Marie touched Gene's arm, he said, "Okay, glance at Jim and do it."

As Millicent brought her arm up, she bumped the table with the vial, spilling the water. "Shit," she said. "That won't do."

"That's why we're here," Gene told her, taking the vial from her.

Refilling it from his water glass, he said, "It may be better if you're leaning back a little more when you lift your arm. And let's leave the cap on for now so I don't have to keep refilling it."

After a couple of more practice runs, Millicent said, "Okay, I think I've got it. It's just a slight sit back as I bring it up and then lean over to pour it out."

"Good," Gene said as she popped the top open and closed it a few times. "Let's have you ladies change places so Marie can practice if Jay decides she's the one he wants."

"I think I can do it with my left hand," Marie said, taking the vial from Gene. "Why don't we try that first?"

"Go ahead," Gene told her. "Pop the top a couple of times to get a feel for that, and when you're ready, Millicent will try to get my attention."

"I'm ready," she said after a few practices. "Should I be looking at Jim when Jay leans over?"

"Yes, that's a good point," Gene answered. "But make it a quick glance. The opportunity to do it unobserved may be short-lived. Jim, what'll you do?"

"I'll be looking at whoever's got the vial and give a single small nod if Jay's head is turned and he's not paying attention," he answered. "If it's not safe, I'll turn my head slightly to the side."

Okay," Gene told Marie and Millicent. "Just remember to glance at him as you're starting to bring the vial up. If he sees any problem, all you have to do is leave your hand in your lap."

"What do we do if he never looks away long enough?" Millicent asked.

"He'll look away," Gene told her. "Especially since you'll be wearing the low-cut dresses we've selected for you. When you lean over to whisper, his eyes will automatically look down when he turns his head."

"You ladies have a knack for getting a man's attention," Jim added as both women turned slightly toward Gene and leaned over a little bit. "I think it's something in a woman's DNA. Call it the distraction gene. It just comes naturally."

Rolling her eyes, Marie looked at Millicent and said, "Let's try this a couple of times."

Three tries later, Marie said, "I'm good. It doesn't matter who my date is; I'm comfortable sitting on Jay's left."

"The only glitch will be if he pulls out a chair for you and wants the chair to your left," Jim told her. "Then you'd have to use your right hand. Do you want to practice it that way?"

"Not necessary," Marie answered. "Maybe Millicent might want to practice with her left hand."

Taking the vial from her, Millicent popped the top a couple of times as she brought it up from her lap with her left hand and said, "I can do it fine."

"Why don't you lead them in?" Gene proposed to Jim. "Then you can pull out the chair for whichever one is your date and take the seat on Marie's left or Millicent's right."

"That'll work," Jim agreed. "As long as Jay's date follows far enough back to give me time to make it obvious which seat I'm taking. I don't think Jay will care as long as he's between both of you.

Now that we're ready for this part, what about the doctor who's supposed to come to our table?" Jim asked.

"It's been arranged," Gene answered. "All he needs to know is what time you'll be there. I'm guessing that Jay thinks he's important enough that he doesn't need reservations. So, you'll signal one of our people sitting around the lounge that you're heading for the restaurant. He'll get word to the doctor, and he'll get to the restaurant before you."

"What if he can't get a table before we do?" Marie asked.

"He'll still be there even if he's waiting for his table," Gene answered. "By the way, Jim will have the vial when he comes into the lounge to meet you ladies. He'll pass it to one of you as you drive to the restaurant, depending on who Jay is with."

"Why don't we have two vials?" Jim asked. "Give them to Marie and Millicent before they come to the hotel. Then, if something goes wrong, we still have a backup."

"That's a good idea," Gene said. "Also, your gun will be in your room, along with a change of clothes and the company material we looked at earlier."

"You don't think my standard layover clothes are good enough for Ole' Dollar Bill?" Jim asked, smiling.

"Jeans and a T-shirt won't do it," Gene answered. "You're a high-level salesman dealing with a man whose ego is as inflated as one of the balloons at the Macy's Thanksgiving Day parade. I almost added shoes, but I'm not sure you remember how to tie them. And because he knows you're from Texas, you get a pass with your boots."

Looking at everyone, Gene said, "If there's nothing else, I'll take care of the bill and meet you guys outside."

Chapter Forty-four

As soon as they returned to the hotel, Gene let the ladies go into the room and closed the door before telling Jim that Marie and Millicent would be going to Denver the following morning and they'd begin their role in the evenings at the hotel.

"I'll be flying the Denver trips starting Monday," Jim told him. "I'm guessing I'll get to my hotel by about four o'clock and then to the Embassy Suites about six that evening."

"Good," Gene answered. "I hope we can take care of Jay on the first night, but it'll most likely be the second night. The ladies should've gotten his attention by then, but your cover story may need an extra night."

"What if we can't get things taken care of on the first trip?" Jim asked. "I won't fly again until the following Sunday."

"We'll just have to wait," Gene told him. "Even if it's your second trip, that'll work. But that's as long as we can wait. The contracts for the WHO event need to be finalized, and the longer Jay is meddling in it, the longer it'll take."

"What about the ladies?" Jim asked. "Will they be working every evening? That's a long time for them to have to play their role and avoid any entanglements."

"We can pull them for a day or two once they've established their reputation," Gene answered. "And I know Jay won't take no for an answer more than once or twice before he gets suspicious. I'll talk to Marie and Millicent and see how they feel about it."

"I'd really like to take care of this Monday night," Jim said. "And as I said earlier, we can use plan B."

"No," Gene said, shaking his head. "We'll have four chances to take care of him without resorting to that. And I can always get another agent if it comes down to that option."

"Okay," Jim said, nodding. "Now, what about Sun and Hua? When are they going to Denver?"

"They'll go Sunday, the day after tomorrow," Gene told him. "Li has had plenty of time to establish some contacts. He was seen talking to a couple of the maids who work at the Embassy Suites, so we're sure they'll be watching for Hua. With a little luck, he'll start maintaining surveillance of the hotel by Monday."

"Has there been any activity that would suggest that another shooter is coming?" Jim asked. "I still think that there's a possibility the PRC will send someone."

"Nothing yet," Gene answered. "We've been monitoring his phone, and Wang is reading every transcript. The other members of the team are following him any time he's not in his hotel. Even if another shooter is coming to take care of Li, it's really no problem. Li sees the accident, makes his call, and the new guy takes care of him."

"I guess," Jim finally agreed. "Maybe I'm overthinking it, as Sun said. But we're counting on Li's propensity to make snap decisions. The other guy may follow up on the accident and discover it was staged."

"I'm going to agree with Sun," Gene told him. "And the fact that the guy that may or may not be here to kill Li knows nothing about Hua or Sun. Let's just concentrate on convincing Li they are dead. Leave the rest of it to the gods."

"You're probably right," Jim replied. "We can always do something later because we'll know what happened to Li since we'll be watching him. That'll give us a look at anybody that's here to remove him. We can take care of that guy then."

"Exactly," Gene said. "Now, about the accident. I had the team do several runs and get the timing down. The real key is how long the truck will block Li's view. The only flaw we can see is if he decides to go around the truck before it makes the left turn. If the truck delays much more than a couple of seconds after the car in front of him moves, Li may get anxious since he's lost sight of his target."

"I can't see him going around the truck on the left side," Jim said. "But, if there's room on the shoulder to pass on the right, it's possible. What about having a car about where the rear of the truck will be on the shoulder changing a tire or something?"

"I'll have them look into that," Gene told him. "We may try to accelerate the operation anyway. If you take care of Jay on your first trip, we'll have everything in place for your next trip. The sooner we can get Li to quit looking for her, the better the folks up in Washington will feel."

"I agree," Jim said. "I'll be glad to finish this one, maybe because I've never felt so out of control or because I've guessed wrong so many times. When are you going back to Quantico?"

"I'll go with Sun and Hua on Sunday and bring them back Monday at about noon," Gene answered. "Then I'll go back to Quantico to make sure everything is on track. If there's nothing else going on, I'll probably come back to Dallas on Tuesday or Wednesday to take Sun and Hua back to Denver for another walk-through at the hotel. That should guarantee that Li knows she's there."

"I probably wouldn't do that more than once again," Jim advised. "Li will probably be there waiting the next time. Once he hears that she's there, he'll probably want to see for himself and start making his plans. The next time, he may be ready to act."

"I agree," Gene said. "One thing we decided was to have them use the Corsica every time. They'll arrive at the hotel in it and leave in it both times. That way, when we're ready to stage the accident, Li won't think anything is out of place."

"That's a good idea," Jim agreed, nodding. "Now, I'll just say goodbye to Marie and Millicent and head home."

Gene opened the door and said, "Hey, guys. Jim's about to leave and wanted to say goodbye."

Both of them came to the door, and Millicent said, "We'll see you in a couple of days, Jim. We've decided that I get to be with you when we go to dinner with Jay, and I'm really looking forward to our first date."

"And I'll be watching to make sure that you don't have a vial of Visine," Jim joked. "You guys, be careful up there. I know how some guys like Jay can be."

"We will," Marie said. "We've got each other's backs. We've dealt with jerks before. We'll see you up there."

Chapter Forty-five

Just after noon on Monday, Jim was flying the third leg of their sequence to Denver. The Captain for the month was a former Air Force C-130 pilot named Tim Carson, whose nickname was Kit. The trip from DFW to Tucson and back had been uneventful, and Kit had spent much of the time talking about growing up in Missouri and his time in the Air Force.

"You want anything from the back?" Kit asked as he picked up the handset to call the Flight Attendant that serviced the cockpit and first class.

"A Dr. Pepper would be great," Jim answered as he took a quick look at the settings on the control panel.

"Merna," Kit said as she answered his call. "Could you please bring Jim a Dr. Pepper and a Diet Coke for me?

Thanks, you're a doll," he said before hanging up. "She'll be here in about five minutes. Do you have anything planned for Denver?"

"I'm supposed to go to dinner with some friends," Jim answered as he heard Fort Worth Center call them with a frequency change.

"American 2344 switching to 132.925," Kit said as he changed the radio to the new frequency. "Fort Worth, American 2344 with you at 320 direct Amarillo.

Roger, now direct Lamar for 2344," Kit acknowledged the new clearance as he watched Jim change the destination in the GPS. "Ride reports?

Copy, smooth until the descent into Denver," Kit repeated, nodding at Jim.

"There're some nice places to eat in Denver," Kit said, leaning back and looking at the low clouds in front of the plane. "I think there's a Del Frisco's pretty close to our hotel."

"I'm not sure where we're going," Jim said, checking the fuel remaining against the flight plan. "I think they're planning on keeping me in the dark until they pick me up."

"Are these some friends from your Marine Corps days?" Kit asked as Merna knocked on the cockpit door.

"Yes," Jim answered, turning to take the glass of ice and Dr. Pepper when the door opened. "Thanks, Merna. How's things back there?"

"Good, Jim," she answered as she handed Kit his drink and glass. "Would you like anything else? I've got some nuts and some pretzels if you'd like."

"Nothing for me," Kit answered, smiling at her. "I'm watching my weight. All of this just sitting in the seat hour after hour is horrible on my waistline."

"If there's a slice of lime or lemon, I'd appreciate it," Jim said, watching her turn her head and roll her eyes.

"I'll be right back," she said as she opened the cockpit door.

"She's cute," Kit said as the door closed. "Maybe you should ask her to go to dinner with you."

"Don't think so," Jim replied as the door opened again. After taking the glass of lime wedges and the door was shut, he continued, "Didn't you see the ring on her left hand? And I already told you I was married."

"I didn't mean anything other than just a friendly dinner," Kit tried to explain. "No different than if you and I went down to dinner."

"That's how a lot of it starts," Jim said, squeezing one of the lime wedges into his glass. "Having a drink with the entire crew is one thing. Asking a Flight Attendant to go to dinner with me is quite different."

"Hell, I do it all of the time," Kit said, pouring his diet Coke into his glass. "I think they like to be asked, even if they say no."

"That's really nice of you," Jim told him. "I just don't want to get the reputation of hitting on the Flight Attendants."

"There's a big difference between hitting on them and just asking them out for dinner on a layover," Kit explained. "If you hadn't had plans for the night, I'd have suggested that we ask the rest of the crew."

"That might have worked," Jim told him as he bit his tongue to keep from saying what he thought. "Maybe next trip."

"American 2344, contact Albuquerque Center on 134.75. Good day," the Fort Worth Center controller directed.

"Albuquerque 134.75 for American 2344. Good day," Kit answered before changing the radio. "Albuquerque, American 2344 with you at 320 and direct Lamar.

Direct Lamar expecting the Quail One," Kit repeated as Jim changed the navigation panel. "Still bumpy on the descent?"

Hearing that it was, he told Jim that he would be off the radio while he called the Flight Attendants. "Merna, my dear," Kit started off when she had answered. "It's supposed to be a little bumpy in the descent, so why don't you tell the other ladies to go ahead and start putting things away? I wouldn't want anyone to spill coffee or something on our passengers."

After hanging up, he turned to Jim and said, "I'll go ahead and make my announcement to the passengers. You've got the radio."

"Got it," Jim said as he put his earpiece in and turned off the overhead speaker.

Kit was still talking to the passengers when Albuquerque directed them to descend and contact Denver Center.

"Denver, American 2344 with you out of 320 for 280, direct Lamar," Jim said as he pointed to the change in altitude to Kit. Seeing him acknowledge the change, Jim repeated the clearance for the Quail arrival and 17 thousand feet and 250 knots at the Quail intersection to Denver Center.

As soon as Kit hung up, Jim told him that they'd been cleared for the arrival procedure and that he'd already requested the current airport information.

"Good job," Kit said as he pulled one of his manuals out of his kit bag. Searching for the one that held the procedures for Denver, he asked, "How did you guys handle the approaches in the F-4? You had a navigator, didn't you?"

"Yeah," Jim answered as he reviewed the approach that was on his control wheel clipboard. "But we didn't have to carry nearly as many approaches as here with American."

"What runway are they using?" Kit asked when he finally found the plates for Denver.

"Landing south, expect 17 Center," Jim answered as the Denver controller told them to cross Quail at 17 thousand, with no speed restriction, and to contact Denver approach on 120.35.

Fifteen minutes later, after they pulled into the gate, Kit parked and opened the cockpit door so the passengers could see them as they got off the plane. As he sat turned in his seat, Jim put everything away and waited for the last passenger to get off.

Once everyone was off and the Flight Attendants were coming up the aisle, Jim grabbed his kit bag and stepped out of the cockpit, saying, "I'll see you at the pickup, Kit. I'm going to hit the head before the ride to the hotel."

"See you there," Kit said as he finished putting away everything. "I'll make sure the ladies don't have to wait out there alone."

Chapter Forty-six

When Jim stepped up to the desk at the hotel to get his key, the clerk handed him a folded slip of paper and said, "Mr. Lashley, this message for you came in an hour or so ago."

"Thanks," Jim said as he turned to follow the rest of the crew to the elevator.

Unfolding the paper as the elevator rose, he saw that it read: *Jim, dinner theater will begin upon your arrival. A car will be waiting for you after 5:30 and will take you back to your hotel after dinner.*

"That sounds mysterious," Merna said, glancing over his shoulder. "I wish my layovers had a little more excitement."

"Not that mysterious," Jim told her, refolding the paper. "My friend has a rather theatrical sense of humor, pardon the pun. He's no doubt referring to some ongoing domestic issue with his two girls.

Anyway, I'll see you guys at pickup in the morning," he continued as the elevator stopped at their floor.

As soon as he closed his door, Jim hung his uniform in the closet and took a quick shower. Checking to see if he needed a shave, he left his shave kit on the counter and slipped on a pair of jeans and a T-shirt. Grabbing his key from the nightstand, he headed down to the lobby.

As he stepped from the elevator, he saw a man wearing a black suit sitting in the lobby watching him. As he approached, the man stood and asked, "Jim Lashley?"

"Yes," Jim answered. "I'm guessing that you're here to take me to the Embassy Suites."

"Yes, sir, I am. I'm Michael, and I'll be your driver for this evening," he answered, handing Jim a room key for the Embassy Suites. "I'll either take you to the restaurant or follow you and then bring you back here."

"Good to meet you, Michael," Jim said as he got in the passenger seat. "How long have you been here in Denver?"

"Almost a week," he answered as he started the car and pulled away from the hotel. "There's also a package under the seat for you. Gene didn't want to leave it in your room at the Embassy."

Jim reached under his seat and pulled out a package wrapped in brown paper. Opening it, he took the small .38 caliber revolver out and looked at it. Flipping the cylinder open, he saw the six chambers were filled with hollow point bullets.

"Thanks," Jim said as he slipped the pistol into the waistband of his jeans and pulled the T-shirt over it. "I'm guessing that I'll leave it with you when you take me back to the hotel."

"Yes, sir," Michael answered. "I was told to tell you all of the bullets have the light load you requested and that it's been test fired to verify the penetration depth."

"Again, thanks," Jim said, smiling at the efficiency of Black Water.

Moments later, as they pulled into the Embassy Suites, Michael said, "I'll be waiting for you guys when you're ready to go."

"Thanks, Michael," Jim said as he opened his door. "I'll see you in an hour or so."

Heading for the elevators, Jim glanced toward the lounge area. Not seeing either Marie or Millicent, he wondered if they were in another area or not here yet.

As he opened the door to his room, he was surprised to see both of them there with Gene. "Good afternoon, guys," he said as he shut the door. "What a pleasant surprise."

"Good to see you too, Jim," Gene said, shaking his hand. "Well dressed, as usual, I see."

"This is about as good as it gets," Jim answered, nodding at Marie and Millicent. "I didn't see anybody in the lounge as I passed. Is anything wrong?"

"No," Gene answered. "We're just here to go over the plan one more time. You've met Michael, so you know about the transportation part."

"Yes," Jim confirmed. "What about if Jay wants to use his car?"

"That's possible," Gene said, handing Jim the folder for Texas Professional Services. "But I'm sure you can convince him that taking your limo would be best considering who you're going out with. I decided that having an extra man would be appropriate in the unlikely event we need to implement an alternate solution."

"How sure are you that he'll be here tonight?" Jim asked, glancing at the business cards and other material in the folder.

"He'll be here," Marie answered, smiling. "He's been coming over every evening since he first noticed us."

"He wanted to go out last night, but we told him that we were waiting for our dates," Millicent added. "It's a good thing we're ready tonight. He was starting to draw too much attention to us."

"What time is he supposed to be here?" Jim asked, looking in the closet at the clothes he would be wearing.

"About six," Gene answered. "We made reservations for 7:30 so there would be time for you to get him interested in your company. And for god's sake, folks, just remember Jim's name is Raymond Fleenor."

"When will Jay be here?" Jim asked, looking at how the ladies were dressed.

"He'll be here between 6 and 6:30," Marie answered. "And Millicent told him she had a date with you this evening to make sure that he didn't bring one of his friends or think that he had the two of us."

"Before I forget it," Gene said, opening his briefcase, "here are the two vials. Unless you ladies have anything else to tell Jim, he needs to get changed."

Marie put her vial in her purse as she stood and said, "I don't think we'll have a problem with him tonight. I thought he was going to snap his neck looking from Millicent to me last night."

"And I don't think his eyes ever got above our necks," Millicent added as she stood. "We'll go on down and entertain him if he's early. But I'm not sure I could stand to be around him again if we don't take care of it tonight."

"That's the plan," Jim said, walking them to the door. "And you both do look terrific, so I don't think we'll have any trouble keeping his eyes off of what we're doing."

Once the door was closed, Gene said, "Go ahead and change while I bring you up to speed on Sun and Hua.

We brought them here as planned yesterday, and they went upstairs to the room we had rented," Gene said as Jim took his jeans off. "They ordered room service for lunch just to have them exposed to another of the hotel staff. That evening, Sun had the car brought around, and they went to dinner.

Right after they drove away, Li received a call describing Hua," Gene told him. "Maybe 30 minutes later, Wang called to say that Li was leaving his apartment. He was here almost an hour before Sun and Hua returned."

"Then he saw Sun," Jim said as he finished putting on his suit jacket.

"Yes," Gene confirmed. "And he definitely recognized him because shortly after he got back to his room, he made a call saying that Sun was here."

"Do you know who he called?" Jim asked, pulling on his boots.

"Wang thinks it was someone in the PRC," Gene answered. "Then he was here when Sun and Hua left this morning. He waited about two hours and finally left."

"Did they say anything about eliminating Sun as well?" Jim asked as he checked himself in the mirror.

"No," Gene said as he rose. "I think this call was just to report the sighting. We're still monitoring his phone, so we'll know if they call him back. Now, you need to get downstairs to be with the ladies when Jay arrives."

"Here's a wallet with several credit cards, your Texas driver's license, and a couple of thousand dollars," Gene said, handing him the wallet and a cell phone. "The phone has the number for Michael, your driver, and me preset. Let me know if you need anything or are having any problems."

Jim put the phone in his pants pocket and the wallet in the inside pocket of his suit coat and said, smiling, "Do I get to keep the credit card and money?"

"Sure, just call it a tip," Gene said sarcastically, opening the door. "I'll be in my room next door when you guys return. Be careful."

"You know I will," Jim said as he walked out patting his jacket pocket where he had put the pistol. "One way or the other, Ole' Dollar Bill is getting devalued tonight."

Chapter Forty-seven

Walking into the lounge, Jim saw that Jay hadn't arrived, and the ladies were sitting casually by a small table. "Good evening, ladies," he said as they looked up. "How are you doing?"

"Good," Millicent answered. "You certainly look better than you did when we left your room." "I can shine up a little," Jim said, taking a seat beside her. "Still no Jay?"

"Not yet," Marie told him. "He'll probably be fashionably late. Keeping us ladies in suspense so he can make his spectacular arrival."

"Tell you what," Jim said, getting out of his chair. "I'll get us a bottle of wine and four glasses. We can at least have something to drink while we wait."

Coming back to the table a couple of minutes later, he sat and told them, "The waiter will bring it in a minute or two. I ordered a bottle of Jadot Le Montrachet Chardonnay if that's all right with you."

"That's fine," Marie answered as she looked toward the entrance. "And I see Mr. Jay William Pride making his entrance."

Turning in his seat, Jim watched him nodding at everybody he passed until he reached their table. He stood and offered his hand, saying, "Mr. Pride, Marie told me you'd be joining us. I'm Raymond Fleenor or just Ray. Please, have a seat. I've got a very nice bottle of Chardonnay coming."

"Why thank you, Ray," Jay said, smiling at both ladies as he took a seat beside Marie. "My, my, my, don't you ladies look lovely tonight."

"Thank you, Mr. Pride," Marie said with a slight nod as the waiter arrived with the wine. "And you're your usual handsome self."

"Shall I pour?" the waiter asked as he pulled the cork from the bottle.

"Of course," Jay said with a dismissive wave of his hand. "And please serve the ladies first."

As soon as they each had a glass, Jay raised his and said, "To two of the prettiest ladies to ever grace the city of Denver. And to a very, *very*, memorable evening."

After taking a sip, he turned to Jim and asked, "So, what brings you to our fair city, Ray?"

"I represent the finest catering business operating in the United States," Jim told him, smiling. "Little company called Texas Professional Services."

"Ah," Jay said dismissively. "A salesman. I assume you're here for the WHO event."

"Yes, sir, I am," Jim told him. "But I'm actually the owner and President of the company, and I'm here to negotiate a contract with the convention center."

"Really," Jay said, becoming interested. "Just what does your company do?"

"Everything from cleaning and serving staff to supplying dinnerware, tablecloths, a selection of wines, along with our own laundry service and dishwashing," Jim answered. "We'll have a truck brought in that has washers and dryers, ironing for the uniforms our staff wears as well as the napkins and tablecloths, and a commercial steam cleaning machine for the dishes. Hell, we'll even polish the shoes our waiters and waitresses wear if the price is right."

"That's a hell of an operation," Jay said, pouring a little more wine into his glass. "What do you charge for something like that?"

"I can't give you information for an ongoing bid," Jim said, leaning slightly closer. "But we had a contract for a weeklong event in New Orleans last year for a little north of a million and a half."

Jay sat back and looked closely at Jim and asked, "How do you think you'll do bidding here?"

"I'm going to say probably fifty-fifty," Jim answered. "I've bid against a couple of the operations here before. I'm generally a little higher, maybe ten percent or so, but our reputation is unmatched in the industry."

"What would you say if I told you that I may be able to help you a little bit?" Jay asked, smiling slyly.

"What do you mean?" Jim asked, sitting back.

"Oh, let's say I may be able to get you better odds than fifty-fifty," Jay said, lifting his glass to his lips. "More like a 95 percent chance that you'll get the contract."

Jim appeared to be thinking about it for a couple of seconds and then asked, "Why would you do that? We've just met, and you really don't know anything about my business."

"I know quite a bit about the service industry," Jay told him, leaning closer. "I'm sort of the go-to guy around here for anyone wanting to do your type of business. Most of the people working here at the hotel are beholding to me. As well as in most of the other hotels and restaurants across Denver."

Jay put his hand on Jim's arm and continued, "I can shut a hotel or restaurant down with a single phone call. And I can do the same with any company that tries to come into my town and take over."

As Jay sat back, Jim tilted his head and asked, "And what would your, let's call it, consultation fee cost me?"

"Not a damn penny," Jay said solemnly. "My normal fee is ten percent. You just add it to your bid, and if you don't get the contract, it costs you nothing."

"I believe I need to give that considerable thought," Jim told him as he finished his wine. "Tell you what, Millicent and I are planning on going to Sushi Sasa for dinner tonight. Why don't you and Marie join us, and we can discuss your proposal?"

"An excellent idea," Jay said happily. "I happen to know the people there intimately, and there won't be a problem getting a table."

"Not necessary," Jim said, taking the cell phone from his pocket and calling Michael. "I already have reservations. I'll just have my car brought around, and we can head over there. Millicent and I are going to come back here after dinner for a couple of drinks, so we'll drop off you and Marie wherever you want."

Jay stood and said, "While you do that, I'll get a bottle of champagne for the drive over to celebrate what I think will be our mutually beneficial relationship."

As soon as he had left the table, Jim turned to Millicent and whispered, "Give me your vial. I'm going to take care of that narcissistic condescending son of a bitch on the drive to the restaurant. You and Marie excuse yourselves to go to the ladies' room when he gets back. Let her know that I'll put the toxin in his glass when I get a chance, and you guys need to distract him when I open the champagne. And try to block his view until I fill the first glass. I'll hand you his glass first and then one for Marie. Just make sure you know which one is his."

"I'll hold it in my left hand," Millicent said, handing Jim the vial as she saw Jay coming back. "It'll work better if he's across from me in the car and to Marie's right when I give them their glasses."

"Just let her know what I'm planning," Jim said, leaning back with the phone to his ear.

As Jay took his seat, Millicent stood and said, "Marie and I need to go to the ladies' room and freshen up before we leave. Will that be all right with you gentlemen?"

"Certainly, pretty lady," Jay answered, looking directly at her breasts. "I do believe that we're all in for an unforgettable evening. But don't take too long; my juices are starting to flow."

"The car will be around front in five minutes," Jim said putting the phone down as the waiter arrived with a bottle of champagne and four glasses. "Do you need to do anything before we leave?"

"Not a damn thing, Ray, my man. Not a damn thing," Jay answered, watching Marie walk away. "Between that lovely lady, our soon-to-be mutual understanding, this champagne, and a little extra special surprise for the drive, I don't need a damn thing. You're about to know why I'm known as Dollar Bill around this town. You don't get shit done without Ole' Dollar Bill."

Chapter Forty-eight

Jim stood as Millicent and Marie came back, saying, "I'll bring the bottle if you ladies will take the glasses."

"I'll get them," Millicent said, picking up the glasses as Marie took Jay's arm. "I'm really looking forward to this evening. Wine, now champagne, sushi, and probably some warm Gekkeikan Sake, not to mention the company of two fine gentlemen."

"It doesn't get any better," Jay said as he headed for the door. "You're about to experience things that most people only dream about. The night's going to be full of surprises."

"I'm sure you're right," Millicent said as she followed him to where the limo was waiting.

"Good evening," Michael said as he held the rear door open for them. "Where would you like to go this evening?"

"Sushi Sasa," Jay answered as Marie followed him into the rear seat. "And take the scenic route. We have plenty of time."

"Certainly, sir," he said as Millicent slid into the rear-facing seat with the glasses. "I know just the route to take."

"Thank you, Michael," Jim told him, following Millicent into the limo. "We'll probably be in the restaurant for an hour or so. If you need to go get something to eat, there should be plenty of time."

"That won't be necessary, sir," Michael said before closing the door. "I had one of the waiters bring me out a sandwich earlier this evening. But thank you for your consideration."

A couple of blocks from the hotel, Jay reached into one of his pockets and held out a small vial filled with white powder along with a tiny silver spoon, saying, "I hope you'll join me in a little mood enhancer."

Watching him fill the little spoon and raise it to his nose, Jim said, "None for me, thank you. But maybe the ladies would like some."

"Maybe later," Marie answered. "Right now, I'm more in the mood for the champagne. However, maybe after we get back to the hotel."

"I agree," Millicent said, watching him snort the cocaine. "It always puts me in the mood after a good meal and a few drinks."

"I guess that's my cue to open the bottle," Jim said, untwisting the wire that held the stopper in. "If the party is about to start, I don't want to be late."

Jay was getting another spoonful as the cork popped and the champagne bubbled out of the top as Millicent said, "Careful, Raymond. Don't get that on your suit."

Marie leaned over, took a handkerchief from her purse, and passed it to Jim, saying, "Here, use this to wipe your hand."

As she started to sit back, she turned to face Jay as he was wiping his nose and kissed him on the lips. Seeing her blocking Jay's view, Millicent held out one of the glasses, and Jim popped the top of the vial, emptying it into the glass. Just as Marie finished kissing Jay, he poured the glass half full of champagne, saying, "I do believe you are right, Mr. Pride. This'll be an unforgettable evening."

Filling another glass the same, he waited for Millicent to hand them to Jay and Marie before saying, "I'd like to propose a toast as soon as Millicent and I have a glass. It's not often that I get to combine business with pleasure like this."

Filling glasses half full for himself and Millicent, he raised his and announced, "I truly believe that I'll enjoy this evening more than any I can remember. To you, Mr. Pride, may this be the one you remember the most also."

"Thank you, Ray boy," he said, tapping his glass against Jim's. "I have no doubt it will be. And to you lovely ladies, may you never forget this night."

Tapping his glass, both of them nodded as Marie replied, "I'm sure I won't. This is the type of evening that I've been looking forward to since I met you."

"To the evening," Millicent said, raising her glass to her lips. "May it fulfill all of our wishes."

Jim looked at Jay as he drained his glass and asked, "Would you like another?"

"Why not?" Jay answered as he turned and lowered his face to Marie's chest. "I'm here for the best night of my life, aren't I?"

"That you are," Jim told him as he took the outstretched glass. "You'll remember this night for the rest of your life."

With Jay's mouth on the top of her breast, Marie looked at Millicent and handed her the vial she had taken out of her purse. "Please fill mine also," she said, passing her glass as well. "I think Mr. Pride is getting ahead of me."

"You've got to run fast to stay up with me," Jay said, lifting his head and looking at her. "The way I feel right now, both of you couldn't keep up."

"I'm sure you're right," Millicent said as she poured the vial into Jay's glass. "I've never met someone like you, and it's a shame that I won't get to spend more time with you."

"Maybe you'd like to join Marie and me later," he told her as Jim filled the glass. "I'm sure Jim would enjoy something different tonight."

"You never know where the night will lead," Jim said, raising his glass. "You just never know."

A few minutes later, as they approached the restaurant, Jay started sweating profusely and gasping for breath. As he bent over, clutching his stomach, Jim got into the seat to his right and said, "Grab his left arm, Marie. Millicent, get the driver's attention."

Tapping on the glass, she waited for the divider glass to lower, and then Jim said, "Take us somewhere quiet. Somewhere you can park, and we won't be noticed for an hour or so."

"You better move over to the side," Jim then told Millicent. "If he throws up, you don't want to be in front of him."

As Jay struggled trying to talk, Marie asked, "How long will this take?"

"Not long," Jim told her as drool started running down Jay's chin. "As much as we gave him, maybe another five minutes."

"Are you going to need my help?" Michael said from the front as he pulled into the darkened lot of a motel.

"Not yet," Jim answered. "Call Gene and tell him where we are and that we won't be going to the restaurant. And let him know I'll call as soon as I can."

"What's wrong with Mr. Pride?" Michael asked as he dialed Gene's number.

"He's having the night of his life," Jim answered as he watched Jay convulse. "Just tell Gene where we are and that the problem is resolved."

A few minutes later, when Jay appeared to be completely paralyzed, Jim took the cocaine container and spoon out of his pocket. "Get the empty vials," he told Millicent. "Pour them together and let me have it."

Once he had the remaining toxin, he put the little spoon in the last drop of the fluid and then filled it with cocaine. As he looked at Jay, he could tell that although he wasn't breathing, he was still alive. "Look what I have for you, asshole," he told him. "When they find your sorry ass body tomorrow morning, they'll find just a wee bit of the poison in this coke that I'm going to stick up your nose. It will match the toxin I put in the champagne you so wonderfully provided."

Jim kept looking in his eyes as he rubbed the little spoon around in Jay's nose, saying, "The only thing the coroner may have a problem with is which killed you, the toxin or the nose candy. Either way, you won't be making any more crooked deals or bothering any little kids."

A couple of minutes later, Jim picked up his phone and called Gene, saying, "I need some information as soon as you can get it. I need to know how fast the toxin will dry and if there's any residue."

"I'll have to call Quantico," Gene told him. "But, first, what the hell happened?"

"Ole' Dollar Bill decided to do a little snort and drink as we were going to the restaurant," Jim told him. "I decided to exterminate him on the way. I told Millicent my plan at the hotel before we left when Jay told me he was buying a bottle of champagne for the drive. I took her vial and told her to brief Marie about the change in plans. She and Marie provided suitable distractions to give me plenty of time to put the toxin in his glass. Then, for good measure, Marie gave me her vial. Now, we need to find a suitable dumping site for the remains of the former City Councilman."

"All right," Gene said, "I'll make a quick call and get back to you. In the meantime, have Michael head back here. I'll have someone else from the team here to take care of the body."

"Thanks," Jim said as Michael started the car. "We should be back within 30 minutes or so."

"I'll have people waiting to go with Michael," Gene told him. "I'll have someone drive you back to your hotel, and the ladies can stay here for the night."

"Did you get that, Michael?" Jim asked as he disconnected the call. "Looks like you're in for a late-night taking out the trash."

"Got it," Michael said, glancing in the rearview mirror. "All part of the job."

Chapter Forty-nine

Gene and four men meet the limo when it pulls up to the front of the Embassy Suites. As Jim got out, Gene looked inside and said, "We'll take it from here. Let me have the pistol, please, Jim. It'll be part of the scene when the Denver Police arrive at where we put his body. With the gun in his hand and a couple of bullets missing, they'll assume that it was a drug deal gone south."

Jim handed the gun to Gene, saying, "I'm sure there's no need to remind your people, but there needs to be some gunpowder residue on Jay's hand if you're going to make it appear that he was shooting at someone."

"Definitely," Gene said as he passed the pistol to one of the men. "The location of the body will be in the same area as other drug-related crimes. And the guys will remove each bullet and put Jay's fingerprints on them before reloading. And there'll be one bullet in the wall of the building across from where the body will be."

"And that'll tie Jay to whatever crime the gun was tied to," Jim added. "Nice touch."

"I think so," Gene said, putting his hand on Jim's shoulder. "All together, a job well done. Maybe even better than the original plan."

"Thanks," Jim said before walking over to where Marie and Millicent were standing, "How are you guys holding up?"

"I'm fine," Millicent answered, looking at the limo. "That was a little more dramatic than I expected, but it couldn't have happened to a nicer guy. What a pig."

"What about you, Marie?" Jim asked, trying to get her to quit looking at Jay's body in the rear of the limo."

"I'll be all right," she finally said, looking up at Jim. "I guess I sort of thought that he'd just, I don't know, sort of like pass out or something. You know, sort of like it was when I worked with you in Chicago."

"Unfortunately, most quick-acting poisons cause a pretty dramatic reaction in the human body," Jim explained as he put his hand on her shoulder. "But that's the price we have to pay if we want quick results. In Chicago, we wanted the man to live for a week or so. In this case, it had to be tonight. I know it's not pretty up close like you had to watch, but it was sort of the lesser of the evils."

"I understand," she said, looking at Jim. "And like Millicent said, the man was an absolute pig. I thought I was going to throw up in his mouth when I had to kiss him."

Jim stood there looking at her for a second as a smile began to form on his face. Finally, he started laughing as he said, "I'd love to have seen the look on his face if you'd done that. That would have been the perfect putdown."

Marie closed her eyes slightly and then began to smile, "Yeah, that would have been a classic. God, I wish I'd just gone ahead and done it. Serve that asshole right."

Millicent joined in on the laughter and added, "And he had the balls to ask if I'd like to join Marie with him. Sure, I'd join her in puking on him. But he was such a pig that he might have liked it."

"Oh, yeeww," Marie said as she lowered her head and gave a slight shiver. "That's just gross."

"Just like him," Millicent said as she put her arms around Marie. "That man deserved worse than we gave him. Much worse. Just think of the women we spared the displeasure of having to deal with him."

"I know," she said, smiling at her and Jim. "I'm just glad it's over. I'll probably have nightmares about that for a while but knowing that he's gone will make it all right in time."

"You'll be all right," Jim told her as Gene walked over. "It was a little more than I'd envisioned, but I've seen worse. And yes, it sticks with you for a while."

"How's everybody?" Gene asked as he joined them.

"We're fine," Millicent answered. "Just a little aftershock. But we'll be just fine. Right, Marie?"

"Yeah, we'll be fine," she answered, looking at Gene. "Like I just told Jim. I was expecting something like that in Chicago. Boy, was this different."

"Yes, it was," Gene agreed. "But, if you'll remember, you guys ended up shooting three guys in a restaurant. And one of them was the guy you had poisoned."

"That's true," Marie said, thinking back. "But I still prefer the more distance thing. You know, where I'm not sitting holding on to the guy's arm as he goes into convulsions."

"I understand," Gene told her, looking from her to Millicent. "But the important thing is how you guys reacted. To pull that off with little to no preparation is exactly why we only hire people like you. No matter how much we plan and practice, it comes down to trusting your people to handle the unexpected. Just like you did in Chicago, you did again here."

"Gene's right," Jim added, smiling at her. "What you two did tonight is the only reason guys like me can do our jobs. Can you imagine what might have happened if you hadn't kissed Jay when you did? I might never have gotten the opportunity to put the toxin in his glass. That little impromptu thing is what makes the difference in success or failure. And sometimes, it's what saves our lives. You have a knack for doing the right thing."

"Jim's right," Millicent added, winking at Jim. "You have a knack for doing..... let's say the right thing. If kissing a pig is ever the right thing to do."

Gene just shook his head and said, "I think you guys need to get to your rooms. I'll book flights for you tomorrow whenever you want to leave. Jim, I'll drive you back to your hotel."

"Good idea," Millicent said, nodding. "Let's go, Marie. A hot shower and a nice soft bed sound so inviting right now."

Looking at Jim, she said, "Good night, Mr. Lashley. Not bad for a first date. Maybe next time you'll actually take me to dinner."

Jim laughed and told her, "As first dates go, I bet you'll never forget this one. You ladies have a good night, and I'm sure we'll run into each other another time."
Marie stepped over to him and said, "Thanks, Jim. I guess it would have been the same even if it had been at the restaurant. I think we did it right. Good night."

As Millicent and Marie headed into the hotel, Gene asked, "Are you ready to get back to your hotel and try to get some sleep before you fly tomorrow?"

"Yeah," Jim said, watching the ladies leave. "Maybe I got a little carried away tonight, but that guy was a complete scumbag. Maybe I should've just shot him. Quicker, same result. Less stress for the girls."

"And more issues for me," Gene said as he led Jim to where he'd left his car. "No, this worked fine. Not to change the subject, but how's your Captain on this trip?"

"Sort of like Jay," Jim said as they got in the car. "But completely classless. I'd say that if Jay had a degree in swineology, it would be at least a Master's degree. Maybe even a Ph.D. My Captain, he's still in the third grade and will never be any better than a low-class pig."

"Remember the TV series Green Acres?" Gene asked as they drove away.

"Sure," Jim answered, looking at him.

"Arnold," Gene said with a quick glance at Jim. "Now there was a pig."

Jim thought for a moment and then replied, laughing, "Arnold was okay. But, in the movie Babe? Now there was a pig."

"Oh yeah?" Gene said, laughing with him. "What about Charlotte's Web?"

"You're right," Jim told him, unable to stop laughing. "Wilbur was, in Charlotte's words, 'Some Pig'."

"Yeah, he was *terrific*," Gene said as their laughter died down somewhat.

"Don't forget *radiant*," Jim added.

"And *humble*," Gene said, finishing the list. "Very humble."

Chapter Fifty

The next morning, Jim was in the hotel lobby having a cup of coffee when Merna stopped by his chair, asking, "How was your dinner party last night, Jim?"

"Good morning, Merna," he answered as he stood up. "Rather mundane. It was more of a cocktail party than a dinner party."

"That's too bad," she said as they saw Kit coming toward them. "But, speaking of mundane, that man's constant innuendos are past mundane and rapidly approaching intolerable."

"I know, and unfortunately, I've got to fly with him for the rest of the month," Jim said quietly. "And I've got to sit right beside him for hours listening to him."

"Good morning," Kit said as he walked up. "Did everyone get a good night's sleep?"

"Fine," both Jim and Merna said almost in unison.

Showing them the paper he'd picked up at the front desk, he told them, "Looks like there was some excitement here in Denver last night. Some famous Councilman or something was found dead not too far from here. Police are saying it was probably a drug deal that ended badly."

"I'm sure that's not the first drug deal that's gone bad here in Denver," Jim said as they saw the other two Flight Attendants coming. "And it's not only here, it's everywhere."

"I know," Kit told him as everyone headed out to get on the van to the airport. "But the desk clerk said he knows one of the clerks over at the Embassy Suites, and the Councilman was seen there last night with a couple of hookers and some salesman."

"Were they involved in the drug thing?" one of the Flight Attendants asked as the van pulled out heading to the airport.

"The desk clerk didn't say and there's nothing about anyone other than the Councilman in the paper," Kit answered.

"I can't imagine having to do that for a living," Merna said, shaking her head. "Why would any woman go into that sort of business?"

"Lots of reasons," Jim answered. "Sometimes it's girls who think they don't have any other options, and I'm sure they only went into it intending to move on quickly.

And, unfortunately, there's a hell of a market for young girls. And some of the gangs or organized crime brings them into the United States with promises of a better life," Jim added. "And then they're sold into prostitution with no real chance of anything else."

"I wonder what a hooker makes," Merna asked, looking at Jim.

"Depends," Jim answered. "I've got a friend whose sister is a lady of the evening, and she gets about $400 per hour."

"That's a lot," Merna exclaimed.

"I'd guess that's about the midrange," Jim told her. "Some of the high-end ladies probably get over $1,000 per hour. And, of course, there are the ones that are more commonly known as street-walkers that make a lot less. When I was overseas, there were always girls at the bars that only charged $10 or $20 for all night."

"I wonder what they'd charge for five minutes?" Kit asked as they approached the airport.

Jim glanced at Merna as she looked down and shook her head before saying, "I don't think they give discounts, Captain. Not for a shorter time or short anything else."

"I wasn't talking about me personally," Kit replied as Merna and the other Flight Attendants covered their mouths, trying not to laugh out loud at Jim's short anything comment. "I heard about places in Asia like that from some of the international pilots."

"I wouldn't know," Jim told him as they pulled to the curb at the airport. "Maybe you should bid for an international slot and check it out."

As they were going through the crew entrance, Merna leaned over and whispered, "You might want to be careful what you say, Mr. Lashley. You've still got to fly with him the rest of the month."

"I know," Jim said as they passed into the terminal. "But, sometimes, my mouth gets ahead of my brain. There must be a medical term for my condition. I just don't know what it is."

"Maybe it's a pedi-oral disease," Merna suggested as they approached their gate. "You know, foot in the mouth?"

Jim laughed and told her, "That's probably as good a diagnosis as any. But the real question is, is there a cure?"

"Cure for what?" Kit asked as he went behind the gate agent to use the computer.

"Stupidity," Merna answered, winking at Jim. "I was just telling Jim how I hate dealing with some of the stupid people on the first flight of the day."

"And it only gets worse as the day goes on," one of the other Flight Attendants said as they started down the jet bridge. "By the third flight, I think the average IQ of the passengers drops by at least half. Especially the men."

"I'll go on down and check out the plane," Jim told Kit as he followed Merna to the jet bridge. "What's the load look like?"

"Full," the gate agent answered. "Couple of non-revenue (non-rev) passengers, including one Flight Attendant trying to get home."

"Sounds good," Kit said, pulling the flight plan and other information from the printer. "At least there's an open jump seat in the rear for the Flight Attendant, if nothing else."

After putting his suitcase in the forward closet and his kitbag in his seat, Jim went down to check the exterior of the airplane. When he was coming back into the jet bridge, he was surprised to see Millicent standing there talking to Merna.

"Jim," Merna said as he started to pass them. "This is Millicent. She's going to be sitting on the jump seat going to Dallas."

"Hi, Millicent," Jim said before going back into the cockpit. "We've flown together before, haven't we?"

"I think so," she answered, handing him a slip of paper as Merna turned and went into the first-class galley. "I can't remember when, but I'm sure we've worked together somewhere."

Putting the paper in his shirt pocket, Jim said, "I'm sure we have, too. Do you have to work today?"

"No," she answered as they stepped into the airplane. "I've got a trip early tomorrow morning, and I've been gone for several days. I just need as much time as I can get at home to take care of everyday stuff."

"I know what you mean," Jim said as he went into the cockpit. "My wife has at least a week's worth of crap for me to do in the three or four days I get off between trips. Anyway, Captain Carson will get you back to Dallas so you can take care of everything."

Millicent rolled her eyes as she said, "Merna told me you guys were super to fly with. Maybe we'll get to work together again someday."

"I'm sure we will," Jim told her as he got into his seat. "It's surprising how you keep running into the same people after a few years. Anyway, like I said, Captain Carson will make sure you get home safely."

Kit turned in his seat and said, "And that I will, miss. Nice to have you on board."

"Nice to meet you, Captain," she told him as she turned to go to her seat. "Please don't hesitate to let Merna know if I can help in any way."

"Wow," Kit said, watching her walk away. "How do you meet these ladies, Jim?"

"Same way you do, Kit," Jim answered as he took the computer papers from the pedestal. "I meet them on the airplane when we work together."

"I guess so," he said, turning back to setting up his instruments for the takeoff. "I just don't get the same reaction from them you do."

"They're probably a little reluctant to be too personal with you because you're the Captain," Jim lied. "Lots of people are still in awe of an airline Captain."

"That's probably it," Kit said, turning to Jim. "I guess it's time for the before starting engines checklist."

Chapter Fifty-one

As they were passing over Oklahoma, Kit excused himself to go to the lavatory, giving Jim a chance to see what was in the note Millicent had given him earlier. Unfolding the paper, all that was written was a phone number and asking for him to call upon landing at DFW.

Once parked at the gate, Jim did a quick walk around of the airplane and headed up the jet bridge to use a phone. As he passed Kit coming down, he said, "Jet's good, and I'll be right back."

Asking to use the phone at the gate agent's desk, he dialed and waited for an answer. Soon, he heard Gene saying, "Barker."

"I figured this would be your number, General," Jim said, smiling. "What can I do for you this morning?"

"I just wanted to give you a heads-up that you're invited to another dinner party this afternoon after you arrive," Gene answered. "I'll have a car waiting at the airport to pick you up when you get here, and the driver will take you back to the airport in the morning."

"Okay," Jim said, wondering what was happening this afternoon. "Is everything all right after the last party?"

"Perfect," Gene told him. "This has nothing to do with that. I'll see you in four hours or so."

Hearing the phone disconnect, Jim looked at the phone and simply hung it up. Thanking the agent, he headed back down to the airplane to get ready for the return trip to Denver.

As he was opening the door to the jet bridge, he heard Merna calling for him to hold the door. As she arrived, she said, "Thanks, Jim. I just ran out to get a book a friend had left for me in operations. I figure I'll have a chance to do some reading this afternoon since we get in so early."

"You're welcome," Jim said as they walked down to the plane. "What's the book?"

"It's called *Genocide by GMO*," she answered, showing him the book. "Supposed to be based on an actual thing that someone created in a lab."

"GMO's," Jim replied as they got to the airplane. "I know some people worry about that, but some people worry about everything. Too much worry isn't good for you either."

"I know," she said as they stepped inside. "My friend is sort of anal about these things. She's always going on about gluten-free, steroid-free, free-range, non-GMO, or whatever. I'm certainly not a vegan or anything, but I try to keep up with whatever the latest craze is. Mainly because people are always asking about what we serve on the plane."

"Well, I hope you enjoy your book," Jim said as he went into the cockpit. "Maybe you'll even learn something. Or maybe it'll be so boring that you get a good nap."

"Maybe it'll just help pass the time this afternoon," she told him as she set the book on her jump seat. "Can I get you guys anything before the passengers get here?"

"Diet Coke, please," Kit said, glancing over his shoulder at her.

"Dr. Pepper for me, please, Merna," Jim answered, smiling.

"And a lime wedge?" she asked knowingly.

"If you don't mind," Jim told her. "As long as it's a non-GMO lime."

"I'm surprised that you're worried about that sort of thing," Kit said, looking at him. "I heard they're creating all sorts of plants and things in the labs these days. And, in some cases, they use DNA from rodents to combine with the plant DNA."

"I wouldn't know," Jim told him as Merna passed Kit his diet coke. "But there're all sorts of things that the labs created in our food today. Just look at the ingredients in your Diet Coke. I don't think the sweetener is from a plant like sugar cane or corn."

Kit tilted his head to read and finally said, "Looks like Aspartame is probably the sweetener."

"I'll bet you're right," Jim told him as he looked at the label on his can. "And I'd bet that it's a lab-created sugar substitute. I'll just stick with Dr. Pepper. High fructose corn syrup. I'm helping out our agricultural business. The farmers of America would be proud of me."

Kit set his can back on the ledge to his left and looked at Jim, saying, "Farmers aside, I guess it's time for the checklist, please."

Three hours later, as they shut the engines down, Kit asked, "Do you have plans for this afternoon, or would you like to go out for a beer or something?"

"I'm going to meet with some friends again this evening," Jim answered as he started putting everything away. "I'm being picked up here, so I'll see you back here tomorrow morning."

"Okay," Kit finally replied. "I guess I'll just ask the ladies if they'd like to do something. It's a shame to be in such a nice town as Denver and not go out."

"Good luck with that," Jim said as he climbed out of his seat. "I really don't think they'll go for it, but I guess it doesn't hurt to try."

"Got plans for this evening?" Merna asked as Jim pulled his suitcase out of the closet.

"Meeting some friends," Jim answered, smiling. "I think Kit said he was going to ask you guys if you wanted to go out. Too bad you brought a book."

"At least I have an excuse," she whispered as the other Flight Attendants came up, pulling their suitcases. "I'll let the others know to start thinking of why they can't go."

"I'm sure they'll appreciate that," Jim told her as he headed up the jet bridge into the terminal. "Look at it this way: just one leg back to DFW, and you're done with him. I've got him for four more trips."

"I feel for you, but have fun tonight," Merna called out as she joined the rest of the crew going up the jet bridge.

Jim spotted the Suburban as he exited the terminal and walked over, pulling his suitcase with his kitbag resting on top. As he approached, Michael stepped out and opened the rear passenger door, saying, "Well, don't you look spiffy in your pretty uniform. Certainly different than last night."

Jim laughed as he put his bags in the rear seat, saying, "Hello, Michael, it's good to see you again. I never really got to thank you for the last night. You were a tremendous help."

"Just doing my job, Jim," he answered as Jim shut the rear door. "I suppose you want to sit up front contrary to company regulations, too."

"Indeed I do," Jim said as he reached for the front passenger door handle. "Indeed I do."

Chapter Fifty-two

As they pulled into the Embassy Suites, Michael opened the rear passenger door for Jim to get his suitcase and said, "Gene's in room 405, and I believe he has the room across the hall for you."

"Thanks again," Jim said, shaking his hand. "I'm sure I'll be seeing you around here until this little assignment is over."

"I know you will," Michael replied, closing the trunk. "I believe we'll be working together this afternoon going out to the route you asked us to look at."

"Great," Jim said, heading to the hotel doors. "I'll see you then."

As he stepped off the elevator on the fourth floor, Jim saw that the room he wanted was down the hall to the left. Approaching it, he noticed that the door to room 406 was open, and a service cart with what appeared to be sandwiches and drinks was being placed on a rectangular table.

As he started to knock on Gene's door, an Asian-looking man he didn't recognize opened it. "Is this General Barker's room?" he asked.

"It is," he heard Gene call out. "Come on in, Jim."

"I'm Wang Jong," the man said, extending his hand. "I'm very glad to meet you, Mr. Lashley."

Jim shook his hand, saying, "Good to meet you, Wang. Please, just call me Jim."

Gene came to the door, holding out a key, and said, "Your room is across the hall, 406. We'll be meeting there in a few minutes after the hotel finishes setting up our lunch buffet. But you can go ahead and get changed before we start."

After putting his uniform in the closet and pulling on a pair of jeans and a T-shirt, Jim opened the bedroom door and saw Sun and Hua talking with Wang. "Sun, I'm rather surprised to see you here," he said, walking over to shake hands. "And you too, Hua."

They both bowed slightly as Sun said, "I convinced General Barker that we needed to bait the hook a little more before we attempt to catch our adversary."

"What Sun really means is that he was tired of sitting around a hotel room down in Dallas waiting for something to happen," Gene said, joining them. "In that respect, he's a lot like you, Jim. Always wanting to take control of the situation. But, in this case, I agree with him."

"And what are we planning this afternoon?" Jim asked as Gene took a plate from the table and started filling it.

"Just a little drive through," Gene said as he took his plate to one of the chairs placed in front of an easel with a map of Denver and the surrounding area. "You guys grab a plate and join me. Michael will be joining us in a few minutes to discuss the route we'll be using."

With a sandwich and a glass of tea, Jim took the chair beside Gene and quietly asked, "I thought we weren't going to expose Hua again until we executed the plan. What happened?"

"I had them brought in yesterday afternoon," Gene explained. "I believe that we can provide adequate protection for the day and again next week when we return. The bigger point is to reinforce Li's thinking that he can remove Hua here, but we want to lead him to where we want. That's the place you selected, and we are going to let him see it ahead of time.

The other reason is to give Sun a chance to see the route and become comfortable with it," Gene continued. "After I described our plan to him, he insisted on having a chance to drive it."

"But you don't need Hua to let Sun see the route and practice," Jim argued.

"No, but Li needs to see her get in the car with Sun for this to be of maximum effectiveness," Gene replied. "If he sees them and follows them, he'll come to the conclusion that where we lead him today and again next Sunday is the perfect spot to assassinate Hua."

Sun came to where they were discussing the operation and said, "Jim, I know Li. I know the way he thinks. He'll be much more comfortable picking his spot, or so he'll think. That's part of why I insisted on coming up here. I want to reduce the chance that he'll take an unplanned shot or something that we may not be able to control. I think you'll understand when we finish the briefing."

Jim looked from Sun to Gene and finally said, "I'm certainly open to suggestions, and Sun is right; he knows our enemy better than any of us. And I also know that no one here would intentionally put Hua in greater jeopardy."

A few minutes later, Michael came in with another man who sat in the back and said, "If everyone is ready, we'll get started, so we'll have plenty of time for questions before we actually go drive the route."

"Anytime you're ready, Michael," Gene said as he returned from putting his plate on the buffet table.

"Yes, sir," Michael said. "The guy who came in with me is Billy Nelson. He'll be driving the truck when we stage the accident."

As everyone turned to look at him, Michael continued, "Today, he'll be riding with me to see the route as well as provide additional security in the unlikely event Li Wei decides to get stupid on us.

Wang has assured us that Li was informed that Hua is back," he told them looking at Gene and Jim. "That was one of the main reasons we're staging this run-through. He'll be informed when she and Sun are about to leave the hotel, and we anticipate that he'll be ready to follow them."

Pointing at the map, he continued, "We'll have the Corsica brought to the entrance just before Sun and Hua go downstairs. Li will see them get in the car and drive away.

We'll take the Suburban and be at the rental house when Sun arrives," he said. "Wang will be following Li as he follows Sun."

"What about the time from when Sun and Hua leave their room and get in the car?" Jim asked. "Whose providing protection if we're already outside?"

"We have four other people here," Gene explained, looking at him. "Two will accompany them down in the elevator and to the lobby. Another will be the doorman who escorts them to their car, which is being brought to the front by another agent. There'll always be at least two people around her."

"And with Li in his car waiting, there shouldn't be anyone else interested," Sun added. "Wang has spent the last few days since Li first saw them following him. When he gets a notification that they are in the hotel, he parks just down the block and waits."

"How does he get notified that she's here and when she leaves?" Jim asked, looking at Wang.

"He gets a phone call," Wang explained. "We've traced it to this hotel but don't know who is using it."

"Who's using it doesn't matter," Gene said looking at Jim. "It's just someone here on the hotel staff that Li's recruited. The important part is that he gets notified and arrives. That's what we're counting on today."

"Okay," Jim said, turning back to Michael. "What's my role here today? I don't expect to be directly involved when we stage the accident."

"No, but everyone here wants to hear what you think," Gene answered. "And mainly because it's your plan. Who else would you want to give the final approval?"

Chapter Fifty-three

"Okay, we've got a couple of hours before we need to go," Michael told them. "Li's car has a tracking device on it, but Wang wants to be there when he gets in to make sure he's the only one in it. Wang will then trail him as he comes here to watch Hua leave the hotel.

One addition we made to your plan, Jim," Michael continued, "is that we'll lead Li to a house a couple of miles from where you planned the accident. We've rented a house on South Lookout Mountain Road that I mentioned. Sun and Hua will go there this afternoon, with Li following. We'll be a few miles in front, and the Suburban will be parked when they arrive. Wang will be following with a couple of our men just in case Li does something unpredictable.

We'll stay at the house for a couple of hours, and then Sun and Hua will come back to the hotel," he added. "We're hoping that Li will believe that they went there for debriefing or a dinner engagement. That doesn't matter. As long as he sees them go there and stay for a little while.

Then Wang and the others will be watching Li as they follow him back here," Michael said, looking at Jim. "We'll give them about 10 minutes head start, and then we'll come back here, too."

"Sun and Hua will be going back to Dallas tomorrow afternoon," Gene told Jim. "We'll bring them back again next Saturday and repeat the process. By then, we're sure that Li will plan on eliminating Hua at the house on Lookout Mountain. It's isolated, and Li will believe he'll have no problem with whoever's inside."

"And then, we'll plan on having the accident the following Monday when you're here," Michael told him. "After two trips, Li will be confident that Hua is going to the same house even if he loses sight of her for longer than we anticipate. There's no other reason for her to be taking that route."

"And, if something goes wrong, we'll push it to your next trip," Gene added. "Since you're coming back Saturday, we'll have you go with us again to make any final adjustments to our plan. Then you'll be here around noon on Sunday when we stage the accident in the afternoon."

"One other thing this does for us," Sun added, "is that after Li sees the white car at the house twice, he'll go by after passing the wreck to see if it's there. When he doesn't see it, he'll be even more convinced that she was in the wreck."

"What about the truck?" Jim asked. "Do we have one?"

"Yes," Michael assured him as he motioned for a man in the back to come forward. "Billy's got hundreds of thousands of miles driving 18-wheelers, and we'll be using his truck. He's going with us to get a good look at the area where we plan to delay Li while Sun takes the side road."

"Good to meet you, Mr. Lashley," Billy said, nodding. "I don't think I'll have any problems with the driving part, but it'll help me with the timing if I can see where the white car will go and how much I need to swing out to make the turn left onto South Grapevine Road."

"I appreciate your help," Jim told him. "Please don't hesitate to let us know if you see something that'll make it work better."

"I will," Billy said, nodding. "I'm going to be making the same run in my truck a couple of times before Sunday. I'll let Michael know if I see any problems or have any suggestions."

"How long will Sun wait on Paradise Road before he comes back to town?" Jim asked, looking at Michael.

"He'll wait until Wang sees Li heading back east on 70," he answered. "Then we'll be sure everything worked when Li calls in that his mission is complete."

"What'll you do with her and Sun after that?" Jim asked Gene.

"I'm waiting for direction from Washington," Gene answered. "I'm looking at taking them back to Dallas. But there's some thinking that she should be a walk-on speaker at the WHO event and break the news of what the PRC is planning regarding their bioweapon program. That may dictate having her stay here."

"What if Li is still here?" Jim asked. "If he gets word that she's still in the hotel, he'll be sure to tell his people back in China. I'd make sure Washington understands that until Li is out of the country, she's at risk, and we've wasted a lot of time and money for no reason."

"I've told them that," Gene said. "They say they may take her down to Colorado Springs and hold her in the Cheyenne Mountain Complex."

"Why would they do that?" Jim asked. "We've done a good job of protecting her up to now."

"They say they're worried about all of the traveling," Gene answered. "I'm even a little concerned that Li may have someone at the airport watching for Hua. Just because he's seen her here a few times doesn't mean he isn't worried about the days when he knows she isn't in the hotel here."

"They have a point," Jim agreed, nodding. "I'd be wondering where she disappeared to if I was him."

"Why don't we worry about that later," Gene said standing. "If there are no further questions, I think we need to get this trial run on the road. Wang, how much time do you need to get in position?"

"About 30 minutes," he answered, coming to the front of the room. "I'll call when Li leaves his hotel."

"Good," Gene said, looking around at the rest of the people. "We'll be ready to head to the rental house as soon as you say he's on his way. Do you have any questions about the route, Sun?"

"None," he answered holding up a map with the route marked. "I'll take 14th Street to Colfax Avenue and US 40 West. Then I'll get on I-70 and follow it about six or seven miles, where I'll take the US 40 exit, turn right on Grapevine Road, and get on US 40. Then, in a couple of miles, there will be a big turn to the left, and Lookout Mountain Road will be on the right. The house is the first on the left, about 500 feet from 40."

"That sounds good," Gene told him and looked at Wang. "If you have any trouble, just keep driving west on 40 until it comes to I-70 in a couple of miles. Get on I-70 going east and come back here. That good with you?"

"That's fine," Wang agreed. "I'll start watching for you to slow down approaching Lookout Mountain Road. If you don't take it, I'll know something's wrong and follow you back here, and we'll try again some other day."

"I guess it's time to go unless there's anything else," Michael said as they headed for the door. "If not, I'll bring the Suburban around to the front, and we can leave as soon as the hotel brings Sun's car to the front."

As everyone else left the room, Jim told Gene, "I'm wondering why we don't just take Hua down to Cheyenne Mountain today and let Washington take care of her. It seems like we're jumping through a lot of hoops just to keep her safe until the end of the month when they may decide to take her there after we stage our little accident."

"They could," Gene explained as they left the room, and Jim locked it. "But they could decide not to let her be at the WHO thing because they don't have enough verification of what she's going to say. That's probably just one of the options they're looking at. For now, our contract is to keep her safe, even if it's only for another week. Let's leave those high-level decisions to the guys that have all the answers."

"I understand," Jim said as they headed for the elevators. "I've executed lots of missions where I didn't know why. And still don't know why we did some of the things we did."

"Like on that hill in Vietnam?" Gene asked as the doors closed.

"Like on that hill," Jim confirmed, thinking back to the men who died on that mission. "And on all the other hills all over the world."

Chapter Fifty-four

Thirty minutes later, as Sun's white Corsica arrived, Michael pulled away from the Embassy Suites with Gene, Jim, Billy, and two other agents headed for the rental house on South Lookout Mountain Road. Heading southeast on 14th street, they came to US 40 and Colfax Avenue and followed it west until it crossed beneath I-70 about six miles west in the area of West Pleasant View.

"Why didn't you stay on US 40?" Jim asked as they joined I-70.

"We need for Sun to make the stop where I-70 exits for US 40 west of Denver," Michael answered. "We looked at just using 40, but we needed the stop just before where Sun gets on Paradise Road. The whole location of the accident you planned depends on that spot. Nothing else would give us time for him to get off 40 and delay Li."

"And I-70 is the most logical way to take the 18-wheeler there," Billy added. "US 40 narrows down to a two-lane road several times west of I-70, and Li could possibly get in front of me. That means that I can't give Sun time to hide."

"Got it," Jim said as they accelerated westbound. "I'm glad you guys were here to drive the route. I might have taken the simplest route and stayed on 40."

As they approached the exit they would take to get on US 40, Jim asked, "What'll you do if Li passes Billy just before the exit?"

"I plan on riding his bumper once we see the first sign for the exit," Billy answered. "That won't give Li a chance to get between us."

"Maybe," Jim argued as he saw a cloverleaf coming up ahead of them. "I think we need another car that'll join you about here as you pass 470. He can then get beside you and make sure Li doesn't get the chance."

"That's a good idea," Gene said as they passed the exit. "After all of this planning, we don't need a stupid move by Li to screw it up. And it gives us another set of eyes and weapons if we need them."

"Speaking of things we need," Jim said, looking at Gene, "what about communications? I think we need a dedicated radio frequency with an open mic for all of them. And Wang needs another radio that is tied to whoever is listening to Li's phone calls. Once we get close to taking the US 40 exit, timing is crucial, and Wang will need to have instant access later to know if Li has reported Hua's death."

"We'll have it for the next run," Gene said as he took out his cell phone. "What else?"

"What about an ambulance for the accident scene?" Bill asked. "I'll be out of the picture once I make the left turn on Grapevine, and the additional car will be miles away on I-70. Who's going to be at the accident when Li comes back from the rental house?"

"That's a good point," Jim said, nodding. "But an ambulance wouldn't have time to respond. We do need someone there when Li comes back just to make sure he doesn't stop and look into the car. What do you think, Gene?"

"What about the car we were going to have sitting beside the road at the stop sign?" Gene answered. "The one that is there to keep Li from making the right turn before Billy makes his left turn. It would be logical for that car to be behind Li and stop to render assistance."

"That'll work," Jim agreed. "I'd suggest that there be a man and a woman in that car. I think it'd be less threatening to Li if he comes back to the accident scene and there's a couple there."

"Okay, I'll work on that," Gene told them before speaking into his phone.

As they took the exit for US 40, Michael said, "Having that car here would also help block Li's view of where Sun will pull off. I'd suggest either an SUV or a pickup that's taller than his car."

"I'll go along with a pickup," Jim told him as they came to the stop sign on Grapevine Road. "That'd be normal out here and having another Suburban-type vehicle might set off a warning bell. And make it some color other than white or black. Maybe bright red. I want Li to have some memory of it being behind him after he turns on US 40."

"Here's where Sun will leave the road," Michael said, pointing at where Paradise Road headed north. "He should be several hundred yards up that road when Li passes it. That, with what we're doing to build a habit pattern of looking for him to continue on 40 to Lookout Mountain Road, should be sufficient."

"And if he doesn't?" Jim asked as they passed Paradise Road. "What if he glimpses Sun's car on Paradise? The main team will be in the Suburban at the rental leaving whoever is in the pickup or Wang to intervene."

Pausing for a few seconds, he continued, "We need the couple in the pickup to have the same communication gear and be armed. If Li just happens to slam on his brakes to follow where Sun actually went, they'll be the only people to stop him from killing both her and Sun."

"We'll also arm Sun," Gene told him, disconnecting his call. "I know he'll feel better if he has some way to protect Hua."

"That's fine," Jim said, shaking his head. "But we need the people in the pickup to be armed with sufficient firepower to ensure Li never gets a shot. Since the entire mission is to safeguard her, even a lucky shot from Li is too much of a risk."

"Agreed," Gene finally said, picking his phone up again. "We'll need another run-through anyway, so we might as well put them in the convoy following Sun and Li."

"We're coming upon the accident site," Michael said as they passed Valley Creek Road on the left, approaching the curve to the right. "This is another crucial point of timing. The more delay we can get back at the stop sign, the more time we have for the explosion and fire before Li gets here."

"I can add some time," Billy told them as they slowed to where the accident would be staged. "I'll take an extra few seconds at the stop sign as if I'm unsure of which way to turn. Then, I'll make a wide right turn before I make the left turn. That should help."

"Anything will help," Jim said as they approached the left curve just prior to Lookout Mountain Road. "The couple in the pickup can advise the explosive guy to set it off as soon as Li makes the turn on 40. It's about a mile from the stop sign, so it'll take him about a minute to get there. If the explosion is, say, 30 seconds from Li making the turn, it should be visible and fully engulfed in flames as he passes it. Then, the first place he can pull off or turn around is here at Lookout Mountain Road. That makes it easy for him to go past the house since it's merely a few yards further."

"There's an ambulance company just up the road from the rental," Michael said as they turned on Lookout Mountain. "If the smoke is visible from there, I'm sure they'll respond."

"That's why I wanted corpses in the car," Jim told him, looking at Gene. "So Li will see bodies. Are they here?"

"Yes," Gene answered as they turned into the driveway of the rental house. "Since the fire will prevent close examination, and the bodies are about the same size as Sun and Hua, we don't think he'll stop and look too closely. We also have Hua's identification in a purse outside of the accident that can be found after the fire is put out."

"Are you using any accelerant?" Jim asked as they got out of the Suburban.

"Yes," Gene answered, approaching the house. "We looked at several different types and settled on Acetone. It has a higher temperature than straight gasoline, which will enhance the combustion of the bodies. It evaporates rather quickly, so there'll be sealed packets of it throughout their clothing. The heat from the initial gasoline fire will set it off."

"Good," Jim agreed as they entered the house. "Now, I guess we wait for Sun and Hua to get here. Then we'll know what Li does when he sees their car here with our Suburban. Did anyone think to stock the house with something to eat or drink?"

"Of course," Gene told him, leading him into the kitchen. "But this is for after Sun and Hua get here. We need to stay here for a couple of hours, and I knew we'd get hungry."

Chapter Fifty-five

Twenty minutes later, Sun pulled into the driveway and parked behind the Suburban. Less than a minute later, as they watched through the curtained window, they saw another car slowly pass that they assumed was Li.

As Jim checked his watch, Gene opened the door, watching them approach, and said, "Come on in, guys. Don't run, but hurry. We don't know if Li will spin around and come back shooting.

How did the drive go?" Gene asked as he closed the front door.

"Fine," Sun answered, looking around at the people there. "I slowed down a bit when I saw the road I'm supposed to take on the day of the accident."

Jim looked from Gene to him and asked, "Did Li see you slow down?"

"I don't think so," Sun admitted, realizing that he may have made a tactical error. "He was just leaving the stop sign, and I didn't slow down very much. Just enough to look at the road."

"It's done," Gene told Jim as he shook his head. "I'm sure Sun will speed right past it next time. I doubt if Li noticed it."

"Let me know when you see Li coming back by," Jim told Michael. "I want to know how long it'll take him to get turned around so we'll know about how much time we'll have at the accident site."

"He's passing now," Michael said, watching from behind the curtains. "He's driving pretty slow and looking this way. I'd bet it'll be considerably faster after he sees the burning car."

"I'm sure you're right," Jim replied as he made a mental note of the elapsed time. "But we've got to start somewhere. Even if he drives faster, it can't be more than a few seconds sooner. It's about a mile back to the crash site, say two minutes at the outside. Add the minute and 15 seconds it took him to pass here, turn around, and get back; that gives us probably three minutes before he's back at the crash site."

"What are you thinking?" Gene asked, watching Jim.

"A couple of things," Jim told him as he was trying to figure out what he wanted. "First, how is the wrecked car going to get here? Next, how long will it take the ambulance from the place just up the road to see the fire and respond?"

"We were going to have the wreck on the truck's flatbed parked up on Paradise Road," Michael answered. "It has a tilting bed, and we can have the wreck off in less than a minute, especially since the driver will unchain it before he goes to where the wreck will be staged.

The driver has been out here and has looked at all the variables," he continued. "He says he can drive off into the ditch just before the curve and start raising the bed. It'll hit maximum tilt about the time he rounds the curve, and the car will slide right off.

He'll continue down the ditch as the bed lowers and then pull back onto the road," Michael finished. "Then he'll just continue west on 40 for about three miles until he can get on I-70 eastbound."

"That sounds good," Jim said, nodding at Michael. "But I think we need him to exit back where he initially got on 40 coming to the crash site. We'll need him to get back to the wreck after Li is gone and hopefully before any law enforcement gets there."

"What about the ambulance?" Michael asked. "What if he arrives before we have a chance to reload the wreck?"

"That's my next point," Jim answered, looking at Gene. "How many ambulances does that station have?"

"I don't know," Gene answered, looking at Michael. "Have someone go up there tomorrow or the next day and find out. I'm sure Jim is trying to think of a way to stall them until we can clean up our accident."

"Exactly," Jim said, smiling at Gene. "Now, what do we do about the random car that may come along?"

"I'm going to say we do nothing for now," Gene answered. "That can be left to the wrecker driver and the couple in the pickup. If someone comes along before we set the car on fire, the wrecker driver can appear to be picking it up until the car leaves. If it's after the fire, the couple can tell them that the ambulance has been called along with the police. That should send them on their way."

"All right, that sounds workable," Jim said, looking from Gene to Michael. "We've only got a few days to do any fine-tuning on the plan, and I'd like for you to have Billy and the wrecker driver make a couple of runs. Especially the wrecker driver. Have him leave a chain or cable attached so he can pull the wreck back up quickly, but do a practice drop in the ditch to make sure nothing drags or catches that would stop it from being where we need it."

"That won't be a problem," Michael told him. "I'll have him out here tomorrow afternoon. When we were initially looking at the site, we came out at different times, and anywhere from 2 o'clock to 4 was the least traffic. Matter of fact, there were generally only two or three cars during that entire period. After 5:30 to 6 o'clock, it picks up considerably."

"It's just after three right now," Jim said, looking at his watch. "We'll plan on having the next run with Sun leaving the hotel about the same time as today. That should give us the best time frame to torch the car, put out the fire, and get it back on the wrecker."

"What about the bodies in the car?" Michael asked, looking at Jim.

"We'll let the wrecker driver take care of whatever's left of them," Jim said. "I'd recommend a tub of hydrofluoric acid. If there isn't much left after the fire, he may be able to just pour the acid over the remaining tissue. If that's too difficult, maybe there's a wrecking yard around here that will crush the car like in Pulp Fiction."

"Is there anything else?" Gene asked everybody. "Jim's brought up some good points, and we have our work cut out for us over the next few days."

Not hearing from anyone, he said, "Let's go into the kitchen and get something to eat. Michael, I want you to stand the first watch in case Li comes back unannounced. Billy can get something to eat and come relieve you."

"Yes, sir," Michael said as the rest of them headed for the kitchen. "Could I get someone to bring me a glass of tea or a Coke before you eat, please?"

"I'll get it for you," Jim said, following the rest of the people. "What's your first choice?"

"Unsweet tea," Michael answered, looking out between the curtains at the parked cars.

"Coming right up," Jim said when Gene handed him the pitcher of tea. Grabbing a glass and adding several ice cubes, he filled it and headed into the living room.

"Here you go," Jim said, handing him the glass. "Sorry, I couldn't get you a slice of lemon."

Michael took a big swig and said, "That's all right, Jim. This is just what I needed."

Lowering the glass, he asked, "What do you really think about the plan now?"

"I'm pretty happy," Jim finally answered. "Given that it's our first practice together and that a few holes have been exposed, I'm still pretty happy."

"But you still have doubts, don't you?" Michael asked, looking at him.

"Yes, I'll always have some doubts," Jim admitted. "Even on the day we actually do it. But, in the meantime, I'd like for you to sort of follow up on everything we've discussed today. I'm not sure exactly what your role is supposed to be, just a driver or something more. But I'm going to talk to Gene and recommend that you take over the practices and implement everything we've discussed."

"Are you sure?" Michael asked, surprised at the request. "I'm really just the driver. Sure, Gene has asked me to sort of watch over most of the transportation issues, but there's a shit load of little things that need to be done."

"Yes, there are," Jim agreed, nodding at him. "And Gene's too busy to get down in the weeds to take care of those annoying little details. I'm going to be back in Texas and won't be back until the next dress rehearsal, probably late Sunday afternoon. Someone has to step up and do it. You've already set up most of it with Billy, the wrecker, and getting everybody out here. I think you're perfectly capable of handling the rest of it. And, if you have a problem, I'll give you my phone number, and we can discuss it. How does that sound?"

"Fine," he answered as Billy came into the room. "I'm sure I'll be calling you 20 or 30 times a day about stuff, though."

"I really doubt that," Jim said as he led Michael into the kitchen. "I'm betting that when I get back in four or five days, you'll have everything in hand without having to call me even once."

"Hey guys," Billy called out as Jim was getting a sandwich. "Li just drove by again looking at the house."

"I'll bet he passes it a few more times before Sun and Hua head back to the hotel," Jim said before taking a bite. "He'll keep watch until their car leaves."

Chapter Fifty-six

An hour later, at the hotel, as they waited for Wang to join them, Jim asked, "Who's handling the explosives, and how will he get there?"

"A guy named Brett," Gene told him. "He was an Explosive Ordnance Disposal (EOD) Technician in the Navy before he joined Black Water. He couldn't be here today due to an assignment in the Middle East, but he'll be back tomorrow or the next day."

"He's going to be with Ron, the wrecker driver," Michael explained. "They'll be with us for the next practice run on Sunday. What time will you get here?"

"About the same as yesterday, 4:30 or so," Jim answered.

"That'll be tight if we want to stage the run to match the low traffic period," Michael told him.

"I don't need to be here for the run," Jim replied. "I'll join you when you get back here to the hotel. If you've already taken care of all the things we've discussed, we'll just make any final adjustments before we execute it Monday afternoon."

"Speaking of final adjustments," Gene interrupted, speaking to Jim, "I want you to be one of the couple that's waiting at the stop sign on US 40. You can pick your partner, but I want you there. Especially since they're going to be the ones who explain the wreck to anyone who stops there."

"Maybe you should use someone else," Jim suggested. "What if my flight is delayed or I'm removed from the trip? That person may also be the one to deal with Li when he comes back from the wreck. Or if he stops to look at it before going to the rental."

"No," Gene said emphatically. "If something happens to you, we'll move it to the next week. And the point about Li stopping is the main reason I want you there. Convincing him that Hua was in the wreck is the point behind this entire operation. I don't want to bring a new man in and try to bring him up to speed or handle a potentially deadly situation. So, who do you want?"

Jim thought for a second and answered, "Millicent."

"All right," Gene said, "I'll have her here Sunday for the practice run. She'll ride with Michael, and he can explain everything as they go to the rental. You'll have a chance to discuss how you guys will operate when we meet back here for the debriefing."

"I'll need a weapon," Jim told him. "And, I'd prefer for her to have a pistol also. But that'll be up to her. If she's not comfortable shooting someone, she doesn't need to be carrying it."

"I'll take care of it," Gene assured him. "What would you prefer?"

"Probably a Smith & Wesson M&P 40," Jim answered. "Load it with Winchester 165 grain PDX-1 Defender. If

Millicent wants a pistol, I'd recommend the same, except the Ranger ammunition because of the lighter recoil. But she can make that decision."

"Anything else?" Gene asked as Wang came in.

"No," Jim answered. "I can't think of anything right now."

"How'd it go with Li?" Gene asked as Wang got a glass of tea from the table.

"About as expected," he answered, taking a drink. "I followed him until he turned on Lookout Mountain, and then I went on past and to the next road, Rockland. I found a cemetery there about 1000 feet from where Lookout meets 40, and I watched him drive up and down Lookout several times. A couple of the times, it took him several minutes to come back, and I figured he may have stopped somewhere to take a walk around the property to see how to approach the house."

"What do you think, Jim?" Gene asked. "Will he try something if we do another practice run?"

"I don't think so," Jim answered. "If it was me, I wouldn't be sure where Hua was going after seeing her go there just one time. I'd wait, but Sun probably knows more about what he may do."

"I think he'll wait," Sun told them. "Although he's somewhat impulsive, he's probably been given instructions to make sure she's taken care of before the WHO meeting. That gives him a few days to make his plans, and I'll bet he knows that he'll only get one shot. So, I believe that he'll want to make sure she's not going shopping or somewhere else."

"Do you think he'll be armed next time?" Jim asked. "We don't know if he was this time or not, but if it was me, I'd be prepared in case the opportunity arose."

"I'm sure he'll be armed," Sun answered. "But he isn't sure of what he'll encounter at the house if that's where he intends to take care of her. I'm betting that he'll want a closer look at the house. Maybe next time, try to see inside since he's probably decided on his approach based on what Wang said."

"That's logical," Jim agreed. "To make a mistake at this point when all it takes is a little patience would be foolhardy. But I'd increase the security around her. Make sure everyone in the security detail can recognize Li on sight. I'd also get some cameras and motion detectors set up at the rental house before the next run. I'd hate for them to be sitting in the house and not knowing that he's creeping up on them."

"I'll take care of that," Gene said. "And I'll put four more agents in the house while Sun and Hua are there next time."

"I disagree," Jim said. "If he sees too many people at the house, he may decide not to do it there. He needs to see a relatively easy target like Sun and her, plus Michael and Millicent. Additional people will probably scare him off. If Michael and Sun are armed, you shouldn't need any additional people."

"I see your point," Gene said, nodding.

"And I'll be watching him," Wang added. "Unless he's recruited additional help, he's still alone, and I'll know if he's got anything other than a handgun. If he's not alone, I'll let you know, and we can make adjustments."

"He'll be alone," Sun told them. "He hasn't had anyone with him yet, according to Wang. And I'm sure he'd have had them by now if he intended to use them. The other thing is sort of what Jim was talking about when we first met. The PRC expects him to do as directed and also wants to keep the number of people that know what happened to a minimum."

"Okay," Gene decided. "We'll get the cameras and motion detectors in tomorrow and have everything ready for the practice on Sunday. Unless there's something else, I'll let you guys go, and we'll meet again then."

"Could you stay a minute?" Jim asked Michael as everyone started to leave.

"Sure," he answered. "What do you need?"

"Just to clear everything we discussed about you being in charge with Gene," Jim told him. "I want everyone involved to understand that you're going to be making the decisions between now and when I get back Sunday evening."

"Did I hear you mention my name?" Gene asked as the last of the people left the room.

"Yes, sir, you did," Jim answered. "I told Michael that I wanted him to be the point of contact when I'm not here. Someone has to implement all the things we've discussed and make sure it gets done. I can't be here, and you don't have time. But he works for you, not me. So, it's your decision, but he's my choice."

"I agree," Gene said, nodding. "The only caveat is that he keeps you informed. If you have any issues with how things are going, I expect you to find a way to get back up here or let me know that we need to delay the operation."

"I'll be in constant contact with Jim, sir," Michael told him. "He's already given me his number, and I plan on letting him know how everything is going. And, if for some reason I can't get in touch with him, I'll find some way to let you know."

"Good," Gene said, looking at both of them. "I'll give you my number also. Just don't use it unless someone needs reminding that you're carrying out Jim's orders or mine."

"I don't think there'll be any problem with that," Michael told him. "These are some of the best people I've worked with since I joined Black Water. Especially Sun and Wang. Even though they aren't connected with our organization, they are exceptionally cooperative."

"Yes, they are," Gene agreed. "Now, before we let Jim go to bed, let's find a nice steak house and have dinner. Then, you can take him back to the airport in the morning before you officially assume the responsibility for this operation."

Chapter Fifty-seven

Late Friday morning, Jim was washing his old 'Vette when a black Suburban pulled up to the curb in front of his house. As he turned the hose off, Gene, Michael, and Millicent got out and started walking up the driveway.

"Nice car," Michael said, admiring the classic 19two Corvette. "How long have you had it?"

"A little over 20 years," Jim answered, wondering why the three of them were here.

"From the look on your face, I'd say you're sort of surprised to see us," Gene said, reaching out to shake hands. "You've got the mouse that got caught eating the cheese look."

"Not really," Jim said as Millicent gave him a quick hug. "I've come to expect the unexpected. This should be a warning for you, Michael. You keep doing well with Black Water, and they'll come to believe they can interrupt your life any time or day of the year."

"Why don't you put your little car back in the garage and go with us to lunch?" Gene asked. "I know you're not quite done washing it, but we don't have all day."

"I guess it'd be fruitless to argue," Jim said, moving the bucket of soapy water from the front of the car. "And I guess it'd be too much to ask for you three to help me finish washing it before we go."

"Correct on both counts," Gene answered, smiling. "And as I've said once already, we don't have all day."

After shutting the garage door, Jim asked, "Any place special for lunch? Maybe a Sushi bar since Millicent didn't get to go last time?"

"How about Venice Pizza?" Gene suggested as he got into the front passenger seat. "I'm not sure Millicent will ever want sushi again."

"It's not the sushi," Millicent said as Michael held the rear door open for her. "It's the ride getting there that I'd worry about."

"Especially if Michael's driving," Jim said, getting in the back seat with her.

As Gene gave directions to the restaurant, Jim said, "I know there must be something major happening, or a simple phone call would've sufficed."

"Sort of," Gene told him. "We'll get into it a little more once we get to the restaurant, but we didn't want to keep practicing something that might not be the best option."

A few minutes later, after they parked at Venice Pizza, Jim led the way inside, telling the owner they'd like a table in the back room. Once they'd taken their seats and ordered, Jim asked, "Okay, what's the main problem?"

"You remember me telling you about Brett, the EOD guy," Gene answered. "Well, he got in yesterday and went with Ron, the wrecker driver, to the accident site. Michael went out also since he was going to check on the surveillance equipment at the rental house.

Anyway, after they got to the site and explained what we were needing, Brett brought up an interesting point," Gene added as their waitress brought a tray with their drinks.

Waiting for her to leave, Jim then asked, "Can't he do what we want? I thought you were going to use acetone and gasoline to torch the car after the wrecker drives off."

"We were," Gene told him. "But that brings up a problem with what to do with the car after we torch it. Why don't you explain it, Michael, since you were there?"

"It's not burning the car or the bodies," Michael told him. "It's the time required to extinguish the fire. Not to mention the smoke from the material in the seats. Brett says that the amount of heat generated from the acetone will set the rubber, plastic, and nylon in the seats and the seat covers on fire. That'll cause an enormous amount of smoke."

"We knew there'd probably be smoke," Jim argued. "That's why we were discussing the ambulance station down from the rental."

"It's not just the smoke," Michael told him. "It's what the fire will do, and not do. It *will* send a large amount of smoke into the air that will attract a lot of attention. It'll most likely be seen from I-70 or any houses within a couple of miles. That'll mean someone will call it in.

The other thing is what it won't do," he continued. "It won't eliminate the bodies, at least not unless we let it burn. And we can't load the car if it's burning. Add to that, even if we did manage to get the fire extinguished and the car loaded, we'd still have the problem with the now charred bodies."

"What we're looking at is probably a major change to the plan," Gene told him. "Michael wants to eliminate the fire part and just go with having Li see the wreck, go by the house, and return to the wreck. Then we can have the wreck, with the bodies still inside, removed as soon as he leaves."

"I was planning on the fire being one of the reasons Li wouldn't stop when he first sees the wreck," Jim told them. "If it's just a wreck, he may stop to look before going to the house."

"That's another thing," Gene said. "Brett and the folks at Quantico say that very few wrecks actually catch on fire. I believe that we need to adjust our plan around just a wreck, no fire."

Jim sat back, thinking as their meals arrived. "Okay," he said as the waitress left. "We're looking at two possibilities if we don't have the fire. First, Li sees the wreck and goes on to the house to see if the Corsica is there. The second scenario, and the one that troubles me, is that he stops at the wreck.

Under the first one, Millicent and I can be there when he comes back," he told them. "Li probably won't get out of his car if he believes that it's Hua in the wreck because he won't want to be placed at the scene. So, he may slow down to take a good look. But I think he'll drive on and confirm her death to his boss.

But if he stops before going by the house, he may get a good look at the bodies and know it's a setup," Jim continued. "Then the whole thing was a waste of time."

"I have a thought about that," Michael told them. "I've driven around that curve several times, and it's perfectly safe at over 70 miles per hour. If Li is trying to catch up with Hua,

I'm betting he'll be pushing it to the maximum. And unless the brakes on his car are better than on the one I was driving, he'll be halfway to Lookout Mountain Road before he can stop. I think he'll continue on because it's only a couple of thousand feet to where he expects to find her car anyway."

"Okay, he drives there and turns around when he sees that her car isn't there," Jim argued. "Then he comes back to the scene where he can get a better look. He may still not believe it's her in the wreck."

"Jim, I think you're overthinking this," Gene interrupted. "I believe that Li will go on to the house. He's already lost sight of her and wants to get there since that's where we think he's planning on killing her. Neither you nor I would stop when we can verify what we need to know by driving on for another few seconds. So, let's eliminate your second scenario for now."

"All right," Jim agreed. "So, he drives by, sees the wreck, goes by the house, and sees no car. He'll still come back to get a better look. I know you said the sizes of the bodies matched Hua and Sun, but if he gets a look at their faces, what then?"

"What if we have the female body half out of the car?" Michael asked. "And there's a large pool of blood around her head as he drives by. If we position it right, he'll only see the back of her head. Since the clothing will match, the car matches, it wasn't at the house; I think he'll come to the conclusion that she's dead."

"I've got to think about this," Jim said, sliding his chair back. "If you'll excuse me, I need to hit the head."

Chapter Fifty-eight

"Okay, the fire's out of the plan," Jim said, coming back to the table. "So, let's go with Li driving by, probably slowing somewhat, then going to the house. What's his next move?"

"I believe it depends on his initial impression as he passed the wreck," Millicent said. "If the body lying beside the overturned car looked like it possibly couldn't have survived the wreck or wouldn't make it to the hospital, he'll probably accept it."

"Worst case, he comes back and takes another look," Michael added. "By then, you and Millicent will be there. Then, if he stops, you can tell him you think they're both dead, but you've called for an ambulance."

"Okay, we'll go with that," Jim said. "I still want Brett there to help Ron unload and reload the car. And since you'll be there with me, Millicent, have you thought about carrying a gun? And using it?"

"I have," she answered. "I've taken some lessons at the Shoot Point Blank range in North Richland Hills. A Captain friend of mine named Rob Sproc took me and another Flight Attendant there a month or so ago. The instructor drilled it into us that if you have a gun and don't use it, someone will take it from you and shoot you with it. Never carry a gun unless you're willing to blow the back of someone's head off from three feet away."

"I know Rob. I flew with him a few months ago. Nice guy, but I think that philosophy is a little dramatic," Jim said, laughing. "I think you should put three rounds in his chest first. Then blow the back of his head off if you need to. But if you want to take the headshot first, go for it. Now, are you happy with the pistol I asked Gene to get for you?"

"It's good," she answered. "But I want the Defender ammunition. I was shooting a 45 at the range, and the recoil didn't bother me."

"Okay then, let's walk through this once more," Jim said, looking at Michael and Millicent, "Ron and Brett drop off the wreck and lay the female body beside the car with her face toward the car. The male is behind the wheel with blood running down his face. There's a shit load of blood. They head west on 40 past Lookout Mountain before they come back and park on Paradise, where they can come get the wreck as soon as we call.

We're a minute or so behind Li in our red pickup," he continued, looking at Millicent. "We stop at the wreck to prevent any lookie-loos from getting too curious. And we're there to reassure Li that Hua's dead when he comes back from the house. As soon as he drives away, we call for Ron to come get the wreck and dispose of it and the bodies."

"That's the way we gamed it," Gene agreed, nodding. "I talked to Sun again about Li's probable reaction, and he agreed. Li will probably accept the accident and call the PRC to tell them about it. The only thing we can't bet on is how far he may go to verify the death. Sun thinks he'll let it drop once he's called it in. He won't want to admit to being wrong. Sun even went so far as to bet that Li will drive past the house and make the call before he comes back to the wreck if we make it look good enough."

"Are we still monitoring all of his calls?" Jim asked.

"Yes, and we think we have the caller from the hotel," Michael told him. "Wang saw Li passing what looked like an envelope of money to one of the housekeeping maids. Since we started suspecting her, we've noticed that she pays considerable attention to Hua whenever she's there."

"I'm with Gene on this," Jim said. "I don't think it matters who it is. But, when this is all over, maybe she needs to get her notice of deportation. What about the surveillance equipment at the house?"

"It's all up and running," Michael answered. "We have coverage from Lookout Road, where it joins US 40 up to the ambulance station. There isn't a square inch of the area in between there 100 yards deep that we can't see. We've set up a monitor inside the house and a relay that sends it to Gene's room at the hotel. There's no way Li, or a little brown tit mouse, can get within 100 yards of that house unseen."

"Do we have the pickup?" Jim asked, looking at Gene.

"Yep. A slightly beat up, but still bright red, double cab dually one-ton Chevrolet," Gene answered. "The rear windows are heavily tinted, and the top of Li's car only comes up to about the bottom of the windows. Between Billy's truck and you, Li can't see a damned thing in the direction of Paradise Road. If Billy delays as much as 30 seconds, Sun will be well off 40 before Li leaves the stop sign."

"That all sounds good. Now, what are you guys' plans for the next couple of days?" Jim asked as they were finishing their meals.

"Billy has made a couple of trial runs already, and Millicent and I will take the truck out there with him tomorrow morning to look at the exact spot we'll need to park," Michael answered. "Ron's happy with how he'll unload and reload with Brett's help. He says he'll just barely have to slow down, and he's got plenty of time if we call him as we're leaving the hotel.

Tomorrow morning, we'll have everybody except Sun and Hua make a trial run," he continued. "Millicent and I'll be in the red pickup. Billy will drive his 18-wheeler, and Ron will bring his wrecker. A couple of agents will be behind us in the Suburban to watch and time everything."

"Have you considered that Li may go out to the house and rig it?" Jim suddenly asked Gene. "That may be the way he intends to get rid of Hua. Blow the house with her in it."

"No," Gene admitted. "But we'll sweep it tomorrow when we get back. Wang has been on his tail night and day and hasn't said anything about his going back out there. But we'll make sure tomorrow. After we do that, I'll relay my feed of the surveillance to Quantico and have someone monitor it 24 hours a day."

"Good," Jim said thoughtfully. "Now, what about Sunday? Are you still planning for Sun and Hua to go back out there?"

"Yes," Gene answered. "You should be in town early enough to be with me monitoring their progress and be there for the debrief."

"Are all of the radios ready?" Jim asked. "I'd like for everybody to have those for at least Sunday evening, if not for the run tomorrow morning. Nothing worse than a radio system that doesn't work."

"They'll have them," Gene assured him. "And, we'll have one tied to them in my room so we can hear minute by minute how things go."

"Well, hell," Jim said, leaning back. "I guess there's nothing for me to do except go home and wash my car. I still don't know why you just didn't call me and say my plan sucked and you'd brief me on the new one when I get there Sunday afternoon."

"Let's go, folks," Gene said, shaking his head and smiling as he picked up the ticket for their meals. "Let's not waste any more of Jim's time. His shiny car is much more important than the life or death of a person that the Secretary of State has charged us with protecting."

Chapter Fifty-nine

When Jim arrived at the airport for his first flight of the trip, he noticed that Kit was no longer the Captain for the leg to Albuquerque. Checking further, he saw that Captain Mike Knox had replaced him for the entire sequence. Smiling as he signed in, he thought about how happy Merna would be not to have to deal with him.

As soon as he arrived at the gate, she was there talking to two other Flight Attendants. When she saw him walking up, she jumped up, grinning, and said, "Guess what?"

"I already know," Jim said, returning her grin. "Captain Carson isn't going to be with us."

"Yes," she almost screamed. "I was debating calling in sick just to avoid him; now I'm glad I didn't. Do you know the new Captain?"

"No," Jim said as he told the gate agent that he was going down to the airplane. "But how bad could he be compared to Captain Kit?"

"You never know," Merna said as she and the other Flight Attendants grabbed their bags. "I guess we'll find out. I'll go down with you and start a pot of coffee. Is there anything else you'd like?"

"A Mrs. T Bloody Mary mix, with a lime if you have it," Jim answered as they went down the jet bridge. "No ice, please."

"You got it, sweetheart," she told him. "I'll even put a little something extra in, definitely not Visine, if you'd like."

"Just the mix will be wonderful," Jim said as he tossed his suitcase in the closet. "Just a little early for me to start celebrating."

"I know," Merna said, pulling out the cart that held the drinks. "But right now, I feel like celebrating."

After turning on the exterior lights, Jim said, "I'm sure you do. Maybe you and the other ladies can sneak a small bottle or two off for this evening in your rooms. One of those bottles that the first-class passengers drank, of course."

When Jim came back from inspecting the exterior of the airplane, he met Captain Knox standing in the first-class galley talking to Merna. "Good morning, Captain," he said as he stepped into the airplane. "I'm Jim Lashley, your First Officer for the trip."

"Good morning, Jim," he said, shaking hands. "Please, just call me Mike. It's good to meet you."

Turning back to Merna, he said, "If you guys need any help back here, don't hesitate to ask. As far as I'm concerned, we're just one big happy family, and if one of us has a problem, we all have one."

"Yes sir, Captain," she told him as he started to go into the cockpit.

"And, like I said, it's Mike," he told her. "And I'd like a cup of black coffee when you get a chance, please, Merna."

"So, Jim, how long have you been on the 80?" Mike asked, taking his seat.

"About five years," Jim answered as he pulled his earpiece and microphone out of his bag. "How about you?"

"About five months, counting the school-house," he responded, laughing. "This is my first trip as a new Captain. I think the reason I got this trip was because you have so much time on the MD 80. So, watch me very carefully and keep us out of trouble."

"Well, if you want, you can fly every leg," Jim offered. "I certainly don't mind."

"Oh no," Mike said. "I'd rather watch and learn something. I already know what I already know. I'm hoping you can teach me some of the finer techniques of flying this plane. How about you fly to Albuquerque, and I'll fly back here and then to Denver? Tomorrow, you fly back here and then to Denver again. I'll take the last leg home Tuesday."

"That's fine with me," Jim said. "There's not supposed to be any bad weather; at least, that's what the weather guessers say. But, if something comes up, just say the word, and we'll change legs. As I said, you can fly every leg or any one you want. I've been in and out of ABQ and DEN several times this month already."

"Good enough," Mike said as Merna handed him a cup of coffee and Jim the Mrs. T Bloody Mary mix. "Thanks, Miss Merna. Did they put meals on for Jim and me?"

"Yes, sir," she answered. "When would you like to eat?"

"I'll give you a call," he told her, smiling. "It's Jim's leg, so he gets his choice. Unless there's chicken fried steak and eggs over medium with hash browns and cream gravy, then I get the first choice."

"You must be a country boy," Merna said, laughing. "And I'm sure you know full well that there's never been either chicken fried steak or over medium eggs on any American Airlines flight. Sometimes there's those scrambled powdered egg things with rubberized chicken parts sausage, which we do have today, and a box of some cereal and fruit."

"Sounds delicious," Mike told her. "I'll give you a call, but don't interrupt the normal service back there for us. Those people get taken care of first."

"I'm sure I'll find time in my busy schedule to take care of you guys," she replied as passengers started to fill the first-class section. "And I guess I better get to work now that people are here. Call if you need anything."

"Nice lady," Mike said as she left. "Have you been flying with her all of this month?"

"Yeah," Jim answered as he put his checklist on his yoke. "And she is very nice. I've flown with her before, don't remember when, but she's always been great to work with."

"Good," Mike said. "Now, I guess we need to get to work, too. Before starting checklist, please."

Five hours later, after taking off from DFW and heading to DEN, Mike asked, "Are you doing anything tonight?"

"Meeting an old Marine buddy for dinner," Jim answered as he took the departure plate from his control yoke and put it away. "What about you?"

"Nothing, just hanging out at the hotel," Mike told him. "I may see if there's a little bar around the hotel somewhere and slip out for a beer."

"I'm sure there's one close by," Jim said. "I'd ask the desk clerk. Probably not while you're in uniform, though."

"I may have slammed my head a few times, landing on the carriers, but I do have a couple of working brain cells," Mike told him, laughing.

"That's right," Jim replied, nodding. "Carrier landings can be a bit abrupt."

"I think that's why it took me so long to become a Captain here," Mike said. "I kept trying to catch the number three wire and slammed it on."

"What's a Navy puke's definition of a good landing?" Jim asked. "Anything you can walk away from, isn't it?"

"Pretty much," Mike agreed, unstrapping. "Now I'm much more genteel with my flying. Don't want to spill the coffee back there. Anyway, you've got the jet while I run to the head."

"I've got the jet," Jim acknowledged, putting his earpiece back in. "See if Merna has a spare Dr. Pepper before you come back if you don't mind."

"I'm sure she does," Mike said, opening the cockpit door. "I'll let her know."

"Direct Lamar, expecting the Quail Four, maintain 320," Jim was saying into his microphone when Mike came back into the cockpit, handing him a glass of ice with a wedge of lime and an unopened Dr. Pepper.

Taking his seat and strapping back in, Mike said, "I've got the jet. Understand Lamar and Quail Four at 320."

"You've got the jet," Jim repeated as he watched Mike change the GPS destination to Lamar. "Everybody happy back there?"

"So it seems," Mike answered as he put his earpiece in. "Have you called for the weather and gate information?"

"Just did," Jim told him. "It should be coming in any minute now."

About an hour later, as they were in the elevator going to their hotel rooms, Jim told Mike and Merna that he'd see them tomorrow and to have a good evening.

As soon as he closed his door, he called Gene's number and said he'd be ready to go as soon as the car got there. Hearing that a driver named Tim would be there in 10 minutes, he changed into his jeans and T-shirt, hoping that the practice run with Sun and Hua was going well.

Chapter Sixty

As Jim walked off the elevator, he saw a guy he didn't know coming through the entrance doors. Noticing the black knit shirt with 'Tim' written over the breast pocket, he walked up and put his hand out, saying, "Hello, Tim. I'm Jim Lashley. Gene said you'd be here to take me to his hotel."

"Yes, sir," Tim answered, shaking Jim's hand. "If you're ready, we'll go now. It shouldn't take but about 15 minutes with the traffic."

"Let's go," Jim answered as they headed out of the hotel. "How's the General today?"

"Normal," Tim said as they got into the black Suburban. "He's always been sort of quiet, never says what's on his mind."

"That's him," Jim agreed as they pulled onto the road. "I've known him for almost 30 years and still can't read the man."

"What is he, maybe 70?" Tim asked as they maneuvered around the slower cars.

"That's probably close," Jim answered. "I'm guessing he was in his early 40s when I met him. So yeah, about 70 or so."

A few minutes later, as they pulled up to the Embassy Suites, Tim said, "Well, you have a nice day. I'm not sure if

I'm supposed to take you back or not, but it was nice to meet you."

"Nice to meet you, too," Jim replied as he got out. "I'm sure someone will let you know if I need a ride back. Take care."

Getting off the elevator on the fourth floor, Jim headed to room 405. Knocking on the door, he waited until he heard Gene saying, "Hang on just a second. I'll be right there.

Good afternoon, Jim," he said, opening the door. "How's your day been?"

"Just fine, sir," Jim answered, following Gene to a table where a computer screen showed several views of the area around the rental. "How's the practice going?"

"Pretty much as expected," Gene answered as one of the radios on the table came to life. Listening to Wang saying that Li was getting back in his car, he added, "Those cameras were a good idea. Li went all around the house and looked in a couple of the windows with binoculars. I think he's trying to decide where to take the shot."

"I imagine you're right," Jim agreed as the view of the front door showed Sun and Hua leaving the house. "I'm willing to bet that the next time he sees them leave the hotel, he'll be ready."

"Yeah, and I wish we knew what he plans to do," Gene said as Hua and Sun got in their car. "I'm not really worried about him trying to blow up the house unless he comes back tonight or tomorrow morning to plant the explosives. And, if he does that, Wang will know."

"He could always bring a small satchel bomb next time he follows Sun," Jim argued. "If a bomb was my plan, I'd probably wait and throw it through the window into the room where they were.

I bet he believes if he brought it out too early, someone might discover it," he continued. "I'm sure he thinks that Hua is meeting with someone from our government and that any safe house would be swept for bugs and explosives before she arrives."

"What's your suggestion regarding the possibility of a bomb?" Gene asked, watching Sun drive away.

"Get a bomb team to sniff Li's car tonight when Wang says it's clear," Jim answered. "If there's nothing there tonight, Wang should be able to see if he brings anything down that might be a bomb. One other thing we could do is get a look at Li's room. See if there's anything that could be used to make a bomb is there."

"I'll get someone on it," Gene said, picking up his phone. "Anything else?"

"Not that I can think of right now," Jim answered, hearing Wang say he was leaving and following Li. "Let's wait until we hear from the team. They may have some new ideas."

A few minutes later, they saw Michael and Millicent come out of the house and get into their Suburban. Hearing that they were leaving, there were a couple of other radio calls acknowledging the practice was over. "Okay, everybody, let's meet at the hotel in 30 minutes. Don't forget to come in one at a time and get off at different floors like we discussed yesterday."

"Looks like Michael has taken over," Jim said, smiling.

"Yes, and he's doing a great job. He recognizes a problem and does something about it," Gene acknowledged as he turned away from the table. "Reminds me of someone I met in Vietnam many, many years ago."

"That brings up a personal question," Jim said, looking at Gene.

"What's that?" Gene asked, leaning back in his chair.

Pausing as he thought about how to phrase the question, he finally asked, "How many more years do you think you'll keep working for Black Water?"

"Fifty, maybe fifty-five," Gene said, laughing. "What about you?

"Fifty, maybe fifty-five," Jim said, smiling at Gene's answer. "I guess I'll stick around as long as you're here."

"You don't think you'll ever want to move up, maybe take over for me?" Gene asked, getting up. "You know that you'll have to retire from American when you're 60. What'll you do after that? Get a job at Walmart selling ladies' shoes? I can't see you as a shoe clerk."

"I haven't thought that far ahead," Jim admitted, following Gene to the couch. "And I'm not sure if Jennifer would like to move up to Virginia if I did."

"That woman will follow you through the gates of hell, and you know it," Gene argued. "You *know* that. The question is really what you'd tell her about your new job."

"Probably the same thing you've been telling her for years," Jim replied, smiling. *"I'm just a consultant to an international security company regarding concerns of our major clients around the world."*

"I don't think that'll work for you," Gene told him. "If my wife was still alive, she'd see right through that bullshit in two seconds. So will Jennifer if you try to pull it on her."

"And your suggestion would be?" Jim asked.

"Probably the truth," Gene advised. "Maybe not all of it. But at least let her know that you work for Black Water. She's smart enough to figure out that it's not just a consultation company. And she's also smart enough to know not to ask questions when she really doesn't want to hear the answer."

"Yeah," Jim said, looking at the ceiling. "She knew that my trips in the Marines weren't to help run a daycare center for underprivileged ragheads. She'd probably be all right with me being a *security consultant.*"

"What brought this about?" Gene asked as someone knocked on the door.

"Nothing," Jim answered, getting up to follow Gene. "I was just wondering if I'd keep working with whoever was your replacement when you decide to retire."

"Good afternoon, sir," the waiter at the door said as Gene opened it. "The buffet you ordered is set up in 406 as you requested. Will there be anything else?"

"Not right now," Gene said, handing him two twenties and a ten-dollar bill. "But would you please stop by in about an hour? I'd appreciate it."

Looking at the 50-dollar tip, the waiter smiled and said, "I'll look in on you every few minutes, sir. Thank you very much."

"Let's go check out our buffet," Gene said, pulling the door closed behind them. "That pack of wolves will get here soon, and they won't leave a shred of lettuce for us. Now, what's this about me retiring?"

Chapter Sixty-one

Jim and Gene were sitting on the couch eating when Michael and Millicent came in. "Did you guys save any for us?" he asked, looking at their half-empty plates.

"Not any of the good stuff," Gene answered. "We left you some sandwich material and a few chips. We're the ones that did all the work today. You're lucky we left anything."

"What do you think, Jim?" Michael asked as he picked at the sandwich makings. "Did you get in early enough to hear everything?"

"Not a lot," he answered, looking at Millicent and back to Michael. "I got here about the time Li was going back to his car. Besides, I'd rather hear what you guys have to say."

"I'm pretty happy with it," Michael said as he built his sandwich and grabbed some chips. "Millicent and I drove the pickup out with Billy and his truck this morning and looked at the best placement to give the maximum blockage. Ron and Brett followed in his wrecker with the accident car on it. I asked them to stop in this afternoon for the debrief. They should be here any time now.

One of Gene's guys led us out there, taking Sun's place," he continued. "We timed how long it would take him

313

to leave the stop sign, turn left on 40, exit on Paradise Road, and drive about 1,500 feet up it to where it curves to the right. Even if Li looks up that road as he passes it, Sun's car will be completely out of sight."

"That was a good idea," Jim agreed, nodding. "How long did it take?"

"A minute and 15 seconds," Michael answered. "He was turning onto Paradise at 40 seconds and was at the curve to the right 20 seconds later. The other 15 seconds put him completely out of sight of the road."

"That's good," Jim told him. "How did delaying Ron behind you go?"

"It went fine," Michael said as Ron and Brett came in. "Since they're here, I'll let them tell you."

"Good afternoon, Jim," Ron said, walking over to shake hands. "How was your flight in?"

"Normal, as usual," Jim answered, standing to shake. "I understand you drove back out today to help Michael with the timing; how did that go?"

"I thought it went well," he answered as he watched Brett fill a plate. "That was only part of what we went out for."

"Yeah, Michael said you took the accident car out with you," Jim replied. "I'm assuming that you and Brett did that to do a little unloading and reloading."

"Yep, I wanted to do it on-site to make sure it slid off easily, and we could pull it back up quickly," he confirmed as Brett came up.

"And?" Jim asked.

"Just fine," Ron said, looking at Brett as they both nodded. "It slid off without a hitch. When we stepped on the road and looked at it, it appeared to have rolled over as it left the road and landed on its top."

"Looked like a normal rollover to me," Brett agreed. "The only thing an accident investigator might think was odd was that there weren't any skid marks or gouges in the ditch leading up to the wreck."

"I'm hoping we don't have to worry about investigators," Gene added, getting up. "What else did you do?"

"Ron had me lay down beside the car like I had been thrown out and positioned me so that anyone on the road would see the back of my head," Brett answered, smiling. "My biggest worry was if someone came speeding around the curve, they might run over me. It's a pretty narrow area between the car and the road."

"That's a concern," Jim told them as he envisioned Li speeding after what he thought was Hua. "Just how far from the road will you put the body?"

"I think it would be better if we stuck her feet in through the car window," he answered. "That might make it look even better, sort of like she may have been part of the way out when the car came to rest on its top."

"I agree," Ron said, heading over to the buffet table. "I don't think Li will be going too fast since he's driven that road before, but the extra couple of feet makes it look better. The only thing that worries me is the blood. It's mainly grass where the car will be, and the blood would disappear in it."

"I think just having it on her head and dress will be good enough," Jim told them. "None of this will stand up to close scrutiny. All it has to do is make Li think it was bad enough to have killed Hua.

Speaking of Hua, how are you?" Jim asked as she walked in with Sun.

"Very well," she replied with a slight bow. "But I'll really be glad when this is over, and I can go back to a normal life."

"I'm afraid our lives will never be normal again," Sun said, shaking Jim's hand. "But at least now we have a chance at life. For that, we both thank you."

"No, we thank you," Gene said, bowing slightly to Hua and Sun. "You've already sacrificed more than could be expected. "We, all of us, thank you and are here to try to give you a somewhat reasonable chance at what we hope will be a long and happy life.

Please, get something to eat while we talk to everybody," Gene told them with a wave of his arm. "Then, we'll see if you have anything to add. We want to get this right tomorrow because we may never get another chance."

"All right, back to the wreck," Jim said to Ron, "what else did you learn?"

"That's about it," he answered, looking from Brett back to Jim. "Brett, do you have anything to add?"

"Not really," he said, shaking his head. "Having two of us hooking up the cables and chains made it go pretty quick. Although we left the wrecker just a few feet in front of the car, it only took a couple of minutes to back up and pull it back onto the bed. I'd say once we get notified to come get it, we'll be pulling away with it on the truck in less than ten minutes."

"I'd agree with that," Ron added. "And, like we talked about, it would look normal to see a wrecker picking up a car if someone drove by. Since we'll put the bodies back in the car as soon as we get back, the only chance someone other than Li will see her lying beside the road will be pretty much when you and Millicent are there in the pickup."

"Speaking of Li, I got out of the wrecker and stood by the right front bumper when the driver of what we call the Sun car pulled away from the stop sign," Brett told them. "I walked along as Ron drove to the stop sign so I could see what it would look like from a lower point of view."

"What did you think?" Michael asked.

"I was at least a foot taller than where Li's vision would be in his car," Brett answered. "I couldn't see over the pickup where you and Millicent will be sitting. I lost view of the car the minute it turned left on 40."

"Okay, that's good work," Jim told them as he saw Billy come in. "Do you have anything else to add?"

"Only that it took us almost three minutes from when we stopped behind Billy's truck until we left the stop sign," Ron told him. "That counts from when the Sun car first pulled up to the stop sign. It was only just a little under a minute before that car left, and Billy pulled up and stopped."

"So, about two minutes from when Billy started making his left turn, you were at the stop sign," Jim replied. "That's about 45 seconds longer than it took the Sun car to get out of sight on Paradise Road. That's great.

What about you, Billy?" Jim asked as he came over with a plate of chips and a sandwich.

"Piece of cake," he answered around a bite of his sandwich. "I could give you a little more time if you think you may need it."

"No, what you did will work great," Jim told him, smiling. "I think that part of our little scene will go all right. You guys have done more than I expected, and the only thing that may screw it up is Li. And we can't exactly predict or control what he'll do. Now, if you'll excuse me, I need to visit the gentlemen's room."

Chapter Sixty-two

"Okay, if everybody's happy with what you guys did this morning, how'd it go this afternoon with Li following you?" Jim asked, coming in from the bathroom.

"Good, I think," Michael answered, looking at Millicent. "We went out in the Suburban about 30 minutes ahead of Sun and Hua. The communication setup works great, as it also did this morning. Everybody could hear everybody else. The only thing I couldn't hear was Wang's communication with whoever's monitoring Li's phone."

"That's all right as long as you can hear Wang," Jim told him. "All we really need from Wang, other than something out of the ordinary, is to tell us when Li calls in Hua's death. That side of the conversation would only be a distraction to you guys. Matter of fact, even when you hear him call in her death, keep doing whatever you're doing until I say otherwise."

"What about us?" Ron asked. "Won't we need to come get the wreck as soon as possible?"

"Not until I call you specifically to come get it," Jim answered, looking at him and Brett. "I want everyone to stay where they are until I can confirm that Li has called in, reporting she's dead and that he's heading back to his room.

Wang will be the one that confirms both of those since he's following him.

What about you guys?" Jim asked Sun and Hua. "What do you think about this afternoon's practice? Anything you want to add?"

As Hua shook her head, Sun said, "I was a little concerned about Li getting that close to the house. I realize that we had to make him believe that we were there, but I thought it was too risky."

"I understand," Gene said, putting his hand on Sun's shoulder. "But I was sitting here watching every step he took. I don't know if he had a gun or not. I'm going to assume he may have had a pistol, but if he had taken it out, I would have been yelling at everyone. Michael and Millicent both had weapons, as did you. I would have told you immediately to take whatever action to both safeguard her and take Li out. This was entirely my decision, and I'll take responsibility for putting both of you in an uncomfortable position. But I truly think it was necessary to give Li the illusion that he could accomplish his task out there where we have control. Otherwise, we may have never known where he'd try to get both of you."

"I appreciate your understanding," Sun said with a slight bow. "It's just that seeing him that close was unsettling. After the problem with your man in San Francisco, I'm still a little cautious when I don't have complete control over where she is or, more importantly, who else knows where she is."

"I'll be fine," Hua said, taking Sun's hand. "You've done so much for me up until now. I trust these men almost as much as I trust you. I'll do as they ask, and I'm asking you to do the same. Maybe you can't truly trust them as I do, but I think you should try. The rest of our lives now depend on these gentlemen and ladies. If things go wrong, then that's fate. At least we did our best. Now it's time to let them do their best."

"We'll do our best," Jim assured him as Wang came in. "I hope that what you've seen will give you some confidence that we know what we're doing. The incident with the man in San Francisco was unfortunate but an isolated event. You've been around these people enough to know that they all want to help. And, if you do see something you think is wrong, Gene will listen and make sure you're satisfied with whatever needs to be done. With a little luck, this'll all be over tomorrow evening and you can start rebuilding your lives."

"Did I miss anything?" Wang asked after bowing to Hua. "I took a little longer than usual to get here to watch Li's house."

"Anything unusual?" Jim asked.

"Someone delivered a couple of sacks," Wang answered. "I couldn't tell what was in them. Could have been groceries or something."

Jim looked at Gene and said, "I doubt it was groceries. Especially since he hasn't ordered any since he's been here, and we're betting that he plans to leave town tomorrow."

"Brett, how much material would you need to build a satchel bomb big enough to blow up a room about the same size as this one?" Jim asked.

"Not much," Brett answered with a puzzled look. "What are you getting at?"

"Gene and I had a discussion earlier this afternoon about Li trying to blow up the house instead of shooting Hua," Jim told him, looking at Gene. "I told him that I would use something I could throw through the window into whichever room she was in."

Brett thought for a minute and said, "I could build one powerful enough to kill everyone here with just a shoebox of material. I didn't go look at the house, but if it's normal single or just double pane glass, a five or ten-pound suitcase would go through the window. Probably have a timer on the detonator to give him time to get away. The only obstacle might be if there are screens on the windows."

"What would you do if there were?" Gene asked. "Would that slow you down?"

"Not really," Brett answered. "Since Li has reconnoitered the house, he'll know what type of screens are there. Probably standard plastic or light wire mesh. Either could be taken care of with a box cutter. Just slice an 'X' in the screen and toss the suitcase in. An extra five seconds, maybe."

"What have you found out about having someone sniff his car for a bomb?" Jim asked Gene.

"The Denver Police Department has a very reliable dog," Gene answered. "They've been notified and are just waiting for Li to come back. I'll make the call right now."

"Do you think we need to run the dog by his room?" Wang asked. "Since the material for the bomb, if that's what was in the sacks, is there and not in his car?"

"No, absolutely not," Jim told him, looking at Gene. "We don't want to disrupt his plan. Right now, he thinks he can approach the house with Hua inside, toss in a bomb, and be done.

We know that she won't be there, and he won't see her car there after seeing the wreck," he continued, looking at each of them. "He'll just go on by and think that he won't need to use it. If we alert him, he'll just change his plans. The only reason I want to know is so that we can be watching for it."

"Do you want to call off the Denver guy's dog?" Gene asked.

"What time does Li normally leave his room?" Jim asked Wang. "More specifically, does he drive to breakfast or somewhere we could walk the dog by without his noticing?"

"He usually leaves around eight or nine," Wang confirmed. "There's an IHOP on Colorado Blvd where he goes for breakfast most of the time. I'll be watching when he comes down in the morning to see if he puts a suitcase or anything in his car."

"That's good, but a suitcase could just be full of his clothes," Jim explained. "I'd prefer to have them send the dog by. Just make sure that the Denver Police don't do anything other than let us know."

"I'll go with them," Michael volunteered. "If Gene can get me clearance, I'll make sure we just walk by and let the dog alert. Then we'll just keep going, and I'll call back here to let you guys know."

"I'll cancel the Denver guys and get someone from down at Cheyenne Mountain's bomb squad to come up here in the morning," Gene told Michael. "I'll have them here at six, and you can check with Wang about where you need to go. I'd rather have complete control than depend on the local guys. Anything else before we break until noon tomorrow?"

Hearing nothing, Gene said, "All right. I want everyone here no later than 12 o'clock. We'll have a final brief to cover anything we find out about the possible bomb and anything else you may think of between now and then."

Turning to Jim, he said, "I'll have Tim take you back to your hotel. Is there anything else you want to know?"

"No, just about the bomb for now," Jim answered. "But you know how to reach me if you need to."

"Yes, I do," Gene said, walking to the door. "I'll go to my room and call Tim. I'll see you around noon tomorrow, and Tim will pick you up at your hotel again. Have a good night."

Chapter Sixty-three

The next morning, Jim was having a cup of coffee from the machine in the lobby when Merna came down, pulling her suitcase. "Good morning, Jim," she said as she parked her rollaboard next to his. "How was your evening?"

"Good," he said, standing. "Did you guys do anything?"

"Mike talked us into going to a little bar down the block," she answered, getting some coffee. "He's such a nice guy. Sort of worried that he might make a mistake since he's a new Captain. Anyway, we had fun. He started telling stories about his life in the Navy, his wife, and his kids. It was fun."

"He's a good guy," Jim agreed as he saw the other two Flight Attendants getting off the elevator. "He'll make a great Captain. I wish he'd be with us for the rest of the month instead of just this trip."

"You and me both," Merna agreed. "Just the thought of Captain Kit makes me ill."

"Holy shit!" Jim exclaimed, laughing. "I never thought of that, Captain Kit. You know, the pirate. Except his name was spelled Kidd. He's the love pirate!"

Merna almost spat her coffee out laughing and said, "That's about the biggest misnomer I've ever heard. A love pirate."

"What are you guys laughing about?" one of the Flight Attendants asked, getting a cup of coffee.

"Jim just figured out that the other Captain, Carson, who called himself Kit, sounded like Captain Kidd, the pirate," she told them, seeing Mike walking toward them. "Then he told me that Kit, now Kidd, was the love pirate. Here to steal your heart."

"Like that would ever happen," the other one said. "Gross. Love pirate."

"Good morning, everyone," Mike said as he joined them. "What a great day to go flying. What say we run down to Dallas, kick everyone off except us, and then head down to Puerto Vallarta for the afternoon?"

"Now that's what an average Captain would do," Jim joked as they headed for the door. "We've decided that you're capable of so much more."

"Such as?" Mike asked as the driver tossed his bags in the back of the shuttle.

"Maybe Belize," Jim offered as they got in the shuttle. "Get each of us our own little cabana, drinking rum out of a coconut, fried bananas, and fresh shrimp on a kabob. That's your style."

"That sounds great," Mike said as they headed to the airport. "I'll give my wife a quick call so she can get the kids ready, and we'll head on down. Wait a minute, do all of you have your passports?"

"I don't," Jim said, going along with the jest. "I'd have to run home and get it. Do you think they'd let us delay an hour or so?"

"Probably not," Merna chimed in. "I always keep mine just in case I need it to fill in an international flight."

"We do, too," the others said.

"Well, shit," Mike said, trying to look despondent. "My wife is going to be very disappointed. And the kids will be heartbroken. They've been looking forward to this trip for almost five minutes."

"I'm sorry, guys," Jim told them with a sad look. "I wish I'd brought mine. You guys go on without me."

"Nope," Mike said, looking around at the Flight Attendants. "We made a pact last night. We stick together. All for one and one for all!"

"Isn't that the motto for the Three Musketeers?" Jim asked. "Looks to me like there're four of you."

"I knew you'd catch us," Merna said, laughing. "But Mike told us you were a Marine and probably couldn't count past two."

"And you'd take the word of a sailor?" Jim asked aghast. "They're all known miscreants. Purveyors of falsehoods. A girl in every port and a hundred inappropriate tattoos that depict their deviant lifestyle."

Mike just smiled and said, "I'll have you know I only have 40 tattoos. Now, who do you believe? Me, a down to earth admirer of that great sailor, John Paul Jones, the man who gave us that famous quote, 'I have not yet begun to fight', or this smooth talking Gyrene that I'm stuck with for the next two days?"

"I'll take one from column A and one from column B," Merna answered him as they pulled into the airport. "I just wish you would be stuck with all of us for the rest of the month. This is the type of crew that I came here to work with."

"Thank you, my lady," Mike said, bowing and doffing his hat. "It's been my life's ambition to toil tirelessly beside such a wonderful group. Unfortunately, I'm of the lowly status as the most junior Captain in the Dallas realm and not worthy of such a splendid crew. Alas, I must retreat into the darkness of reserve status after tomorrow. Such is my fate."

"And I thought I was full of crap," Jim said, laughing as he got off the shuttle. "Good thing I'm wearing boots. I'll just have to tuck my pant legs in the tops."

"My oh my," Mike said as they were getting their bags and tipping the driver. "A Marine *and* a shit kicker. I thought scheduling was supposed to take it easy on us new guys."

"Oh, Grasshopper, you are so naive," Jim told him as they headed into the airport. "You are unwise in the ways of the world. Although I only have three more legs to complete your transition from larva to a magnificent butterfly, I shall do my utmost to make you a Captain among Captains. It's my burden, yet I carry it proudly."

"Okay, guys," Merna whispered. "I think the people in here are starting to wonder if maybe they should take the bus."

"Well, it *is* Jim's leg to DFW and back," Mike told them softly. "Maybe we should go with them."

"All because I didn't bring my passport," Jim told them as they cleared the security. "Now, you blame me for missing out on the Belize trip. Isn't it enough that I have to share the cockpit with such a scoundrel?"

"Arrgh. Ye could have been sharing it with a swarthy mate," Mike said, trying to sound like a pirate. "A mutineer he be, and he swang from the yardarm as the treasonous should."

"I guess you overheard our discussion about our last Captain," Merna said as they approached their gate.

"That I did," Mike answered, smiling as he stepped behind the desk. "My great great granddaddy told me to keep my ears open and my mouth shut. He said the only things you'll ever catch with an open mouth are flies. But that's all right. Most of us who've been around long enough to become a Captain have heard about most of the ones that either the First Officers or the Flight Attendants don't want to fly with. And we had to fly with a lot of them when we were First Officers."

"Aye, Captain," Jim said smiling, heading for the jet bridge door, "I'll be checking the ship by your leave."

"Take your time, Jim. I'll be right down," Mike answered as the gate agent came up. "How are you doing this morning, ma'am?"

"Just fine, Captain," she answered, signing into her computer. "Looks like a full load heading to Dallas this morning."

"I just saw that," Mike said, tearing the computer sheets off. "Any nonrevs?"

"Only one, a Captain commuting to Dallas for a trip," she told him, nodding to a man wearing an American Airlines uniform with four stripes on his sleeves.

"No seats in the back?" Mike asked before leaving.

"Doesn't look like it," she answered, rechecking her list. "I'll wait until we finish boarding if you'd like."

"No, go ahead and give him the jump seat," Mike told her. "Tell him to come on down at his convenience."

"Yes, sir," she said, motioning to the man. "I'll let him know."

"Thanks," Mike said, going to the jet bridge door. "Let me know if I can help you."

Chapter Sixty-four

After returning from Dallas and getting to their layover hotel, Jim noticed a familiar black Suburban parked under the portico as they got out of the hotel van. Entering the hotel, he saw Michael sitting in the lobby reading a newspaper.

After getting his room key and saying good evening to the crew, he quickly went to his room, changed clothes, and came back down to the lobby. "Been waiting long?" he asked Michael as he walked over to where he was sitting.

"Not long," Michael answered, standing and shaking Jim's hand. "I just checked the arrivals and then looked at how long it took you to get here last time. You're only a couple of minutes off."

"Airport traffic can be somewhat unpredictable," Jim told him as they headed out of the hotel. "Anything exciting happening so far today?"

"Not really," Michael told him as they got in the car. "Everyone's checked in, and they'll be coming by the hotel in the next hour or so."

"What did you find out about a bomb?" Jim asked as they headed for the Embassy Suites. "Did the dog hit on Li's car?"

"Yes, he did," Michael answered. "Wang met with the Air Force guys and showed them his car. When they led the dog around it, he reacted to the trunk. They walked down the block and came back by. As they went by the car again, the same thing happened again."

"Okay, we know how he plans on killing Hua," Jim said, nodding. "Now my biggest worry is what he'll do with the bomb after he sees the accident."

"What do you mean?" Michael asked as they pulled into the parking lot at the Embassy Suites. "We've already factored in that he'll drive on by and go look at the house. Why would he do anything after he confirms that the wreck was her?"

"It's just an unknown," Jim said as they headed into the hotel. "For instance, he may come back by the wreck and toss the bomb at the car just to make sure."

"Isn't that why you and Millicent will be there?" Michael asked, getting on the elevator.

"Sort of," Jim acknowledged. "It's actually to get the bodies out of sight and to discourage other drivers from stopping by until Ron gets back with the wrecker. Li could still drive by and do something stupid. Makes me glad we kept Brett with us. He may be needed to defuse the bomb later."

"Don't you plan on letting Li go once he calls in that Hua's dead?" Michael asked as they got to room 405.

"Maybe," Jim answered as he knocked on the door. "Sun really wants to shoot him. And I guess it sort of depends on what he does after he thinks Hua is dead. If he books a flight back to China, I'm in favor of letting him go.

If he stays around more than a day, I may recommend that Sun gets his way."

"Sun gets his way on what?" Gene asked, opening the door.

"On killing Li," Jim answered, walking in.

"I thought we'd discussed that," Gene said, going over to the desk where the computer and radios were.

"We did," Jim said, looking at all of the screens showing the area around the rental. "I'm talking about if he doesn't leave soon after the accident this afternoon. That might mean that he's waiting to verify Hua and Sun's death."

"I guess we'll just have to wait and see what he does," Gene acknowledged. "Do you have any other questions or recommendations?"

"No, unless there have been any changes since I left yesterday," Jim answered.

"Not really, just verification of the bomb," he told Jim. "And I assume Michael told you about that."

"Yes, he did," Jim answered as Sun and Hua came into the room. "Hey, guys. Are ya'll ready for this to be over?"

"Definitely," Sun said for both of them. "Our only real concern is what we'll do once this is over. Do you know what your government has in mind?"

"Not really," Gene answered. "We think they'll take you down to Cheyenne Mountain until the WHO meeting is over. They'd planned on you being at the meeting if they could get some additional information on what Hua has told them, but they haven't so far."

"At least you'll be safe down there," Jim added, looking at them. "Regardless of what the government plans for you later on, you need to disappear for a while. Especially if we convince Li you're dead, and he tells his boss."

"And after that?" Hua asked. "What'll happen to us?"

"I'd wanted to get this over with before we talked about the future," Gene told her, motioning to the couch. "Please have a seat, and I'll try to explain what we, by that, I mean my company, have in mind.

Jim and I talked about this last month," he continued, looking at each of them. "We're both concerned with what happens to people like you who give up their lives to help our country. My company has been setting up a couple of options.

We'll get deeper into your desires over the next week or so, but I asked them to see if we couldn't keep you in your chosen fields," he continued. "That's pretty easy for you, Hua. There are universities that could benefit from your knowledge. As well as the Center for Disease Control, or CDC.

You're a little more difficult," Gene told Sun, smiling. "It would be difficult to put you in our military, even if there was a service exchange between the US and China, which there isn't."

"I don't expect you to take care of me," Sun argued. "I did this because I thought it was the right thing to do. I really didn't have any plans for once Hua was here safely, but I'm sure I can go back to San Francisco, where there are relatives of my family. I'll be all right."

"Maybe for a while," Jim said, looking at Sun. "What about in a year when you see someone you knew from the army back home? Will you wonder if he saw you? How many years do you want to spend looking over your shoulder every time you go out? Is that the way you want to spend the rest of your life?"

"That's not what you want," Gene told him. "And it's not what we want. You have skills that'll come in useful for my company. We have a branch that does a lot of work overseas, much of it in Southeast Asia. You could be a tremendous asset to us. But we'll discuss that more fully at a later date. For now, we're looking at using you as a security guard at a small university in Oregon.

There's a small college just south of Portland, not too far from Salem, called Linfield College," Gene continued. "They have a wonderful biology department where we have arranged for Hua to be an associate professor. You would be one of the security personnel there until we make arrangements for both of you in something more suitable."

"I thought I'd get a chance to work in more of a research capacity," Hua said, looking at Gene. "I don't know what type of virology labs you have here, but that is what I'd really like."

"We'll talk about more options later," Gene assured her. "For now, we just want for both of you to disappear for a year or so. The college I mentioned is out of the way, has a small student population, and about one and a half percent of the city's population of 32,000 is Asian, so you won't stand out.

Anyway, as I said, this is just temporary," Gene reiterated as Wang came in. "And we'll have Mr. Jong there along with you if he chooses to stay in the US. I'll let you guys talk about it when we get rid of Li."

Chapter Sixty-five

"What do you say, Wang?" Gene asked as he shook his hand. "Would you like to remain here in the US with Sun and Hua?"

Wang looked at them and answered, "I came here expecting to remain. There's nothing left for me back in China. The PRC may not know of my involvement yet, but sooner or later, they will. It would be my great pleasure to remain with my friends here regardless of where it is."

"Good, we'll include you in our plans," Gene told him. "Now, what's going on with Li?"

"It looks like he's checking out of his room," Wang answered. "He carried a couple of suitcases down to his car this morning and put them in the trunk. As we've suspected, I think he plans on completing his mission today and is ready to head back to China."

"Can you check on that?" Jim asked Gene. "Have the company do a quick check of the airlines to see if he's purchased a ticket?"

"I'll take care of that," Gene said, picking up the phone. "Of course, he may be using a false name. But, I have them run checks to see if there's another name that came here about the same time Li did."

"What do you plan on doing after you pass the wreck following Li?" Jim asked. "I'm sure you realize that if you turn on Lookout Road behind Li, he'll see you."

"Yes," Wang answered. "There's a little road about 200 feet past Lookout where I can turn around and wait. From there, I'll be able to see Li when he comes back. I figured I'd just follow him back to town and see what he does."

"That sounds good," Jim agreed as he saw Gene hanging up the phone. "Then, if he goes to the airport, you can let us know."

"They're running a name-matching program," Gene said, looking at Jim. "If there are matching names for anyone purchasing a ticket today or tomorrow to China that came from there in the last week, we'll know."

"I really hope he leaves," Jim said as Billy came into the room. "Anything other than that could cause us problems with those people back in China still wondering if she's been taken care of."

"I agree," Gene said, looking at Sun. "One thing I want to emphasize. Once you and Hua are safely hiding on Paradise Road, I don't want you coming back until either Jim or Michael comes to get you. Once Li passes the wreck, he can do any number of things, including looking in the house on Lookout or sitting there while he makes phone calls. I just don't want you or your car seen until we know he's gone. Do you understand?"

"Yes, sir," Sun answered with a slight nod. "As much as I'd like to be more proactive, I'll wait. As you've pointed out, Hua's safety is the most important thing, and my wishes don't count."

"Good," Gene told him, turning to Billy. "How's your part coming?"

"I'm ready," Billy answered. "I parked the truck at a Park and Ride just off I-70 about where 40 heads west. The other guys that are driving the blocking car will be there and follow me when I pull out. I'll head over there after Michael goes to the house and be ready to leave when Sun calls that he's passing the cloverleaf, where 70 goes over 470. I'll be getting on 70 about the time he's passing where I'll be getting on."

"And I'll slow down if I get there before he's on 70," Sun added. "If he's already on 70, I'll pass him, and the blocking car will pull up beside Billy to prevent Li from passing him."

"Great," Jim said, envisioning how it would work. "I want everybody to make sure their radios are working and keep a running conversation about where you are all of the time. Once Michael leaves heading to the house, I want everyone to check in with their location and let us know if they see any problems with completing their part of the operation. Just remember, we need everyone at the exit from I-70 to 40 on time. That's the crucial part.

What about the wrecker?" Jim asked, looking around. "Has anyone talked to Ron this morning?"

"He called in a couple of hours ago," Michael answered. "He and Brett had the car loaded with the bodies inside. They were going to leave it at Denver Scrap Metal just north of I-70 on Washington Street. They'll join 70 a couple of miles later, where it crosses over I-25. Then they'll follow me to where they'll be waiting for everyone to get to 40."

"When will they get here?" Jim asked, wanting to talk face-to-face with everyone before the plan began.

"I'll check," Gene said, picking up one of the radios that tied everyone together. "Ron, where are you right now?"

A couple of seconds later, Ron answered, "Brett and I are just getting on I-70 heading your way. We should be there in 15 minutes."

"Is the wrecker safe where you left it?" Jim asked.

"Perfectly," Ron told him, laughing. "The guy that runs the yard understands that nobody touches my wrecker, or he'll be in the trunk of the car when it's crushed this evening."

"Just how did you ensure that?" Jim asked.

"You'll be getting a bill for it," Brett said, coming on the radio. "It turns out that a few thousand dollars will buy a certain amount of loyalty and cooperation. That and the fact that I served with his brother in the Middle East a few years ago."

"How did you find that out?" Gene asked.

"I saw a picture of him and his brother when we went in to discuss disposing of the wreck when we came back," Brett answered. "I recognized the brother, and one thing led to another. Bottom line, he'll watch over the truck and make sure it goes straight into the crusher the minute we get back."

"Amazing how our lives keep intersecting with our former lives, isn't it?" Jim asked, smiling. "You just never know when you'll run into someone from your past."

"That's what binds so many service people," Gene added. "Bonds cemented in blood in the service seem to remain regardless of the time apart. Something about shared misery."

"Misery loves company," Michael said as Millicent came in. "Isn't that the old saying?"

"Who's miserable," she asked, nodding to everyone. "I thought today would be more of a joyful occasion."

"It is," Jim assured her, giving her a quick hug. "Just some old military guys talking about our past. Don't pay any attention to us. Are you ready?"

"Yes," she answered, smiling at Hua. "A little nervous, but ready."

"If you have any doubts, now is the time to voice your concerns," Jim told her.

"I've just been running every possibility of what'll happen at the wreck when Li comes back by," she answered. "Not really doubts, just hoping that he goes on by without stopping."

"Unfortunately, we can't control that," Jim told her. "But we'll deal with whatever he does. Are you comfortable with your part, or would you rather remain in the truck?"

"I'll stay with you," she said, shaking her head. "If we need to be standing on the road, I'll be there. All I have is a little stage fright right now; it'll pass."

Jim looked at her face for a couple of seconds and said, "You'll be fine. You wouldn't be here if I didn't have all the confidence in the world in you."

Chapter Sixty-six

Just as Ron and Brett came in, Gene's phone rang. "Barker," he answered. Listening for a couple of minutes, he finally asked, "If this happened early this morning, why are you just now informing me?

How sure are you of your analysis?" he asked when he heard the answer and motioned for Jim to come join him. "All right. Thanks for the update.

We may have a problem," Gene said to Jim looking for Wang. Seeing him, he motioned him over.

"That was Quantico," he told them both. "It appears that Li went out to the house late this morning. Did you see anything, Wang?"

"No, but I didn't follow him once we had the dog sniff his car," Wang answered. "I was going to return to watching him after we finished here. What happened?"

"It looks like he took the bomb into the house," Gene answered. "He was seen carrying a briefcase size object through the area behind the house, entered it through the back door, and came back out without it."

"That probably means he plans on a remote detonation," Jim said, looking at Brett and waving. "We need to get Brett and Ron back out there as soon as possible."

When Brett got to them, Jim said, "I need you to go out to the house, find the bomb we believe Li left there, and take care of it."

"Do you know anything about it?" Brett asked.

"Not, really," Jim answered, looking at Gene. "Maybe we can get Quantico to send us a shot of the briefcase Li was seen carrying."

As Gene picked up his phone, Jim asked Wang, "Do you know where his car is right now?"

"Just a second," Wang answered, taking out his phone.

"Ron, have you guys loaded the bodies in the wrecked car?" Jim asked as he waited for Gene and Wang to answer his questions.

"No, we were going to have them brought to us before we went out this afternoon," Ron answered.

Pointing at one of the computer screens, Gene said, "Here's the video of Li approaching the house. You can see what he's carrying, and it looks like a normal size briefcase."

Brett bent over and watched it for a few moments and then said, "I'd guess that it's a remote triggered devise, probably C-4, and all he has to do is call the receiver that's part of the triggering mechanism."

"How much damage could he do with a bomb that size?" Ron asked. "It's not that big."

"Depends on how much explosive is in it," Brett answered, looking at the close-up of the briefcase. "Potentially enough to level the entire house."

"Wow," Ron exclaimed. "I always thought it'd have to be like one of those bombs you see fall out of a B-52 or something."

"Nope," Brett told him. "Today's explosives are a magnitude higher than the old TNT days. A one-pound block of C-4, easily contained in that briefcase, could level the house."

"Can you disarm it?" Jim asked as he saw Wang hang up.

"Probably, but I'd like to have my equipment before I try that," Brett answered. "For now, I'd just check for an anti-lift trigger, pick it up, and move it somewhere far enough away that it won't get the detonation signal. Or at least get it to an area where it won't do any damage if it goes off."

"Li's car is at his hotel," Wang told them when Brett finished. "I've asked for the guys at Quantico to notify me when it moves."

"Good," Jim said, nodding. "What I want right now is for Ron and Brett to get the wrecker and go out to the house and find that bomb. If you don't want to try to disarm it, just get it the hell out of there. I damn sure don't want it going off if Li drives by and blows it even though Sun's car isn't there."

"What about getting the bodies?" Ron asked, thinking about how it would affect the staged accident. "Should we go get them before we leave?"

"No, I'll get the bodies to you out there," Jim answered as they headed out of the room. "Just get out to the house and take care of the bomb however Brett thinks is best. Give me a call when you get out there."

Jim turned to Gene and said, "We need to call whoever wanted us to take care of that city problem and have them find us an ambulance we can use. Have them bring it here to the hotel and leave it. Then we need two of our guys that can drive it over to where the bodies are and load them this afternoon. After that, they need to be provided Emergency Medical Technician (EMT) uniforms and come out when Ron and Brett unload the wreck. The four of them can position the bodies and do whatever else is required to set the scene. If anybody sees them, they'll think they are picking up the victims.

And get them a radio with the common frequency," Jim said as Gene picked up his phone again.

Turning to Michael, he said, "I need you to keep track of Brett, Ron, and the guys Gene's getting for us acting as EMTs. I don't want you going out to the house until they've got that bomb disposed of and the ambulance out there to help get the wreck staged. If you think you need to leave earlier than we thought, go ahead. But stay out of the house until Brett gives you the all-clear. You can keep me updated by radio."

"I'll wait here for now," Michael said. "But I'll stay on the radio with Brett until he's finished clearing out the house. How is this going to impact the operation?"

"I'm not sure yet," Jim admitted, signaling for Billy to come over. "Maybe just delay us as long as it takes Gene to round up the ambulance and EMTs. Or worse case, if it gets too late, we delay until tomorrow."

"What do you want me to do?" Millicent asked, watching everybody scurrying around, trying to get a handle on the changing situation. "I can at least monitor radios or something.”

“Thanks, Millicent,” Jim told her, looking for Billy. “Right now, I can’t think of anything. Maybe ask Gene if he needs help finding two guys to be EMTs or finding uniforms for them.”

“Okay,” she said as Billy walked up.

“What can I do?” Billy asked. “I’ll go pick up the bodies if you want me to. That way, they’ll be here when the ambulance gets here.”

“Let’s hang on a second with the bodies,” Jim said, nodding. “Is delaying for an hour or so going to impact you?”

“Not really,” Billy answered. “I was going to wait at the Park and Ride until I got the call to get on I-70 anyway.”

“Are the guys driving the blocking car coming here?” Jim asked, signaling for Millicent to come back.

“I believe so,” Billy answered. “They checked in an hour or so ago, and they knew we were all meeting here for the final go-ahead.”

“Millicent, when Gene gets off the phone, ask him if he wants to use the guys that were driving the blocking car to be the EMTs,” Jim told her. “It might save some time instead of trying to find two new men.”

“I’ll ask him,” she answered. “But who’ll drive the car that keeps Li from passing Billy before Sun gets off I-70?”

“You and I’ll do it with the truck we’ll be driving if I have to,” Jim answered. “We’ll just cut in front of Billy as we approach the turnoff for 40 and pull over on the shoulder as Sun stops.”

“Okay,” she said, turning away.

"Do you want me to try and contact those guys?" Billy asked. "I'm sure they're driving the car they were going to use."

"If they aren't here in the next few minutes, call them. For now, check with Gene or Millicent to see if they need to be the EMTs," Jim said as he headed across the hall to room 406. "I'll be back in a minute."

Chapter Sixty-seven

When Jim came back in, Billy was talking to two guys Jim hadn't seen before. As he approached, Billy said, "Jim, this is Harry and his partner Art. They were going to be the ones driving the car that blocked Li from passing me."

Jim extended his hand and said, "Good to meet you guys. Did Billy tell you what changes we're planning?"

After shaking hands with Jim, Harry said, "Yeah, he said you may need us to drive an ambulance and go pick up a couple of bodies instead of driving the car."

"That's right," Jim confirmed. "Have you ever driven an ambulance?"

"No," Harry said, looking at Art. "But we've driven all sorts of panel trucks, delivery trucks, and a shitload of others. It's just a truck."

"As long as we don't have to know how to operate the stuff in the back," Art added. "We can drive it."

"Good, that's the plan for now," Jim told them, signaling for Millicent to step over.

"This is Harry and his partner Art," Jim told her when she got to him. "They were the drivers of the car that was to block Li. Has Gene decided if he wants to use them, or has he found other men?"

"He hasn't said," Millicent answered, looking back at Gene. "He was just finishing talking to somebody about the ambulance and uniforms. I'll go ask him."

"Just have him come over here when he finishes his phone call," Jim said. "It'll be easier to do this with all of us standing here."

Seconds later, Gene disconnected his call and followed Millicent to where Jim and the others were standing. "The ambulance will be downstairs in 15 minutes," Gene said, looking at everybody. "There'll be two uniforms, big enough to fit an average-size guy, in the rear."

"Good," Jim said, looking at Harry and Art. "These two guys, Harry and Art, will drive it instead of driving the car to block Li from passing Billy. They both appear to be average size. They'll also go get the bodies and take them out to Ron and Brett."

"You plan on using the ambulance to block Li from passing Billy?" Gene asked after nodding at Harry and Art.

"No, they'll go meet Ron and Brett at the house after they pick up the bodies. Millicent and I'll block Li, and I'll explain how in a minute," Jim answered. "But they need to know where the bodies are and if they need anything authorizing them to get them."

"The bodies are at Rose Cremation Society on 14th Street," Gene told them as he walked over to his desk and picked up a file.

"You'll need these papers," he told Harry, handing him the file. "It has all the death certificates and other information about the bodies that have been kept refrigerated since we brought them here. I don't expect any problems, but just ask for Pat Tavor if you have any trouble."

"We'll go as soon as the ambulance gets here," Harry said, handing the file to Art. "Where do we meet Ron?"

"Michael, can you come give Harry and Art directions to the house on Lookout?" Jim asked. "If you think it's necessary, you can head out there after they pick up the bodies, and they can follow you."

"I think that's best," Michael answered. "There's not a lot left here for me to do, and I'd like to see how things are progressing with Brett. If you guys will just let me know when you're ready to go, I'll follow you to get the bodies and then you follow me out to the house."

"Make sure you get your radios out of your car before you go," Jim told them as they headed for the door. "Please check in with Gene as soon as you change into the uniforms and head over to get the bodies."

"How's the timing looking?" Gene asked, looking at his watch.

"Maybe a little tight," Jim answered, thinking about what needed to be done. "But we've got a couple of hours before we pull the plug. Michael said there was very little traffic between 2 o'clock and 4 o'clock. And, he said it was really not too busy until after 5:30 or 6."

"What'll you do if we have to delay?" Gene motioned for Sun and Hua.

"Couple of options," Jim answered. "None of them good. We could shut down 40 for an hour or so because of the 'accident.' Or we could postpone until tomorrow."

"How would you manage tomorrow?" Gene asked as Sun and Hua came over.

"I get on the first flight back here after I get home," Jim answered. "Then, I'd catch a flight home after we get done."

"That would put you home after Jennifer gets off work, wouldn't it?" Gene asked. "What would you tell her?"

"Maybe," Jim admitted. "I could say something about being late and then stopping by Venice for a beer with the Captain."

"You're right about no good options," Gene finally said, looking at him. "What about next week?"

"I don't want to push it that far," Jim told him, shaking his head. "We've got to move Sun and Hua again if we wait. Also, Li will probably go back out and get his bomb. Too many little things could go wrong if we don't do it today or tomorrow."

"What's causing the problem?" Sun asked, looking from Jim to Gene.

"I'm assuming that Wang told you about the bomb, didn't he?" Jim asked.

"Yes, he told me," Sun replied. "I don't see why that would cause a delay. Li would have no reason to use it if he doesn't see my car at the house."

"Possibly," Jim agreed, nodding. "But he could also blow it because he thinks someone Hua has been talking to is in the house. It's a chance I don't want to take, even if nobody is in the house."

"It's ultimately my decision, and I'll make it when Ron and Brett call in," Gene told them. "If they get the bomb out of the house before 3 o'clock, we can still be done by 4. And there's still a slight chance that there won't be much traffic until after 5. Jim's right, though. We need that bomb gone and if it's not there after tomorrow, Li will know something's up."

"We're at the house," Ron just then called in on the radio. "Brett is checking out the front door to see if it's rigged. I'll call back when he gets inside."

"All right," Jim said, relieved that they were finally there. "We'll give them 30 minutes to disarm or move the bomb. That should give Harry and Art plenty of time to go get the bodies and be driving out there."

Looking around, he saw Billy and told him, "You better go to the Park and Ride and get your truck ready to roll. Just stay on the radio and keep us informed if you're having any problems."

"Got it," Billy said, nodding. "I'll make a call when I'm in the truck, and you can let me know when Sun is headed my way."

"Now, what about you and Millicent blocking Li instead of a different car?" Gene asked as Billy left.

Chapter Sixty-eight

"Since we're using Harry and Art for the ambulance, I think it's too late to get anyone else," Jim explained. "I can go out with Millicent when Billy is ready to leave the Park and Ride. I'll be right on his tail as he gets on I-70. Then, when we get close to the exit for 40, I'll speed up and pass him getting behind Sun."

"Then when Sun stops at the stop sign, I'll pull over on the shoulder like I'm checking directions," Jim continued. "Then I'll pull out right behind Li and stop at the wreck. That way, if Li stops, I'm right there. And I'll stay there until he passes on his way back."

"That'll work," Gene agreed, looking at Millicent. "Is that all right with you, Millicent?"

"That's fine," she answered. "That's not really any different than what we'd planned anyway. And in some ways, I think it's even better."

"So, what now?" Gene asked as his phone rang. After listening for a moment, he said thanks and hung up.

"The ambulance is downstairs," he told Michael. "Why don't you go with Harry and Art to make sure everything is good? Give me a call when you're satisfied with the uniforms and stuff and let me know when you're heading over to get the bodies."

"We're on our way," Michael answered as he ushered Harry and Art out of the door. "I'll give you a call when we're headed out to meet Ron and Brett."

"I think you need to head over to Li's place," Jim told Wang. "I don't want to wait for Quantico to call us when he moves. I'd rather you be right behind him, and then you can call us."

"That's fine," Wang said as he walked over to Sun and Hua. "I'll be watching out for you guys. With everyone here ready to step in if anything goes wrong, you'll be safe, and we'll be on our way to Oregon before you know it."

Hua put her arms around his neck and said, "Thank you, Wang Jong. You're more than just Sun's friend. You're a special friend to me, too. I'll see you back here later this afternoon. Everything will turn out just fine."

Sun put out his hand to shake and merely said, "Thank you, my friend. May we both have a long and happy life in the future."

"Where's the red pickup?" Jim asked as Wang left. "I think I'll head over to the Park and Ride so that we don't waste any time once Wang says Li is on his way here."

"It's in the underground parking lot," Gene answered. "Just call the front desk, and it'll be brought up. Have them bring up Sun's car also. We might as well get ready for everyone to head out. I'd hate to have to put this off until tomorrow, so every minute we can shave off of the time to get Li out there is to our advantage."

"I'll head on down," Jim said, looking at Millicent. "Are you ready?"

"As ready as I'll ever be, I guess," she answered, walking over to Hua. "Don't worry, Jim and I, along with everyone else, will make sure you're safe. And I'll see you back here in a couple of hours for a bottle of champagne."

"Thank you," Hua said, giving Millicent a hug.

"And thank you, Mr. Jim Lashley," she said hugging Jim also. "Sun and I'll always be in your debt."

"Like Millicent said, we'll see you back here for champagne in a couple of hours," Jim said, nodding at Sun. "You guys will be able to relax and enjoy life with Wang before you know it and all of this will be a distant memory.

I'll give you a call when we meet up with Billy," Jim told Gene as he and Millicent headed for the door. "I'll be listening on the radio, but please bring me up to date on anything once I check in from the pickup."

"I'll be waiting to hear from you," Gene said, watching him go. "Just yell if you or Millicent see or need anything. And remember, we can always try again another day if this one heads south."

A few minutes later, Gene heard Jim on the radio saying that he was on his way to meet Billy. Billy then called in to say that he was almost to his truck.

Gene then radioed Michael, asking, "Where are you guys?"

"We're on our way to get the bodies," Michael answered. "The uniforms aren't a perfect fit, but with luck, nobody will notice. We should be there in about five more minutes. I'll call when we're on our way to meet Ron."

"Ron, are you listening?" Gene asked, keying the radio.

"Stand by, please," Ron answered. "Brett's just now coming out with the briefcase. I'll let you know what's happening when I get a chance to talk to him."

"Good," Gene told him. "Michael should be there in about 20 minutes or so with the ambulance. You guys just stay at the house until everyone meets."

"Roger that," Ron answered as Brett got to the wrecker. "Hang on, Brett's here."

A moment later, Brett came on the radio saying, "It's defused. After I determined there weren't any exterior triggering devices, I took a chance and opened the briefcase. I figured it couldn't be too sophisticated since Li made it in his hotel room with material bought locally. Anyway, it's inert now. What would you like for me to do with it?"

"If you're positive it's safe, give it to Michael when he gets there," Gene answered. "I wish you'd just taken it out in the back and left it until we could get a bomb squad out, but thanks."

"Not my first rodeo, General," Brett told him. "I wouldn't have touched it if I didn't think I could handle it. I still have some use for most of my body parts, and I'd like to keep them all together."

"You EOD people are nuts anyway," Gene said, chuckling. "Getting your kicks playing with stuff that'll take your head off if you sneeze at the wrong time. But, again, thanks."

"I'm at the Park and Ride," Billy called in. "I'll be in my truck and ready to roll in 10 minutes."

"I'll be there in about 10 minutes," Jim added as he headed west on Colfax Avenue. "Where's the ambulance?"

"We're just picking up the bodies," Michael answered. "We should be out of here in another 15 minutes."

"Is Sun's car ready downstairs?" Jim asked as he looked for Kipling Street to turn north.

"Standby," Gene said as he picked up his phone. Seconds later, he said, "It's out front, ready to go."

"Where's Wang?" Jim asked as they passed Wadsworth Boulevard.

"I'll be at Li's in five minutes," Wang answered. "Unless Quantico has called, he should still be there waiting for his informant in the hotel to tell him that Sun and Hua are leaving."

"Well shit," Jim said as he realized that the hotel informant might have called Li when Sun's car was brought around front. "Hurry your ass over there, Wang. Li may already know that Sun's car is ready to move."

"Got it," Wang said, accelerating down the street. "Even if he leaves now, he'll pass me heading to the hotel, and I can turn around."

"Folks, we may be hitting the crunch time," Jim announced. "Michael, you and your guys are now the critical line. We need you guys to haul ass out to the house and meet Ron and Brett. Have Harry run the lights and siren. Looks like we made a good call getting the ambulance."

"We'll head for the accident spot if that'll help," Ron offered.

"Not yet, stay at the house," Jim ordered. "You don't need to be seen on the road with the wreck any longer than necessary. Michael, call when you get on I-70."

"Got it," Michael answered as he saw Harry coming out with the attendants to load the bodies. "We may be out of here in about five minutes now."

"Li's headed for the hotel," Wang called excitedly. "I'm turning around to follow him."

"Gene, send Sun down to the car when Wang tells you Li is in place," Jim said as he turned north on Kipling Street. "Then have him wait for Hua. It shouldn't be more than a couple of minutes, and then you can send her down. We can stall a little bit until Michael and the ambulance are out where the accident will take place. Billy, I'm about four miles from you. Are you ready?"

Chapter Sixty-nine

"I'll be ready to pull out when you get here," Billy answered.

"What's your status, Michael?" Jim asked as he approached I-70.

"We'll be pulling out within two minutes," Michael answered, watching the bodies being loaded into the ambulance. "With the lights, we should be pulling off I-70 onto 40 in less than 10 minutes."

"All right, Ron, you guys leave the house in 10 minutes and be ready to drop the car when the ambulance gets there," Jim directed as he approached I-70. "Wang, where are you?"

"I'm about a half block behind Li," Wang answered. "We'll be at the hotel in two minutes."

"Call when you get there," Jim directed, getting on I-70 westbound. "Gene, as soon as you hear Wang say Li is in place, send Sun down by himself. Billy, I'll be with you in two minutes."

"Take the Ward Road exit, and you'll see me on the north side of the parking lot facing east," Billy replied. "Just swing around behind me when you get here, and we'll be ready before Sun gets to I-70."

"I see the exit now," Jim told him. "Michael, status?"

"The ambulance is loaded, and we're on our way," Michael told him. "Estimated Time of Arrival (ETA) now eight minutes to 40."

"One minute to the hotel," Wang called. "He's hauling ass."

"Sun is on his way down," Gene announced, motioning for Sun to leave.

"Good; Li should be in place when Sun gets off the elevator and leaves the building," Jim said, taking the Ward Road exit. "How long will it take you to be ready to dump the car, Ron?"

"We can be there in two minutes from when you call, ready to unload," Ron answered.

"Michael, give me a call when you get on I-70," Jim said as he passed beside Billy's truck. "That should be about three minutes from the exit for 40."

"Got it," Michael said as he followed the ambulance west on Colfax Avenue. "Should be there in about five minutes."

"Ron, when you hear Michael and the ambulance are on I-70, go ahead and leave the house," Jim directed, pulling in behind Billy. "That should put you at the curve just seconds ahead of the ambulance to have the wreck unloaded, waiting for them to drop off the bodies."

"We'll be there when he gets there," Ron acknowledged.

"Li is at the hotel," Wang reported. "He's watching Sun coming out and going to the car."

"Okay, guys, we'll be basing everything on Sun now," Jim said. "I'm looking at probably two minutes before he leaves the hotel. We can make some minor adjustments to slow him down if necessary as he drives, but it's only good for a minute or so since it's only nine or ten miles from the hotel until we all meet at the stop sign."

"Are you ready for me to send Hua down?" Gene asked, seeing how nervous she was getting.

"Thirty seconds," Jim answered. "Sun, are you on the radio?"

"Yes," Sun replied. "I'm ready anytime now."

"Hua should be getting off the elevator in a minute," Jim told him. "By the time she gets to the car, you should be good to go."

"Six minutes to I-70," Michael announced. "What do you want me to do once I drop off the ambulance?"

"Stop by the wrecker and get the bomb from Brett, and go on to the house," Jim told him. "We still want Li to see the Suburban there as if waiting for Hua.

"Are you damn sure that thing's not going to blow my head off after you give it to me?" Michael asked, following the ambulance west on Colfax Avenue.

"Pretty sure," Brett joked. "If you'd like, I can open it and show you what it looks like before it explodes."

"Why don't we just put it in the trunk of the wreck?" Michael asked. "I'd trust Brett with my life, and it appears that's exactly what I'm doing, but why are we keeping it?"

"One, to make sure it gets disposed of correctly," Jim answered, smiling at the gallows humor that seemed to come out when people are under stress. "But also to use as evidence against Li if we need it."

"Hua is coming out," Sun told them. "We'll be leaving in about a minute."

"Okay, call crossing Wadsworth," Jim directed. "Billy and I'll leave then and should be passing where you'll join I-70 when you get there. Give us another call when you cross Kipling, and we can adjust a little."

"Will do," Sun said as Hua got in the car.

"Looks like Li is on his phone," Wang reported. "I'm standing by for Quantico to tell me what he's saying."

As Sun pulled away from the hotel, Gene said, "Quantico says Li just told someone that he'd be on his way to San Fran within four hours. Did you hear them, Wang?"

"Yes, I did," Wang answered. "I'm pulling out to follow Li now. Do you still want me to park on that road just before I get to the cemetery?"

"Yes," Jim told him. "For everybody, we are now just following exactly what we practiced. If everybody sticks to the schedule we just modified to account for the ambulance, everything should fall in place. If anyone sees a problem from this point on, let me know immediately."

"We're about a minute from I-70," Michael said as they sped west. "Five minutes now from getting on 40."

"Does Harry know where the wreck will be?" Jim asked. "Or are you going to pass him before you get to the exit for 40?"

"Michael told me about where it will be," Harry answered as he drove the ambulance. "I'll be looking for it as soon as I leave the stop sign to get on 40. Shouldn't be hard to spot a wrecker beside the road."

"Good," Jim said, smiling. "It wouldn't look good for a car to be passing a speeding emergency vehicle, and lord knows we don't want to attract any attention."

"Let's see," Gene mused as he sat back in his chair by the computers and radios. "A speeding ambulance with a black Suburban appearing to be in a race with it, a wrecker with a wrecked car on its bed sitting beside a semi-busy road with a bomb, nope, nothing worthy of any attention here."

"Good to know you've still got your sense of humor, General," Jim said, laughing. "But the point is clear. Let's try not to draw any more attention than necessary at this point. Ron, can you give us an estimate of the traffic on 40?"

"Pretty sparse," Ron answered. "I've only seen a couple of cars pass by on 40, and nobody has gone by us on Lookout Road."

"Great," Jim said, smiling at Millicent. "We may pull this shit off yet. How's it coming, Michael?"

"Pulling onto I-70," Michael responded. "ETA four minutes."

Chapter Seventy

A couple of minutes later, Sun called, "Approaching Wadsworth."

"We're rolling," Jim radioed as Billy crossed Ward Road onto the access ramp to I-70. "We should get there as you get on. Just look for an 18-wheeler with a maroon truck pulling a white trailer with a tiger on the side. We'll be looking for you as well. If we see you in front of us, I'll let you know, and you can slow down for us to pass."

"Understand," Sun responded. "Where will you be?"

"I'll be behind Billy until he passes you," Jim answered as they pulled onto I-70. "Then I'll pull up beside him and stay there until we get to the exit for 40."

"Li's about a half block behind Sun," Wang called. "I'll let you know if we fall behind too much."

"We're at the wreck site," Ron radioed. "I'm ready to unload the car as soon as Michael gets here."

"The ambulance just took the exit for 40," Michael said. "We'll be there in about a minute."

"That's good," Jim radioed. "Ron, go ahead and unload and disconnect. Harry, stop behind the wreck for now. Let's leave the bodies in the ambulance until Billy and I cross 470 with Sun. That'll give all of you three or four minutes to pose the bodies and drive away."

"Got it," Harry responded. "I'll be there in about one minute."

A couple of minutes later, Michael radioed, saying, "I've got the bomb, and I'm heading for the house. Do you want me to do anything else?"

"Nope, just leave the bomb in the Suburban, go inside, and wait," Jim told him as they got on I-70. "With luck, Li will be there in less than 10 minutes unless he stops at the wreck."

"Looks like I'll be on I-70 in a couple of minutes," Sun called. "Should I slow down, or is the timing still good?"

"Still looks good; I think we'll be slightly in front of you when you get on," Jim answered, seeing the sign for the exit to Colfax Avenue a mile away. "Wang, anything new with Li?"

"No," Wang answered. "I'm still a little way behind him, and he seems happy with being behind Sun. I think he's just going to follow him like he did in the practice runs."

"Ron, how's the traffic on 40?" Jim asked as he stayed close behind Billy to prevent anyone from getting between them.

"Nothing," Ron answered, looking both ways up and down the road. "Do you want us to place the bodies now?"

"Give me a minute or so," Jim told him as they approached the exit for Colfax Avenue. "I'll let you know as soon as Billy and I team up with Sun."

"I'm getting on 70," Sun called. "I think I see you about half a mile in front of me."

"That sounds about right," Jim said. "Do you see my red truck behind Billy?"

"Yes, I see you," Sun answered.

"Are there any cars between you and me?" Jim asked, looking in his rearview mirror.

"Just one, and he looks like he's going to pass you," Sun answered. "Do you want me to speed up?"

"Yes, just a little," Jim told him, seeing the car Sun was talking about. "I'm going to pull up beside Billy as soon as that car passes me. Then you just match Billy's speed, but don't get too close."

"What if another car passes me and gets between us?" Sun asked as he saw Jim swing into the left lane.

"Don't worry about it," Jim said, seeing him in his mirror. "There isn't an exit until we get to 40. I'll just pull in front of Billy to let him by if he's trying to pass. If he takes the exit for 40 behind Billy, I'll still be in front and parked on the shoulder beside the stop sign. I can pull out in front of Li to give you a chance to get off 40 as we planned. But let's not worry about things we can't control.

Ron, go ahead and put the bodies out and send Harry down to the road just before the cemetery where Wang's going to park," Jim said as he saw the sign for the 40 exit a mile ahead. "We'll be there in about three minutes, so you head to Rockland Road when the stage is set and be ready to come back for the wreck when I call."

"Got it," Ron answered. "Brett just finished pouring the blood over the female's head and on the driver. We'll be out of here in 30 seconds."

"Okay, guys, we're close," Jim said as he started to speed up to get in front of Billy. "Sun, pass us and be ready to take the exit as soon as you get there. Wang, let me know if Li does anything unexpected."

Just as Sun got beside Billy's truck, Wang called, saying, "Li's speeding up! I think he's going to try to pass you and get behind Sun."

Jim glanced in his rearview mirror and saw Li gaining on them quickly and said, "Sun, get in front of me as fast as you can. I'll see if I can prevent him from getting right behind you."

As Sun sped by him, Jim looked again and saw that he couldn't get back in the left lane without possibly hitting Li. "Sun, go ahead and take the exit," he yelled. "I'll be right behind you. Billy, don't bother following. Just keep going west and turn around after you see Li get off. Wang, keep Li in sight and let me know if he doesn't take the next exit."

"What now?" Sun asked as he pulled up to the stop sign.

"Go up Paradise Road as we planned," Jim told him. "Wait there until I figure out what to do."

"What's happening?" Gene asked, hearing that the plan was falling apart.

"Li didn't make the exit on 40," Jim answered as he turned west on 40 behind Sun. "I think he'll keep going west on I-70 until he can come back east on 40 about five miles down the road."

"Then what?" Gene asked.

"Then I think he'll come back and go up Lookout Road to see if the car is at the house," Jim answered as he saw the wreck coming up ahead. "Then he'll probably come back toward the wreck trying to find Sun."

"Harry, are you where you can see Li when he comes east on 40?" Jim asked as he pulled over behind the staged wreck.

"Yeah," Harry said. "I can see the road that leads to the house, too. What do you want me to do?"

"Wait until you see Li turn north on Lookout and pull out onto 40 heading east with your lights and siren," Jim said, getting out of the pickup with Millicent. "Then he'll see you heading this way and probably assume something happened when he doesn't see Sun's car at the house. "You should have a couple of minutes to get here and pretend to be working the accident."

"Where will you be, Jim?" Gene asked, trying to envision how the plan was changing.

"Millicent and I'll be here making sure no cars stop before Harry gets here with the ambulance," he answered as he walked up and looked at the bodies. "Harry, when you and Art get here, park on the road beside the wreck. One of you needs to be at the back of the ambulance when Li approaches.”

“I’ll have Art at the back,” Harry told him, nodding at Art. “What do you want him to do?”

“Watch for Li to stop,” Jim answered. “My truck is across from the wreck, and that only leaves one lane for a car to pass. When Li stops, have Art bring a sheet out of the back and cover the female body as if you’ve decided she’s dead. But give him a chance to see her dress and the blood first.”

Chapter Seventy-one

"Li's taking the exit," Wang said as he watched Li pull off at the Mt. Vernon Road exit. "He's coming back down 40."

"He'll be at Lookout Road in about two minutes," Jim advised everyone. "Be ready to roll, Harry. Michael, keep a look out of your window and let us know as soon as you can tell that Li is coming back here to the wreck."

"Got it," Michael told them.

"What do you want me to do?" Wang asked as he followed Li.

"Go ahead and park at Rockland Road," Jim told him. "Gene, you and Wang need to be paying close attention to Li's phone right now. I'm hoping that he'll make a call to his boss when he gets here to the wreck. The trick now is to let him see enough to make him believe that Hua is dead but not let him get too close. That's why the timing of covering her body is so critical."

"What if he gets out of his car and comes to look?" Harry asked.

"Just ask him to stay back," Jim answered. "Don't confront him. But make sure the sheet is over the body before he gets too close. I don't think he'll go so far as to lift it, but I'll be there with Millicent.

We'll be standing in the road at the front of the ambulance looking at the wreck," Jim said, looking at Millicent for her consent. "I'll try to intercede if he starts coming too close."

"Li just turned on Lookout," Wang said as he stopped by the cemetery.

"I see him," Michael said, looking through the drapes. "He's looking at the house and slowing down. Looks like he's going up to where the Feed Zone is to turn around."

"Let us know the minute you see him coming back," Jim directed. "Harry, make sure you're running and ready when Michael says he's turned around."

A minute later, Michael radioed, "I see him coming back down the road. He's still going pretty slow and looking at the house. Wait a second, I think he's going to stop."

"Go now, Harry," Jim said, looking west on 40. "I want Li to see you coming here. Brett, are you damn sure that bomb Michael has is safe? Li may be planning on blowing the house thinking that Hua got out and the car went on."

"It's safe," Brett said. "I disconnected the receiver from the charge and cut the wire leading to the detonator. It's just pieces and parts right now."

"We're on our way," Harry said as they headed east to the wreck. "We'll be there in less than a minute."

"What's Li doing now?" Jim asked.

"Just sitting there," Michael answered. "Now, he's looking at something in his car. I can't tell what he's doing."

"Shit," Jim exclaimed. "I think he's trying to figure out why the house didn't explode. Keep watching. He may get out and come to the house."

"No," Michael said a second later. "He's leaving. I guess Brett was right. At least I'm still here. And I just heard the ambulance go by. I think that's what pulled him away."

"Good," Jim said, watching Harry and Art coming at him. "We'll know in a couple of minutes if he's going to buy the accident thing."

As Harry came to a stop, he killed the siren and left the lights flashing as he and Art got out of the truck. "Where do you want me?" he asked as Art headed to the rear of the ambulance.

"Go to the driver's side and look like you're examining him," Jim answered. "Li should be here in another minute and this has to look convincing."

Seconds later, Jim saw Li coming to a stop a few yards from the rear of the ambulance and sit looking at the wreck. Watching him, Jim could tell that he was using his phone and said, "Wang, he's on the phone. You and Gene let me know what he's saying."

"He just told someone that he thinks Hua has been involved in an accident," Gene said over the radio. "He said he's going to try to get a closer look, but it looks like she's dead."

"Cover her, Art," Jim said quietly as he walked down the road with Millicent toward Li's car.

"Do you have your gun?" Jim asked Millicent as they watched Li talking.

"In my waistband in the back," she answered as Li opened his car door. "Why?"

"Just in case," Jim whispered. "If Li starts toward the bodies, I'll get between him and Art. I want you to stay on the road and let me draw his attention. But be ready if the shit hits the fan."

"I can do that," Millicent replied, watching Li come toward them. "What do you plan?"

"Hopefully, just get him to go back to his car," Jim answered. "We'll see what he plans first."

Li was almost to Jim when Art pulled the sheet over the body. "Sorry, mister," Jim said when Li got to him. "There's been an accident, and I'm trying to help the EMTs keep the road clear. If you'd please just go back to your car, it'd really help us."

"What happened?" Li asked trying to get a better look at the body.

"I'm not sure," Jim answered, moving slightly to block his view. "I just came down the road and saw the car there. I called 911 and waited to make sure another car didn't come by and block the road before the ambulance got here. So, please, just get back in your car and let these guys do what they can."

"I was supposed to be meeting some friends out here," Li said, trying to look around Jim. "They were driving a white car like that one. Maybe I can help identify the people to see if they're the ones I was meeting."

"Then I'll be glad to take your name and phone number to give to the EMTs," Jim said, moving once again. "They can give you a call when they get to the hospital."

"This one's dead, too," Harry called from the other side of the wreck. "Let's load them up and head to St. Anthony.

We'll let them make the pronouncement, but it's too late to do anything for them."

"I'd like a quick look at this one," Li shouted, pointing to the sheet-covered body. "I think I know her."

"Sorry, buddy," Art said as Harry joined him. "We've got to get them loaded and to the hospital. Now, if you'd just stand back, you can follow us to the hospital and see the bodies there."

Li took another look toward the body and then looked at Jim before turning back toward his car. Just as he was walking past Millicent, he stopped and asked, "Do I know you? You look very familiar."

"No, I don't think so," she answered as she saw Jim slip his pistol out of his jeans. "I've never been out here before. My husband and I were just heading to Lookout Mountain Park for the afternoon."

Li stood staring at her for a moment and then exclaimed, "Lookout Mountain. That's where I saw you. You were at that house on Lookout Mountain Road."

Taking a step back, Li asked, "What are you doing here? What's going on? I want to see who's under that sheet."

Turning toward Jim, Li pulled a pistol out of his pants just as Jim pointed his at his face, saying, "No, Li. You don't get to look under that sheet."

"That's not for you to decide," Li said, pointing his pistol at Jim. "You get out of my way before I shoot you and everyone else here."

"I don't think so," Millicent said as she quietly stepped behind Li and put her pistol against his head. "You have two choices right now. Choice number one, you can lower your gun and let Jim take it, or choice number two, I'll blow your friggin' brains across the road. Choose wisely, Grasshopper. It could be the last choice you ever make."

Chapter Seventy-two

Li stared at Jim for a second and finally realized that he had no choice other than to do as Millicent had said. Raising his left hand, he let the pistol rotate around the finger of his right hand until the barrel was pointing down. Extending it to Jim, he asked, "How do you know who I am?"

Jim kept his pistol pointed at him as he took the gun and answered, "A very old friend of yours, Sun Bin, told us about you. Now, drop to your knees and put your hands behind your back. If you do anything besides that, either the pretty lady behind you or I will most assuredly blow your brains out.

Harry, radio for Ron to come pick up the wreck, please," Jim said as he stood with his pistol still pointed at Li's face. "And ask Art to scrounge around in the ambulance and get me some tape or quick ties. Then, if you don't mind, let's put the female's body either in the car or, better yet, put both of them in the ambulance."

Art climbed into the rear of the ambulance and quickly came out with a roll of four-inch-wide cloth tape, asking, "Will this do?"

"Perfect," Jim answered. "Now, squeeze his wrists together and wrap the tape around them as tight as you can about ten times. Then lay him on his stomach and do the same with his ankles."

"Ron is on his way," Harry said as he came over to where they were tying up Li. "Gene's been calling. What should I tell him?"

"Tell him I've got Li, and I'm taking him to the house on Lookout," Jim said as Art began wrapping the tape around Li's wrists. "And tell him I'll call when we get Mr. Wei under control."

"Got it," Harry said as he stepped back. "Do you want me to call Michael also?"

"Please, and tell him that we'll be there in a few minutes," Jim answered as Art eased Li forward onto his stomach. "And tell Sun and Wang that they can meet us there as well."

"How are you doing back there, Millicent?" Jim asked, looking up as Art taped Li's ankles.

"Pretty good," she answered as she lowered her gun. "That was rather unexpected, though."

"Yeah, unexpected," Jim said, chuckling as he put his gun back in his jeans. "I guess that's as good a way of saying it as any. Now, if you don't mind, put your gun away. We don't need anyone driving by and seeing this little three-ring circus and you standing there with your gun. It might draw attention. And, as I said earlier, we don't need attention right now."

Walking back to the front of the ambulance to get the radio he had left there when he went to confront Li, he looked both ways to see if there was anyone driving toward them. Not seeing anyone, he picked up his radio and called, "Excuse me, General, are you still just sitting there in your cozy room?"

"What the hell just happened?" Gene demanded. "Harry said you're tying up Li and going to take him to the house. Is that right?"

"That's the plan for now," Jim answered walking back to where Li was lying on the road. "Unless you have a better idea, that's the best one I could come up with on short notice. But I guess we could bring him to your room."

Gene paused several seconds and then said, "I'll meet you at the house in about 30 minutes. Is there anything you need me to bring?"

"Not that I can think of right now," Jim said, checking the tape around Li's wrists. "Oh, on second thought, can you get me some flex cuffs?"

"Okay, it might take a minute or so. Anything else?" Gene asked as he reached for his phone.

"Hang on a second," Jim said as he looked at Millicent and the others. "I think a bag of hamburgers, some fries, and a cooler of drinks might be in order."

"Are you sure you don't want me to call a catering service?" Gene asked, shaking his head. "Maybe there's a pizza delivery service that would come out."

"Pizza, burgers, anything will suffice," Jim said, smiling at Millicent. "It's been a rather long day, and someone will be spending the next few hours cleaning up this mess. I think the folks out here would appreciate anything you can bring."

"I'll see what I can do," Gene told him. "Is everyone all right?"

"Hang on a second," Jim said, turning to Harry. "Let's get Li in the back of the ambulance, and please get the lady off the road. There's still a chance someone will drive by. We need this cleaned up so Ron can load the wreck as soon as he gets here.

Okay," he continued, walking down the road. "Yeah, everyone's all right. Millicent's a little stressed, except she doesn't know it yet. But I can see it in her eyes. The same look I've seen in others the first time they're faced with killing another man."

"I know what you mean," Gene agreed. "Not so easy when it comes down to it. Especially for someone who hasn't had the training. Like her. Shooting at the range doesn't prepare anyone for the reality of watching someone's head explode right in front of you."

"Yep," Jim agreed, turning back to watch them load Li. "But she'll get through it. Might make her a damn good field agent. We'll have a beer and laugh about it one of these days. But for now, I've got to get this shit off the road, and I'll talk more when you get out here."

"Oh, before you go," Gene said, "Quantico sent me the tapes of Li's last phone call. I think Sun may be able to listen to see exactly what Li meant. I'll bring it with me."

"Good," Jim said as he saw Ron coming down the road. "We definitely need to know what the folks back in China think happened to Hua. Otherwise, we're going to need a new plan."

"Indeed," Gene said before using the phone he had picked up. "I'll see you as soon as I can get the flex cuffs and something for the folks to eat. Shouldn't be much more than 30 to 45 minutes."

"How's it coming?" Jim asked as he walked to the rear of the ambulance. "Is Mr. Wei comfortable back there?"

"I put a strip of tape across his mouth," Harry told him as they looked at Li lying on the floor of the ambulance. "I didn't want him to start yelling if someone came by."

"Good idea," Jim said, seeing Millicent sitting in the pickup. "Why don't you go ahead and put the bodies in there with him? Might improve his attitude for later."

"No problem," Harry said, turning to Art. "Jim says to load everyone in the ambulance. Let's start with the guy in the wreck so Ron can get it loaded and gone."

Jim walked over to the pickup and put his hand on Millicent's arm and said, "You did good, lady. You did good."

"What now?" she asked as she put her hand on his.

"Now we clean up the mess," Jim said, smiling. "Always the worst part of the operation is making sure nobody ever knows what happened. Rule number one of the company, don't leave shit behind that'll let anyone know we were involved. Ever."

Millicent smiled faintly and said, "You're full of shit, Mr. Lashley. There isn't any rule like that."

"Maybe not written," Jim said as they watched Ron back up to the wreck. "But I guarantee you that it's their number one rule. Do you want to go back to the hotel, or do you want to hang out with us at the house for a couple of hours?"

"Can I go to the house with you and decide later?" Millicent asked, looking Jim in the eyes.

"Of course," Jim told her, putting his other hand on her shoulder. "Take your time. I'll have Michael take you, or you can go with either Gene or me if you decide you need to go."

"Thank you, Jim," she said as she squeezed his hand. "I think I'll stay until you're ready to go."

"Brett, I need you to drive Li's car back to the house when you finish helping Ron get the wreck on his truck," Jim said as he left Millicent. "If you don't mind."

Chapter Seventy-three

A few minutes later, as Jim got out of his pickup after following everyone from the accident scene to the house, he looked around, telling Millicent, "Looks like they're all here. Gene should be here soon with something to eat."

"That's good," Millicent said as she came around the truck to join him. "I'm getting a little hungry."

"Me too," Jim said, walking with her to the house. "I haven't had anything to eat today since that little fruit cup I had on the flight down to DFW this morning. And a good juicy cheeseburger sounds really good right now."

Michael met them just as they were about to open the door and said, "Not what we planned, was it?"

"Not really," Jim admitted as they walked into the house. "Millicent was pretty succinct, calling it unexpected. But it is what it is, as my great, great grandfather always said."

"What now?" Michael asked, taking a quick look at Millicent.

"First," Jim said, "let's get Li separated and wait for Gene to get here. If you'd take care of Millicent, get her a chair or something. I need to talk to Sun really quick."

"Come with me, Millicent," Michael said, leading her to the kitchen where everyone was congregating. "We didn't plan for any extended stays, as you'll remember coming out here before, so the only chairs are in here."

Jim walked over to Sun and asked, "Can we step outside and talk?"

"Sure, Jim," he answered, pushing himself off the countertop where he had been leaning. "What do we do now?"

"That's part of what I want to talk to you about," Jim told him as he motioned for Wang to follow them.

"Gene's bringing a copy of Li's phone call," he told them as they stood outside the house. "I'd like for both of you to listen to it very carefully and let us know if you think China believes Hua is dead."

"I think he said that," Wang said. "I know he told them that she was in an accident, and it looked like she was dead."

"That's good," Jim said. "But the key is if they believe she's dead or still waiting for confirmation. That's why Gene's bringing up the entire conversation. Things were getting a little rushed with the way things were not going according to our plan, and people sometimes miss a critical word or two. So, that's why I'd like for both of you to listen to the tape, and we'll decide what to do with Li after that."

"That sounds reasonable," Wang replied. "I was rather occupied trying to figure out just what I should do when he made the call. But I believe he said he thought she was dead. I could be wrong. It'll be good to listen to it again."

"What'll we do with him now?" Sun asked as Michael came out of the house.

"Not sure yet," Jim told him, shaking his head. "A lot depends on the tape. If we don't get an answer from it, we'll need to figure out how to make sure China believes she's dead."

"I guess you're talking about Hua," Michael said as he got to them. "She's talking to Millicent right now. Do you think Li didn't tell them she died in the accident?"

"That's what we're talking about," Jim told him. "If they don't think she's dead, they'll just send someone else to take care of her. Hell, he could already be getting on a plane in Beijing right now."

"I see your point," Michael said. "What do we do with him if he didn't tell them?"

"Maybe convince him that he has no other choice," Jim answered. "By the way, did you get his phone out of his car?"

"Brett brought it in," Michael answered. "What do we do with him after we figure out what Beijing knows?"

"Depends," Jim told them, looking at Sun. "I don't think we can ever trust him not to tell them she's still alive if we let him go. And I wouldn't trust him not being able to get word to them if we just lock him up somewhere."

"I have the solution," Sun said, looking directly at Jim. "And I'll be glad to ask him what he told his boss."

"I know you do," Jim told him. "And you may get your chance. But, as I told you before, this has to be done so no one knows what happened. That may take a little planning."

"Gene's here," Ron called from the back door. "I believe he's asking for you, Jim."

"Please ask him to come out here and join Michael and me," Jim told him. "Sun, why don't you and Wang go get something to eat while we discuss what we need to do next. And I'll let Gene know what you want."

"Thank you, Jim," Sun said with a slight bow. "I think you'll find that eliminating him is the only real answer. Hua has gone through too much to let that man have any possibility of putting her in danger again."

"I know," Jim said, putting his hand on Sun's shoulder. "And I agree with you. It's just a matter of how we do it."

"I brought you a Dr. Pepper," Gene said, handing Jim the can. "Thought you might want one. Too bad I don't have any Jack Daniels to top it off."

"Thanks, Gene," Jim said, pulling the tap. "I think I'll drink it straight and save the Jack for a Coke later this evening when you take me back to my hotel."

"I left the tape on the table, and Hua will give it to Sun," Gene said as Jim took a drink. "I hope they can figure out that those people who sent Li here think he did his job."

"I do, too," Jim replied. "That'd solve one of our problems right now. But the other problem is what to do with him afterward. Sun wants him eliminated, and I agree. I don't know how long the company, or the government, plans on keeping Hua a secret, but having the PRC think she's dead is the only way to stop them."

"I agree," Gene said, nodding. "And it needs to be done soon. It appears that he's already made plans to go back, so we need to figure out what to do before they start looking for him there."

"I think we have two options there," Jim told them, looking at Gene and Michael. "I don't have time to do either, so I'm suggesting that you let Michael take over everything from this point on."

"What do you think, Michael?" Gene asked, looking at him. "Do you want the job?"

"What do you mean by *everything*?" Michael asked Jim.

"Just the little things," Jim said, smiling. "Taking care of the two bodies we collected. Getting rid of Li. Taking his car back to where it came from. Getting rid of the wreck. Sanitizing the ambulance for fingerprints, DNA, hair…anything that could identify our people or those we put in the back. And helping Sun get rid of Li."

"Ahhh," Michael said, nodding and smiling at Gene. "Just the little things."

Chapter Seventy-four

"General," Sun said, coming back outside with Wang. "We've listened to the tape several times and have both come to the same conclusion."

"And that is?" Gene asked as Jim and Michael looked at them.

"He left it open," Sun answered, with Wang nodding in agreement. "His comment was exactly as Wang remembered, he told them that she was in an accident, and it *looked* like she was dead."

"What do you think the PRC will do?" Jim asked. "Will they take that as a possibility, or even a probability, or wait for confirmation?"

"I believe they'll wait," Sun answered. "In all my years of being part of that organization, I've learned one thing. They want, no, they expect an absolutely positive result. And, in a matter this important, they won't take *it looked like* as an answer to an order."

"What do you suggest?" Jim asked. "You know him better than anyone here. What'll it take to get him to provide confirmation of her death?"

"Especially now that he's seen her here," Gene added.

"You may not want to hear my suggestion," Sun answered, looking at Wang for his agreement. "But I believe that there's only one way to get him to make a call saying she is dead."

"What's that?" Gene asked, already knowing the answer wouldn't be in line with the Geneva Convention.

"Have you ever heard of waterboarding?" Sun asked.

"Yes," Gene answered, looking at Jim. "It's a form of simulating drowning. It's been around for centuries. We used it during the Philippine-American war around 1900, the Japanese and Germans used it during World War Two, and we used it again during Vietnam."

"And you think you can use it on Li?" Jim asked.

"Yes, if you want quick results," Sun answered, nodding. "Li has seen it used several times and knows that it'll go on and on until the subject finally answers the questions. And he knows I've used it before. So, yes, I think he'll make the call."

"You know that once the call is made, he can say anything," Jim told him. "And once he says it, it can't be taken back. Is that a risk you're willing to take?"

"That's not my decision," Sun said with a slight bow. "That's your decision. You asked if I could make him make the call. The answer is yes, but he may grow a set of balls at the end and disappoint us. Especially if he thinks he'll die anyway."

"Hold on a second," Jim said, thinking. "What if we do the waterboarding, fake the call to see what he does, and then waterboard him again? Gene, can you get us a recorder that looks like his phone?"

"I think so," he answered, taking his phone out of his pocket. "Let me call Quantico and see if there's an electronics shop around here that can put one inside his phone."

"What's your idea?" Michael asked as Gene walked away, talking on his phone.

"We can waterboard him, pretend to dial China, and hold the phone up to his lips," Jim explained, looking at Sun and Wang. "Then, if he doesn't say the right things, we pull the phone back and start over. Sooner or later, he's going to say Hua's dead."

"What about if he doesn't hear China's response?" Sun asked. "He'll know you didn't really make a call."

"I'm hoping that the electronic geeks can bypass the microphone part and leave the speaker intact," Jim said, thinking about how it would work. "Then, if he says the wrong thing, we just hang up, and China will think it was a disconnect."

"What about if Wang comes in after a couple of sessions and promises him we'll let him go if he just cooperates?" Michael suggested.

"You're talking about the good cop/bad cop thing," Jim said, shaking his head. "We'll still have the same problem. He may say yes to Wang but still alert his boss to the fact that Hua isn't dead. I don't want to take that chance. And the only way I can make sure he doesn't screw this up is by recording him and then playing that back to whoever sent him here."

"They can do it," Gene said, coming back to them. "They're contacting a company here in Denver that'll meet me at the hotel. They guess it'll take an hour or less to remodel the phone so that the microphone connects to a recording chip, but the rest of the phone acts normal."

"Okay, we're looking at two hours from now until you can get back," Jim told Gene. "Here's my suggestion. We let Sun start on Li while we wait for the phone. He can start and stop several times with a good break in between so Li can think things over. All he has to tell Li is that he's not going to quit until he does what he's going to be asked to do. Then, when you get back with it, Sun can start over again using the phone. What do you think, Sun?"

"That's a pretty good technique," he answered, nodding. "We always started with just a little water, enough to make them cough when they finally take a breath. Then, we increase it more and more until they believe that the next time, the water may never quit. I can use the two hours to build up the amount of water and ask simple questions to get him to realize that the only way to stop me from pouring the water is to do as I ask."

"Okay, that's what we'll do," Gene told them. "Michael, you're in charge here. Get Sun anything he needs and work with the rest of the guys to start wrapping everything else up. You know, the little things."

"What do you think I should do about the bodies?" Michael asked Jim.

"Take them back to Rose," Jim said. "Make sure you wash all the blood from both bodies and put the gowns back on they had on when you picked them up. Explain that the people who were supposed to receive the bodies for cremation aren't available, and you need him to perform the cremation. Get a couple of nice urns, and then dump the ashes along the road after you pick them up."

"What about Li's car?" he asked, making mental notes.

"Have Brett drop it off tonight after hours," Jim answered. "Are the rental papers in the car?"

"I'll check," Michael told him. "And the wreck and the ambulance?"

"Ron knows what to do with the wreck," Jim answered. "Just have Harry and Art bring the ambulance back to the hotel after they clean it. Anything else?"

"What about Hua?" he asked.

"We'll take her with us," Gene answered. "A team will take her down to the Springs until the government decides what to do. Anything else?"

"I guess that's it," Michael said, looking at Jim. "But I still have your phone number if I think of anything else."

"Good luck with that," Jim told him, laughing. "I won't get home until tomorrow afternoon, so I won't be there to answer your questions. And this shit needs to be done today."

"I forgot about that," Michael said, smiling. "I guess I'll have to call Gene."

"I don't think so," Gene said as he turned to leave. "Earn your pay, son. Figure it out. If you screw it up, fix it. Time to pull up your big boy pants if you want to keep playing in this league."

"I guess you know you need to get Quantico to find Li's ticket home and make some adjustments to give us time," Jim said as they walked to the house.

"Of course," Gene told him, smiling as he opened the door. "And as always, you go running back to that pretty little wife of yours and leave the heavy lifting to me."

"Just keeping you sharp, General," Jim said, looking for Millicent and Hua. "I think we need to get Millicent back home. She's going to realize sooner or later what she was about to do, and it could hit pretty hard. And I assume you know you need to take me back to my hotel."

"I know all things, Jim, my boy," Gene said, smiling at him. "How do you think I got those stars? I'm more than just a pretty face."

Chapter Seventy-five

The next morning, Jim was sitting in the lobby having a cup of coffee when Merna came down dragging her suitcase. Seeing Jim, she came over and asked, "Would you watch my bag for me while I get a cup of coffee, kind sir?"

"It would be my extreme pleasure, lovely lady," Jim said with a slight nod. "If it would please my lady, I'll get ye coffee from yon pot."

"That'd be a kind gesture, noble sir," she said with an exaggerated curtsey. "However, it'd be beneath such a lofty gentleman such as yourself. May I refill yours?"

"No, thank you, madam," Jim said smiling as Mike got off the elevator. "But I see the King of the Realm exiting yon portal. Perchance, you could offer him a goblet of elixir."

"Good morning, guys," Mike said, pulling his suitcase up beside Merna's. "How were your evenings?"

"Rather boring," Merna said. "We ladies had a toenail party in my room and had a bottle or two of......Sprite. Good time to gossip. Painting each other's toenails and drinking.....7 Up."

"I thought it was Sprite," Jim said, picturing his wife with them. "But I get the picture. And before you offer, I really don't need to hear the gossip."

"Even if it's about a couple of the male Flight Attendants?" she asked, winking at Mike. "Pretty juicy stuff."

"No, thank you," Jim repeated, standing up. "Now, I think I need another cup of coffee just to get even the thought out of my mind."

"It'll take more than coffee for that," Mike said, following him to the coffee pot. "That's one aspect of this job that I just have to grin and bear."

"Don't you mean grin and *bare*?" Merna said, laughing as she followed them to the coffee.

"Oh Merna, Merna, Merna. Why aren't you going to be with me for the rest of my time with American Airlines," Mike said, shaking his head. "We could have such a good time. Especially if we could get this old Marine to join us."

"It'd be fun," Jim said, pouring coffee into the cup Mike was holding. "But that's not the way of the world according to AA. The odds of us being together again before I retire are about a gazillion to one."

"It's surprising though," Merna told them. "I seem to fly with the same people more than you'd expect, given the number of pilots and stuff."

"I know what you mean," Jim said, pouring Merna some coffee. "It's just that I keep having to fly with the assholes. Why's that?"

"Because you can put up with them," Mike said as he saw the other Flight Attendants get off the elevator. "Most of the First Officers use the 'Do Not Pair With' option so they never have to fly with the real assholes. You seem to be one of the few that'll fly with anyone."

"That's probably why I'm with you this month," Jim said with a straight face. "I can bet there're half of the pilots at American that have you on their do not fly with list."

"Impossible," Mike said with a hurt look on his face. "This is my first trip as a Captain. Nobody except you knows what an ass I am."

"Oh no," Jim quickly replied. "I've already gone on the pilot website and spread the word. But the real reason behind my treachery is so that I'll end up being the only one that'll fly with you."

"You are a devious bastard," Mike said as they went to get their bags. "I think that's why I like you. Whose flight is it back to DFW anyway?"

"Yours," Jim said as they followed the Flight Attendants out to the van. "I got a call from the Chief Pilot last night saying that you needed all the practice you can get. It seems that the controllers in the tower have been taking bets on whether or not the airplane will be able to taxi to the gate after one of your landings.

"It's not really about your landings, though," Jim said as the driver tossed their bags into the back of the van. "It's just that he keeps betting on you and losing."

The next morning, Jim was sitting at the kitchen table having coffee with Jennifer when the doorbell rang. "I'll get it," he said, sitting his cup on the table.

"Good morning, Jim," Gene said as he opened the door. "Is the coffee ready?"

"Of course, General," Jim said as Gene walked in. "I think there's still a cup or two left in the pot."

"Good," he said, walking to the kitchen. "How's that lovely wife of yours this morning?"

"I'm fine, General," Jennifer said, getting up to hug him. "To what do we owe the pleasure?"

"Just thought I'd stop in and take my favorite people out to breakfast this morning," Gene said, getting a cup from the cabinet. "Unless you prefer to cook here."

"Going out sounds good," Jennifer said. "Jim never takes me out anymore."

"Bullshit," Jim said, grinning. "The pans here all have cobwebs, and I'm not sure if the oven even works any longer."

"Whatever, Jim Lashley," she said, putting her cup in the sink. "I'll be out in 20 minutes, so a real gentleman can take us out for breakfast."

As soon as she left, Jim turned to Gene and asked, "Did you guys get everything wrapped up?"

"Of course," Gene said as he sipped his coffee. "Michael is turning out to be a good agent. He was a little hesitant at first, not wanting to make a wrong decision. But he finally figured out that there aren't really any wrong decisions, just opportunities to learn."

"What happened to Li?" Jim asked, putting his cup in the sink.

"He finally made the phone call," Gene told him. "Unfortunately, he got very sick when he got back to San Francisco. It appears that he had dinner with Sun the night before he was to leave for Beijing and ate some very bad sushi."

"That's terrible," Jim said, smiling. "At least Sun got his wish. And Hua?"

"I don't know," Gene told him. "Some people from the State Department came and picked her up at the hotel the day after the accident, and I haven't heard from them."

"What about the Oregon deal?" Jim asked.

"We're working on it," Gene told him. "Sun and Wang will be there next week, and I've gotten assurance from the Dean of the College there that Hua will have a position whenever she gets there."

"I guess it all worked out even after I screwed everything up at the start then," Jim said as he heard Jennifer coming back down the hall.

"I wouldn't say screwed up," Gene said, smiling at him. "Just another chance to learn from our mistakes. Don't forget, I was there with you. So, I learned a lot too."

"Jennifer, my dear," Gene said, standing and putting his cup on the table. "You certainly do know how to brighten a room. Are you sure you want to have breakfast with a couple of old knuckle-dragging grunts this morning?"

"Nobody I'd rather be with," she said, taking Gene and Jim's arms. "My two favorite men in the world."

www.ingramcontent.com/pod-product-compliance
Lightning Source LLC
Chambersburg PA
CBHW070642310726

48982CB00001B/387

9 781964 289960